RESCUING MARIA

GUARDIAN HOSTAGE RESCUE SPECIALISTS

ELLIE MASTERS

JEM PUBLISHING

Editor: Erin Toland

Proofreader: Roxanne Leblanc

Published in the United States of America

JEM Publishing

This is a work of fiction. While reference might be made to actual historical events or existing locations, the names, characters, businesses, places, and incidents are either the product of the author's imagination or are used fictitiously, and any resemblance to actual persons, living or dead, business establishments, events, or locales is entirely coincidental.

Paperback ISBN: 978-1-952625-35-0

DEDICATION

This book is dedicated to my one and only—my amazing and wonderful husband.

Without your care and support, my writing would not have made it this far.

You pushed me when I needed to be pushed.

You supported me when I felt discouraged.

You believed in me when I didn't believe in myself.

If it weren't for you, this book never would have come to life.

ALSO BY ELLIE MASTERS

The LIGHTER SIDE

Ellie Masters is the lighter side of the Jet & Ellie Masters writing duo! You will find Contemporary Romance, Military Romance, Romantic Suspense, Billionaire Romance, and Rock Star Romance in Ellie's Works.

YOU CAN FIND ELLIE'S BOOKS HERE:

ELLIEMASTERS.COM/BOOKS

Military Romance

Guardian Hostage Rescue Specialists

Rescuing Melissa

(Get a FREE copy of Rescuing Melissa

when you join Ellie's Newsletter)

Alpha Team

Rescuing Zoe

Rescuing Moira

Rescuing Eve

Rescuing Lily

Rescuing Jinx

Rescuing Maria

Bravo Team

Rescuing Angie

Rescuing Isabelle

Rescuing Carmen

Rescuing Rosalie

Military Romance

Guardian Personal Protection Specialists

Sybil's Protector

Lyra's Protector

The One I Want Series

(Small Town, Military Heroes)

By Jet & Ellie Masters

EACH BOOK IN THIS SERIES CAN BE READ AS A STANDALONE AND IS ABOUT A DIFFERENT COUPLE WITH AN HEA.

Saving Abby

Saving Ariel

Saving Brie

Saving Cate

Saving Dani

Saving Jen

Rockstar Romance

The Angel Fire Rock Romance Series

EACH BOOK IN THIS SERIES CAN BE READ AS A STANDALONE AND IS ABOUT A DIFFERENT COUPLE WITH AN HEA. IT IS RECOMMENDED THEY ARE READ IN ORDER.

Ashes to New (prequel)

Heart's Insanity (book 1)

Heart's Desire (book 2)

Heart's Collide (book 3)

Hearts Divided (book 4)

Hearts Entwined (book5)

1

MARIA

A HUGE SMILE FILLS MY FACE AS I HUG MY BEST FRIEND. "GET ALL pampered so I can sell your ass and make a ton of money for the kids!"

"Will do." Sybil hugs me tight. "I wish you were coming with me." She puffs her lower lip out into a fake pout and looks at me with dopey eyes. "Please ..."

My phone buzzes in my pocket, making me jump. The screen lights up with my mother's name, taking my mood from cheerful to tense in less than a second.

The incoming text flattens my smile into a slash of apprehension. In less than five minutes, my bright and cheery day will turn dour and depressing.

"I've got lunch with MD." I take a step back and respond to the text.

"I don't envy your weekly luncheon with your mother."

"Wish I could play hooky."

Muriel Rossi, matriarch of the Rossi family, is a formidable woman. Our weekly luncheon is an event I can't escape.

I've tried.

Luncheon doesn't quite capture the gist of our weekly interaction. It's more of a sparring match, where we trade verbal blows.

Trade?

If trade means I'm her verbal punching bag, then I've got that bit down. It's a one-sided battle, where she fires volley after volley, and I soak it all in with little to no retaliation.

I put a lot of effort into winning our war of wills. Each time, I fail.

Is that a dramatic statement? Maybe?

But it's true.

A real sense of dread twists at my insides. Time to put my emotional armor in place.

Sybil senses my unease and wraps me in a hug. "It's one hour. You'll survive." She releases me, clasps both my hands, and gives a squeeze of support. "I'd come with if I thought it would help." Sybil's smile shines bright with the power to turn any frown upside down.

It works wonders on me. Before I know it, my cheeks hurt from the grin she puts there.

"You're right. I can survive anything, even lunch with Mommy Dearest."

"There you go." Sybil playfully punches my arm. "I'll see you later tonight. You can tell me how horrible she was to you. As for tonight, I never thought you'd be my pimp."

"Pimp?" I say. "Who's calling who a pimp? You're the great matchmaker."

"Got me there. Although, it never did any good with you."

All through college, Sybil tried again and again to set me up. Nothing lasted more than a few dates.

"Not my fault. You know my mother ..."

"Yes, MD is the very definition of a kill joy."

MD is the term we use when speaking about my mother, Mommy Dearest. It's not an endearment.

"For the record..." Sybil holds up a finger. "I never asked anyone to pay for a date with you, so you can't call me your pimp. You're literally making these men bid on me."

"It's for a good cause. Besides, you're well compensated."

After graduation, Sybil came to work as an intern at the Belvedere.

Which is funny.

It's an entry-level position.

The funny part is that, like me, her family owns an exclusive resort in Hawaii. She'll be stepping into the same CEO shoes I wear, but her father wants her to work a year someplace else—to see how things are done differently—before heading home to run her family's business.

"Not complaining, and with the Belvedere picking up the tab, I'm all in. Besides, it's for the children." Sybil flicks her luxurious, dark hair over her shoulder.

I envy that hair.

"As for pampering," Sybil says, "I booked the full spa experience —on you."

"The hottie who bids on you tonight is going to be one lucky bastard." I can't help but tease.

"I wish. With my luck, I'll get a fat toad who sweats like a pig."

"I don't think pigs sweat, and who cares if he's a fat toad? Not to mention, that's a horrible thing to say about anyone. You grew up in the hospitality industry, girl, and know better."

"I'm kidding." Sybil rolls her eyes, dramatically flicking her lashes, then fluttering them suggestively. "I'll make his night."

"I'm sure you will. Consider this a test of everything you've learned."

"Oh, I know." Sybil props a hand on her hip. "Why aren't you in the lineup? Bet you'd be the biggest draw of the night. The only Rossi heir? Men will be tripping over themselves to get to you."

If only that were the case.

"Three reasons." I hold up my index finger and begin counting. "First, only interns get auctioned off. Two, I'm the CEO, and three ..."

Sybil cuts me off. "Mommy Dearest would be aghast if her daughter ever hit an auction block, even if it's for charity." She presses her hands to her cheeks with dramatic flair. "The scandal."

"Exactly." I shove Sybil playfully. "Now, hurry up or you're going to be late for your very important date."

"You quoting the White Rabbit?"

"Goofball."

"Spoilsport."

"MD's going to be here any minute. Unless you want to suffer her disapproving glare, I suggest you skedaddle." I squint, attempting to match my mother's signature look of disapproval. It's a sharp edge that cuts deep.

Always has.

"Oh hell no." Sybil spins toward the door. "I'm out."

Sybil and my mother never bonded. Not like I did with Sybil's mom.

At first, my mother welcomed Sybil into our home. She was wonderful about making sure my friend felt like she was part of our family, but something changed after Sybil and I turned sixteen.

We never figured out what happened, what unforgivable crime Sybil committed, but after our sweet sixteen, mom's demeanor did a complete 180 when it came to Sybil.

"With the threat of running into MD, I am over and out, boss." Sybil snaps to attention and rewards me with a goofy salute. Her lilting laughter is as pretty as her *hapa* roots.

Hapa.

That's a word I learned when we first met.

We were almost twelve.

My father, God rest his soul, booked a trip for me and my mother to Hawaii for the summer—the entire summer. As a twelve-year-old, I found that mortifying. They wanted me to leave my friends behind and head to a godforsaken island where I knew nobody. Not to mention, I would spend my birthday alone, surrounded only by adults.

To a preteen, it was the kiss of death. I hated my parents for subjecting me to such unwarranted punishment. I begged to stay behind, but my father wanted me to have an experience that didn't involve spending yet another summer at our house in the Hamptons.

I like our house in the Hamptons.

That trip to Hawaii turned out to be the best thing that ever happened to me.

Sybil and I hit it off right away. Daughter of the resort owners, Sybil's mother is native Hawaiian by birth: dark hair, tanned skin, dark eyes. Her father is as Scandinavian as they come: tall, piercing blue eyes, fair skin, and handsome.

Hapa means mixed.

The combination of Hawaiian and Scandinavian genes created an incredible beauty in my friend. Eyes the color of the turquoise waters of her island home—a sea foam green—she's blessed with the thick hair of her Polynesian heritage. It's long, wavy, and hangs all the way to her ass. Sybil is a siren, born to break men's hearts.

Not that I cared about any of that at the time. She knew all the cool places to hang out at her family's exclusive resort. We were inseparable preteens, united against the adults by the end of day one.

When I found out she was leaving for a camp on the Big Island the next day, I had a complete, and epic, meltdown. I didn't want to spend my summer with boring grownups.

Mother said no, but Sybil came to my rescue. Together, we convinced my father to let me go. He said yes. Mother fell in line like the dutiful wife she was.

Sybil and I have been besties ever since.

"You sure you can't come with me?" Sybil asks for the tenth time. "It'd be so much more fun."

"You know I can't." I glance at my watch.

"I wish you could cancel on your mother, just once. She never lets you have any fun. You're practically a prisoner here."

Sybil's not wrong about that.

"I've learned how to keep the peace. I give her this and she leaves me alone."

"Alone to do what? You're not allowed to date like a normal person. You barely go out at all."

"She just wants what's best for me."

"She keeps you locked in an ivory tower."

"Come on, just because I live here doesn't mean ..."

"Live, work, and eat." Sybil's brow arches. "Hey, just worried about you. You haven't dated anyone since we left Cornell, and now that your uncle has his goons following you 24/7, you'll never meet a man on your own."

"MD is challenging at the best of times ..."

"Most times? She's downright brutal and cruel." Sybil doesn't pull her punches, but things between her and my mother definitely hit arctic cold several years ago.

"You really should have it out with her. You're a grown woman. CEO of the Belvedere. You run a multi-million-dollar company, but your mommy refuses to let you date? Do you hear the words coming out of my mouth?"

If the decision had been left up to my mother all those years ago, she never would've let me hang out with Sybil. She would've forbade me from going off-island to a no-name horse camp filled with average kids from average families.

My mother's nose is stuck high in the sky. Growing up beneath that prejudice made life complicated, to say the least.

"I hear you just fine." I blow out an exasperated breath. "Let me deal with my mother. You need to hurry up before she catches you, or you'll find your spa day transformed into a luncheon of judgment."

"Okay. Fine." Sybil lifts her hands in defeat. "I'm leaving without you, but I'm going to text every minute."

"Please don't. You know how MD hates the obnoxiousness of cell phones."

"Which is why ..." Sybil wraps me in another hug and whispers in my ear, "I'll only text you every ten minutes. Is she staying for the banquet?"

"She didn't say, but I assume so. It's our most popular fundraiser of the year. She'd hate to miss the pageantry."

"I just wish you could come and go as you please. You know, some people actually leave the hotel. Instead of lunch downstairs, why don't you take her someplace in the French Quarter? You know, knock her off her game? Level the playing field? Why not pretend you've got a secret boyfriend you've been keeping from her for months. Now that would be scandalous."

"Scandalous and deadly." I can't help but laugh. "There's no way you'll get her to walk those streets. If there's not a red carpet rolled out to the curb, it's beneath her station."

"I know." Sybil gives me a look. "I wish she wasn't so hard on you."

"I wish she was more like your mom."

Sybil's mother is the most amazing person on earth. Warm and welcoming, she's the definition of Hawaiian hospitality.

When she saw the friendship between Sybil and me blooming, she did everything she could to encourage it, even when that meant sending her daughter halfway across the globe to spend every summer with me in the Hamptons. They even enrolled Sybil in the ultra-elite Prescott Academy, a boarding school for children of wealthy families, so we could go to high school together.

Sybil's mother recognized the value of a lifetime friendship. In many ways, Sybil's mother is more my mother than my own.

I hate admitting that, but it's true.

Sybil's phone chirps. "Okay, I gotta go or I will miss my appointment. Give your mother my love."

"I will." We hug one last time.

"Bye-ee!" She waves, bouncing with excitement.

"I'll see you tonight." I blow Sybil a kiss.

A smile fills her face as she spins around and leaves my office with a bounce in her step.

As for my office, a private set of stairs leads up one floor to the spacious living quarters my uncle commissioned for me after my graduation from Cornell.

Uncle Marco calls it a graduation gift. It took several months, and Sybil mentioning it, before I realized I live in a gilded cage. If I want to head outside, a highly skilled team of security professionals always accompanies me. Another gift from my uncle, they never get in my way, exactly, but they do report everything I do directly to my uncle.

Not that I haven't slipped out from under their protection from time to time. Sybil is my bestie, after all. She figured out a way to free me from my unwanted shadows.

But I'm not complaining, and I'm not fighting it. The Belvedere is my legacy, passed down to me by my father. I live, eat, sleep, and work all within the walls and halls of the hotel casino built upon some of the priciest land in New Orleans.

After four years at the prestigious hotel school at Cornell University, I graduated with honors and stepped directly into the role of Chief Executive Officer at the Belvedere. I maintain my position with a controlling interest in company stock and a seat on the board of directors. That's the only reason my uncle hasn't kicked me out.

He can't.

It's also topic number one of the weekly luncheons I endure with MD.

As for Uncle Marco, he's old-fashioned, unlike my father. Marco grew up in my father's shadow. The younger brother to the Rossi empire, friction heated the air between brothers. Marco made no secret he coveted his brother's position as head of the Rossi family, but he stood back, obedient to tradition.

But then, my father died.

Marco stepped up and fulfilled his obligations to the family. He did so in many ways, none nearly as shocking as when he married my mother. But that was the promise he made to my father. At least, that's what he claims was said between them.

No one really knows. It's his word against a dead man.

In addition to other Rossi holdings, he wants control of the Belvedere, but the trust my father set up gives controlling interest to me.

Marco wants to take that from me; says my place is in the home, raising children. Did I mention traditional?

If my suspicions are correct, and they are when it comes to my mother, that's exactly what she wants to discuss.

Once a week, precisely at noon, we meet for a mother-daughter luncheon. It's a battle of wills, and I dread it all week long.

2

MARIA

WITH SYBIL GONE, I HAVE A FEW MINUTES TO PACE BESIDE THE FLOOR-
to-ceiling glass windows of my office. They look out toward the
French Quarter. My sensible heels tap against the stone floors, setting
up a monotonous rhythm I find soothing.

I'm going to need that in a moment.

If Sybil is fast enough, she'll miss my mother. I listen for the
unmistakable *tap, tap, tap* of my mother's signature walk in her five-
inch heels and breathe deeply when I don't hear them.

I do hear the elevator ding. A quick peek shows Sybil getting onto
the elevator. Two other employees join her.

"Have fun!" I wave, but Sybil doesn't see me.

I wish I was in that elevator with her instead of here. Executing a
precise pivot, I spin around and march down the length of my office
again.

MD is late. If it were me, I'd find myself at the wrong end of a
tongue lashing about how tardiness is an unforgivable sin, but I am
not my mother.

She doesn't answer to me.

And so, I pace.

Each week, we fight the same battle. She wants me to leave the corporate world. Despite the phenomenal success of the Belvedere, the idea of her daughter involved in an industry of service, the hotel business, grates on her nerves.

It's okay for a man, but not her daughter. Each week, I defend my decision to put my career first. Is it wrong of me to want praise from my mother?

According to her, I'm an embarrassment to the family.

The sound of my mother's stilettos clacking against the marble in the hall outside my office sends a shiver racing down my spine.

It's time, and I brace for our weekly battle.

She'll gently suggest I step down. I'll dig in, demanding she acknowledge my accomplishments. We'll end in a stalemate, lick our wounds, and wait until next week when we'll go at it again.

It's exhausting.

With a deep breath in, I spin around and fix a smile to my face. My mother's footsteps echo down the long hall outside my office while I head to the door to properly greet a woman of her stature.

My assistant is not present. I gave her a long lunch, protecting her from MD's harsh criticism.

"Mother," I throw my arms out wide, "you look absolutely amazing."

And she does.

My mother is stunning. A natural beauty, she's got one of those bodies designers salivate over. Golden hair sweeps up off her neck in a perfect up-do with naught a hair out of place. Her crystalline-blue eyes are deep and radiant, carrying the power to stop men in their tracks. Her luminescent skin is flawless, with not one blemish to mar her beauty. Her hourglass figure, perfectly proportioned, makes men take a second look, every single time.

I'm merely pretty in comparison, although my rare sapphire eyes have been known to turn a head every now and again.

My mother closes the distance with a regal air. Arms held stiffly out from her sides, we hug the air, never actually touching, and exchange air kisses to each cheek. I can't remember the last time my mother gave me a real hug.

"You lost weight again." She leans back. Hand to chin, her brows tug tight. "I told you this job is too stressful for a woman. When are you going to realize this isn't for you?" Her mouth pinches tight. "Where is your assistant?"

"At lunch." I keep a false smile plastered to my face during her wonderful greeting. She wastes no time getting right to the heart of the matter.

"You need to be stricter with the help. Give them an inch and they'll walk all over you. If you were a man, your assistant would never leave you unsupported."

"Mother, my employees need to eat."

"They need to be here, greeting those who think they can waltz right on in and disturb the CEO. You don't understand how important appearances are." There goes her head, shaking side to side. It's only one of many digs I'll endure.

"I love my job and part of that is treating my employees well. It encourages them to work harder, then when I have to ask them to stay late, it's not a problem."

"You shouldn't have to ask them to do their job. Marco would never stoop so low. He never asks. He tells them what to do and expects them to stay."

"I'm doing fine, Mother. My employees love me."

"No ... the stress is showing." She peers at my face. Her harsh gaze seeks every imperfection. "Your suit is sloppy. Send it to my dressmaker. She'll do what she can to make it flatter a woman's figure." Another scorching gaze sears a hole in my heart. "That blouse is not doing you any favors. I'll send something over. Put that one in the trash."

Trash?

I look amazing in my suit, and I got it tailored to perfection. As for the blouse, it's silky and feminine. I'm not throwing it away.

"Marco said you left your security behind again." Her arms fold under her breasts as she looks down her perfectly upturned nose at me.

"I did."

"That Sybil is going to be the death of you. Those men are there to keep you safe. You have no idea what someone would do to get their hands on you and hurt you."

Maybe not, but I know what my mother will do to keep me safe. I live in a glass tower, a princess of circumstance, and prisoner of the Rossi name.

Resentment builds within me, snarling and spitting, as I whirl toward my mother. The urge to give her a piece of my mind rages within me, but I swallow the words the moment her hard eyes latch onto me.

"I don't need a bodyguard, let alone half a dozen."

"I didn't raise you to be ungrateful. Marco cares about you. He wants you to be safe. He can't do that if you constantly resist his efforts and leave your security team scrambling to find you."

"It was one night out on the town."

Sybil and I try to go out at least once a month.

"It's one night too many." She snaps her fingers, ending our conversation. "We must hurry. You know how I feel about tardiness."

"Yes, Mother." I am very aware of what she thinks about a lot of things.

"When you disrespect your uncle, you disrespect me. That's not how I raised you. That friend of yours encourages you to sneak away. How are we going to find you a suitable match when you flirt with scandal? You know better."

My mother would love it if she could lock me up like a nun. The idea of scandal touching the Rossi name terrifies her.

"I'm not disrespectful."

"That is not what Marco says to me. As head of the family, he deserves your allegiance and your respect."

Allegiance?

There's so much I can say in response to that, but I swallow my words and respond with a nod.

"He has my respect."

"Then show it." Her biting comment makes me flinch. "Give him your father's shares in the Belvedere. Stop this nonsense about running a company you know nothing about."

"Mother, I know what I'm doing. My degree is in hotel management." I would remind her I graduated with honors, but it would do no good.

"Not another word." She stops and holds up a finger. "I don't want to ruin our luncheon with one of your tantrums. We'll speak of this later." Her phone buzzes with an incoming text.

In an unusual break in character, she takes a look at the screen. With her vision getting worse, and refusal to wear glasses, I can't help but see the message.

Package acquired. Delivery as discussed.

Her eyes dart back and forth, rereading the message several times. It's almost as if I cease to exist.

"Is everything okay?"

For my mother to interrupt a conversation to look at her phone, I imagine the worst has happened. Her lips turn up into one of the scariest smiles I've seen in my life. It's predatory.

"Everything is fine. In fact, it's going to be perfect."

It may be my imagination, but her cheeks flush and her eyes gleam. Her lips slide into a triumphant smile.

Okay, that's creepy.

"Fine?" I don't understand. "What does that mean?"

"It means things are exactly as they're supposed to be." She shoves her phone back into the depths of her purse and spins to face me. "Chop, chop, we're going to be late."

She spins in her stilettos and marches toward the elevator, chin held high, back ramrod straight; she glides with a gait envied by the most talented runway models. My mother is perfection personified, but why does she look so incredibly pleased after that text?

I don't like odd when it comes to my mother.

In fact, the last time I saw that look on my mother's face was when she told me about my father's death. In an uncharacteristic move, she used a video call to tell me the news.

At nineteen, I couldn't stop the tears from falling. I idolized my father and couldn't believe he was dead. My mother scolded me and told me Rossi women never cry. My tears, according to her, were scandalous and proof of weakness.

Above all, a Rossi can never be seen as weak.

Her husband of twenty-one years died, yet she didn't allow one tear to mar the serene perfection of her face. She told me it was because she refused to give the gossips anything to talk about.

I don't believe she mourned my father. As much as he loved me, their relationship remained cold and distant. I don't know why they got married. Any spark that may have existed died long before I came along. I always thought they'd be happier with a divorce. Not that my mother would consider it. Divorce leads to gossip and scandal.

Then a year later, she shocked everyone when she married my uncle. It was a year to the day after my father's death. It was as if she read the societal rule book, completed a year-long mourning period, wearing black every day, declining social invites, and making my life miserable. Once that year was over, she moved on.

I expected people to talk, to churn the rumor mill, but either I wasn't privy to the gossip train, or it got stopped in its tracks.

3

LIAM

One of the things I've learned as a Guardian is to expect the unexpected. There's no such thing as a normal rescue operation. Which means rescuing kidnap victims requires adaptability and finesse.

Such as this mission.

Instead of a six-man team, Wolfe and I team up with Lily and Jinx. The four of us execute one mission while the rest of Alpha team heads out on another one. The ops run concurrently, spreading Guardian HRS resources thin.

Which requires out-of-the-box thinking.

"You're thinking about it again." Wolfe nudges my knee as the driver navigates through the thick traffic of New Orleans.

"I can't *not* think about it." I shake my head. "Did you ever think this is what you'd be doing when you became a SEAL?"

"I don't know. It's kind of cool. Like James Bond cool." His grin is a mile wide.

"James Bond cool?" I shake my head. "I don't believe you just said that."

"What else would you call it. We've got cameras in our tie pins, some funky tech in our cell phones, and exfil?" Wolfe huffs a laugh. "You'll get to put your Fred Astaire moves to work. If we pull that off, it's going to be epic."

And if we don't?

"It's certainly out-of-the-box thinking." I scratch the back of my neck.

"Stop complaining about the op." Lily kicks my foot, dislodging it from its perch on my knee.

I shoot her a dirty look and kick my heel over my knee again. "Not complaining, just trying to wrap my head around it."

I'm also doing my damned best not to be a chauvinistic prick to Jinx and Lily. I've spent my fair share of time on the sparring mat looking up at Jinx. Lily's yet to throw me down, but she's getting better every day. The thing is, I've never operated with a woman before.

My instinct is to defend and protect. If I do that to either one of them, they'll chew me up and spit me out. But they're still chicks. Not to mention, the prep work on this mission is basically non-existent. There wasn't time for it.

That makes me itchy.

Working with chicks? On an op that hasn't been fully vetted? My spidey-senses tingle big time.

"How am I supposed to be your date and not touch you?" I glance at Lily.

Wolfe laughs again. "Knox will cut your balls off if ..."

"He'll do no such thing." Lily crosses her arms. "Knox understands undercover work. Don't overthink this."

"She's right about that," Jinx chimes in.

"Agree." I spread my arms out wide. "But you didn't hear what he said to me."

"What did he say?" Lily blows out a frustrated breath.

"Let's just say him cutting off my balls is the least of my worries."

"It's going to be fine. We hold hands. You put your arm over my shoulder. We stare intently into each other's eyes. We don't have to kiss to be on a date. Leave that to the love birds." Lily jabs her thumb toward Wolfe and Jinx.

Their relationship is nothing short of combustible. They fought tooth and nail, denying their attraction for each other, and thank the Lord they sorted through their shit.

Wolfe looks up at Jinx and that grin of his turns positively sinful.

"Don't you have undercover experience?" Lily arches a brow.

"Liam is the king of undercover," Wolfe chimes in, pulling his gaze off his woman to join the conversation. "He's the one who gave Max and Knox pointers on their mission."

"That's true."

Knox went undercover as Max's bodyguard. The two of them infiltrated Benefield's estate in Colombia, posing as buyers. They were there to rescue Eve Deverough, daughter of a shipping mogul. Deverough is the one who surrendered the information, which brings us to the Belvedere tonight.

Six names were scrawled on Benefield's ledgers. Through expert intelligence work by Jinx and Wolfe, we know those women were kidnapped and brought to the Belvedere. Deverough confirmed it and added the additional note about the women being split into two separate batches. One group is to be sold. The other group is meant for something far worse.

Our job is to get in the Belvedere and rescue the women slated to be sold at auction. The rest of Alpha team is tasked with rescuing the others.

"I'm not worried about the date part of the evening. Knox can fuck himself if he thinks I'd do anything to you. I'm worried about getting *out* of the Belvedere. Are we really expected to walk out the front door?"

"That's Mitzy's plan." Lily taps the window and watches the city go by. She's probably thinking about Knox. His mission is far more dangerous than ours.

Operationally challenging, he'll be boarding *Caviar Dreams*, an exclusive cruise line operated beneath the Belvedere corporate umbrella. With no knowledge of where the three women are being held on board that ship, they'll need to improvise on the fly.

We have that knowledge, courtesy of Deverough, our criminal turned star witness. Not that our operation is without risk. We're working on a zero-footprint op. The whole point is to *not* draw attention, which is kind of silly considering that's exactly what Wolfe and Jinx's initial marching orders dictate. But that phase of the operation is critical to embedding Mitzy's technology into the servers of Belvedere's security system. After that, low profile is our *modus operandi.*

"It's insane." I pinch the bridge of my nose and tilt my head back.

"It's Mitzy Magic." Jinx pokes me in the ribs. Or tries to. "Damn, that hurt. Forgot you're wearing Kevlar."

Wolfe and I wear Kevlar vests beneath our dark suits. The girls do not. There's simply no place to hide it in the skimpy, sprayed-on dresses they wear. Although, if what I heard the other day is correct, Mitzy and Forest are working on a side project that embeds the bulletproof advantage of Kevlar into fabric itself. It'll be a game-changer. I feel guilty wearing Kevlar when the girls go without.

It feels all kinds of wrong.

"You've got nothing to worry about as far as I'm concerned. We're just two friends having fun." Lily takes my hand in hers and laces our fingers together. "Let me deal with Knox and his jealousy issues."

It feels like holding hands with my sister.

Not a good vibe.

"Fine. You deal with him, and I'll keep my hands to myself." I extricate my hand and shove it under my leg.

"Looks like we're here." Wolfe leans forward. "Check your weapons." He's taking lead for this mission.

The four of us complete a quick weapons check. We're kitted out with tranquilizer darts and sidearms. Jinx hides her tranq gun and knives down her boots. Lily squirreled away a few knives in her boots; she also wears a thigh holster with a Walther PPK—a nod to James Bond's iconic weapon.

I respect that.

"Everyone ready?" Wolfe waits for our affirmatives, then he jumps out of the car, helping Jinx and then Lily out. I climb out my side and circle around to join them. I drape an arm around Lily's shoulder. It feels weird, but I dig deep and man up.

Our out-of-the-box operation is officially active.

We enter the Belvedere looking like two couples out for a bit of fun. Instead, we're here to rescue several women who were ripped out of their perfect lives and shoved into the horrific world of human trafficking.

Lily looks amazing in her little black dress and combat boots. She totally pulls off the gothic vibe despite her ivory skin and white-blonde hair. Knox's warning runs through my head. He gave me an earful of what I could and couldn't do with *his* woman.

It's basically a look but don't touch kind of thing.

Which is totally cool.

Anything other than holding hands, maybe slinging my arm over her shoulder, delves into creep territory. Fortunately, he trusts me with his life, which means he trusts me on a mission with his woman.

Things are totally different for Wolfe and Jinx. They can barely keep their hands off each other.

I'm happy for Wolfe, glad he found the woman he was destined to love, but I'm kind of frustrated too.

I'm the last man standing. A happy bachelor nowhere near ready to settle down. I like being free to do as I want, see who I want, and fuck who I want. The thought of settling for one woman the rest of my life feels constricting.

Like suffocating slowly.

I'm happy the guys found their women, but that leaves me flying solo. It's not nearly as fun as it used to be. I'm happy Wolfe finally stopped fighting with Jinx and got his head out of his ass. The success of tonight's mission rests heavily on their shoulders.

Lily and I are merely the lookouts.

Wolfe and Jinx are tasked with going behind enemy lines and planting a bit of Mitzy Magic. It's some kind of tech that basically cracks open Belvedere's incredible security system like an egg.

Mitzy will have access to turn cameras on and off, reset their security feeds, and plant alternate video streams. There will be no door she can't unlock. The elevators will be hers to control, which will figure heavily in our exfil. Getting out of the Belvedere is the one piece of this operation that I'm not sold on.

I thought my plan was pretty sweet, but it got vetoed by practically everyone. I wanted to jump off the roof. That sounds dangerous, but the Belvedere is more than high enough for a base jump. Not to mention, it fixes the biggest issue we have: getting caught with hostages in tow.

I thought soaring off the roof presented the best chance for success. Only, CJ vetoed that. Evidently, Jinx and Lily haven't completed their qualifications on the wingsuits. After we rescue the women, there will be seven of us we need to get out of the hotel. So, we're going with Mitzy's crazy scheme.

Step one, enter the Belvedere.

Jinx is on fire with her sprayed-on red dress. Lily looks equally amazing in her tiny, black dress. All eyes follow the girls into the Belvedere while Wolfe and I prowl behind them, checking out the crowd. We're decked out in black suits, outfitted with the Kevlar vests underneath. Our tie pins hold tiny cameras Mitzy uses to track our movements. We pack heat in our shoulder harnesses. Our watches hold gear designed to cast a disruption field around us. It's supposed to mess with the cameras.

The evening crowd pulses with activity as Wolfe and I steer our *dates* deeper into the crowded casino. All around us, lights flash, disorienting the gamblers while the incessant ringing of the slot machines encourages them to feed more money into a losing proposition.

Waitresses dressed in practically nothing weave through the crowd, delivering alcohol to those who gamble. The drunker the guests become, the more the house rakes in.

We stop at the slots. Lily and Jinx play a few rounds. Jinx loses ten bucks in less than five minutes, but Lily comes away a winner.

"Oh my God, I won a hundred bucks." She and Jinx jump up and down, showing off their sexy bodies to everyone nearby. I get a peck on the cheek from Lily. "Luv, did you see it?"

"You're my lucky lady." Wrapping an arm around her waist, I pull her to me and plant a kiss on her forehead. Her lips are forbidden territory, according to Knox.

"Great job. Keep moving." Mitzy uses the comm links buried in our ear canals to direct us through the gaming floor with laser-focused targeting. *"Hang out at the craps table."*

"You want us to play?" I hate craps and Wolfe isn't much of a gambler.

"No, just pretend to be interested. I'm pulling up building schematics. Hang on."

It shouldn't surprise me she acquired the building schematics. Mitzy is a wonder when it comes to technology.

"Let's hit the bar." Jinx tugs on Wolfe's arm, begging him to follow her to the bar. At least, that's what it looks like.

"That's right. Keep heading toward the bar."

As we head in that direction, Wolfe and Jinx play things up. Lily grasps my upper arm, letting me lead, while Wolfe grabs Jinx's ass. He twirls her into his embrace, kissing her. Their public display turns from dirty to practically indecent.

"Get a room." I slap Wolfe on the shoulder as Lily and I squeeze by, taking the lead.

"I'm so damn happy they finally got their heads out of their asses." Lily's grip on my bicep tightens. "I was getting tired of their constant fighting."

"You and me both." I loop my arm around her shoulder, tugging her close. She leans her head on my shoulder and places her hand over my chest.

"My, my, you're so—rock *hard*." Lily runs her hand over my chest, shamelessly feeling me up, but all she feels is the hard Kevlar plate beneath my shirt.

I can't help but laugh. With the way Wolfe and Jinx heat things up, Lily and I are left in the dusty wasteland of platonic friendship.

But that's okay.

Our job is to be the lookouts for Wolfe and Jinx. Theirs is to make a scene to set up their upcoming performance.

Every move is being watched and recorded by hundreds of cameras embedded in the ceiling and the walls. Which makes the *undercover* bit kind of funny.

4

MARIA

OUR WAITER REMOVES OUR LUNCH DISHES BENEATH MY MOTHER'S disapproving glare and sniffs of disgust. She berated him during the entire meal, complaining about anything and everything.

Most of those things were well outside his control. She'll leave no tip, Mother rarely does, but I'll see he's rewarded handsomely for the verbal abuse my mother subjected him to.

The plates and glasses clink as his hand shakes. Chin tucked, he escapes before my mother can dress him down for his sloppy service.

I take in a steadying breath, bracing for the real part of our conversation. Until now, Mother has been almost bearable, but her sharp tongue no longer has a target in our helpless serving staff.

I dig in, determined to once again beg for reason.

"You can tell Uncle Marco to pull back his men. I don't need them, and I'm sure he needs them elsewhere. Not to mention, following me around is a waste of their skillset."

"Your safety is important to Marco."

"And you."

You need to stop poking the bear.

It's bad enough I have to endure my mother, but my inner voice needs to cut me some slack. This isn't easy.

"Excuse me?" Her lips pinch tight as her left brow arches with offense.

"My safety is important to Uncle Marco *as well as* you." Will she get the hint?

Unlikely. But she will take offense.

"Oh please, you're trying to start an argument with me. I'm not going to tell Marco what to do. It's not my place."

Called that one.

Sure did.

"I don't care if it is, or it isn't your place. He'll listen to you, and as your *daughter*, I'm asking you to help me out."

"If you think I'm on your side of that discussion, think again. Despite what you think, you are important to me."

Only because I forced her to say it.

"I don't need to live in a prison."

"Don't be dramatic. You're not a prisoner. That kind of behavior is unseemly in a lady. As for your security detail, they're there to keep you safe. Honestly, you live with your head in the clouds. How you ever made it through college is beyond me."

She turns her hand over, examines the perfection of her manicure, then makes a show of fiddling with the twenty-karat diamond my uncle shoved on her ring finger. She does that to forcibly draw the eye.

If she thinks I care one bit about the rock on her finger, she can think again. The diamond is so massive, it's grotesque.

"Unseemly?" I bite my tongue. There are many things I can say about that comment.

"Yes." She slaps her hand on the table, making the crystal rattle. "You need to stop acting like a child."

"How is any of what I said acting like a child? I can take care of myself."

"You are heir to the Rossi fortune. You act like you don't know what that means. With no idea of the danger all around you. If only I'd had a son. A male would understand."

"Of course, Mother, my fragile female brain can't comprehend such complicated things, and as far as being in danger? How the hell am I in danger?"

"Now, you're twisting my words. The business world is complicated. Unscrupulous men will do whatever it takes to get an advantage over their competitors. It takes a degree of aggression you simply don't possess."

"Aggression is different from danger. I spent years learning everything I need to know and being aggressive isn't the end all and be all of success."

"Book smarts are not the same as experience." She dismisses my comment with a sniff of indifference. "You lack experience. Who else in your graduating class stepped into the position of CEO? Even if you were a man, it would take years to learn everything."

"Well, unfortunately, Dad died before he could pass on his knowledge. But I'm finding my way."

"No need to *find your way*. Your uncle is more than willing to step in. Besides, you're not getting any younger."

Younger?

Here it comes ...

"I don't need him stepping in." Leaning back, my arms cross over my chest. Yes, it's a defensive mood. Yes, she sees it for what it is.

She may not be a Wolf of Wall Street, but my mother is the Empress of Expression.

The *not getting any younger* comment is one I'm not touching with a ten-foot pole. My purpose in life does not begin and end with my uterus.

"You're too stubborn to ask for the help you need." She flicks her fingers as if getting rid of something distasteful. "You should've paid more attention to your lessons in finishing school. Decorum and manners were never your strong suit."

"I had other things to learn."

"Of course, but letting you waste all your time on the martial arts messed with your brain; gave you ideas and blurred the lines between men and women."

"If you mean it taught self-confidence, self-reliance, and self-discipline, then you're right."

It's also perfect for keeping in shape. To this day, I practice my moves religiously and train with an instructor several times a week. It keeps the mind sharp, the reflexes on point, and it's a great way to work out my aggression.

"You're a beautiful woman, Maria. That's the power you wield. It's your best attribute, and someday, you'll understand what that means. Not to mention, that's what we're going to capitalize on. Running the Belvedere is a fantasy that's run its course and has come to its end. It's time to turn your attention to the future."

"Wow, I'm sorry you're so disappointed in me. I suppose graduating with honors means nothing to you, and have you looked at our financial reports?"

"Why should I? Marco tells me what I need to know."

"That's exactly my point. Who's he to decide what you need to know?"

"He's my husband."

Your second husband.

What kind of woman marries her dead husband's brother? It's twisted.

But I get it. My mother is looking to the future. I'm her only child. Marrying my uncle, when she did, ensured no other children would be born into the Rossi family.

I *am* the future of the Rossi family.

As for *He's my husband,* yet again, I'm not touching that with a ten-foot pole. Or rather, I shouldn't.

I know going in that it's a mistake, but I can't help myself.

"Well, I'm killing it, and I don't need a man to tell me what to think, what to do, or how to do it. I have a backbone, and I'm not stuck in the past when it comes to outdated, sexist thinking. Our last two quarterly reports are nothing short of spectacular."

I press my finger on the table, emphasizing my point. Not that it does any good, judging by her indignant snort.

Since when is it *ladylike* to snort?

"That's my doing." I can't help wanting my mother's praise. It's instinctual for a child to seek a parent's approval. "Those are my business decisions, and my strategic plan, implementing the changes the Belvedere needs to move into the next century."

"Your father made a mistake." Mother picks at nonexistent lint on the white linen tablecloth.

"Excuse me?"

"He spoiled you. Put ideas in your head. He wanted a son but got a girl. He *overcompensated.* I tried to tell him no man wants to marry a woman who competes with him at work, but he didn't listen. He filled your mind with this drivel. A man wants a wife who supports him. Not a woman who opposes him and fights him on every little thing. You're making my job harder than it should be."

"Your job?"

"Finding an appropriate match for you."

"For me?"

"Yes, darling. A husband."

"Need I mention, again, that it's not the 1950s? Those kinds of outdated ideas are gone for a reason. I don't need you to find me a husband."

"A woman of your social stature needs to be extremely selective when choosing a husband. I have several candidates in mind. We can talk about them next time you come to brunch."

"I'm not discussing this further. I'm not getting married to some cretin you think will make a good match for the Rossi's. When I marry, if I marry, it'll be for love."

"You're being difficult."

"I'm not being difficult. Money, and social status, are not the end all and be all of happiness. Who I marry is my choice. Not yours."

"Who you marry affects the Rossi's. Love is an illusion. You'll marry an appropriate match for both you and the Rossi's." Her perfectly upturned nose fits her prejudices like a glove. "We need to be selective and careful who we allow into this family."

"Well, thanks, but no thanks, for the matchmaking help. I don't believe in great families merging resources by forcing eligible bachelors and bachelorettes into loveless and lifelong unions of despair and regret."

"Your job is to further the family's interests. You'll marry an appropriate match. Someone I approve. That's the end of it."

"Is that what you did? Did you marry Father to further family interests?"

"I did what was expected of me."

"Were you ever in love?"

The strangest expression comes over her face: intense anger mixed with something even more frightening, deep-seated hatred.

Too afraid to say anything, silence stretches between us. Is it possible she hated my father? If so, why marry him in the first place?

Mother takes her napkin off her lap and folds it into a neat square. That's the signal our luncheon is at an end.

"I know getting a degree was important to you. I know running your father's company is important too, but this is not the life he meant for his daughter. You've had your fun. You've honored his memory, but this nonsense needs to end."

"Excuse me?"

"Marco and I have been patient, but it's time to make a few changes. If you're not going to look out for your future, I will."

Resentment rampages through me as I bite my tongue trying not to snap at my mother.

"You can't force this on me."

"I can and I have. It's time to fulfill your obligations to the family."

My eyes sting with the threat of tears. I'm a strong, independent woman, but that doesn't mean I don't crave the love of my mother.

"But my job ..."

"Rossi women don't have jobs. It's beneath us. The decision's already been made. Don't act like a child. This isn't an argument you can win." With that, my mother departs.

There's no goodbye. No hugs filled with air and very little tenderness. There's no kiss on my cheek that shows me I'm loved.

I emerge from lunch emotionally scarred. It's a wonder I'm not bruised and bleeding.

It hurts.

It always does. I rub my breastbone, trying to erase the fresh wounds inflicted by my mother and fight to breathe against the constriction in my chest.

But I will not cry.

Not where others can see.

My mother turns innocuous comments into the most vicious weapons ever wielded. There's no way I'll live up to the unobtainable standards she puts in place.

I watch her depart, tears pricking at my eyes, and clutch my phone. I've kept it on silent the entire time, honoring my mother's wishes about intrusive texts during a meal.

Hopefully, Sybil's having a much better time than me. I look forward to reading her texts. She can be obnoxious about it, especially when she knows such texts annoy my mother.

I expect to see well over sixty texts from Sybil, one for each minute I endured. To my surprise, there are none.

I leave a tip equal to the cost of our meal, then fire off an email to the waiter's manager, singing his praises when dealing with difficult customers. Then, I fire off a string of texts to Sybil and anxiously wait for a reply.

I get nothing.

I send another handful of texts, detailing my mother's plans to saddle me with a husband I hate in a marriage I loathe. It's sure to get a response.

Nothing.

That's odd.

I head up to my office on the twenty-second floor. My personal suite of rooms, my apartment, aka prison, is easiest to access through the private staircase in my office. If I take the elevator to the twenty-third floor, I have to weave my way through our extensive security suite.

Somehow, making that commute is distasteful. I don't like that they all know I live in an overly spacious apartment occupying nearly a quarter of the twenty-third floor.

Of course, it's nothing like the twenty-fifth floor. That floor belongs to my uncle; all of it. Not to live in. He uses the floor to run his businesses. The Rossi family is involved in a lot of businesses.

By the time I make it upstairs, there's still nothing from Sybil. My insides churn. Sybil and I have been inseparable since the summer we met.

If we aren't with each other, we text nonstop. We text all day long. I'm talking scores and scores of texts. That doesn't count the many phone calls.

Something's terribly wrong.

Over the next hour, I begin to pace. I haven't heard from Sybil since she was in my office, heading to the spa.

The spa.

It takes half a second to get the number and one minute to learn Sybil never showed up for her appointment.

Real fear punches me in the gut.

"Sybil, where the hell are you?"

5

MARIA

With my overly active imagination, I have Sybil kidnapped and headed for horrible things within a nanosecond. My imagination is not my friend.

There's a perfectly reasonable explanation why Sybil never made it to the spa.

What if she got in a wreck?

My hands fly to my face, squishing my cheeks together and pushing my lips out. A wreck is far more likely than a kidnapping. It's equally bad and potentially worse.

Think. Think. Think.

If Sybil got in a wreck, they would notify next of kin.

Do I call her parents?

I don't want to bother them. Her father is in and out of the hospital, dealing with leukemia. The last thing he needs is a panicked phone call from me.

What else?

I tap my fingers on my desk, but for the life of me, I can't think where she could be. Sybil was headed to the spa. Maybe something happened in the garage? She hates garages; says they're spooky places where nefarious men wait on pretty girls heading to their cars alone.

What if some guy nabbed her and shoved her in the back of his trunk? What if she's there right now, banging on the trunk and screaming for help?

Okay, that's simply ridiculous. He wouldn't leave the car in the garage. Mr. Nefarious would hightail it out of there.

See? This is where my mind goes.

The urge to run to the garage overwhelms me, but what am I going to do?

I could call security and have them take a look.

But what am I going to tell them? I have no proof Sybil got nabbed in the garage. There's no way to know if she was involved in an accident. I could call the hospitals, but again, I'm not immediate family. They won't release any information.

Now I pace.

Up and down the long bank of floor-to-ceiling glass, I stop at the corners and peer out at the city below. Can I see any signs of an accident? No, of course I can't.

So, what can I do? What can I do that doesn't make me look like a raving lunatic?

Another glance at my phone reveals the same thing from the last hundred times I looked.

Nothing.

No texts.

No calls.

Nada.

It's as if Sybil vanished off the surface of the planet. My hands tremble as I shove my phone back in my pocket. My stomach twists in knots, churning until I'm sick to my stomach.

I'm a total mess. There's probably a simple explanation and I'm working myself into knots over nothing.

What can I do?

Of all things, my mother's voice speaks in my head. *If you lose something, the best way to find it is to go to the place you last saw it.*

Okay.

The last place I saw Sybil was my office.

That doesn't help.

No. That's not right. The last place I saw her was at the elevator.

I race to the elevator and mash the down button.

My heart bangs away inside my chest, sending adrenaline-fueled fear coursing through my body. My hands shake. My breaths become shallow and rapid. That queasy sensation in my stomach turns into a full-on riot.

I'm going to be sick.

I race to the bathroom, barely making it in time.

Holding my hair to the side, I empty the contents of my stomach. I hate throwing up. My entire body shakes with this weird, unsettled feeling. When I'm convinced there's nothing left in my stomach, I head to the sink, where I wash my hands and splash cold water on my face.

Staring at my reflection, I barely recognize the woman looking back at me. All color is gone from her face. Red lines her eyes.

Not a good look on me.

I put myself together and head back to the elevator.

Technically, the last place I saw Sybil was when she entered the elevator. She would've gone down to the employee levels of the parking garage. I remember her saying something about a particular level, but for the life of me, I can't remember which one. There are three employee levels of the garage sitting beneath the Belvedere.

I jab the button marked EL-1: employee level 1. The elevator doors close so damn slowly, and the elevator drops the twenty-plus floors moving with the speed of molasses. Each floor I pass comes with a little ding until I finally look out onto employee parking.

"Okay." I brush back the hair from my face. "Sybil drives a ..."

Shit! I have no idea what kind of car Sybil is driving today. I mean, I know what her car looks like, but her car is in the shop.

She drove a loaner.

Shit. Shit. Shit!

"Miss Rossi?" The deep timbre of Gerald's voice pulls me up short. My ever-present security team followed me down. They're sneaky shits like that.

I wipe the tears on my cheek and slowly turn around.

"Yes, Gerald?"

"If you want to head out, I'm happy to take you."

Dear Gerald, you don't deserve my anger.

"Um, I wasn't trying to go anywhere. I just remembered my friend said she brought me something for tonight's event. It's in the trunk of her car, but silly me, I left the keys upstairs."

"Of course," Gerald gestures toward the elevator.

Gerald's nice.

Let me qualify that. As a human, he's a nice guy, but as one of the many security tasked with watching over me, I hate him for taking the job. Yet again, I don't know how they followed me, or how they got here so quick, but sure as shit, three of them are here.

"Sorry, guys." I wave to Stefan and Duke. "No need to bother yourselves. I'll just head back upstairs and give her a call. I should have her bring it to me anyway." I give a goofy shrug.

Shit.

The Gala.

I roll my wrist to check the time. I've got a little over an hour before my presence is required. The Gala starts promptly at five. There's an hour of meet and greet, followed by a silent auction, then dinner is served. The intern auction follows.

The whole thing shuts down by nine.

Most of our donors are older couples who prefer heading home before the bewitching hour. It also serves the needs of the younger crowd. Most of them don't head out to the clubs until at least nine or ten. They get to go to the Gala *and* have a night on the town. It's win-win for all involved.

Except for me.

Nine is hours away.

As the CEO, my presence is required, and Mother will be there. She'll arrive promptly at five and leave no later than eight. That leaves me less than an hour to find Sybil and get dressed for the Gala.

Stefan and Duke return polite smiles. I don't know if I convince them or not. All that matters to them is that I'm not allowed to leave without them by my side.

Nice guys. Shit job.

I hate them for contributing to my imprisonment.

Duke pushes the button for the elevator and all four of us ride back to the twenty-second floor. They walk me to the door of my office, then politely excuse themselves.

A glance at the clock reveals too much time has passed.

I barely have time to get ready. My hairdresser and makeup specialist will be here in less than half an hour.

Sybil, where the hell are you?

I knock my fist against my forehead. I need to figure this out, but I'm trapped by my role as CEO and my position as the *only Rossi heir.*

"Sybil, this had better be a joke. If not, I'm going to kill you for making me worry."

With societal obligations I can't ignore, I spend the next hour getting glammed up for the annual charity auction. At five 'til five, I meet my mother and uncle downstairs.

"Good evening, Maria." My mother's lips pinch, disappointed by something. I don't know what and I don't care.

I'm the spitting image of my mother, except for my eyes. She wears a ruby-red gown adorned with glittering crystals. The fabric drapes her willowy frame in elegant falls and the embedded crystals glitter in the light of the chandeliers. That's not all that sparkles.

Diamonds encircle her neck, wrap around her wrists, and adorn her fingers. The twenty-karat monstrosity, however, takes center stage, flashing its brilliance for all to see. Millions in diamonds cling to her frame, but her only security is the imposing presence of my uncle.

Black shoes. Black pants. Black shirt, tie, and jacket; he's a pillar of black on black. His evening attire matches his black hair and coal-black eyes. A handsome man, his face is chiseled perfection, square jaw, hawkish nose, brooding brow, piercing eyes, the slightest hint of a five o'clock shadow that never goes away.

Power radiates from his body. His hardened gaze vibrates with authority, making me want to curl into myself, or slink away. There's something wild about him, something feral. Everything about him screams danger.

Intimidation.

Power.

The air buzzes around him, a warning to beware and proceed with caution. The firm set of his lips and his hardened gaze trigger alarms in my head. There's always been something off about my uncle.

"Maria." My uncle takes a step forward. Grasping my elbow, he leans in and places a kiss on my cheek. "You look lovely as always." He delivers his comment mechanically, cold as hell, and releases me as quickly as he can.

His eyes say something else entirely. Full of criticism and judgment, his cold gaze sends my pulse racing. There's no compassion in those eyes.

"Thank you." I keep my reply light, welcoming, and friendly. "This looks to be a great year for the charity. Do you want to grab drinks before the silent auction begins?"

"You go ahead." Mother clutches my uncle's arm. "We'll be along shortly."

Summarily dismissed, I don't see either of them until dinner is served, which is fine by me. The meal is extravagant. The conversation cursory. Honestly, a conversation about the weather would be more exciting.

The first part of the evening consists of silent bidding on various donated items: trips to exotic locales, crates of fine wine and finer whiskey, resort getaways, jewelry, and many other things. There's something for everyone and we expect to bring in six figures for the first auction alone. We hope to double that for the intern's auction: the one Sybil fails to make.

She's officially MIA and I'm losing my ever-loving mind.

I do everything in my power not to fidget. Trapped by my position and obligation as CEO, I can't leave the banquet until the end. Even worse is the smile I can't let slip. On the outside, I'm the perfect host, gracious and welcoming. I shake hands, laugh at stale jokes, and work the room while my insides churn and fear takes root.

Inside, I'm dying. Something is officially wrong. Days too early to file a missing person's report, I don't know what I can do, but I must do something.

Mother and Uncle Marco excuse themselves moments prior to the intern's auction. I get no goodbye other than a brief fluttering of my mother's fingers. As usual, Uncle Marco barely says a word to me.

There's definitely something different about my mother. She's anticipatory, almost gleeful. I can't put my finger on it, but she doesn't insult me one time. That alone is noteworthy.

Whatever excites her is enough to ignore her daughter. To make matters weirder, that same eagerness slips past my uncle's normally stoic exterior. Those two are up to something.

Hopefully, it has nothing to do with me.

I close my eyes and pray my overly active imagination is just that. I hate that I'm such a worrier. The entire dinner, my stomach knots with dread. Each minute is an eternity where anything can happen to Sybil.

As with all things, eventually the Gala comes to an end. I say my goodbyes, thank everyone for coming, finish up with a short speech, then hightail it out of the ballroom and race to my office. Up the back set of stairs, I remove the constrictive ball gown and slip back into the business suit with my favorite blouse I wore earlier.

If I'm supposed to look where I last saw Sybil, there's only one place to go, and it's just outside my door.

6

LIAM

"*Found it,*" Mitzy calls out through the comms. "*Veer left. You'll see an employee access door.*"

Wolfe guides Jinx over to the door Mitzy indicates. Nondescript, it's colored the same deep, ruby red as the rest of the walls. There's a small doorknob that breaks with the camouflage, but otherwise, there's nothing to distract eager gamblers from the glam and glitz of the slots and gaming tables.

Lily and I redirect our bar intersection, following now, instead of leading. Wolfe puts Jinx's back to the wall and props his hand over her head. They kiss and grope while we wait for an employee to come through the door.

Lily stands beside me, leaning against the wall. She kicks up a boot, pressing the sole against the wall. I mirror her pose, crossing my arms over my chest. Next to me, Jinx and Wolfe are a mess of roaming hands and passionate kisses.

"Here." I hand Lily a bunch of flyers I pulled from the displays by the door. "Pretend you're looking for what to do."

The flyers are a mix of shows, nightlife, restaurants, and thrill rides.

My gaze shifts to Jinx and Wolfe for a microsecond, then I focus back on the crowd. Overhead, there are far too many cameras to count.

"How long do you figure they'll have?" Like me, Lily pretends to look at the flyers, but she's watching the crowd. "I count seven. How about you?"

"Twelve."

"Twelve?" She arches a brow. "No way I missed that many. There are two by the bar. Four at the tables: three watch the players, the other one watches the dealers, and one by the entrance."

Our job is to identify the security personnel working the floor. The moment Jinx and Wolfe slip away, we're on the clock. Their presence in the employee-only areas will draw attention, but we're prepared for that.

Not wanting to attract too much attention, I show Lily who she missed. Since coming to Guardian HRS, her mind has been a sponge, trying to soak up as much information as possible before being placed on active status.

Recently recruited onto Delta team, she'll be working domestic hostage rescue after her orientation and training are complete.

"Two by the entrance, not one. That couple over there are undercover."

"How ..." Lily glances at them. "Ah, I see. Shoulder harnesses. She needs a looser fitting jacket."

"Agree." It didn't take a second for the bulge in the woman's jacket to give away her purpose.

"Check out the slots. The other two are there. See how they walk the rows?"

It takes Lily a second. "Got it. You've got a good eye."

"As do you."

"I missed too many." Her brows knit together, frustrated with her performance.

"You'll always miss something. Expect the unexpected and you'll do just fine."

I'm surprised she found as many as she did. Although, I shouldn't be. Lily comes to the Guardians with years of DEA experience under her belt. Jinx too.

"And if they catch Jinx and Wolfe before they ..." She tugs on her earring and pushes off the wall. Spinning to face me, she loops her hands around my neck. Her fingers play with my hair. I place a hand over the small of her back and pull her in for a kiss. Beside us, Jinx and Wolfe haven't stopped pawing each other.

"Jeez, how long is this going to take?"

"No way to know." This is the one piece we don't control. We're blind when it comes to the movements of the Belvedere's employees. "But it shouldn't be too long. With as many employees that work the floor, someone's either coming on shift, getting off work, or taking a break."

"Just makes me nervous." She lifts on tiptoe and kisses my cheek. "Security makes me nervous. The moment Wolfe and Jinx slip through that door, what's to keep them from going after them?"

"They won't."

"How can you be so sure?"

"Human nature."

"Meaning?"

"The house is interested in the gamblers. Their entire focus is on the gaming floor. Watching those at slots, making sure they're not messing with the machines. They watch the players at the table, making sure no one is counting cards or cheating. Their entire focus is on the room, not what's happening at the edges ... or who slipped into employee-only areas. You don't think this is the first time the house catches a couple looking for a bit of a thrill."

At least that's the entire premise. Mitzy says it'll work. We'll see about that.

"It's a big risk." Lily continues to scan the room, looking for security teams who show any interest in the two couples holding up the wall.

"They can't afford to pull security off the floor. They'll send someone else after Wolfe and Jinx."

"I hope so."

"Me too."

It doesn't take long before two cocktail waitresses come through the door. As they head to work, Lily discretely blocks the door from closing with her boot.

"You guys are on," I whisper to Wolfe and Jinx, but there's no need. Wolfe takes Jinx's hand. He glances out into the crowd, looking like a guilty fucker, then he and Jinx slip through the doorway and disappear.

Meanwhile, Lily and I listen to their progress as Mitzy navigates them to a cleaning closet and talks them through uploading the code she needs to access Belvedere's security systems.

As I suspected, none of the security on the floor go after the amorous couple, but they are aware of the breach. I catch several of them speaking into their communication gear. They're fucking obvious about it too. Honestly, it's comical.

A few minutes later, I hear the magic words.

Mission success. Wolfe's gruff voice sounds in my ear.

The code was uploaded moments before Wolfe and Jinx got caught by a security patrol sent to find them. They're escorted out by the guards where Lily and I wait.

Jinx hugs Lily. "I'm so going to kill you! We got caught." Jinx grins at the two security guards. "Thanks for not busting us."

"Just get a room next time." One of the guards rolls his eyes. As I suspected, this isn't the first couple he's had to deal with.

The guards let Wolfe and Jinx off with a warning.

"Thank you, you're the best." Jinx gives each of the guards a quick peck on the cheek.

"Now, how about drinks?" Lily drags me away. "I hear this place has the most amazing rooftop bar with an awesome view."

We head to a set of elevators and crowd on board with nearly a score of other people. The Belvedere definitely knows how to move large groups of people efficiently.

"Checkpoint Delta achieved," Wolfe reports our progress to our team.

"Copy that. Head over to the southern corner. You'll see a maintenance hatch which leads down to the HVAC floor." Mitzy guides us once again.

Our intelligence says the women are being held in a room two floors beneath the rooftop bar. Our job is to free them, extract them via the rooftop bar, then walk them out the front of the Belvedere.

Walk out of the front entrance!

It's a crazy mission.

Wolfe's eyes practically bugged out of his head when Mitzy suggested it. I don't know how she can pull it off, but that's why we call it Mitzy Magic.

The bar is hopping. The music thumps. The dance floor pulses. It's a warm night with enough breeze to keep things comfortable. Unlike the gaming floor, where cigarettes are discouraged, the smokers take it as a challenge to keep a smoke cloud over our heads. I hate the noxious fumes and blink against the sting in my eyes.

Over a hundred people party it up on the rooftop while the city lights stretch out toward the horizon. It's a really cool bar with fluorescent lighting on the dance floor and around the edges of the rooftop railing. The lights pulse to the beat of the music as eager dancers bump and grind on the dance floor.

"T-minus ten. You guys ready?" Mitzy calls out to us.

Technically, Wolfe is the lead of this op, but all four of us answer.

We wait for Mitzy's signal as things become more organized on the dance floor. People cluster together, then they begin to form lines. The rooftop bar turns into a massive line dance. More people arrive via the elevators as Mitzy counts us down.

Someone reaches out from the crowd, handing me a duffel bag. I sling it over my shoulder and nod to Wolfe. The contents are our ticket out of here.

The table we occupy sits next to an equipment access door with an electronic lock. On Mitzy's mark, the door remotely unlocks, and the four of us move. I hold the door while Wolfe, Lily, and Jinx file in, then close it behind us. We wind our way through a maze of machinery until we reach another door leading to a stairwell.

"Take the stairwell down one flight." Mitzy keeps us moving, calling

out the locations of the guards. In the background, she scrambles the feeds of the surveillance cameras. She inserts a loop of an empty hall as we engage an enemy who never sees us coming.

Using silent, non-lethal darts, Jinx and I take out the men guarding our objective. Behind that unobtrusive door, our kidnap victims have no idea we're here to rescue them.

Mitzy's remote access unlocks the door. Wolfe and I look at each other, counting down silently from three to one. We kick down the door.

I sweep right. Wolfe sweeps left.

7

MARIA

I BARGE INTO THE SECURITY SUITE AT THE BELVEDERE. MEN LOOK UP from the camera feeds they monitor, but otherwise ignore me. Since I've made it a habit to visit all divisions within the Belvedere, my presence isn't abnormal.

I head to an unoccupied terminal in the corner and sit down. Before I can log in, Bert Ruben, Assistant Chief of Security, waddles over to me. His grin is as large as the rest of him.

"Miss Rossi, what a pleasure to have you back with us. Is there something I can help you with?"

"Oh, thank you, but no." I lower my voice to a whisper. "There's a guy at the Gala and well ..." I don't finish my sentence because I have no idea what to say. I'm a horrible liar. All I need is for Bert to leave me alone.

"Do you need any help?"

"You're so sweet, but I remember what to do. Thank you." I smile and flutter my lashes.

Burt is sweet and easy to manipulate. Just like with the maids, I spent a week behind a computer screen with security, monitoring the gambling floor, the guest halls, the loading docks, and every other piece of the Belvedere.

"If you need any help ..." He clasps his hands together, hopeful.

"Thank you so much, but you're an excellent teacher. If I run into problems, I'll call you."

"I'll leave you to it, Miss Rossi."

"Thank you." I wait for him to leave before rolling up my sleeves and digging in.

Sybil got on that elevator. What level of employee parking did she exit on? If I know that, I can focus on that level.

Still nothing from Sybil.

I pull up the footage from outside my office and wind back the tape to just before lunch. I follow Sybil to the elevator where two other employees join her. The men enter the elevator with Sybil and I switch security cameras to the one inside the elevator, only it's on the fritz.

I lose the feed. I scroll the timestamp forward. Whatever the malfunction, it appears to be fixed an hour later.

With thousands of cameras scattered throughout the Belvedere, malfunctions are not uncommon. I rewind, note the time, then jump down to the cameras in the garage.

Eyes glued to the screen, I wait for the elevator door to open on EL-1, but nothing happens. I fast forward the feed.

Nothing.

Switching to EL-2, the same thing happens. The elevator door never opens. I move to EL-3, hoping this is the right floor. Clutching at my gut, tension builds within me.

Nothing.

Leaning back, I blow out a breath, wondering what I'm missing.

Okay, think it through.

My fingers tap the desk as I try to piece together the puzzling disappearance of my friend. She didn't vanish inside the elevator.

What about the two men? Is there any sign of them exiting the elevator?

Only one way to know.

Backing up the feed again, I note the time stamp. I check each floor, looking for the elevator door opening. The cameras show two views where they're mounted. One points into the elevator, the other points the opposite direction down the hall. All I need is to search floor by floor and wait for Sybil to exit the elevator.

I will find her.

Starting at the twenty-first floor, I'm systematic in my search.

No Sybil.

Not only is there no Sybil, but there's no sign of the two men who rode with her exiting the elevator. I check the feed inside the elevator again. It cuts out the moment the three of them boarded it.

If no one got out on any of the floors below, did they go up instead?

I flex my fingers and lean in, determined to solve this mystery. But there's nothing on the closed-circuit monitors which show her exiting the elevator.

Sybil simply vanished.

Okay, don't panic.

Bert comes by several times to check on me. Each time, I flip over to the banquet hall and pretend I'm looking for my mystery man of the evening.

The moment he walks away, I lean in and double down. In a casino, where every square inch of the building is monitored and recorded, it should be impossible to lose anyone.

I set a thirty-minute window, fast forward all the feeds, and check everything out from the parking garage to the laundry room, to the entrances, loading docks, and even the rooftop bar. There are no cameras on the HVAC floor and none on the twenty-fifth.

That floor is restricted. Even I'm not allowed up there, which says something considering I'm the CEO. Uncle Marco uses that floor for his business dealings and doesn't want the intrusiveness of surveillance cameras in that space. Not that they aren't there.

I pull at my chin, thinking.

An idea comes to me. It takes a moment to remember the pass-code, but I think I've got it right. I enter a code I once saw my father type into his computer at home. He needed to access the Belvedere's security systems from outside the building for some reason. I remember it because my father seemed nervous that night.

He died later that night, and it's my hope the code still exists within Belvedere's systems.

It's a Hail Mary move, but I've got nothing left to try.

I type the code, squeeze my eyes tight, and press Enter. Prying my eyes open, I stare at the screen.

Success! I'm in.

Knowing I don't have much time, I search the twenty-fifth floor. Marco may not want surveillance on his floor, but that doesn't mean there aren't hundreds of cameras. And it doesn't mean they aren't recording everything they see. All it means is they operate on a separate server, a server my father's old access code cracks wide open.

The elevator feed cuts out the moment Sybil enters the elevator. I flip over to a camera directed toward the elevator on the twenty-fifth floor. Oddly, those feeds are also affected. It's too much of a coincidence.

I stare at the feed, letting it fast forward. The interference cuts out after a minute or two, leaving me staring at a closed elevator. Switching to the hallway view, I nibble at my lower lip hoping something happens. The time index counts upward. Thirty minutes pass and the hall remains empty.

Bert is on patrol again, heading my way. I've spent too much time here and draw his eye. Time to give up. As I reach to cut the feed, three men exit a room at the far end of the hall. They stride toward the elevator, heads down, very purposeful in their gate. Each man carries a laundry bag slung over his shoulder. As someone who's worked with the housekeeping service, they aren't carrying laundry.

They carry something far worse.

Not that I'm an expert, but those are bodies in those bags, and none of the bodies show signs of life.

With my heart pounding, I track them to the elevator. From there, I follow them to the loading dock where a panel truck waits for them. They load the bodies and shut the doors. The truck drives off while I gulp air.

My overly active imagination is a curse, except this time—this time it got everything right.

I don't know if Sybil is in one of those bags, but I feel it. I feel it in my gut. I feel it in the shattering of my heart. Somehow, I simply know.

Sybil didn't vanish.

She was taken.

Bert angles in my direction. Quickly, I shut down the feed, only my finger slips. Instead of a replay, the cameras reveal a live feed of the twenty-fifth floor.

Two men in dark suits and two women in cocktail dresses creep down the hall. As if that's not weird enough, each of them carries a gun.

They take out two men posted as guards outside that same room, then kick in the door and rush inside.

One of the security technicians calls Bert over to review a potential cheater at the craps table. Bert pauses to review the file. The technician points at the screen and they discuss what they see.

Meanwhile, I look back at the room. The two men and two women exit, but now they wear bright orange tee-shirts with a smiley face on them. In addition, they escort three women out of the room. They wear the same shirts but are dirty, disheveled, and wear no shoes.

What the hell?

I follow their movements, but instead of heading to the elevator, they take the stairs. Whoever those people are, they know something about Sybil. And if they're taking the stairs, I strongly doubt they're walking down twenty-five flights.

Which means I know exactly where they're headed.

As I close down my screen, several of the technicians call out to Bert. All I hear is something about bright orange shirts. I race to the rooftop with no idea what I'm going to do, but I stop in my apartment and grab my gun.

I'm prepared for anything.

8

LIAM

Jinx and Lily follow us into the room.

I take out one guard. Wolfe gets another. We expect two but find six instead.

The remaining men rise from their game of cards, reaching for their weapons. Lily and Jinx don't hesitate. The girls are fucking fierce. Together, they take down two men, leaving only two standing.

Or rather, two rushing toward me and Wolfe.

They completely ignore Lily and Jinx, which is an epic mistake.

Jinx moves into action. In a flowing dance of death, the men go down. We work seamlessly as a team, which is amazing considering neither Wolfe nor I have ever operated with a female before. To my surprise, it's just like working alongside Max, Knox, Axel, and Griff.

Who knew?

"Where are the women?" Jinx scans the room. Two doors lead out of the room. One goes to a bathroom, which is empty. Jinx heads to the other door. "Found them."

I yank the duffel bag off my shoulder and toss it on the table. We work on borrowed time. Once open, I yank out a stack of bright orange shirts with a garish white *Be Happy* smiley face smack dab on the front.

Our goal is no longer about stealth.

It's about blending in.

Wolfe heads into the room with the women. Rose Hunt, Julie Gant, and Lori Black are filthy, scared, and afraid. They huddle together, unsure if we're there to help, or to harm.

But they're alive and not too damaged to move.

Jinx hands each girl a shirt, calming the girls and soothing them by explaining who we are and what's happening. None of the women wear shoes, which complicates things.

We'll make it work.

All the women look comical because the extra-large shirts hang down to their knees. Wolfe gives me a look as he dons his shirt.

"We need to move." I keep my voice low, for Wolfe's ears only.

"Copy that." He glances at the women. "Ten seconds."

"Gotcha." Jinx helps Rose Hunt with her shirt while Lily moves to the other women.

While Wolfe gets the women ready to move, I watch over our sleeping guards. When we head out, Wolfe's on point and I take the rear. Jinx holds hands with Rose. Lily has Julie Gant on her left and Lori Black on her right.

"Which direction? Up or down?" Wolfe asks for direction.

"Back to the roof," Mitzy responds.

"So, we're really doing this?" I ask.

"Trust me." Mitzy's voice is terse. Strained.

Wolfe looks back at me and shakes his head. I'm with him. What Mitzy plans is absolute insanity.

"We know." Jinx squeezes Rose's hand, lending support.

"I'm scared." Rose sniffs, but she's steady on her feet and ready for whatever comes next.

The woman is a fighter.

All three women were brutally taken and traumatized. They're strong where it counts.

Wolfe counts us down. On his mark, we move as a group, heading back to the stairwell and up the flight of stairs.

I remove the duffel bag from my shoulder, pull out the white masks, then tie the door closed. It won't stop anyone, but it'll definitely slow them down. Tucking the masks under my arm, I take the stairs two at a time.

Wolfe steers the women through the maze of the machine room, then stops at the service door where we entered. A deep thumping bass sounds from the other side accompanied by the stomping and clapping of dancers.

While I hand out the masks, Wolfe peers through the slats of the service door. "Fucking amazing."

We exit onto the rooftop bar and come to a halt, stunned by what we see.

A flash mob has taken over the entire roof. They wear identical orange shirts with that damn garish white smiley face on it. In addition, they wear white masks as they dance to the song "Happy" by Pharrell Williams. It's absolutely chaotic and perfect.

We move into the sea of orange, the four of us with our three rescues. We do a bit of rearranging. Wolfe takes Rose's hand. I grab Julie. Jinx and Lily put Lori between them.

Definitely not a stealth op.

We move into the crowd, dancing with the flash mob as we make our way across the roof to the elevators.

"If you like this," Mitzy's voice rings in my ear, *"you're going to love what's downstairs."*

Halfway across the dance floor, the elevator doors open and half a dozen security guards pour out.

"Time to move." Wolfe presses forward.

The dance steps are easy. Wolfe is a bit awkward. Lily and Jinx carve up the floor. Rose, Lori, and Julie stumble through the steps, still in shock and unsure about the rescue.

My attention sticks to the guards. When they head to the periphery, moving away from the elevator, I breathe in. They were probably sent to keep an eye on the crowd and make sure it doesn't get too crazy.

We make it to the elevators, unmolested, when all of a sudden, every cellphone goes off. The crowd shouts and moves en-mass for the elevator. We push in, keeping our group together, where we hide in plain sight.

People jostle one another. As a big man, I keep my elbows in while protecting my charge. I accidentally bump into a woman beside me.

"Sorry." My gruff apology is met with a piercing glare from the beautiful woman.

She stands out because she's not wearing an orange shirt like everyone else. Or a mask.

And the stare she gives me is filled with unrestrained hatred.

I do a double-take because her eyes are the color of sapphires.

Fucking stunning.

I shift Julie to my other side, protecting my rescue.

The people inside the elevator vibrate with excess energy. It's a palpable force. Everyone wears a white mask. We're all in the same garish orange shirt.

Except for the woman with sapphire eyes.

Her attention bounces around the crowd, but I swear her look lingers on our rescues.

I pull Julie in tight, sheltering her within my protective umbrella. With a step to the left, I move away from the unusual woman.

That creates a hole in the crowd, which an excited partygoer immediately fills. The man shouts, holding up his phone. "It's going viral!" He shows Wolfe his screen. "Look."

I peek and see a video of hundreds of people on the rooftop dancing.

"Ten thousand views and climbing," the man says. "We're going to break the record."

Everyone shouts at his comment. Record? It's insane, but I wouldn't put it past Mitzy to try to break a flash mob record in the middle of an operation.

The express elevator slows and comes to a stop. I take Julie's hand as the doors open to a sea of orange. "Happy" blares through the speakers as the crowd gyrates toward the exit.

I can't help but shake my head.

Mitzy Magic, indeed.

The brilliance of her plan astounds me. In addition to our mission, she's also running a rescue operation with the rest of Alpha team. How the hell did she do this?

One thing I'll say, as far as operations go, this is easily the most fun I've ever had.

We merge with the crowd, keeping pace with those around us. We're jostled about and struggle not to be separated as we walk and dance our way outside. The woman with the sapphire eyes gets tossed against me again.

"Sorry." One look into her eyes, and I struggle to breathe. I steady her on her feet, then turn my attention back to my charge as we near the exit.

Soon, we're outside the Belvedere. That stupid song blares over loudspeakers parked outside, and the crowd grows and grows, spilling out, up, and down the street in all directions, and not only from the Belvedere. It appears to be a mass event.

Everyone's dressed in orange. Most wear the white masks. All dance the exact same steps.

"Cross the street. Head left. You'll see a van." Mitzy gives us final directions.

Wolfe heads toward the van while I scan the crowd for threats.

My gaze finds the woman with the sapphire eyes some distance back. I was able to push through the crowd while she got stuck in the flow.

Behind her, emerging from the Belvedere, half a dozen security guards force their way through the crowd, making a beeline straight toward us.

Fuck.

9

MARIA

THE TWO COUPLES HURRY THE CAPTIVE WOMEN OUT OF MY HOTEL, herding them like animals. The group is hard to follow, considering the entire street basically exploded into one massive flash mob.

My best friend was kidnapped and held with those women. They're my only chance to find out what happened to Sybil.

And I'm not losing them.

All around me that damn "Happy" song blares overhead. Hundreds of people in bright-orange shirts, with the same dorky white smiley face on the front, kick up their heels, oblivious of the abduction occurring right under their noses.

As if that's not bad enough, there are the masks. A *thing* in New Orleans, the whole dang mob wears nearly identical white masks, making my rescue nearly futile.

But I'm tenacious and determined.

I chase after the kidnappers. It's just me and my Colt .45.

The two men stand head and shoulders above the crowd. That's the only reason I follow the kidnappers at all. The two women who are with them, the men's *dates*—and I use the term loosely—are impossible to follow. That goes for the three kidnapped women as well. They all wear those same loose-fitting orange shirts along with the masks, making them virtually indistinguishable from the crowd.

The kidnappers push the women through the excited flash mob, arrowing directly toward a nondescript van parked a street away. As they near the vehicle, the side door slides open. A man leans out and waves vigorously for them to hurry up.

The woman wearing combat boots jumps in. She's followed by a second woman, also wearing shoes. Those are the ones working with the men. The second woman helps one of the kidnap victims into the van. The second follows, practically leaping inside, almost as if she's willing?

My brows scrunch, confused by that. The third victim is right behind the second, jumping in and disappearing inside.

I'm going to lose them.

I yank out my Colt .45 and sprint with everything I've got.

Just a little bit further...

The first man climbs inside. The second turns his back to me.

A burst of adrenaline rushes through me, fueling the muscles of my legs. I close the distance.

"Don't move." I press the muzzle of my gun against his back. It connects with solid muscle. My voice isn't nearly as firm as I'd like, but he gets the message.

Holy hell, I did it.

Hands up, he slowly turns around. Despite the orange shirt and mask, he's a shock to my senses, and not one bit concerned about my gun. My brows climb up my forehead as he slowly removes the mask.

Holy hotness and Hollywood gorgeous, like, shoot-me-dead-and-stick-a-fork-in-me-I'm-done-kind-of-H-O-T, he decimates my ability to think. My gun waivers when the tall, freakishly handsome, Hollywood heartthrob takes me in from head to toe.

The deadly combination of surfer blond hair, mischievous eyes, and a body ripped right off a blockbuster movie poster, are a triple threat weakening my knees.

The Colt .45 wobbles.

Beneath the obnoxious orange shirt, a dark suit clads his hard physique. Not only tall, he's well built. The fabric of his suit molds around his toned and sculpted body, barely containing the flexing and bunching of his muscles.

Focus!

I'm trying to be a fucking badass.

Instead, I drool like a star-struck idiot.

Midnight-blue eyes. Strong jaw. Taller than tall. Broad chest. Trim waist. His body is chiseled perfection. Seriously, this guy can't be real.

"Where's Sybil?" My voice comes out steady, which is a surprise. I'm way outside my comfort zone, but, for Sybil, I'll do whatever it takes to get her back.

As for the Hollywood heartthrob staring at me, there's no fear in his gaze. Instead, his eyes round with surprise. Like how dare I draw a weapon on him?

I have an answer for that.

He took my bestie, and I want her back.

I tighten my grip and remind myself I'm here to rescue my best friend. My sister from another mother, Sybil, was taken, and these sad sacks are involved.

I know it, and I'm going to make them give her back.

Despite his holy hotness factor, I press the muzzle of my gun, pushing hard against the man's chest.

"Where is she?" My voice comes out a low growl.

"Whoa, hold up and calm down." The guy looks at his chest, totally chill.

Hello? I'm pointing a gun at you.

"I am calm."

"Maria Rossi?" The woman with the combat boots leans forward. Her brows pinch together then her attention snaps over my head to the crazy flash mob behind me.

"How do you know my name?"

The woman holds up her hands. Once again, her focus shifts to the crowd behind me.

"Maria, you need to pay attention." She once again looks over my head. "We don't have much time. Sybil isn't here. She's not one of the three we rescued, but we know where she is."

"Where?" I'm moments from shooting Hollywood heartthrob.

"We can explain, but we have to move." The other man speaks up. He wears the same silly shirt as everyone else, an obnoxious orange with a white smiley face on it.

The entire flash mob behind me gyrates to the music in the same damn shirt. Only instead of trying to escape in a van like these assholes, the crowd kicks up their feet.

"No one is going anywhere." I glance over my shoulder and groan.

My security detail are tenacious assholes. My uncle charged them with one thing: keeping me safe, and they don't want to piss off my uncle.

Fuckers follow me everywhere.

Honestly, they're a pain in the ass. They hound my every move, but instead of keeping me safe, they're there to keep me from looking too deeply into what my uncle is doing right under my nose.

For the first time ever, the monkeys assigned to protect me might actually do something worthwhile. I glance over my shoulder to track their progress.

The moment I check on them, I regret it.

Hollywood heartthrob grabs the muzzle of my Colt .45 and rips the pistol out of my hand. My mouth gapes, shocked by how easily he disarms me, but he's not done. He grabs me by the waist and yanks me inside the van. A girlish screech escapes me as I fly through the air.

"Go!" he shouts and pulls his legs and feet inside the van.

The other man closes the sliding door shut. The van lurches forward, moving fast, with me trapped inside.

Well, shit. This isn't part of the plan.

10

MARIA

Hollywood spins me to my back, then straddles my hips. A cocky smirk fills his expression. He's got the upper hand and knows it. I want to slap the smug look right off his face.

No one manhandles me like that and gets away with it.

I pummel his chest. Goddamn that hurts. His upper body is protected by one of those bulletproof vests. The bastard takes my wrists and pins them over my head.

Fucker.

"We've got a bit of a snafu." The man who slammed the door shut gives me the eye, like I'm some kind of puzzle he needs to sort out.

"Now aren't you a pretty thing?" Hollywood leans down until our faces are a breath apart.

His minty breath and husky laugh shouldn't be legal. Combine that with a chiseled jaw, all blunt angles with a dusting of a five o'clock shadow, and he's the kind of man women get stupid around.

There's a roughness to him; danger lurking beneath his outward perfection, authority vibrating in every breath, and lethality prowling the depths of his expressive gaze. Warning bells ring in my ears, triggering my fight or flight instincts.

Intimidating, his gaze pins me far more effectively than his grip on my hands, or the power of his legs straddling me. He can do anything to me and there's precious little I can do to fight back. If that's not bad enough, he challenges me with his hard stare, daring me to try and free myself.

I fight back the only way I can.

I head butt the sexy heartthrob.

Crack!

Score one.

Pain becomes my universe and dark spots dance in my eyes. But it's worth it.

"Fuckin' A." He releases my wrists, placing his palm over his forehead, which frees me to karate chop the side of his neck. I go right for the bundle of nerves that will wreak havoc on his senses.

Score two for me.

And I'm not done.

I rock my hips, giving me room to move. My knee slams home. Score number three; a direct hit to his nuts.

He grunts and rolls to the side, curling into fetal position, huffing in pain.

"Maria!" The woman who seems to know exactly who I am moves forward and restrains my arm.

I plan on punching Hollywood's lights out and don't appreciate the interference. I grab the chick's wrist, apply pressure on a different nerve bundle, and flip her to her back. For the first time in my life, all that training in martial arts serves a purpose.

"Okay, that's enough." The man who shut the door aims my gun at my head. "Everyone take a time out."

I take my hands off the woman.

"We're the good guys." The woman coughs and rolls to her side.

The man with my gun gives it a little shake. I puff at my hair. There's always that one bit which always seems to fall into my face. With my gun trained on me, I scoot until my back presses against the back of the front passenger seat.

"Where the hell is my friend?" I give Hollywood a look then peer into the back of the van.

The three women huddled in the back look more relieved than scared. The others stare at me, respect dawning in their expressions.

I'm having a really hard time sorting out what the hell I'm seeing. There are two others in the van. People I've ignored thus far: the driver and the man sitting in the passenger seat.

"Looks like we're having a failure to communicate." The man holding my gun narrows his gaze. "We have a team on the way to rescue your friend. As to why *you're* here, I need an answer right now."

I'm not ready to answer his questions, not when I have so many of my own. I firm my chin and deepen my voice, trying to take back control.

"Someone better start telling me what's going on, or I swear ..." I stare at the man holding my Colt .45.

"Swear what?" Hollywood is no longer bent over double. "You gonna knee me in the nuts again?"

My kneecap still stings from slamming into his groin. He's going to have bruised nuts for days. Gingerly, I feel my forehead where a lump is beginning to form. I'm going to have one epic headache after this.

"If that's what it takes." I wrap my arms around myself.

When my father was alive, he insisted I learn how to defend myself. I know several ways to incapacitate a man with nothing but my hands. A knee to the groin is but one of the tools in my arsenal.

With what I'm suddenly learning about my family—and here, I refer to the past few hours since Sybil disappeared—my father's insistence makes much more sense.

She's not the only thing I lost tonight.

"Who are you?" I have questions that need immediate answers.

"The good guys." The man with my gun makes a show of lowering it.

"That's debatable." I turn my attention to the three people in this van who I trust to tell me the truth. I look to the women huddled in the back. "Are they who they say they are?"

"I don't know who they are, but they saved us." One of the women wipes her tear-streaked face.

Okay, maybe these people are the good guys?

But it's not enough. Sybil is still missing.

"I thought they were kidnapping you." My attention shifts to the man holding my gun. "Taking you where they took Sybil."

The man cocks his head. He places a finger to his ear then speaks. "Can't do that."

"Can't do what?" I ask.

His response makes no sense, but then I see the earpiece.

Belvedere's security team wears something similar, hooking them up to the security suite where every square inch of the Belvedere is highly monitored.

Well, almost every square inch.

There's the whole twenty-fifth floor where my uncle held at least six captive women. I'm too numb to process what that means.

The van rocks violently as it navigates through the congested streets. I brace to keep from careening inside the back of the van. There are no windows, which makes me queasy.

"You knew about the girls. You knew they were kidnapped?" The man gives me one hell of a look.

I slide back and glare. How dare he accuse me?

"You knew and did nothing to help them?" Hollywood turns his magnetic blue eyes on me. His angry stare sends currents of electricity shooting into the air. "Of all the cold-hearted ..."

The fine hairs on my arms lift as the air sizzles between us.

"Don't bother finishing that sentence." It pisses me off for him to think that, let alone say it. The problem is he speaks the truth. Those judgmental eyes make me want to curl in on myself, but I firm the trembling in my jaw. "What was I going to do? Walk in there myself and set them free? That's not how things work."

I've been expressly *forbidden* from accessing that particular floor. Uncle Marco's orders are not questioned, and me being as new as I am to my position, the last person I want to piss off is my uncle.

Now that I'm suspicious about what the real family business might be, questioning anything is downright dangerous.

Lethal comes to mind.

"Ever think to call the cops?" Hollywood leans in, closing the distance between us.

The Chief of Police was recently at a meeting hosted by Marco at the Belvedere. I may be slow at putting two and two together, but I'm not stupid.

My entire life is a sham. I thought my family was in the hotel business. My eyes and ears are open now. The truths I've discovered are uncomfortable and dangerous.

I'm part of a crime family, a stooge who until very recently was completely and totally oblivious about everything.

I hate that the most.

The people, who are supposed to love me, kept me in the dark my entire life. They lied to me, and I don't know what to do about it.

I've never felt this lost in my life, and the one person I can talk to about everything is missing. I lift up a silent prayer; *please keep Sybil safe.*

I straighten my spine and firm my chin. I'm ready to go to war to save Sybil. I don't care who's responsible for her disappearance. I don't care what these people think about me. None of it matters. I need allies, but I don't know if I'm with friend or foe.

What matters is Sybil, and I'll move Heaven and Earth to rescue her.

11

LIAM

THE RAVEN-HAIRED BEAUTY WITH SAPPHIRE EYES IS SOMETHING ELSE. Tough as nails and fucking fierce, she grabs a man's attention and holds it tight.

But she's a Rossi, and the Rossi's are as dirty as they come.

In other words, she's dangerous, but she's also afraid. Her voice trembles, revealing her fear.

I should keep my trap shut, but there's something about her that makes my blood boil. Maybe it's her zero fucks attitude? Or her unbridled tenacity to find her friend. Her animosity for all of us thickens the air.

She's fierce, fragile, and phenomenal.

"The cops?" Her caustic laugh is not what I expect.

"Yeah, princess. The cops." I can't help but push. "That's what you do when you see something illegal."

Her gaze drops to the floorboard, where it settles. I get it. She's unwilling to spew her filth to my face.

Typical.

But then her huge, expressive eyes lift, challenging me. Her raven-black hair tangles around her shoulders and falls down her back in gentle waves. Strands of hair fan across her face, caught in those long, thick lashes of hers which sweep across her sculpted cheeks.

Her fingers curl, balling her tiny hands into vibrating fists, and fury builds in her gaze.

"Most of them are bought and paid for, so no, I didn't go to the cops."

Her outrage explodes, making me suck in a breath. I stagger with the betrayal swirling in her eyes. That's honest pain, unable to be faked.

Who hurt this woman?

"You should've done something." I should back down, but I don't.

The woman is a Rossi. Despite her pain, she doesn't get my compassion.

She flinches with the way I sling my words at her, using them as weapons. Her shoulders slump as if physically wounded, and her knees pull up to her chest. She wraps her arms around her shins, seeking solace in her own embrace.

"You have no idea what it means to live in my world." Her eyes shimmer in the dimly lit interior of the van. "Take your judgment and shove it up your ass." Her words bite and sting.

Wolfe clears his throat. "We have a problem." When Maria looks up, he points at her. "You need to fix it."

"Me?" Maria's eyes widen. "I'm not the one stealing women."

"We're not stealing them either, princess." I lean in, knowing my size will intimidate her, but she holds her own, staring me down like a fighter. "We're rescuing them."

"The men following you, are they your security detail?" Wolfe rolls right over me.

"That's funny." Her caustic laugh returns, but there's pain rimming her eyes. "They're unwanted protection."

"That's one and the same, sweetheart." I rub at my neck where she karate chopped me and refrain from cupping my balls. They pulse with residual pain, the kind that twists my insides.

"It's totally different." Maria crosses her arms, defiant and holding up rather well, considering we basically kidnapped her.

Not our best moment, but there wasn't time to have a sit-down and chat with armed security barreling down on us. The worst possible outcome would've been a firefight in the middle of Mitzy's flash mob.

I say *we basically kidnapped her*, but I'm the one who dragged her into the van. Circumstances dictated what happened next.

"Doesn't matter. From their viewpoint, it looks like we abducted you." Wolfe leans back, dark eyes simmering with irritation. "We don't need that kind of heat breathing down our necks, especially from the Rossi's."

"What are you going to do? Pump me full of lead and drop my body in a dark alley?" Maria responds with a flippant retort.

Damn if her ire and spite aren't sexy.

As for the rest of her, she's smokin' hot.

I'd do her in a heartbeat.

"We could dump her on the street." I offer an obvious solution.

Wolfe gives me the eye. It's a really bad idea, especially considering the neighborhood we're driving through.

"We're not dumping her on the street." CJ, who's been quiet up to now in the passenger seat, takes command.

"Then what are you going to do with me?" She cowers on the floor, tugging her arms and legs close, making herself as small as possible.

It kind of makes me feel like a jerk, intimidating her. In general, I'm chivalrous when it comes to women. I adore the fairer sex and put them on a pedestal. I don't generally threaten them and make them feel like shit.

"We're taking you with us." CJ gives me, Wolfe, and Maria the same hard look. It says to shut up and deal with it. His word is final.

But bringing Maria back to Rose Manor, temporary headquarters for the Guardians while we're in New Orleans, is crazy. He's basically inviting the enemy into our home base.

"Liam, bind her hands and put a blindfold on her." CJ issues orders, and I follow them.

"Give me your hands." I grab a few zip ties and point at her hands.

"No." Maria sniffs with indignation.

"Look, princess, CJ says you're getting hooded and bound. Don't make me gag you, too."

"You'd just love that, wouldn't you?" She's got spunk, and I love every bit of it.

"You don't want to know what I love, princess." I gesture again at her hands. "We can do this the easy way or the hard way."

"There's no way in hell you're touching me." Maria glares at CJ.

It's the perfect distraction. I launch at Maria, spinning her around in a flash. Facedown, cheek pressed to the floorboard, I yank first one hand, and then the other, behind her back.

Zip. Zip.

In less than a heartbeat, I truss her up.

"You're going to regret this." Maria thrashes beneath me.

"I seriously doubt that." I spin her around and loop my hands under her arms. Pulling her up, I place her in a sitting position against the side of the van. Her knee rears up, but I'm ready.

No way is she doing that twice.

With my hand firmly on her knee, I lean in close. "Princess, you and I are going to have a little conversation. Knee me in the groin again, and I won't hesitate to swat your very fine ass."

"Only bastards hit women."

"I never hit a woman in anger, but if she begs for it, I'm more than happy to oblige. Since you know what will happen if you knee me in the nuts again, I'll know you're begging for it."

"Fuck you."

"Such foul language from a princess."

"I'm no fucking princess."

"I guess we'll see about that."

Damn if that little exchange doesn't make me hard as a damn rock. This is not the time for shit like that. I'm on an active mission and getting hard? I need my fucking head examined.

What I need is to get as far away from Maria Rossi as I can get.

Unfortunately, that's not happening.

12

LIAM

Since I have no hood, I use the next best thing and strip out of the dang *Happy* shirt. Her eyes practically bug out of her head when I pull off the shirt. I'd say she was enjoying my well-defined six-pack, but I wear a full suit underneath the garish shirt.

There's nothing to see. Although, I can guess what she's thinking.

"Yeah, it's bulletproof." I tap the material with my fist.

"So, the whole time ..." She's cute the way her forehead scrunches.

"You've got spunk, sweetie. Gotta admire that. While a slug from your Colt would've kicked like a motherfucker, I was never in danger."

I was.

A shot fired at point-blank range would be enough to contuse my heart and concuss my lungs. It likely would've killed me, but she doesn't need to know that.

"You're a cocky asshole." She huffs and puffs beneath my shirt.

"Careful, sweetie, or I might take that as a compliment."

For the rest of the drive back to Rose Manor, an old plantation home Guardian HRS appropriated for our use while in New Orleans, we ride in silence.

We being me and Maria.

The rest of the van is quite talkative.

Jinx and Lily speak to the three women we rescued, reassuring them and preparing them for what to expect when we get to the manor. Wolfe keeps looking at me, shaking his head like I'm a goddamn fool.

Fucker is having fun with me.

CJ carries on a conversation on a private channel with Mitzy, our technical lead and bona fide wizard of all things tech. The term Mitzy Magic is well earned. No doubt, they're discussing what to do about Maria Rossi.

The ride through the city and then out to the plantation takes a little more than an hour. When we get to Rose Manor, Wolfe and I, along with CJ, join Sam, head of Guardian HRS, in the carriage house garage.

I lead Maria, bound and hooded, to an uncomfortable chair and push her down into the seat.

Wolfe moves off some distance with Sam and CJ. Jinx stands by Wolfe's side. I'm happy to see the two of them finally got their heads out of their asses and figured shit out. While they do a quick debrief out of Maria's hearing, my fingers absently knead Maria's neck and shoulders. I don't realize I'm doing it until she jerks away with a hiss of venom.

"Didn't ask for a neck massage, asshole."

Damn but she's a feisty one. I lift my hands like I've been stung.

Bad move.

Maria launches out of the seat. The guys glance over as I burst into action. I fling my sorry ass after her. Still hooded, she takes two steps before tripping over a rock.

I lunge, catching her on the way down. Maria shrieks as I tug her tight to my body and twist us in the air, shifting our positions. Landing on my back, I break her fall.

A sharp rock digs into my shoulder, along with another one at my hip. I grunt with the impact while Maria's thrashing dislodges the makeshift hood. Her wild and frightened eyes stare down at me, unfocused and terrified.

Not too terrified that she doesn't try to head butt me again.

I dodge and flip our positions. Lying on top of her for the second time in as many hours, I cradle the back of her head to protect her skull from hitting one of the small rocks littering the ground.

Garage is too modern of a name for the carriage house. Built over a hundred years ago, it's where the carriages and horses were housed. The stalls are long gone, but the dirt floor remains, along with all of its rocks.

Nose to nose, eye to eye, Maria and I trade stares. I'm easily twice her size. Her chest rises and falls as her breaths rush in and out. The musty smell of the ground fills my nostrils but layered on top of that is something I can't quite describe. Lilac and rose, it's a heavenly perfection. I lean down, sniffing Maria's neck.

No idea why the fuck I do that, but damn if she doesn't smell good.

Good?

It's fucking intoxicating.

"Stop sniffing me." Maria wriggles. Her dark eyes blaze with fury.

"Stop trying to get away," I fire right back.

"So, I *am* a prisoner." Indignation darkens her sapphire eyes, turning them a deeper shade of purple.

"Hey, you're the one who jumped inside our van."

"I didn't jump. You yanked me inside."

"Only because you were being a little shit, waving your gun at me. We needed to get out of there before your goons arrived."

"They're not *my* goons." She breaths out a frustrated breath. "Seriously, can you get off of me? This isn't comfortable."

"Are you going to behave?"

"Are you going to let me go?"

"Not until we have a chance to chat, princess."

"Please stop calling me that." Pain flashes through her eyes again. "I'm no princess. If anything, I'm a damn stooge." Her inner lip curls.

The moment she notices me staring, her eyes close and she blows out a breath.

"Stooge? Why would you say that?"

"Because it's true."

"Liam, get off the girl." CJ saunters over. His expression stern, arms crossed over his chest, but a smile tugs at the corner of his lips. He not so subtly kicks the heel of my boot.

I remove myself from Maria, then hold out a hand to help her to her feet. She gives me a look like I'm an idiot. That's when I realize how foolish I look. Her hands are secured behind her back.

Maria rolls to her side and slowly takes to her feet. She gives the chair an irritated glare, then primly walks over as if it's her choice to sit on it.

"You gonna keep me tied up like a criminal? Or do you think you can cut these off?" She shifts to the side and wriggles her fingers.

I look at CJ. He gives a nod.

"Are you?" I pull out my pocketknife.

"What?"

"A criminal?"

"Not in this life nor the next. Unlike you, I don't kidnap strangers and hold them hostage."

"You weren't kidnapped."

"Wanna tell that to the cops and see what they think?" She sniffs at me.

"You pulled a gun on me. Wanna tell that to the cops?" I can't help but get in a dig. "I've got you on aggravated assault. Maybe attempted murder."

"You're an asshole." She looks away, dismissing me.

"And you're a—"

"Liam." CJ cuts me off. "Cut her free."

I cut the ties. Maria glares while rubbing her wrists.

"Thank you." She spits out the words.

"You're welcome." I return her thank you with a snarl.

CJ shakes his head as he strolls over to grab a folding chair for himself. He snaps it open in front of Maria and takes a seat.

I get to stand.

"If the two of you are done, it's time for a conversation." CJ rolls up his sleeves.

I know what he means by conversation.

CJ's going to interrogate Maria.

I'm not sure how I feel about that.

"Maria Rossi." CJ glances at his cuticles, speaking as if reciting her dossier by memory. "Only daughter of Milo Rossi. Sole niece of his younger brother who took over after your father's death. Marco Rossi is involved in the vilest industry on the planet. You're the sole heir to the Rossi empire. Somewhere inside your head is the knowledge to bring the whole organization crashing down."

"That's not true." Maria's voice trembles. "I know nothing about any of that."

"You're going to tell us what we need to know." CJ leans forward and lowers his voice, turning ominous and deadly.

13

MARIA

I'm a knee-knocking, leg-bouncing, nervous wreck. My stomach's got that queasy, shaky, unsettled feeling that makes my whole body tremble.

We're not going to mention Hollywood. He looms with bridled ferocity and restrained lethality simmering in his gaze.

The three rescued women are gone, ushered away the moment we arrived. I can only hope they receive a much warmer welcome than the one I currently enjoy.

Instead of letting the men begin their interrogation, I fire the first shot. "Where's Sybil Niles?"

"We ask the questions." Hollywood has the *menacing thing* down to a tee.

"That's not how this is going to work." Spine straight, shoulders back, chin lifted, lips steady and firm, and eyes on the target, I breathe while projecting strength I don't feel.

Strength is necessary. I need to tip the balance of power between myself and these men before I'm completely overwhelmed.

"And how is this going to work?" The man sitting across from me arches a brow.

"What's your name?" I'll pepper them with questions, learning as much about them as I can.

"CJ."

"Well, CJ ..." I draw out his name. "We both have questions. You answer mine and I might answer yours."

"You see this as a negotiation?" CJ's smooth Texan drawl sends shivers down my spine.

Liam moves around to stand behind me, which puts him out of my line of sight. No more stargazing at his lethal beauty.

He places his hands on my shoulders, making me jump. Instead of holding me down, his fingers dig in, massaging my neck.

The way CJ looks at me makes me squirm. He lets the silence stretch while Liam's fingers work magic, releasing the tension in my neck.

"Rather than a negotiation, let's consider this a simple conversation." CJ exchanges a look with Liam.

"Conversation?"

"I want to talk about what happened." CJ leans back.

"Which part?" My eyes close as Liam's fingers attack the tight knots in my shoulders.

"Let's start with how you knew to follow us." Liam's got great control of his voice. Before, it was authoritative and commanding. Now, it's got a slow-rolling, sultry vibe to it. Deep, resonating, and sexy as fuck.

"You mean through that freaky flash mob?" I twist to look at Liam.

"Yes." There's that smirk again. How is it possible that a simple smirk makes Liam look even more handsome?

"I watched the whole thing." If he can do deep and resonating, I can do flippant and snarky.

"Maybe we should back up a bit." CJ settles back, looking far more comfortable than I feel. "If you knew about the women being held, why didn't you call the cops?"

"I don't trust the cops. Not now."

"What changed?" CJ cocks his head, interested and confused.

"Everything."

"Explain."

"How do I explain?"

"Usually, people start at the beginning and continue on through to the end." Liam's touch grounds me. The massage soothes me.

"The beginning? There is no beginning."

"There's always something." Liam's fingers stop the massage. His hands rest on my shoulders. It's a gentle touch, but if I try to get out of this chair, he'll make sure that doesn't happen.

I know nothing about these people, except they saved three women. For that reason alone, I feel I can trust them.

"Fine. My entire life is a lie."

"Go on." CJ relaxes. Leans back.

My body mimics his, relaxing and leaning back against the uncomfortable wooden back of my chair.

"Everything I thought was true is so incredibly twisted and wrong."

"The women?" CJ cups his chin. "You didn't know about the women?"

"Hell, no."

What do you do when the people you love and trust aren't who they seem? When you've been so damn blind that you didn't see what's happening all around you?

After a long stretch of silence, CJ continues his questioning. "How did you know your friend was being held in that room?"

I clear my throat, needing more time to collect my thoughts.

"Are you the cops? Is that how you rescued those women? Or FBI?"

"We're not." CJ leans back, settling in.

Strange.

"Vigilantes? Mercenaries?"

"No and no." Liam's husky laughter is like sin rolled in chocolate. He puts more vigor into the unsolicited shoulder rub. Tiny jolts of electricity shoot down my spine.

"Then what are you?" I direct my question back to CJ.

"We're the men who do whatever it takes to rescue you." CJ's voice rings with truth. Something about this whole operation just makes me believe what he says.

"But you kidnapped me. That makes you the bad guys."

"The world is not so black and white, Miss Rossi." CJ turns over his hand to examine his cuticles. It's a measured move, something designed to off-balance me.

Liam moves from my shoulders to my neck. Those thumbs of his find every tiny knot and forces them to give in.

CJ clears his throat. "Miss Rossi, I asked if the men following you were your security detail and you said ..."

"I don't remember what I said. My uncle orders them to watch over me. They don't work for me."

"Watch over? Not protect?" CJ's mouth twitches. He doesn't believe me.

"They're there to make sure I don't go where I shouldn't."

"And where is that?" CJ keeps his voice low and controlled, encouraging me to speak freely.

"The twenty-fifth floor for one thing." The moment I blurt that out, I regret it.

"Oddly specific." Liam's fingers sweep across my shoulder, sending a flurry of chills fluttering down my back.

"What's special about that floor?" CJ leans forward.

"It's where my uncle conducts his business."

"Such as abducting women?" Liam's voice turns back into that threatening growl.

"Evidently." I don't care one bit that my reply is flippant as shit. "Welcome to my shitty life."

Was my father involved? Or is it only Marco?

My dad was the best dad in the world. Sure, he didn't let me pursue frivolous things. His words. Not mine. He wanted a son. Got me instead. He groomed me to take over the Belvedere. Why would he do that if he was a monster involved in human trafficking?

Have I been a fool my entire life?

"Miss Rossi, I'd like to know *why* you were watching that room." CJ's voice snaps me back to the present.

"Why?"

"Correct."

We're in a stable of sorts, painstakingly maintained. The air is damp, full of musty smells. My mind conjures images of horses stamping in stalls to my right and grand carriages getting ready to take out the master of the house.

"Because of Sybil."

"Your friend?" Elbows on knees, CJ clasps his hands and props his chin on the tips of his fingers.

"My *best* friend." These men need to understand what Sybil means to me.

"Why did you think Sybil Niles was in that room?" CJ wants an answer, and I'm okay with giving one.

My heart tells me any chance I have of getting Sybil back rests with these people. I'm not sure why I trust my gut on this, considering how epically it's failed me in the past, but I go out on a limb. I'll do whatever it takes to rescue Sybil.

"Tonight was our annual charity auction. Sybil, along with our other interns, was getting auctioned off. The last time I saw, or spoke, to her, she was heading to the spa, along with all the other interns as our treat. When she didn't answer my texts, I got worried. When she was a no show for the Gala, I went looking."

"And what did that entail?" Liam, who's been quiet for a spell, chimes in. There goes that voice of his, melodious, multi-tonal, rich, and layered with all kinds of heavenly hotness.

I shake free of the spell he seems to have over me and think back to what was going through my head earlier today.

It feels like Sybil's been missing for weeks.

CJ lowers both his hands and rests them in his lap. His sympathy is almost too much. It's real. Not imagined. Not made up.

When I fail to say anything further, CJ clears his throat.

"Miss Rossi, this whole situation is as unusual for us as it is for you."

"Enlighten me." There's a shift in the conversation, a sense of wrongness being righted.

"Our mission was to rescue those women. Your security detail was closing in. We didn't know if they were after you, or after the women we rescued." CJ leans back.

His gaze shifts to Liam, the man I feel all the way down to my bones. The one man who stands out from all the others. And it's not because of his Hollywood-heartthrob looks. It's in the way Liam looks at me, like I'm some tasty morsel he can't wait to devour.

"I'm not certain of anything anymore. Maybe they followed me, or maybe they were after you. I just don't know." My shoulders slump, defeated and overwhelmed. At lunch, life was good; happy and bright, full of so much promise. Less than ten hours later, it's all gone to shit.

Liam removes his hands from my shoulders and takes a step back.

CJ stands and presses out the wrinkles in his slacks. "I'd like to continue this conversation in more comfortable surroundings. I'd appreciate it if you would join us as our guest."

Their guest?

CJ's smile is genuine. It's the kind you get from long-lost friends happy to see you after too much time spent apart. Friends who are thrilled to have you once again in their lives.

But I'm a stranger to this man.

I sense great warmth beneath his stony exterior.

Compassion.

He's the kind of man who takes all the broken pieces and puts them together again. Not because you asked, but because he's compelled to help.

I try to clear my throat, but there's a lump filled with sadness and tears. A cough fails to dislodge it. A swallow only settles it firmly in place. I sniff to push back the sadness welling up from deep within me and one lonely tear trickles down my cheek.

"Your guest?" I croak out a weak reply.

How did I go from prisoner to guest in the span of a heartbeat?

"Yes." There's no lie on his lips. No duplicity in his eyes. Only kindness shines from his face. It makes me believe he truly wants to make the world a better place. "Sometimes, it's necessary to extend a bit of trust. I'm willing to do that for you, and hope you consider doing the same."

"A guest means I'm free to go if I want. Right?"

"If you decide to leave, no one will stop you." CJ gestures to Liam.

Liam moves around to stand directly in front of me. "If you want to go back, I'll take you." His head tilts to the side, assessing, judging, peeling me apart layer by layer. "But if I do that, we won't be able to update you about your friend."

"Sybil?" My heart leaps to my throat. "What do you know about Sybil?"

Liam does something that completely wrecks me. He reaches out and cups my cheek with his hand. The rough pad of his thumb brushes against my cheek where that single, lonely tear dares to slip past my restraint and reveal my sorrow.

"I'll be in the library with the team." CJ walks past us, headed to a door, which leads out of this place.

Something releases in my throat. Tension drains out of me, and it takes my fear with it.

"You're not the enemy, are you?" I blink to clear my vision and force the tears away.

"Not in this life nor the next."

Liam intrigues me. I might stick around if only to spend more time trying to figure him out.

14

LIAM

There's something about Maria. She's resilient and tough under pressure. That kind of strength is admirable.

"What do you know about Sybil?" She clears her throat and bunches her fingers, curling them into tiny fists.

"CJ and the others will tell you what they can about your friend."

"Why won't you tell me about Sybil?" Frustration bleeds through her expression. "You know something."

"What I know isn't of value to you."

It's the truth.

Tonight consists of two rescue missions; one at the Belvedere and one onboard *Caviar Dreams*, an exclusive luxury cruise liner and subsidiary operation of the Belvedere.

"If it involves Sybil, I have a right to know."

Frustration and fear bleed through her tough exterior. It's in the trembling of her chin, the shaking of her hands, and in the way she covers her stomach like she's moments from getting sick.

I close the distance and place a finger beneath her chin. Lifting gently, I force her to look me in the eye. Tears brim in her turbulent gaze and she jerks away as a tear rolls down her cheek.

Maria is strong but fragile when it comes to her friend.

"I don't understand why you won't tell me." Her fingers curl again, forming tight fists.

"I don't have the details. If I did, I'd tell you. CJ invited you to a conversation. You can choose to hear what he has to say or return to the Belvedere."

"Aren't you afraid I'll blab about everything I've seen?"

"If what I think is true, I strongly doubt that will happen. I *see* you."

"See me?" She sniffs and swipes at her nose with the back of her hand. "You know nothing about me."

"I know more than you think."

I clasp my hands in front of me, letting my body relax. It's the only way I know to be less threatening. I want her to feel comfortable opening up to me.

CJ wants me to gain her trust. It's why he left me alone with her; to establish the groundwork before we can turn her to our side.

"Impossible." She shakes her head, negating what I said.

I take a step toward her, curious whether she'll stand her ground, retreat, or mirror my actions.

"Not impossible. You know your family is dirty." I begin with a truth. Her response will determine what comes next.

Her chin lifts in challenge. Maria is miles away from extending any degree of trust, but if I can get her to turn on her family, it could be a total game changer.

This is a pivotal moment.

"You discovered that tonight. Worried about your friend, you uncovered an unsavory truth, and you're reeling with what you've discovered."

"Is that a guess?" She flicks her long hair over her shoulder. It's a dismissive gesture, diminishing what I said.

It's hard not to stare. Nearly black, her hair shimmers with the deepest blue, each layer darker than the one before, all gradually deepening to black. It's mesmerizing, much like the woman herself.

What makes you tick, Miss Maria Rossi?

"Not a guess." I thrust my hands in my pockets. "Your trust was gone the moment you realized Sybil was kidnapped."

Maria ducks her head.

That's the crux of it.

It's the beginning and end. The moment when Maria realized her perfect world was rotten at its core.

"If you trusted the cops, you would've gone to them, but you didn't."

"You're making a lot of assumptions." She dismisses me.

"You didn't call the cops. Instead, you chased after your friend. That kind of loyalty is rare."

"Then tell me what you know about Sybil."

When she reveals her emotions, the pain and hurt, along with her love for her friend, my protective instincts fully engage. I want to help this woman.

"I can't tell you anything about Sybil because I don't know how that op's going."

"Op?"

"The operation to rescue her."

"So, they are doing *something*?"

"Yes."

"That's incredible. It's everything." A sob escapes her.

Overwhelmed, she lunges toward me. Her arms loop around my midsection and wrap around my back. "Thank you. Thank you. Thank you." She buries her face against my chest as deep, soul-crushing sobs pour out of her.

I fold my arms around her slender frame as the delicate scents of lilac and rose flood my senses. I can't help but breathe her in, filling my lungs until they're bursting with everything that is Maria Rossi.

I cup the back of her head, holding her while she cries. She fits perfectly in my arms.

I don't know how long we stand there—it feels like forever—but the moment she pulls away, it's as if I imagined the whole thing. Maria takes a step back and swipes at her cheeks. Her eyes focus on the ground, unable, or unwilling, to look at me.

Maybe she's embarrassed by that sudden rush of emotion.

Entranced, I can't tear my gaze away while she rebuilds her protective walls. It happens with a sniff of her nose, a curling of her fingers. Her hands tighten into fists. Her weight shifts forward then falls back. Slowly, she lifts her chin. Those stormy eyes of hers find my face and zoom in on my eyes.

"Sorry." She wipes the tears away. "It's a relief knowing someone's doing something. I was ... overwhelmed." Another sniff and she unlocks our gazes. There's a pull, then a snap, as if she takes a piece of me with her.

"We're going to do everything we can to rescue your friend." It's important Maria knows *something* is being done. "Tell me about Sybil. What made you go looking for her?" My goal is to encourage her to open up.

Maria takes in a breath, holds it, then slowly exhales.

"Sybil and I are close. Sisters of another mother kind of close. We met when we were twelve. Share the same birthday. Went to the same prep school. Spent all our summers together. We went to Cornell together, and we're both taking over our family's business. Me with the Belvedere and Sybil with her parents' resort in Hawaii. We text all day long. We call even more often."

"I take it she didn't text you?"

"She didn't text me when she got to the spa. Didn't text me pictures. Nothing." Maria presses her lips together and takes in a deep breath. She tells me how she tried to find her friend.

Each time she speaks, I get a glimpse of the complexities that make up Maria Rossi.

"When she didn't text me back or return my calls—and I left tons —I lost it."

What were the clues that drove Maria? What is it that tipped her hand and sent her digging? She tells me everything she did to find her friend. I'm beyond impressed.

Her pain is real. It's fresh and raw.

"Your brain and heart finally connected." I feel sorry for Maria. Her entire life, everything she believes to be true, is gone.

"What do you mean?"

"The gap between what you knew versus what you wanted to feel. You wanted to feel the goodness around you, but it wasn't there."

"I guess that's one way to put it." Her entire expression falls.

It's like watching a light go out, taking away her happiness and joy. Maria looks back at me, eyes dark, expression flat. Hope erased.

"Want to know the worst of it?"

"Sure." I can't imagine what could be worse than finding out your family is involved in human trafficking.

"All my life, the other kids teased me about my family's wealth. They said my family was nothing more than a bunch of crooks. Our money was bad money. Tainted money. I thought they were jealous. Their family fortunes may come with prestige, but many of those families are struggling while my family was rising."

"And you never once thought they might be right?"

"Never." Maria shakes her head with absolute conviction. "I had no reason to think otherwise."

I can see her much younger self getting teased by those kids. Knowing what little I do about her, she likely went toe to toe with them, defending her family's reputation from those eager to tear her down.

"My mother said kids were cruel and to ignore them. That they were jealous of what the Rossi's built. My grandfather made our family what it is now. My father took what my grandfather built and created an empire. My uncle took the reins when my dad passed. I've never once seen anything suspicious."

"But some part of you had to suspect?" It's a stretch, but I can't believe she's been clueless her entire life. "There had to be things that didn't add up. The disconnect between heart and mind?"

"I was never let in on any family business growing up. The only things I participated in were the parties. We had councilmen, representatives, senators, and industry giants all attending my family's events. Celebrities came. Bankers and lawyers. There was never a reason to think things were anything other than what they appeared."

"But Sybil?" I circle us back around to her friend. "Your gut told you something wasn't right."

"There were other things. Recent things." She looks down, ashamed.

"Like what?"

"Irregularities in the books. I've been in my position for a very short time. There's so much to learn. Some of what I saw didn't make sense, but I figured that was because I was new and still learning the ropes. There are people who take care of all of that. Uncle Marco kept joking with me about letting my employees do the jobs they were hired to do and stop micromanaging everything. Not once did I realize what my real job was."

"And what is that?" I've already figured it out. Has she?

"I'm the pretty face to put on the business, while all kinds of filth swims below me." She rests her hands on her knees. Her fingers curl into fists, clench, then relax.

"I'm sorry." I reach out and gently place my hand on her knee. "I can't imagine how that feels. The betrayal alone ..."

She wipes her face. "I should've seen through it long ago." Slowly, she shakes her head.

"I'm still curious about one more thing."

"What's that?"

"How did searching for Sybil lead you to me and my team? If restricted, how were you able to see anything?"

"The cameras on that level are normally turned off. I turned them on."

"Wouldn't the security staff have reported that?"

"Remember how I said I've made it a point to work in all the areas within the Belvedere?"

"Yes."

"Security was the first department I worked in. I spent a week learning the job. It wasn't unusual for me to stop in from time to time. I stopped in tonight."

"To look for Sybil?"

"I had to do something."

This woman has a head on her shoulders. Smart and pretty, I'm hooked already.

"And?"

"I went for a Hail Mary and put in one of my father's codes. I used to hang out in his office at home and peeked when he logged in for work. I didn't think the code would work. All trace of my father has been scrubbed, but the password worked. I saw your team take out the guards. You brought out the women, and you know the rest."

"I hope you've seen enough to know, we're on your side. If you still want to go home, no one will stop you. I'll take you back." I hold out my hand. "But I sincerely hope you decide to stay."

I hope she'll stay.

My fear is what will happen after she does.

15

MARIA

Liam extends his hand. It's a strange about-face considering not too long ago, I kneed him in the nuts.

Without thinking, I reach out. It's a natural reaction. The moment Liam's hand wraps around mine, a jolt of electricity shoots down my arm. In the wake of that startling sensation, a rush of heat follows, wrapping around me like a hug. He gestures toward the door.

"If there's anything I can do to save Sybil ... I'm in."

Swallowing past the constriction in my throat, I realize what I mean and the lengths to which I'll go to save my friend.

Liam leads me outside the carriage house. Instead of a prisoner, he welcomes me like a friend.

The lingering heat and humidity engulf me the moment we step outside.

Normal for New Orleans this time of year, the sultry, evening air stubbornly refuses to provide relief to its residents. Cicadas buzz at near deafening levels, joined in by thousands upon thousands of tree frogs and crickets chirping in a dissonant chorus that somehow feels right.

These are the sounds I love, and the oppressive heat is something I welcome.

"Don't be nervous." Rough and calloused, Liam's hand engulfs mine.

I'm way beyond nervous. I'm still trying to figure out Guardian HRS.

Can they be trusted?

Liam says nothing about Sybil, but confirms the Guardians are on the job. Whatever that means. If I lose her, I don't know what I'll do.

Hug Liam again?

Is it sad I haven't felt the comfort of a good hug in years? It may be decades.

The last hug I received from a man was my father. That was years ago. Uncle Marco never touches me. He can barely stand my presence. My mother's hugs stopped years before that.

Actually, I can pinpoint the day. Summer of my sweet sixteen. Dad took the family to the Hamptons, where we threw dazzling party after party. It was a momentous summer for me.

For Sybil as well.

We made a pact to lose our virginity, and like most things in our lives, we conquered that milestone together.

I found a cute busboy to usher in that new phase of my life. He popped my cherry in one of the many guest rooms that no one ever sleeps in. It was wild, unhinged, and free; exactly how I imagined sex should be.

Sybil ditched her virginity with the help of an older man. Despite asking, to this day, she's not divulged who the older man was. I'm not sure if that's because she's ashamed she never got his name, forgot it, or something else.

What I do know is my mother never once hugged me after my sixteenth birthday.

"How are you holding up?" Liam's warm voice washes over me, stirring me from my thoughts. "Don't be nervous. These people are some of the best on the planet." He guides me across the open space between the carriage house and the manor proper.

Fueled by the lingering rush of adrenaline screaming through my bloodstream, my heart bangs away like a kettle drum. I'm both terrified of what waits for me behind that door and anxiously hopeful for what I might learn.

I walk a few feet inside, then wait for Liam to lead from there. Despite the massive size of the home, the back hallways are narrow; built for servants to use. There's not a lot of room for him to pass by me, and when he does, I shamelessly take in a deep breath.

I've never met a man who smells dark and delicious. Most men reek of cologne or body odor; two scents I particularly dislike.

But Liam?

He smells good.

"This way." He takes me to a huge dining room.

A massive table fills the room, seating ten to a side. Every other seat is occupied, but not a single person looks up as we pass through.

Cluttered on top of the table, an assortment of computers and monitors emit a steady blue glow while multicolored wires stretch between them.

We pass through the dining room and head to the front of the house. Liam stops in the foyer.

He gestures to a dark, paneled room filled floor to ceiling with books. Several groupings of leather couches and armchairs fill out the floor. Sitting in those couches, an eclectic group of people wait for us.

For me.

A slender woman, with hair I can only describe as a riot of color, turns at my entrance. Styled in a short pixie cut, her hair shimmers in the light of the chandeliers overhead.

She sits beside her complete opposite. If I thought Liam was a tall man, that's nothing compared to the giant who slouches in the leather chair. Where the woman's hair is bright with a rainbow of colors, his is white upon white. His pale blue eyes steal my breath, they're icy, hard, and formidable.

He picks me apart with that stare of his. Unlike most men, however, he confines his examination to my face and eyes, not once dipping lower than my neck. He's definitely *not* interested in me like that.

His examination makes me feel like a bug beneath a microscope, peeled away to my most basic self.

Lounging on the sofa next to him is another contrast. A woman about the same height and build as me, her hair is long like mine. Instead of deep black, hers is chestnut brown, warm like her eyes and the instant smile on her face. It feels as if we've known each other for years, rather than meeting for the first time.

Occupying the other end of the couch is CJ, who I'm well acquainted with. The other occupant is a man with a look and build similar to CJ and Liam. He puts down the book he's reading and approaches me.

"Miss Rossi, it's a pleasure to meet you." He sticks out his hand, which I automatically take. Like Liam, his hand is rough and calloused, and engulfs mine. "I'm Sam, head of Guardian HRS. Let me introduce you to the others." He spins around to face the room. "You've met CJ, head of our Guardians."

CJ lifts his hand and smiles. It's a strange thing to see on his face, considering not too long ago he sat across from me, interrogating me. Sam gestures to the woman with the pixie hair.

"Mitzy leads our technical team."

Mitzy pops up and crosses the room. When I stick out my hand, she stops and props her hands on her hips. She gives me one look, then approaches with her arms out wide.

"Girl, you deserve a hug. I can't imagine how you must be feeling right now."

Before I can do anything, Mitzy wraps her arms around me. Her hug is brief but welcoming. I slowly lift my arms and give an awkward squeeze in return. Mitzy releases me, then spins around to the rest of the room.

"These men aren't nearly as scary as they look, especially once you get to know them. For example, Forest looks all icy and fierce, but he's a total teddy bear."

"I really wish you wouldn't call me that." The massive man rises from his chair, even taller and more massive than I initially thought. He must be nearly seven feet tall, maybe a few inches shorter, but damn if he isn't gigantic. He makes me think of a Viking, and he's scary as hell, at least until he turns his grumpy face into a smile for me.

"It's nice to meet you, Maria." So far, he's the only one to address me by my first name. The others have been entirely too formal. "I'm glad you decided to talk with us." Unlike Mitzy's hug, he keeps our contact to a brief handshake.

"And this is Skye." Mitzy continues. "She and Forest are brother and sister, not related by blood. They're the reason the rest of us are here." Mitzy spins me toward the other woman.

Skye rises to greet me. Unlike Mitzy, she extends a slender hand, and that warm smile of hers chases away my fear.

"Mitzy's right about the guys," Skye says. "Don't let their tough exteriors fool you. Each one of them is a total softy at heart."

"It's nice to meet you?" I don't mean for that to sound like a question, but I can't help the rising inflection in my voice.

"Forest," Skye turns to the white giant. "Why don't you get Maria something to drink?" She points to Liam, completely at ease ordering the men around. "Pull that chair around. It'll be easier to talk if we're all facing each other."

Liam, Sam, and CJ work as a team to rearrange the furniture.

"I thought it would be more comfortable talking in here rather than in the dining room." Skye sits in one of the plush armchairs. "If you walked through it, you know what I mean."

"It's a mess of computers and wires strung all over the place."

"Hey," Mitzy interjects. "It's not a mess. It's color-coded perfection."

"This is true." Skye's gentle demeanor makes me feel like a guest instead of a star witness.

"Wine, whiskey, or bourbon?" Forest calls over his shoulder as he heads to a table in the corner full of crystal and booze.

"Whiskey sounds just about right." Not normally a whiskey drinker, I need something strong to take the edge off and settle my nerves. I swallow, happy to see that lump in my throat is gone. "How are the women doing? The ones you rescued."

Skye cocks her head, pauses, then gives a nod as if reaching a decision. "They're in shock but recovering. I don't think it's hit any of them what happened. Thank God they don't know what waited for them."

On that ominous note, I want to ask what was going to happen, but I hold my tongue. Too many questions swirl around in my head. Questions demanding answers that will change my life forever.

Hell, my life is irrevocably changed.

My head and heart fight a war. My head knows the truth, but my heart desperately clings to the hope it's all one big misunderstanding. In the end, my heart curls inward, beaten, battered, bruised, and broken.

After Liam and the others reorganize the furniture, he guides me over to one of the leather chairs. It's one of those plush ones with buttery soft leather and high arms that wrap around you. I'm glad to be offered one of the few single chairs. If I had to share the couch, my unease would only rise with my beating heart.

With two sofas and three chairs, the others get comfortable. I sit across from Skye and Forest. Sam and CJ sit on the couch to my left, while Mitzy and Liam take the remaining couch.

"What happens now?" I sip the whiskey, letting the burn flow through me.

"We're presented with a problem and a potential opportunity," Sam speaks while the others look at me. "I'm hopeful you'll help us."

"I understand I'm the problem, but what do you mean by opportunity? And can someone tell me something about Sybil?" I'll take any small nugget about my friend.

They can ask a million questions, but I'll always circle around to what matters to me. The whole reason I'm here—the reason I'm a problem—is because Sybil is missing.

"Is she here?" My gaze bounces from person to person. There's a stiffness to their postures, which doesn't feel like good news.

"She is not." Sam leans forward, intently watching my reactions.

"Please tell me you're doing something to find my friend." My fingers claw at the leather armrest and my other hand flies to my belly. That queasy-shaky-going-to-get-sick-any-minute sensation returns.

"I can't divulge anything at this moment." That must be Sam's way of telling me not to delve too deep into what they're doing.

I understand. I've done nothing to make them trust me. As far as they know, I might be involved in the whole disgusting business. I try not to react, but it's hard. I feel vulnerable and helpless.

"Miss Rossi, we need to discuss the problem you present." Sam taps the leather armrest.

"I'm not comfortable having you call me a *problem*." I use finger quotes to emphasize my point.

"The armed security team in pursuit ..." Sam cuts straight to it. "What would be their immediate response to your abduction?"

"They'd call my uncle."

"And then?"

"With the money and resources at my uncle's command, he won't stop until he finds me." A chill runs down my spine. I may very well have led my uncle straight to the Guardians' front door.

16

LIAM

I say nothing while the others speak with Maria, keeping my own council. There's something about her, a vulnerability beneath her steely exterior, which intrigues me.

She's a trooper, strong under pressure, she recovers quickly when out of her element, and she's incredibly brave.

"That's what I was afraid of." Sam exchanges a look with Forest and Skye.

"How did you know who to follow on the roof?" Mitzy pipes up, interrupting Sam. She looks up from her tablet. "I have a feed with you by the elevator. The flash mob was already in progress. It was chaos. How did you get there?"

Yeah, Mitzy Magic created that chaos, which gave us the perfect escape from the Belvedere.

Maria's gaze cuts to me. I give a nod of support which Maria takes. "I was looking for Sybil ..."

She repeats what she told me, how Sybil failed to check in, what Maria did to find her friend, and how that led her to us.

"Where was your security detail?" Sam presses his hands together, holding them in front of his face. "Why weren't they with you?"

"They only follow me when I leave the Belvedere. When I got on the rooftop elevator, they weren't able to join me because of the crowd."

"That explains why they were behind you out on the street." He nods, putting the picture together in his head.

"I suppose. I don't pay attention. I rarely do. It's not my job to keep up with them." Her mesmerizing gaze jumps from person to person, barely landing on me.

That stoic exterior of hers shows signs of weakening. Her friend is important to her, and Sam isn't giving her answers.

Which I get.

Right now, Alpha team is somewhere on the Mississippi River attempting to rescue her friend and two others. Anything can happen. Anything can go wrong. He won't confirm anything until those women are safely in Guardian HRS custody.

"Why are you assigned a security detail?" Forest's glacial gaze is fierce. His temperament odd.

"For my safety, I suppose." Maria holds her own against Forest's barrage of questions.

Forest leans forward, making the leather seat creak. "Since being assigned a security detail, have you ditched your security team before?"

"Sometimes." Forest's final question brings a light to Maria's face, brightening it and making her look even prettier than before.

I'm curious where he's going with this.

"You mean what did my uncle do?" She blows out a breath. "He was pissed. Said I needed them for my safety. That I was being irresponsible and acting like a child."

"How is your relationship with your uncle?"

"Why?"

"Please answer." Forest isn't as smooth as Sam and CJ with his questions, but that's a part of his personality. Neurodivergent is one term. High-functioning Asperger's is another.

Either way, Maria responds better to his line of questioning than she did to CJ's mini-interrogation.

"My uncle's always been distant."

"Why?" Forest presses his point.

"I don't know." She puffs out her cheeks and stares at her lap.

"There has to be a reason."

"I mean nothing to my uncle. No reason why." Pain threads through her words.

"Your uncle married your mother not too long after your father's death. He's your stepfather." Forest continues his questioning.

"He did, but he's not my stepfather." Her arms cross, closing herself in. "At least, we don't use that term."

"Don't you find that odd?" Forest presses his point, whatever that might be.

"Not really." Maria's brows scrunch together. "Are you asking if it's odd I don't call him stepfather or that he married my mother?"

"That he married your mother?"

"He told my father he would take care of us." Maria shrugs, like the whole arrangement isn't as odd, and fucked up, as it appears.

Personally, I find the whole thing somewhat grotesque.

"But marrying your brother's wife is a few steps beyond simply taking care of you." Forest drums his fingers on the armrest of the chair.

"I don't know what you're looking for." A hard tone edges into her voice.

"It's important." Forest snaps his fingers. "Mitz, I need a deep dive into the Rossi brothers. Anything you can find."

"On it, boss." Mitzy's practically attached to that tablet. She carries it with her everywhere.

"Dig deep."

"I always do." Mitzy's tablet glows as she fires it up.

"Back to your security detail. You have ditched them before?" Forest kicks back, getting comfortable. Sam and CJ haven't said a word since Forest took over. Skye's rather quiet.

"Yes." Maria blows out a breath. "I don't like them looking over everything I do and reporting it back to my mother and my uncle. I like to go out and not worry about what I do."

"And you go out with your friend, Sybil?" Forest shifts in his seat, attention fixed solidly on Maria.

"We do everything together."

"How would you ditch them?"

"Different ways. Sometimes, after work, Sybil and I would decide to go clubbing, or we'd go to the bars in the French Quarter or Market District. It depends really. She'd call for a car or have her friends pick us up. I'd wander out the front of the Belvedere, security detail in tow, then make a break for the car."

"It's safe to say ditching your security detail is not that far out of your usual behavior? Is that an accurate statement?"

"I don't do it all that often, but yes."

"That's our answer." Forest turns to his sister. "And our solution."

"Our answer to what, Bean?" Skye cocks her head sideways. "What are you thinking?"

Bean? I've never heard Skye use that name before. It echoes with distant pain.

"Easy." Forest shifts his glacial gaze in my direction. "We're going to take advantage of it."

"How?" Skye doesn't sound convinced.

"We send the two of them out on the town." Forest points at Maria, then his pale gaze swings straight at me.

"Me?" I point to my chest. "Me and Maria? Out on the town?"

Such a bad idea. Like, epically bad.

"Don't be a dunce, lover boy. It's not a good look on you." Forest shifts focus to Maria, who hunches into the massive leather chair that's intent on swallowing her whole. "Maria used the flash mob to get away from her security team. She's been seeing Liam for weeks ... maybe months. Mitz, build a backstory for them."

"Wait a minute?" I clear my throat.

"That would fit into your established behavior?" There's a thawing in Forest's glacial gaze. "Yes or no?"

"Yes, but ..." Maria holds her hands tight in her lap.

"Good." Forest claps his hands. "This is how things will play out.

All those times Maria ditched her detail were to hook up with Liam. They've been secretly dating for months, and she's been keeping her relationship with him a secret." Forest blows out his breath. "But things are heating up between them. It's time to introduce him to the family."

"Whoa." I can't help but interject. "Can we slow this train down a bit?"

"No. The one thing we don't have is time." Forest's pale eyes pin me in place. "We need to get Maria back under the watchful eye of her security detail and her family, especially her family. Mitz—"

"You know I'm already on it." Mitzy doesn't bat an eye.

Forest's heavy gaze sweeps back to Maria. His lips press tight together. "Lover boy over here will post on social media. Mitz, I'll need a few months going back. Tonight though, things are different for them ..." He taps the leather armrest while the rest of us wait.

"On it." Mitzy's fingers dance over the tablet.

His eyes suddenly widen, lit up with an idea I know I'm going to hate.

"Congratulations, the two of you are officially engaged." Forest leans back and claps his hands, as if it's all said and done. "That's why tonight is special. And it's perfect for inserting Liam into the Rossi home."

"Whoa, hold up." Again, I point to my chest. "Engaged? Don't I have something to say about that? I don't have a ring."

Not only that, but I don't think Maria is okay with any of this.

"No. You don't." Forest gives me a look. "Mitz—"

"Forest, I swear, if you ask me to produce an engagement ring out of thin air, I'll pull it out of your ass, and then I *will* quit." She gives a shake of her head, which makes her psychedelic hair swish. It glitters despite the dim lighting. "Magic only goes so far ..."

The rest of what she says is unintelligible, spoken beneath her breath, but it's clear she's not happy.

I don't blame her. In the span of a few minutes, Forest's asked her to do several impossible things.

As for me, and my take on this, my job is with my team. Doing what Forest says will take time. If I stay behind, how will I operate with my team? And what the fuck will I do all day long?

"This is how we're going to fix things." The look Forest gives me makes me feel two feet tall. He leans forward, palms pressed together, fingers steepled under his chin while I feel the world closing in around me.

17

MARIA

Forest's words hit me hard. What he says is insane.

"You want me to pretend to be engaged?" I look directly at Forest and close my gaping mouth. "To him?"

"Look, I'm not happy about it either, princess." Liam snorts with indignation, delivering his words with scathing irritation.

It hurts. It shouldn't, but it does.

"Make it happen, lover boy." Forest's attention shifts from me to Liam.

Behind me, Liam chokes.

I pick at my clothes, removing lint that's not there, smoothing wrinkles that don't need smoothing and try not to look as uncomfortable as I feel. The whiskey makes my throat burn, but I don't care. I toss back the last of the alcohol and close my eyes.

I would ask what it is that they want from me, but it's obvious, and I'm not stupid. They want to use me to get to my uncle.

The kingpin behind everything.

"Tell me about Sybil." I've cooperated. I've answered their questions, but they've answered none of mine. I look to Forest. He glances at Sam and gives a little bump of his chin.

"Sybil was taken from the Belvedere and placed on *Caviar Dreams*," Sam explains. "Two other women were taken with her."

"*Caviar Dreams?*" My heart leaps in my chest, running a breakneck speed with nowhere to go. "That's one of mine; a subsidiary at least."

"Correct." Sam's gaze softens.

"You believe my uncle's responsible, and you want to use me to get to him." I press my lips together and swallow against the lump in my throat.

"We have a team inbound to rescue Sybil and the others." Sam glances at Forest who gives another nod. "Just like we sent one to the Belvedere to rescue the three women left behind. As the mission is ongoing, there's nothing else I can tell you."

Caviar Dreams is the flagship of Belvedere's C&C cruise lines. That sickening sensation returns. Lightheaded, the room spins around me. I grab at the armrest, needing something solid to hold onto.

"If you bear with me for a moment ..., can you tell me more about your relationship with your uncle?" Forest's deep voice rolls like thunder and takes on a softer edge. He looks tired, fatigued, and keeps pinching his eyes as if in pain.

"When I was a kid, he was distant. Not mean, but difficult to approach. I always felt there was something off between him and my dad, or that he didn't like kids."

"And your relationship now?"

"Even more distant."

"Why are you running the Belvedere instead of him?"

"My father mapped out my life's trajectory before he died."

"How?"

"He set it up in his will. My uncle tried to change that, but because of how my father's estate worked, transferring his seat on the board and his stocks directly to me, there wasn't much my uncle could do about it."

"Your father placed you in a difficult position."

"Only because he didn't have a son."

"Why the Belvedere?" Forest pinches the bridge of his nose. "He had to know that would put you in direct opposition to your uncle."

"Maybe it was the only thing he could give me?" I shift in my seat, nervous and tired. "You believe my uncle is at the heart of this and I may agree." All evidence points to my uncle. "But I can't believe my father knew about any of this. If he did, he never would've given me control of the Belvedere. He would've known my uncle would try to take it away from me."

I'm sharing way more than I should.

"Last night, I went to sleep the CEO of the Belvedere. Today, I woke up, living a nightmare."

"Mitzy tells me never to assume, but do you understand what we're asking of you?"

"You want me to spy on my family."

"We need you to get our operative close to them. You don't need to spy, or lie, or anything else."

"You want me to pretend to be engaged to a man I barely know."

"Hmm ..." Forest leans back. He steeples his fingers and rests his chin on the tops of his fingers. "Maybe one little lie."

"I won't pretend to understand who you people are, but I want Sybil back, safe and sound. You make that happen, and I'll do whatever you need."

"You don't yet know what that will cost you." Forest slants his head, giving me a way out.

"Does it matter? My perfect life is in shambles, and there's no way I can return to the Belvedere knowing what I know."

"We need to get you back, and soon, but I have a story to tell you first." Forest props his elbows on the armrests of his chair, then tips his head back to stare at the ceiling. "It's my hope, and I think I've judged you right, but I hope you might be willing to work with us."

There goes the Earth again, shifting beneath my feet.

Liam lifts out of his seat. He takes the tumbler out of my hand.

"You're going to need another drink for this part." His smile is warm. His voice rock steady. His presence lends me strength. Yet, he remains a mystery. Most importantly, he's not happy getting stuck with me.

I glance around the room, stating the obvious. "You do realize one word from me to my uncle about any of tonight's events is enough to destroy your organization?"

"We're aware." Forest's glacial gaze thaws. "But I believe we can trust you."

"How can you be sure?"

"Because you cared enough about your friend to risk your life and your safety to find her. You tracked four elite operatives into and through a crowd because all you could think about was saving your friend. You didn't worry about your safety, and that says a great deal about your character."

"I'll do anything to find Sybil."

"Here, I poured you a double shot." Liam returns with the tumbler.

Our fingers brush against each other as he hands me the whiskey. Like before, warmth rushes up my arm. Instead of returning to the couch, he hitches a hip on the back of my chair. Oddly, I feel less alone.

"Are you sure about this?" Skye reaches for her brother but stops short. Her hand hovers over his, but he pulls away. His hands fall into his lap as she sighs and leans back.

"You disagree?" Forest glances at his sister.

"No." Skye takes in a deep breath and slowly blows it out. "This needs to end."

"What needs to end?" I look between them, confused and nervous again.

I'm terrified of what he's going to tell me.

The foundations of my world are in constant upheaval, delivering one shock after the next and making me question everything.

What's true? What's false?

Who do I trust? Who's lying to me?

It's dangerous jumping in too quickly with people I don't know, but I sense a gravity to this situation. This is important. Whatever *this* is.

I have a feeling my entire world is going to change.

Again ...

Forest stares down at his hands. Clasped tightly in his lap, the knuckles turn white as he shakes.

While my insides churn, he sits in complete silence, barely moving except for the slow rise and fall of his chest. The rest of the room does the same, as if everyone waits for him to begin.

I'm right there with them, but my attention bounces around the room, taking in the reactions of the others.

Skye looks on with love shrouded by some great pain. Mitzy's look is one of compassion. Sam and CJ are more stoic in their responses. They sit absolutely still, barely moving, focused completely on the man who created this amazing organization.

I can't see Liam. He sits behind me. But I feel him. I feel every pull of his breath. Every measured exhale. His body radiates heat, which my body absorbs. Like the others, he's incredibly still.

With one hand on my stomach, which does nothing to stop the sinking sensation that's going on in there, I watch Forest too.

His deep rumbly voice begins with a clearing of his throat, boulders grinding together, then turns into words carrying an incredible burden.

"There was once a time when Skye and I had other names. She was Elsbeth and I was her Bean. We've shed those names, but they're still very much a part of who we are today."

Bean.

That's the name Skye used not too long ago.

"Our story is not a good one. There's nothing light or fun in our past. It's deeply tragic and horrifically painful." Forest looks up and stares at me. His glacial gaze shimmers, almost as if there are tears. "I want to tell you about a man named John Snowden."

18

MARIA

LIAM PLACES A HAND ON MY SHOULDER AND GIVES A TINY SQUEEZE.

"Skye doesn't want me to tell this story, but in order for you to make an informed decision, you need to know everything." Forest gives an agonizingly slow blink. His white hair makes his complexion look pale, sickly almost.

"It all began when I was a boy. I lost my family and entered foster care. The first night, I was brutally raped by my foster father. Skye held me while I bled. She held me every night thereafter."

My hand flies to my mouth. The images those few sentences convey are horrifying.

This man is massive, stronger than strong, taller than tall, broader than broad, and fiercer than any warrior I've ever imagined. I can't imagine him ever being small, but I feel his pain. I see the scared little boy inside.

Forest weaves together a story too horrific to be real, but I sense no lies. Through the abuse both he and Skye endured year after year, my heart breaks for them.

And just when I don't think things can get worse, Forest tells me about John Snowden.

"He intended to make Skye his personal sex slave and wanted me to fight in the pens."

"Fight?" I want to say something here like *you mean boxing* or *cage fighting?* But I know to hold my tongue. Whatever horrific thing I imagine in my head, what he says next will be far worse than I can imagine.

"But Skye saved me. She saved us." Forest glances at Skye and a serene smile comes over his face. He reaches out a hand, holding it palm up between them. "She still does."

Skye tentatively leans forward and places her hand in his. Forest flinches, but then breathes out a shaky breath.

"This is huge for me." He stares at their hands.

I feel like I should ask *What's huge?* But the look on Forest's face says the answers to my questions are forthcoming.

"For years after the abuse, I couldn't touch Skye, or stand to have her touch me, without triggering a crippling PTSD episode. The things they made me do to her ... to us ..." He shakes his head and closes his eyes again.

The room once again hangs on his next words.

My first impression of Forest Summers was that he is a formidable force, but I see the tender, and defenseless, child he once was. There's weakness beneath his strength. He takes in a deep breath and continues.

"We both suffered PTSD from what we endured. It's taken us years to heal. Skye found an amazing man to love her, and with time, he helped her heal. My journey took a turn for the worse before things got better. While we were free from the horrors of foster care, John Snowden was still out there in the world." Forest takes in a breath and shudders. "I made it my life's work to take him down. I created the Guardians. Hired Sam to run the whole thing. Had to hire him away from the FBI, but he came."

"After he explained his vision for Guardian HRS, I had to be a part of what he wanted to build." Sam glances at me. "There was not one hint of hesitation."

Sam's words carry weight and meaning. It feels like he's trying to tell me something, but I can't decipher that right now. I'm too entranced by Forest's story.

"Sam brings his FBI connections to the Guardians. Our Delta team works mainly with the FBI in domestic hostage rescue scenarios. Alpha, Bravo, and Charlie are our main hostage rescue teams."

"Don't forget The Facility." Mitzy reaches out to lightly push on Forest's arm then turns to me. "He built this amazing place."

"The Facility is a rehabilitation halfway home for those we rescue. They're given the counseling they need to heal and the skills needed to survive. I gathered what I needed to take Snowden down."

"By *what*," Mitzy makes finger quotes and shakes her head, "he means people. He gathered the people he needed."

"Whatever, Mitz." He gives her a playful grin. "Mitzy came to me through a mutual friend. She worked one case with me and never left."

"You can't get rid of me now." Mitzy folds her legs beneath her and beams at Forest.

There's real love between those gathered here.

"Snowden was ... a monster."

I take particular note of the tense Forest uses.

"If he wasn't sending young boys to fight to the death in his fighting rings, he sold them. It wasn't just young boys either. He sold girls as well. But where he really made his money was in the acquisition, and sale, of young women. He didn't do that alone. In the vacuum left behind after his death, his business thrived. Since then, we've rescued scores of those who've been taken and discovered the range of ... *acquisitions* ... offered has expanded."

Forest pauses to sip at his drink. His brows pinch together, and he stares at the amber liquid swirling in his glass.

"Mitch Lancaster, one of our clients, hired us to rescue his daughter who went missing during Spring Break while she was in Cancun." His expression darkens. "When we did, we were made aware of the newest *offering* for those willing to pay."

"What does that mean?"

For some reason, that name sounds familiar. I make a mental note to look into it.

Something happens to the atmosphere in the room. Tension builds until it vibrates with barely restrained hatred.

What could be worse than selling women? Sending boys to fight to their death is one, but I sense there's something worse. I feel it in the suffocating weight of those gathered around me.

It's in the way they lean forward and listen to Forest. It's in the tension girding their frames and in the tiny movements they make. A tic of their jaw. An eye that twitches. Lips pressed tight together.

Forest's gaze hardens, and I sink back into my chair.

"Do you know what a snuff film is?"

I asked what could be worse and Forest delivers.

There goes the room again, spinning around me. That sinking sensation returns with a vengeance. While my stomach goes into free fall, I wet my mouth, because somewhere along the way, it got incredibly dry.

"Y-yes." I answer his question with a shaky voice.

"Zoe Lancaster is the only survivor out of seven women kidnapped, then brutally murdered. We later discovered it was a special request. Since that day, we've been looking for not only who that client is, but who fulfilled that request."

"And that brought you here?" My hand flies over my mouth. The depravity and evil that exists in this world is unbearable.

"It did."

"And the girl? Zoe?"

"Fortunately, she survived. By pure chance, another young lady was kidnapped with Zoe. Eve Deverough was taken to a compound buried deep in the jungles of Colombia."

"Deverough?" Now there's a name I recognize.

"Yes."

"There was something in the news about her father."

"Correct."

"He was executed."

"Correct." Forest nods. "When we rescued Eve, she had the foresight during her captivity to keep her eyes open. That resulted in us acquiring a ledger which details every transaction going back years. There's more to the story, more than we have time for in the very few minutes left to us, but that ledger brought us to your doorstep."

"Mine?"

"To Carson Deverough. From him to the Belvedere and subsequently to the Rossi's."

"My family." My shoulders slump.

The gravity of what these people fight against overwhelms me.

"I'm not privy to my uncle's business dealings."

"No, but you have access to his most personal space. That's an opportunity we can't ignore."

"Tell me what you need me to do."

I'm in. I'm all in.

"First and foremost, you *must* draw attention away from the three women we rescued tonight. Your security team saw Liam pull you into that van. My hope is they didn't see the three women get inside of it first. We send you and Liam back."

"How does that help?" My brows scrunch together.

"It takes their attention away from who was in that van. This is very important. I can't emphasize it enough." Forest pauses to cough into his fist. "Having Liam in a position close to your family allows us access we wouldn't otherwise have."

No one wakes up one day hoping to find out their entire life is a lie and those closest to them are monsters.

I've said it before and I'll say it again, I don't know these people, but their connection is overwhelming. Their mission to make this world a better place is beyond admirable. Their dedication to helping others is a palpable force.

Today, after Sybil was taken, I no longer knew who I could trust.

Now, after Forest's tragic story, I know one thing without any doubt.

I want to be one of them.

I want to be a Guardian.

19

LIAM

THE TENSION IN THE LIBRARY IS AT AN ALL-TIME HIGH. I'VE HEARD Forest's story before. Who hasn't in Guardian HRS? But this is the first time I've heard him tell it.

Chills race down my spine when he mentions Snowden. That operation was a Clusterfuck with a capital C. Not Guardian HRS's finest hour. We went in, guns blazing. We left, tails tucked between our legs.

Using Forest and Mitzy's virtual reality technology, we mocked up the compound Snowden was using in the Philippines. We anticipated every scenario. Troubleshot every contingency.

But there was one thing no one could foresee.

Snowden forced a terrible choice on Forest, and it came at a horrific cost. Forest didn't balk. He made the trade. He surrendered himself and was lost to us.

Guardian HRS redeemed ourselves later, rescuing not only Forest but his aide as well; the woman who would later become his wife. Snowden died during that second raid, put down like the rabid dog he was by Paul, the third member of Forest's unique triad.

We thought we destroyed Snowden's human-trafficking ring.

We were wrong.

In telling his story, Forest's stoic exterior fades. There's a tiredness in the way he carries himself; a bone-deep fatigue I've never seen before. A victim of unspeakable cruelty, endured as a child, then again as an adult beneath Snowden's reign, Forest is a survivor.

Now, he dedicates his life to rescuing others.

The man's a legend, but that kind of intensity can wear anyone down.

Skye takes over the story, with Mitzy interjecting, detailing how Maria can help Guardian HRS. I gesture to CJ and Sam, needing to speak with them in the hall.

I'm not good with abandoning my team, and an operation like they're proposing takes time.

"Want a little more?" I lean down, asking Maria about her drink.

The shaking in her hands is worse. No surprise. Forest and Skye make no secret of asking Maria to go to war against her family.

But there's one massively huge problem.

Maria knows nothing about undercover work. She doesn't know how to live a lie. That makes her unreliable: the very definition of *the weakest* link.

Chances of this whole thing turning on us is more likely than not.

Just as she picked up on the tension between her father and uncle when she was young, her family will sense a change within her. They may not know what it is at first, that Maria's loyalties shifted, but they will notice something's off.

That will prove lethal if not addressed and contained.

"I'm good." Maria twists in her seat and cranes her neck to look at me. "Thank you."

Her soft smile hits hard, lodging smack dab in the center of my chest. It tunnels under my skin and wraps around my heart, stirring up all kinds of protective instincts.

I gesture for the glass and take it out of her hand. While I return the empty glass to the bar, Sam and CJ excuse themselves. Mitzy follows. Which is no surprise.

They've spent the better part of an hour with Maria; an hour away from watching over Alpha team's rescue efforts aboard *Caviar Dreams.*

Mitzy, Sam, and CJ wait for me in the foyer while Skye speaks to Maria. Forest appears to be done for now. Retelling his story took a lot out of him. He reclines in the chair and closes his eyes.

"What's going on?" Mitzy looks between Sam and CJ while I exit the library.

On my way out, I close the heavy wooden doors.

"Ask Liam." Sam jabs a thumb in my direction.

"Don't have time for that. Alpha team is with CDR Fisher on the *USS Charles Sexton.* I'm needed back at Command and Control." She says she needs to go, but Mitzy's as curious as a cat. She'll stay because she can't bear to miss out on whatever it is I want to say.

"This won't take long." I glance over my shoulder. "Am I the only one who thinks this is one hell of a bad idea?"

"You mean putting you and Maria together?" Mitzy's lips twist into a smirk. "With all the sparks flying between the two of you, it's perfect."

"Sparks? There are no sparks." I give her a look. It does nothing to erase the shit-eating grin on her face.

"There's a distinct *vibe* going on between the two of you. How is putting the two of you together a bad idea?" She couches her question as a simple thing but taunts me with the sparkle in her eyes. Mitzy's having fun with me.

"There's no vibe. No spark. No nothing."

"Whatever." She gives a little flap of her hand, dismissing my comment. "Doesn't change a thing."

"Maria won't be able to pull this off." I can't be the only one who sees how big of a problem that creates.

"Not my problem, lover boy." She rolls her eyes and that grin turns into a smirk.

"Don't you start." My words come out as a growl.

"What?" Mitzy gives a flippant shrug. "When the boss man speaks, we fall in line. Or don't you trust Forest?"

"Of course, I trust Forest." My eyes bug out a little.

Everyone *trusts* Forest.

The man's brain doesn't operate like the rest of ours, and it never stops. Whenever he comes to the Guardians with a hair-brained idea, we fall in line. Even when his tech gear does questionable things.

Memories of *Rufus*, Forest's Robotic Ultra Functional Utility Specialist, aka robotic sentry dog, humping me during a test scenario in B-town, one of Guardian HQ's mocked-up training towns, brings a frown to my face. That's something my teammates have tons of fun with and not something I'll live down anytime soon.

Forest's tech is cool. His VR suite is beyond compare. The night vision tech is far superior to what we had in the Navy. Our weapons and protective gear are designed with one thing in mind: kill the enemy while keeping us alive.

What he's not good with is people.

He thinks he can simply issue an order and Maria will fall in line. He doesn't understand the tenuous minefield human relationships must navigate. He doesn't comprehend the hundreds of hours required to train an undercover operative.

I have the training. Maria does not.

This is doomed from the start, and I have every intention of shutting it down.

"If you trust Forest, then what's the problem?" Mitzy props her hands on her hips and stares me down.

"Maria." I look to Sam and CJ for a little moral support and get nothing. Frustrated, I turn back to Mitzy. "Maria is the problem."

"Whatever. I don't have time for this. I'm going to let these idiots deal with whatever issue you're having with your girl." Her attention shifts to Sam and CJ. "Good luck."

With that, Mitzy spins around and flits back to the dining room, where her technical team follows the progress of Alpha team.

I'd give anything to be with my team right now, instead of standing in the foyer of Rose Manor with my thumb up my butt staring at my boss's boss and his boss.

"You have a problem with your assignment?" Sam shifts his attention from Mitzy's retreating backside to me.

"It's a shit assignment. My place is with my team, not babysitting Maria."

"Your place is doing what Guardian HRS needs," CJ jumps in. "What's bothering you?"

"She's not qualified for the kind of undercover work this requires. Her family will see right through this bogus relationship. That puts her in danger, places me at risk, and destroys any advantage we might have."

"She'll learn what she needs to learn." Sam rocks back on his heels.

"How?" I glance back at the library with its closed doors.

"You'll teach her, for one thing." CJ chews at his lower lip.

"I'm a fighter, not a teacher." I defend my position, already aware I wage a losing battle.

"One of the biggest parts of being an operator is teaching those who are new to the team. You're an excellent instructor, and need I remind you that we have no one else who can do this?" That's CJ's way of telling me to fall in line.

"But ..." I run my hand through my hair, frustrated. I'm not getting out of this.

"Look ..." CJ places a hand on my shoulder. "I get you want to stay with your team. After this operation, we'll be packing it up here in NOLA and returning to California."

"Exactly. I need to be with Alpha, not left behind in New Orleans. Bravo is still operating short. Delta is busy as fuck. Charlie is your only team operating at full strength."

"We'll pull from Bravo like we've done in the past." CJ doesn't mince words.

Bravo's had it rough. They walked into a shitstorm in Cancun. No one died, but the injuries they sustained are not insignificant. Since then, they've supplemented our team when we've had men out with injuries, like Griff when he got shot in the leg.

"Not if I'm with my team." My case is lost, but I'm not ready to accept defeat.

"You are the one Maria's security team saw pulling her into the van." Sam states all the reasons why it must be me, and I hate that he's right. "The only person it can be is you. Fortunately, we've been blessed."

"How's that?"

"Previous pattern of behavior." Sam shrugs. Neither he, nor CJ, will force me if I absolutely put my foot down.

Sending me on a mission I can't get behind is a recipe for disaster, but they both know I'll obey the chain of command. My ego is not that big, and there's no argument left to be made.

"Exactly." CJ stands with Sam. "You're it."

"It's a shit assignment."

"What's a shit assignment?" Maria's soft voice makes me palm my face. Of all the things she could overhear, why did it have to be that?

"Nothing." I spin around and fix a fake smile on my face. "Just talking about Guardian stuff."

"By *stuff* you mean getting stuck with me?" Her left brow arches as fires swirl in those sapphire eyes of hers. "For the record, *Hollywood*, I'm not happy about it either."

Behind me, CJ and Sam snicker.

"Now wait a second. That's not what I said."

It's a no-go getting out of this. Best to put on a smile and do my damn job.

Grin and bear the suckage.

It's a saying a few of us had during BUDS. We did whatever we had to and made it to the end of another horrible day with a smile on our faces. We did that because we didn't ring the bell. Each day we didn't ring out was one day closer to joining the ranks of the most elite warriors in the world.

"You said, and I quote." She lifts up her fingers and hooks them in the air. "It's a shit assignment. Shit meaning me." Maria glares at me. Arms crossed. Lips pressed together. There's a storm brewing in her eyes.

"Hey, I never said it was you." I hold up my hands in surrender. She's nearly a foot shorter than me, but damn, what a tempest when mad.

"Did too." She doesn't back down.

"Did not." Can't help but fire one back at her.

I blow out a frustrated breath, very much aware Maria dresses me down in full view of not only Sam and CJ, but Forest and Skye as well. They join us in the foyer and listen to every word.

"You're in for a rough go, lover boy." Forest huffs a laugh, but fatigue pulls at his shoulders and makes his smile sag.

"Come on Bean, you should get some rest." Skye places her hand on Forest's arm. "We've got it from here."

"I'm not sitting this one out. If we don't get those girls ..." His gaze cuts to Maria.

It takes a second for it to sink in, but Maria gets it. Like watching a wreck in slow motion, she gets it.

"Is there a problem with the rescue?" She grasps my arm for support.

I think she forgets she was dressing me down not two seconds previously.

"No problem. Just more moving parts than the Belvedere operation." Forest points between me and Maria. "The two of you need to hurry up and start date night. We need lots of smiling pictures of the happy couple."

"Do we have to fake an engagement?" I look to Skye for support.

"A fiancé will be given more leeway to move freely." She crushes any hope I have left.

Shoot me dead.

Maria gives me the eye, then takes me in from head to toe. I wear the black suit from earlier in the evening when I escorted Lily into the Belvedere as my date. I know exactly what she's thinking.

"Uh-oh." I smack my hand over my forehead. "Houston, we have a problem."

"What's that?" Skye keeps hold of Forest, grasping his arm with a delicate touch.

"They have me on camera with Lily when we entered earlier."

"That's no problem." Forest's rumbly words end in a cough.

"How's that. It's all captured on their security feeds."

"I know Knox and there's no way you did anything but hug Lily. Figure something out. She's your sister, or a cousin." Forest looks between me and Maria. "Play nice."

"Can't make any promises." Maria's stormy expression shifts to me. "Remember, lover boy, I'm doing the Guardians a favor."

"Don't you dare start with that." I've descended into some kind of personal hell.

"Fine. Hollywood it is." Maria's gaze cuts to Skye. "How are we getting back? Anything specific you want us to do?"

"Just look like a couple having fun. I'm sure Hollywood can figure out the rest." Skye winks.

Figure it out?

I can do that and more. It's time to have a little fun at Maria's expense, and it's always best to just dive in.

20

MARIA

THE PAST FEW HOURS HAVE BEEN A COMPLETE WHIRLWIND. I'M DIZZY with the sudden changes in my life; a victim of whiplash as I go from loyal Rossi family member to Guardian conspirator, all within the span of a few hours.

I fear what happens next.

That sinking sensation in my gut doesn't look like it's going away anytime soon. If anything, that twisting, gnawing apprehension builds and builds until I feel like I'm going to be physically sick.

Again.

My hand sits over my belly, pressing in. It does nothing to ease the sinking sense of dread swirling in my gut.

I'm going to lie to my family.

I've never lied to them before, not about something this big. Not only that, but I'm going to cover up the rescue of three women. I mean, that's a good thing—rescuing others—but I don't like this new world I find myself in.

"What happens now?" I look to Liam for guidance.

Evidently, I'm stuck with him for the time being.

"Guess we're engaged." He doesn't look happy about this either.

In fact, he gazes longingly toward the dining room where all the computers report back status updates about his friends.

A fake relationship?

"I'm not good at pretend. Never have been. It's one of the reasons I rarely got away with anything growing up."

"Is that so?" His husky voice whispers across my skin, lifting the fine hairs as it sinks in and wakes up my nervous system. There's simply too much of him to process.

"My father always saw right through me."

"What about your mother? She's the one we have to convince."

"Mother?" I give a shake of my head. "Not so much. But my father always knew when a lie touched my lips." I turn my attention to CJ and Sam. "I don't think I can do this."

"If you don't convince them, the lives of those women are at risk." CJ doesn't sugarcoat it.

That makes me take a step back. I try to swallow, but there's a thick lump of fear closing off my throat. If I don't pull this off—it's not just those women who are at risk. What's to keep my family from thinking I'm working with the Guardians?

You could tell them the truth ... Liam abducted you.

I could, but that would start an all-out war. The Guardians are not the bad guys in this twisted and fucked up world. It's the ones closest to me who are evil. They kidnap, then sell, women. Children too, if I understand what Forest said.

Sam glances at his phone. "The car will be here in five." His attention shifts back to Liam. "Mitzy sent a list of places if you need ideas. You know the drill, keep moving."

"Got it." Liam runs his fingers through his hair.

Why something like that is so damn hot perplexes me, but a tiny shiver of anticipation shoots through me.

"Behave out there." Sam gives Liam a look, then shifts his attention to me. "You've got this, Maria. Tonight is simple. All we're doing is covering up your disappearance, but keep in mind this isn't a first date between the two of you."

"What does that mean?"

Liam saunters up to me, the man has the sexy swagger down pat. When he slides an arm around my waist, I flinch and push him away.

He leans down and whispers in my ear. "A couple like us touches ... intimately."

He runs his hand through my hair, twirling the strands around his fingers. Softly, he tucks the hair behind my ear and leans down to press his lips lightly against my earlobe.

My mouth dries up like the Sahara, and I gulp when I get the meaning of what he says.

His heated breath against my skin sends a riot of sensation shooting through me, accelerating my heart rate, deepening my breathing, and heating the skin of my cheeks.

"For example ..." Without warning, Liam backs me up against the wall.

Bracing one arm over my head, the tiny sliver of air left between us is a fragile thing, vibrating and humming with need. Like a string stretched taut, it plays a melody that is uniquely him and me.

My heart kicks into overdrive. My skin flames white hot, spiking temperatures in *other* parts of my body.

He's magnetic. Unstoppable. He's determined and dangerous.

What he is ... is overwhelming.

And he's going to kiss me.

He takes my senses and puts them in overdrive, like a drug-fueled high lifting me up. That's not good because there's always a precipitous drop on the other side, and I'm terrified of heights.

My head tips back, staring up at him while he leans down. I know where this is heading. I'm unable to stop what comes next. There's too much power vibrating in the space between us, stirring up physical needs and wants best ignored rather than indulged.

I don't do pretend, which means I can easily fall for him if I don't keep my head in the game. Liam's not only attractive, he's also a protector, a defender, and a warrior. He's walking sex on a stick.

I'm in a terrifying free fall. Too vulnerable to be in a position to make rational decisions.

I will fail.

I'll do something stupid like tumble into his arms, maybe even his bed, and my heart will gladly follow when it should remain locked up tight, safe from his charms.

"Please, don't." I press my hand against his chest, pushing him away. Not that I can. The man is a solid wall of muscle, steel beneath skin.

"Princess, if we're to be believed, this is necessary."

By *this*, he means kissing.

Touching.

Intimate things.

How intimate?

"I don't see how shoving your tongue down my throat proves we're a couple when there are other things that involve far less slobber."

"Slobber?" He pulls a face. "What kind of men have you been dating? Trust me, princess, there will be no slobber when I kiss you."

When.

Not if.

Liam makes that clear.

"How about we table that?" The sudden shakiness in my voice isn't something I can hide. That right there is why we're doomed to fail. I'm incapable of covering up my reactions.

"Table what?" He pulls back.

"The kissing."

"Princess, tonight you and I are going to a few clubs. We'll visit some bars and stroll down the street. I'll hold your hand, kiss you senseless in the bar, and grind suggestively against you on the dance floor. My hands will be all over you, and yours *should* be all over me."

He already said babysitting me was a shit assignment.

"It's a bit much, don't you think?" Maybe I can get him to agree to hand holding and a hug?

"You do get what we're trying to do here? Kissing is just the beginning." His left eyebrow lifts and a smirk fills his face.

Our whole goal tonight is to cover up my *abduction* by pretending Liam and I have been secretly dating.

Shit, he's right.

The whole groping hands and kissing thing needs to be convincing. I inhale in a deep breath.

"Do that again." Liam's low, sultry voice should be bottled as an aphrodisiac. It's potent, sensual, and smooths away all the rough edges. He's got the kind of voice you want to wrap your whole soul around.

"Do what?"

"Breathe." He takes in a deep breath, gesturing with his arm as he sweeps up from his diaphragm all the way to his mouth. His gaze pins me in place while I follow. His hand moves down as he exhales. "Two more times."

"I don't—"

"Humor me." The smile tilting the corners of his lips is soft and gentle, impossible to resist. He takes in another breath while I join him.

We breathe together. Each time, his hand moves from his diaphragm to his mouth and back out again, almost as if he's pulling and pushing the air in and out of his lungs.

It works.

I hate to admit it, but the slow breathing soothes my anxiety.

At some point during our exchange, CJ and Sam leave us. Too focused on Liam, I miss their departure. I open my eyes after the last breath in time to see headlights flickering through the window as a car pulls around the stately drive.

"That's our ride." Liam extends his hand. "How about we slow things down? Begin with holding hands? Graduate to wrapping my arm around your shoulder? Your waist? Move to a hug? I'll try not to slobber on you when we kiss, but we will kiss."

He makes it a promise, and while I'm nothing more than an assignment to him, there's heat in his words. Is it possible he *wants* to kiss me? Not because that's what he's been ordered to do, but because he might want to as well?

"I'm not dressed to go clubbing."

"Luv, we're in New Orleans, you fit in just fine."

"I'm wearing a suit." I run my hands down my body while Liam snickers. I'm garbed in business professional gear: a modest skirt, silk blouse, and a suit jacket.

"You have no idea, do you?" He cocks his head, flagrantly staring at me.

"About what?"

"How hot you are?"

Heat rushes to my cheeks. I hate the way I blush. It's too revealing, broadcasting my emotions to anyone and everyone around me.

"You're a knockout." Liam takes a step back and folds his arms across his chest. He takes his time checking me out. "Ditch the jacket. You don't need that."

I peel off the jacket. Liam takes it, folds it gently, and places it on the massive entry table standing in the middle of the foyer.

"Definitely hot." He tilts his head and cups his chin. "There's nothing about your clothes, your shoes, or your jewelry that's flashy and screams money, but the absence of it broadcasts class. You pull that off well."

"That's the result of years of finishing school."

"Is that even a thing anymore?"

"If you're my mother's daughter, it's that and more. I was the kid who went from karate to finishing school, and only then hit the books."

"Karate?" His brows tug together. "Got the rainbow?"

"Huh?"

"The rainbow of belt colors?"

"Maybe." Why does his comment make me defensive? Angry? Insulted?

Because it's dismissive, that's why. I'd say something, but I don't need to defend my abilities. He can think what he wants, but my training is extensive.

Maybe he forgot what happened in the van?

It's what my father demanded. He didn't want his only child, a girl at that, to be defenseless. I'm well versed in how to handle a weapon as well as defending myself against multiple attackers.

What I'm not prepared to handle is the man standing opposite me.

Rainbow of colors, my ass. I'll show Liam what I can do.

21

MARIA

"COME HERE." LIAM'S VOICE DIPS TO THE LOWER REGISTERS.

It's a swoon-worthy sound that makes the butterflies in my belly take flight. They flit around, anxious little things, waiting for what comes next. Meanwhile, I'm barely holding on, too terrified by recent events to take a breather.

My perfect little world lies at my feet; a million shards of lie piled upon lie. There's no way to put it all back together.

My life's a ruinous disaster.

"Maria?" Liam's voice washes over me.

That expressive face of his fills with compassion. I detect a hint of sorrow tugging at the corners of his eyes, although I don't know what he has to be sad about.

Christ, his eyes will be my undoing.

"Shouldn't we get moving?" I rub sweaty palms on my skirt, a nervous mannerism I wish I could stop.

"There's no rush." Liam's gaze casts over my shoulder. "We have all night."

"That's what scares me." I tuck my chin and mumble.

"Here. Let's try this." Liam grabs me by the waist, then pulls me close until we're a hairsbreadth away from each other.

My hand goes to his chest, to the steel beneath his skin, where I push against him.

I can't breathe standing this close.

"Not like that." He lifts my hand off his chest.

The skin of his hand is rough, the palm and fingers calloused from hard work. One breath pulls his unique scent deep into my nostrils. It's not cologne or overly scented deodorant. He smells good: dark, mysterious, and uniquely Liam.

"Put it here." Gently, he places my hand on his shoulder. "Put your other hand on my shoulder as well." He bends his knees, stooping down to my eye level. "I'm not going to do anything you don't want. If kissing's off the table, it's off the table. There are many ways for couples to be intimate."

"When you say *intimate*, what do you mean?"

"I see the fear swirling in your eyes, princess, but relax. Like I said, nothing happens that you don't want."

I'm glad he says that.

"We want your family to think we're together, but we're only putting on a show in public. The engaged, not-engaged thing is something we can discuss. Does that help?"

"Maybe?"

"For the next few minutes, I want you to trust me."

"Why?"

His low chuckle lifts the corners of my mouth into something almost masquerading as a smile.

"That's not trusting. It's questioning." Liam playfully presses his finger against the tip of my nose, teasing me.

"I'm inquisitive by nature." I cock my head to the side and look up at him through the fringe of my thick lashes. It's a coy look, one which never fails me. I use it to get men to do what I want, only it slides right off Liam.

He tilts his head back and his husky laughter rolls over me with pure devastation. I should count myself lucky he's willing to hold me in his arms. Outside of the catastrophe which has become my life, I'd never have a chance with a guy like Liam.

"I'm going to try something." Liquid warmth. That's what his voice sounds like. "We haven't given you any time to stop and think about what's happened. Unfortunately, we don't have time for slow and easy. I need you to pretend we aren't complete strangers. For the past six months, we've been secretly dating, which means we hold hands. We get in each other's personal space. We laugh. We hug. And we kiss. I'm going to kiss you, and I'll try my best not to slobber."

"I didn't—"

"Trust me." Mirth swims in those magnetic eyes of his. "But try not to slobber on me, okay?" Liam's having fun with me. "Loop your arms over my shoulders."

"The car's waiting. Shouldn't we go?" I glance out at the car patiently waiting in the drive.

"Don't worry about the car." Liam places his finger beneath my chin and gently turns my head back to him.

"I hate making anyone wait."

"If we go out there with you stiff and standoffish around me, we lose before we begin. I promise, I don't bite." His lips twitch with that comment telling me he does exactly that. "It's one kiss. A trial run, minus the slobber."

My hesitation must be new for him. I'm surprised he's not more frustrated than he is.

I can do this.

I take in another deep breath and blow it out nice and slow. "Hand on your shoulder?" I place my hand on his shoulder.

"Don't make it sound like a chore, princess. You might actually have fun if you let yourself go."

"I'm scared as shit right now. Give me a little grace, please?"

"Grace given." The way he looks into my eyes makes my heart bang away inside my chest. Whoever snags him is going to be a very lucky girl.

"Wait a second." I lean away from him. Or as much as I can, considering he hasn't released the grip he has on my hips.

"What now?" This time, Liam blows out a frustrated breath. I'm definitely getting on his nerves.

It feels like we're rushing the whole *getting to know you* thing. Which is hysterical, considering that's exactly what we're doing. I need more of a warmup before we move full steam ahead.

So, I do what I do best.

I stall.

"You're not married, are you?" I have to tilt my head back to look at his face. He's easily a foot taller than me. "Engaged? Dating?"

"No. Why?"

"Because I don't kiss someone who belongs to someone else."

"I'm free and single. Last man standing."

"What does that mean?"

"Only that all the other guys on my team are no longer on the market." The way he says it sounds wistful, almost as if he lost something precious to him.

He misses hanging out with his friends. It's a tiny peek behind the curtain, revealing more than he realizes. Definitely more than he wants me to know. I play it off, pretending I didn't catch everything he meant with those words.

"Okay ... Hands on your shoulders." I place my hands stiffly on his shoulders. It's more like awkwardly bracing my hands on his broad shoulders.

Nibbling my lower lip, I wriggle my toes, unsure what to do next. This feels awkward.

"Not like that." Liam grabs my wrists, lifts my hands off his shoulders, and loops them around his neck.

Because of his height, I'm forced to lean against him. It's intimate. Far more than I'm comfortable with. He's so tall, there's no space between us at all.

While I stretch, trying to reach around his neck, Liam places his hands on my waist. His fingers wrap around to splay against the small of my back.

Our bodies press tight against each other from shoulder to shoulder and hip to hip. My breasts squish against his chest, soft to his hard.

He steals my breath and makes me sway on legs suddenly weaker than they were moments before.

I'm exceptionally uncomfortable. That feeling radiates throughout my entire body as I lock my knees and try to breathe without expanding my chest any more than I have to.

I'm acutely aware of my breasts and how they're completely pressed against his chest. Each breath only accentuates my discomfort.

"Close your eyes." His voice softens, which makes that weakness in my knees ten times worse.

Instead of stiff legs, I stand on noodle legs now.

"Why?"

My entire body is on high alert, exquisitely sensitive to every sensation. From the delicious timbre of his voice to his incredibly unique scent, he drowns me in sensation.

"Because I said so." There goes that husky laugh again. It rumbles around inside my chest, vibrating within me. "You really don't know how to trust, do you?"

"I guess not." I blow out a breath and can't help but grin.

I don't trust myself around Liam.

His thumbs dig in at my waist while his fingers slide down over the curve of my ass.

Holding firm, he rotates his hips back and forth, then side to side, making a figure-eight motion. I have no choice but to follow because his hands act like clamps fixing my hips to his.

The man has moves, and he's good. He's good enough to compensate for the stiffness in my body.

It's almost as if we're dancing.

"Try not to resist my movements."

"I'm a horrible dancer."

"You're going to be the death of me, princess." His low throaty chuckle is like liquid warmth spreading through me. It's the only reason I let the *princess* comment go.

His hips swirl in a figure eight, taking me with him. If I let him guide me, I follow just fine. If I try and think about following his movements, I get in my own way. It's harder than it looks.

"If I step on your toes, sorry in advance." My voice shakes like every other part of me.

I can do this.

Since I'm plastered against his broad chest, his rumbly laughter settles beneath my ribcage.

Liam is not a threat.

Maybe if I repeat that over and over, I'll believe it.

There's zero reason not to trust him, and about a million reasons why not trusting him is a really bad idea.

His hands move from my waist to settle on my hips. "Lift up on tiptoe and kiss me."

"Kiss you?" My eyes widen with surprise. When he presses the pad of his finger over my lips, my brows bunch together, confused.

"If you can't do that when no one is around," he says. "How are you going to do it when we're being watched? And trust me, we will be watched."

"This is impossible."

"It's just a kiss."

I'm going to blow it.

Frustrated, my fists clench and I squeeze my eyes shut. Liam removes his fingers from my lips, leaving an emptiness there.

My lids fly open, however, when the sudden heat of his lips touch mine. It's a light, barely perceptible sensation. My knees buckle and he holds me tight as a shiver races down my spine.

Gasping, I pull back, but then something happens. My heart pounds like thunder and that low fire burning deep within me explodes outward in a rush of heat. His lips feel good on mine. I suddenly want more.

I lift up on tiptoe and press my lips against his.

Suddenly, I feel him everywhere, every place our bodies touch, my nerve endings wake up, craving more of the delicious sensation.

His palm slides up my back, a magical caress along my spine that sends waves of pleasure pulsing through my body. The stiffness in my body melts away as the magic of his fingers kneads my flesh.

Instead of pulling away, I'm captivated and entranced. His touch continues dancing up and down my spine, commanding my muscles to relax, igniting my skin in a rush of heat, and lighting my nerves up like the Fourth of July.

This is dangerous.

Liam is dangerous.

Much more of this and he'll turn me into an addict, with him being the drug I crave.

We just met, and yet he already knows exactly how to touch me, when to stroke me, and how to command my body to bend to his will.

Or maybe, he's just a really good kisser and it has nothing to do with me?

I'm terrified, but not enough to want any of this to stop. With the magic of his fingers wrecking my self-control, a contented sigh slips out of me.

I've never felt a kiss this tender.

A kiss this relentless.

A kiss that devastates and devours while promising to protect and shelter. My blood heats as his firm lips slide against mine.

With a diabolical sweep of his tongue, he parts my lips and lays claim to my mouth.

He tastes like he smells: dark, tantalizing, and deliciously male. The determined assault on my mouth sends sparks of electricity racing down my spine. My insides twist and heat as his greedy mouth takes and claims. I cling to him, wanting more, yet unable to voice my desires beneath the overload of stimulation.

No one has ever kissed me like this.

No one.

If this is what a real kiss feels like, I've been ripped off my entire life.

Liam doesn't just kiss. He hijacks my entire body. Those talented fingers of his continue kneading the muscles along my spine, turning my knees to jelly. I cling to him out of necessity. There's no way I'm capable of standing on my own.

Not now.

Not with his lips pressed to mine.

Not with his tongue probing and exploring, teasing and tempting. His hand flattens against the small of my back, pulling me against the hardness of his body.

And he is hard.

His rigid length presses against my belly, unashamedly aroused and powerful.

Liam will cause serious damage if I don't find some way to protect myself from his inherent charms. One kiss and he's already ruined me for other men.

Passion fuels his entire soul.

And holy hell, if this is what Liam's kiss feels like, what will it feel like when we have sex?

When?

Yes.

I said it.

God willing, if that's where this leads, I'm more than happy to follow Liam.

Every nerve in my body thrums in anticipation, leaving me wholly unprepared when his mouth releases mine and those lips of his travel to the angle of my jaw.

22

LIAM

Maria's strung out from everything that's happened tonight. That tension vibrates in her breath. It pulses in the way she carries her body. She's so keyed up, she's forgotten how to act normal. That kind of agitation broadcasts itself to the world.

My job is to turn that negative energy around. Until I do, our mission is a no-go. It's dangerous for us both; that's a risk I won't accept.

So, I kiss her, and holy hell, the woman burns beneath my lips. It's unexpected and fascinating. Strokes my ego just fine, if I do say so myself.

Christ, her breathy moans are addictive as shit; a mainline of adrenaline shooting through my veins. Maria tastes like heaven, light and fresh, a hint of mint and strawberries. She's perfection and has no idea how desirable she is to a man like me.

The chemistry between us is a palpable thing, crackling between us, waiting for the right spark to ignite.

Which makes kissing her dangerous.

I can get lost in this woman if I'm not careful.

But Maria isn't a random hookup.

She's my job, and my job is to get her to a point where she's comfortable with me touching her.

She's a puzzle I get to figure out—a challenge—and I love a good challenge. Put all the pieces in the right places and there's no doubt in my mind, this woman will turn into a raging inferno beneath my skilled hands, mouth, and cock, if she decides to take things that far.

I'll lead as far as she lets me, but there's no way I'll force something like that. It's no fun and just plain wrong.

I string a trail of kisses from the corner of her mouth to the angle of her jaw. From there, I nibble on her earlobe before working my way down the gentle curve of her neck. I trace a path to the soft spot at the hollow of her throat. A signature move of mine, it never fails to drive a woman crazy.

"Liam ..." The way my name fills her breathy moan is a total turn-on.

My dick takes notice, moving from interested to fully engaged. Meaning, I go from soft to hard in the span of a heartbeat.

"Don't think too hard, princess. Let it happen." Unfortunately for my dick, kissing Maria won't lead to the good stuff. That's not what this is.

"But ..."

I silence her rebuttal by kissing along her collarbone to the corner of her shoulder.

If we were in a club, my nose would be deep in her cleavage by now. My hand would be under her shirt or under her skirt. Considering this isn't a club, and we're practically strangers, I'm trying to be a gentleman about this kiss. Damn, if she's not temptation overload.

I stop at her shoulder, leaving my lips pressed to her skin while she regains control of her breathing. Once she steadies herself, I give one final press of my lips and relinquish the kiss.

"That wasn't that bad of a kiss, was it?" My goal is to make a dent in her personal armor. Crack it wide open and find a way to slip inside. I not only need her to be comfortable around me, but the more time I spend with her—especially kissing her—the more I *want* her to enjoy her time with me.

"It was a good kiss." She breathes the words out on a contented sigh.

"Good? I can't believe my ears. Just good?" I place my hands over my ears and widen my eyes in mock horror. "I've spent decades perfecting that kiss. You wound me. Quick, we need to do that again."

"You're a goofball, and decades? How old were you when you started perfecting that kiss? And I doubt there's anything I can say that can wound you."

"What about my fragile ego?"

This is good. Banter is good. It's just what we need.

"Fragile?" Her laughter is a beautiful thing. It dances in the air and brings a smile to my face. "I seriously doubt your ego is *that* fragile."

"Well, when my kissing skills are in question, my ego gets a little sensitive."

"Well, your ego has nothing to worry about. Your kissing is off the charts hot." She folds her arms over her chest. Normally, that would tell me she's closed off, but exactly the opposite is happening.

Maria is having fun with me. She's loosening up. Those crossed arms are a part of the fun.

She mocks me.

I almost want to pump my fist in the air. I'm making progress.

"Whew!" I make a show of wiping fictitious sweat off my brow. "I can rest easy tonight knowing my epic kissing ability met the mark." I grip her arms, lightly, and pull back a tiny bit. "No slobber, right?" My gaze darts from one sapphire eye to the next. Damn, but those eyes are mesmerizing.

Instead of pinching together, her brows kind of wiggle and her cheeks turn the faintest shade of pink. "No slobber. You did good, Hollywood."

Definitely making progress.

"Are you saying my epic kissing ability superseded the mark?"

"I'm saying no such thing. The last thing I need is to stroke your ego any more than I just did."

"I'm not against a little stroking." A quick glance at my crotch forces her gaze to drop. "Ego or otherwise."

"No doubt about that." This time, she props her hands on her hips, loosening up and smiling for the first time. Not a fake smile, but an honest expression of amusement.

"Hey, I'm a guy. It's not my fault we think about sex every seven seconds."

"Seven seconds? It's amazing men have time to do anything else."

"I should kiss you again."

It's a cautious test. The more I can get her to relax around me, the more normal she'll act when put under pressure. I need her to turn to me for support rather than stand on her own.

"About that kiss."

"I'm all ears."

"Decades of perfection?" She arches a brow, questioning me. "You had to be a fetus when you started."

"Maybe I'm older than I look?"

"Fine." There go her hands again, propped up on her sinfully sexy hips. "How old are you?"

"How old are you?" I turn the question around, but I know her age. It's in the briefing files we all received.

"You're not supposed to ask a woman how old she is." Her quick retort makes me smile.

Definitely warming up to me.

"Hey, you started with the age crap." I hold my hands up and out in defense. "Only fair to answer your own question."

"You said you've been perfecting your kiss for decades. That's at least *two* decades. If you were ten when you first kissed a girl, which is arguably young, to be honest, that would put you in your thirties."

"Twenty-eight, actually."

"Really? So, you were ..."

"Eight. Third grade. Lacy Cooper dared me to kiss Margery Beck."

Wow, that's a memory that pops up out of nowhere. I haven't thought about Margery in a very long time. I can't help but wonder what happened to her over the years.

"A dare? Your first kiss was because of a dare?"

"Don't judge." I waggle my finger. More teasing. More lightening of the atmosphere between us. Things are going well.

I like this. It's a safe topic.

"Not judging, just surprised. When I was in third grade, the boys weren't interested in me." Her matter-of-fact statement is filled with the conviction of false-truth. She knows nothing about a young boy's mind.

"I can tell you, with one hundred percent certainty, those boys were definitely interested."

"Not at eight, they weren't." She defends her comment.

"You don't know boys." I can't remember a time when I wasn't curious about girls. They always fascinated me. "The boys may not have known what to do, but they were definitely watching."

"That may be." She hesitantly agrees, then negates it. "The ones in my third-grade classroom never talked about kissing."

"You're wrong. Or maybe I was a third-grade perv?" I shrug. "Who knows? It's possible. I watched all the girls, and I *studied* the sixth graders who shared our recess period. Those boys not only hung out with the girls, they touched them. They held hands, and they kissed. Never where the teachers could see, but I saw what they did."

"Oh my, you were a perv." Her eyes shine with amusement. Better yet, she leans forward and taps me on the shoulder. "And you were eight when you kissed a girl for the first time? I have to hear this story."

Score one for the win. She touched me. Not because I told her. It was unplanned, uninhibited, and completely natural.

"Well, Lacy said I had a fish mouth and slobbered like a dog. Maybe the two of you talked?" I arch a brow.

"You're a goofball. Why did you kiss Margery? That doesn't make sense. Why didn't you kiss Lacy?"

"Because Tod Thomson kissed Margery under the slide. He was a fifth grader, and you know what that meant."

"No. I don't know. What could that possibly mean?"

"Margery was the only girl in our class who could prove Lacy

Cooper wrong. I figured I kiss Margery and do better than Tod Thomson. He was the meanest kid in school, a royal prick. Although I didn't know to call him that at the time."

"You didn't know what *royal prick* meant, but you knew he kissed Margery?"

"Everyone knew he kissed Margery."

"How?"

"Because he blabbed it to everyone." My lips twist with the memory. "Tod was a tool. A total bastard."

The longer we talk, the more I enjoy her company. There's an easiness with her. She's both vulnerable and mentally tough. I love the contrast. Makes her that much more interesting.

I no longer regret getting stuck with her. In fact, I'm looking forward to spending more time with Maria Rossi.

"You're absolutely stunning, and I don't mean just on the outside. Your mind is a rich tapestry I can't wait to unravel."

"Unravel? I don't know if there's anything left to unravel, not that I'm terribly complex."

"Come here. After everything you've learned about your family, you need a hug."

I draw her into my embrace. Her arms wrap around me, and she places her cheek against my chest. There's no resistance.

One hurdle down.

"You're not what I expected." Maria takes in a deep breath.

"And what is that?" I continue holding her but leave space between us. This isn't something I can force. Maria needs to feel safe in my arms.

This close, her sapphire eyes mesmerize me. I could get lost in them for days and still need more. Tiny flecks of blue, green, and gold dance in those captivating depths.

Truly an unusual beauty.

"It's not complimentary." Her lashes flutter with that comment.

Maria tightens her hold on me, snuggling against my chest. As for me, I keep my grip loose. I'll lose her if I push this.

"I bet I can guess." I brush her hair off her shoulder.

"You think so?"

"Yes." I can't help it. "You believe I'm the kind of man who goes to a bar, snaps his fingers, flirts, then fucks, then leaves."

"Flirts, then fucks? Props for great alliteration." Her soft laughter warms me from the inside out.

"Great alliteration would be flirts, fucks, and flees."

"You win." Her laughter comes freely, not forced at all. She punches me lightly on the chest. "Definitely *not* what I expected."

"Princess." I cup the side of her face and draw my thumb across her cheek. I want to press it against her lips, but I'm in no rush.

"Yes?" Her eyes close as I trace the gentle curve of her cheekbone. It wouldn't take much to lean down and steal another kiss.

"How about you give me that kiss I asked for?" I keep my tone neutral, injecting as little emotion into my words as possible.

"I already did." She counters, a defensive move.

"No. I kissed you." Time to remind her. "I asked you to trust me. Or did you forget about lifting up on tiptoe and kissing me?"

"You're going to be the death of me." She nibbles on her lower lip while I hold incredibly still, trying not to spook her.

She's either going to rise to the challenge or take a massive step back. If she does that, I'm sending that car away. There's no way we can be seen in public if she's that uncomfortable around me.

However, if she takes the bait and ...

Maria lifts on tiptoe and very gently brushes her lips against mine.

"Well, hello, sunshine." My arms wrap around her and tug her in close.

I don't do what I want, which is to pursue that kiss further. Instead, I hold her tight and thread my fingers through her silky hair.

"You, Miss Maria Rossi, are the bravest woman alive. Fierce and loyal, I'm definitely falling for you."

"Goofball." She punches me in the chest. To my surprise, it kind of hurts.

"You've got some *oomph* in that punch of yours."

"I should. Got my black belt at the end of that rainbow of colors, then moved on to Krav Maga. Or did you forget how I took you down in the van?"

"You continue to impress me, Miss Maria Rossi."

She nibbles on her lower lip, unsure and insecure.

"That's what we teach our rescues."

"Your what?"

"The women we save. Well, the women, the kids, and the young men who would kill me if they ever heard me calling them boys. We call them our rescues and teach them how to defend themselves at The Facility. We do a whole hell of a lot more than that, but that's what the Guardians do."

"I feel like there's so much more to know about the Guardians."

"There's layers upon layers."

"That story Forest told ..." She hesitates. "Is it true?"

"Every word."

"Damn."

"Yeah."

"He seems so normal."

"There's nothing normal about Forest Summers."

23

MARIA

"ARE YOU READY?" LIAM GAZES AT ME, HEAT BANKED FOR THE MOMENT; male arousal simmers in the background.

I'm not the only one affected by that kiss.

"I'm terrified."

"It's just a night out. Let your hair down, have a few drinks. I'll take you to the dance floor. We'll have fun. That's all this needs to be."

I run my hands up and down my arms when a sudden chill overcomes me. My attention shifts from Liam to the door leading outside.

I do that on purpose because I don't want my gaze to slip down to the prominent bulge between Liam's legs. That's a dangerous path for my eyes to travel, let alone my mind.

I know very little about Liam, but the whole alliteration thing ... flirts, fucks, and flees ... is something to be cautious about.

Although, who am I kidding? Am I any different?

My virginity went out like that the summer of my sweet sixteen: flirt, fuck, and flee. I didn't date while in college, but I was far from abstinent. When the urge arose, I took care of the itch.

When Sybil and I go out, invariably it's because that itch is back. I'm a young woman with needs. Men aren't the only ones who can engage in meaningless sex.

As for relationships, is it odd I've never been in a serious one?

"You have nothing to be scared about when I'm around." The low, husky sound of Liam's voice sends warm tendrils of anticipation rushing down my spine.

Hot licks of fiery passion spark and sizzle, they're promises of what things might become if I let them.

If I let myself believe Liam can be something other than what he is ... a man doing a job assigned to him.

"Does nothing scare you?" I look into the turbulent depths of Liam's eyes.

Evidence of his arousal lingers, but there's something else there as well; a ferocious protector lurks in the background.

No wonder the man is a Guardian. He's dedicated to making the world a better place, safer for those of us who lack his tenacity, strength, and ability to make a difference.

"Fear is a mind-killer." The words roll off his tongue, deep, rumbly, and sinfully addictive.

"Are you quoting Dune to me?"

His laughter warms the air, wrapping around me like a soothing blanket.

"You read Dune?"

"Guilty as charged and proud of it. I'm a voracious reader of all things sci-fi."

"I devoured the series as a child. That phrase always stuck with me." Liam glances over my shoulder, looking outside at the car waiting for us.

"Me too."

"The few times I faced fear, I let that passage rumble through my mind. It never failed to give me the strength I needed. I truly believe what separates us from animals is the ability to stare fear in the face and conquer it."

"I wish I had that kind of strength."

The phrase is iconic among science fiction Dune fanatics. It's a truth seldom expressed but foundational.

Fear is a paralyzing force. If not confronted, it can be incapacitating.

"You're stronger than you know." The way Liam looks at me makes me want to believe.

"I've never felt real fear." My gaze bounces down to his chest, seeking solace.

"Then, you've never been tested. All fear is a manifestation of your mind. As the master of your mind, you control your fear."

"You say it like it's easy."

"I say what I know. Believe me, I've been in plenty of situations where fear nipped at the fringes of my mind." Liam taps the middle of my forehead. "Believe it here." His hand moves over the middle of my chest. "Feel it here."

I want to believe him. My life's been easy. Not one time have I been afraid.

But Sybil?

She faces a fear I can't imagine.

The idea of being kidnapped and sold is terrifying and paralyzing but academic to me. I can think about it. I can imagine it. But I have no understanding of what true fear feels like.

"Do you think there's any news about Sybil?"

I hope he knows something I don't.

"My brothers are on it, and Guardians never fail."

"You have incredible faith in your team."

Liam doesn't respond. Although, what kind of response do I expect?

Sybil, I hope you're safe. I pray the Guardians pull through and rescue you.

"You've got this, princess."

"Then we'd better hurry up before I lose my nerve."

"After you." He gestures toward the door.

While I pivot, he opens the door for me. He places his hand on the small of my back, gently guiding me as I exit Rose Manor.

New Orleans is hot and humid during the day, sweltering and

sultry at night. The moment I walk out, a wall of heat slams into me. I breathe in the moist air and close my eyes.

I can do this.

We cross the short distance to the car. Liam opens the door, and I slip inside. The driver looks up from his phone and glances at me through the rearview mirror. He waits for Liam to walk around to the other side of the vehicle and get in. When Liam sits, the driver looks at him.

"Where to?" He swipes the screen of his phone, loading up a map, and inputs the information as Liam rattles off an address in the French Quarter.

Liam and I sit in relative silence as the driver takes us back to the city.

My cues come from Liam. He's quiet; therefore I remain the same. I assume it's because of the driver, and it makes sense. We need to be careful talking about anything to do with Guardian HRS and the foul business my family's involved in.

Liam's long legs barely fit in the back of the car. His shoulder brushes against mine. His arm presses against me. His muscular thigh touches mine. Heat radiates from him, warming the entire left side of my body. The one thing which doesn't touch me are his hands.

He folds those in his lap, fingers loosely clasped as he stares out the front of the car. When not looking at him, I watch the city close in on us and think about that kiss.

Swoon-worthy comes to mind.

Eventually, my thoughts turn to my uncle.

When I stand across from Marco's disapproving frown and attempt to hide everything I've learned about my family, how will that play out?

Do I return to the Belvedere? Both my office and my apartment are there. My commute each day is one short flight of stairs. I live, work, eat, and play all within the walls of the Belvedere.

Rather than think about what comes next, I reach for Liam's hand and take it in mine.

He shifts beside me, tossing his arm around my shoulder and

pulls me to him. When he leans down to kiss the top of my head, my eyes drift closed, and a sigh escapes me.

That kiss in the foyer ... Liam's kiss, fabulous and hot, unexpected and intense, and oh-so-sexy-I-want-more, does far more than break the ice. It ignites the air between us.

A simmering heat swirls around us, an inferno that promises to erupt into something truly spectacular if I'm brave enough to fan the flames.

Despite what's happening between me and Liam, there's a hollowness sitting within my chest.

It's a vacancy of emotion when it comes to my uncle.

My uncle sits at the heart of the human-trafficking operation operating from within the walls of the Belvedere.

My hotel.

My home.

Terrible crimes occurring beneath my nose.

I can't believe my father was involved in such a despicable trade, but how could he not have been?

There's one thing I hold onto. My mother may be bristly at the best of times, but there's no way she's involved.

I press my palm against my breastbone, trying to erase the painful ache welling up within me. So engrossed in my thoughts, I miss the moment when the car pulls up to a curb.

"You're going to like this ..." Liam hops out of the car and circles around to open my door.

His chivalry surprises me. He circles around the car while I awkwardly wait for him to open a door I'm more than capable of opening myself. Hand extended, the light in his eyes is bright, eager, and excited.

Why can't I feel the same emotions?

Because this isn't a date. It's fake.

Our evening begins with a late dinner. I should call it a midnight meal, but this is New Orleans. We may not be the city that never sleeps, but we are the city that knows how to party all night long.

It's nearly one in the morning by the time we finish and Liam pays the tab. Holding hands, he leads me out of the restaurant. With a bit of wine taking the edge off my anxiety, I feel much more comfortable than I did going in.

Easily twice my size, the alcohol barely touches Liam, while I wobble in my heels. Good thing he holds me tight against him for support.

I'm tired. More than a bit strung out and perfectly happy having the night end here, but it can't. We have a job to do.

During the entire meal, Liam asked the waiter and waitresses to take our picture, shamelessly posting the whole thing to a social media account created hours previously with a bit of Mitzy Magic.

"Doing okay in those heels?" Liam glances down at my footwear. "Next stop is three blocks over, but I can get a car if that's too far."

In any other city, I'd be worried about walking around this late. Hell, I never do that alone in New Orleans. Somehow, having a man the size of Liam by my side makes all my concerns about drunks, muggers, and other unsavory characters drift into the background.

"I'm good." My heels are reasonable, meant for a day at the office rather than clubbing all night. I've got several blocks in me.

With his arm looped around my shoulders, Liam leads the way. We stop where crowds gather around street performers. Liam snaps a few selfies, posting to social media. Each time, he tags me. Then he drops a few dollars into the till, and we move on.

This doesn't feel like a job and soon I relax. I even laugh at a few of his jokes. He likes to make fun of himself and appears completely oblivious of the gaping stares he attracts from every woman regardless of age.

He's a man on a mission with that phone of his, snapping pictures nonstop. We stand cheek to cheek. There are a few tentative kisses, pictures sent out to the world. He plays with the street performers, drawing larger crowds, and fills their hats with coin and cash. A natural performer, he never fully steals the show, but his gregarious nature is a natural force all its own.

"You ready for some dancing?" Liam scans the crowded street.

He's perpetually alert, looking for threats, shielding me, and completely relaxed the entire time. Not that I'm an expert, but I see beneath the veneer. He's a consummate professional, protecting me while getting the job done. The man is wired tight, ready to defend, or attack. There's an undeniable lethality slumbering in his frame.

"Maria?" Liam wraps his arm around my waist and pulls me tight against him. "You're daydreaming again."

"Sorry."

"You think too hard." The pad of his finger taps between my eyes. "Need to breathe with me again?"

Oh, my lord, the thought of breathing with him is not what I need. We didn't even touch, yet that moment felt as intimate as a kiss to me. All of his intensity? Focused on me? It was a mainline of sensation surging within me.

"Sorry, I'm good." I shrug. "I'm a thinker, not a fighter."

"Well, my secret source says you worked through the rainbow and are a force to be reckoned with. Krav Maga? I don't know what I'm most eager to experience: taking you on the dance floor or sparring with you on the mat."

"Goof." I'm that secret source of his.

He's being corny.

"And you're sexy as fuck. It's time we hit a club. I'm eager to get you on the dance floor."

"I told you I'm no good. Two left feet. They're only good at stepping on my date's toes."

"Don't worry about my toes." He glances down and taps the toe of his boot. "Steel toes. I'll be perfectly safe. Besides, every woman looks amazing when they dance with me."

"Because of your heartthrob looks?"

"No, because they're the sexiest thing on the planet when they're in my arms. Beauty is in the eye of the beholder, and there's a reason for that. In my arms, you are perfection. Every male within sight of you will fantasize about taking you from me and claiming you as their own."

"What do you mean?"

"The sexiest thing about a woman isn't her looks, it's the confidence she shows the world, but more than that, it's the way the man who holds her looks her in the eye."

"That makes no sense."

"Luv, you're amazing and beautiful, desirable and coveted. In my arms, you're that and so much more. No man in his right mind will be able to keep his eyes off of you. Every one of them will envy me."

"You?"

"Because I'm the one holding you."

"Like I said, you're corny."

"I'm simply being honest." He stares deeply into my eyes, and for a second, I almost believe him.

"Liam," I place my hand on his chest. "You don't have to pretend. Let's just get through this night."

He gives me a look, one I can't decipher, then continues on without a witty comeback.

24

LIAM

It's a dark night, darker than it should be. Or maybe, it's my mood that's bleak. I'm not happy operating without backup.

It's like walking out onto the field without a jockstrap on. All the important bits swing free: unprotected, vulnerable, and susceptible to physical harm. It's like asking to get kicked in the nuts.

Which means, I'm hyper-alert and cranky.

I miss my team.

I miss the confidence they instill.

I miss knowing I'm not out on my own with nothing but my ass to back me up.

Some guys are meant for the solitary fight. Brett and Sawyer, our new Guardian Protectors, were specifically recruited because they work best alone.

I'm not like that.

I prefer a team backing me up.

Instead, I'm out here swinging in the wind with an unknown female tied to me. The sinful curves of Maria Rossi, my enemy who is not my enemy, do not inspire confidence. Those curves inspire all kinds of indecent thoughts, like that kiss which was nuclear hot.

Don't get me wrong, I like the chick, but she's not a member of my team.

As for this night, humidity tenaciously clings to the air. The temperature dropped a few degrees while we enjoyed our dinner. It's balmy, comfortable, and perfect for a late-evening stroll.

I eye Maria with caution.

Pretty enough to knock me off my game, she's a dangerous distraction. We're reluctant teammates thrust together out of circumstance and necessity with insane chemistry swirling between us.

A quick check of my phone reveals no status update on her friend, Sybil. Knowing how Sam and the others are going to play this, the chances for a tear-filled reunion are slim to none.

Let's go with none.

We're too damn close to figuring out who's responsible for the kidnappings, the sales, and the deaths of innocent women. We know the Rossi's are involved, the result of insane intel work by Wolfe and Jinx, but all we know is that the money connects.

We don't know who's in charge—although we assume—and we don't know who the clients are—which we need—especially the one ordering snuff.

We're not taking down the Rossi operation until we ID that buyer and rain a whole lot of hellfire down on their pathetic life.

"How are you holding up?"

I look to Maria like I have a hundred times already this night. Each time, it's like getting sucker punched. My breath catches. My heart skips a beat. She strikes awe in me.

With her world falling down around her, she's fucking fierce. Calm. Cool. Collected. She's not whimpering in a corner and useless. Instead, she's on the street, doing what she can to help her friend.

"I'm good." Maria does a little pirouette, spinning around on her toes as she takes in the sights and sounds of the French Quarter late at night.

Her purse swings out wide, putting me on high alert. It won't take but a grab and a yank to rip that purse off her shoulder and run off with it through the crowd.

As for crowds, it's well past midnight, heading towards two, and it's past time to hit some clubs.

"It's a beautiful night." Maria spins again, this time slower. Her purse doesn't swing out nearly as wide. "The temperature is perfect. The breeze is just right. It's enough to cool down without being too chilly." She looks up at me through the dark fringe of her lashes. "The company is F-I-N-E, fine."

"Glad I pass the test." I can't help but chuckle.

"Liam, you're lickably hot. You'd pass any woman's test."

"Lickably hot?"

I'm certainly interested in licking her. I'd start at her toes, move up her legs, spend eternity between the juncture of her thighs, then move up to nibble on her perfect breasts.

Yeah, lickably hot.

"Definitely." She spins in front of me, then stops.

Hands propped on her hips, she gives me the once over, sliding her hungry gaze up and down my body. It's exaggerated and fun.

"If I'm lickably hot, you're a raging inferno. A sensual siren men can't resist."

"Now that is over the top."

"Is it?" I tug at my chin, having fun with the playful back and forth.

"So, where are we going?"

"To a club."

"I *know* that." She rolls her eyes and spins back around to my side. Leaning in, she grabs my hand and interlaces her fingers with mine. "Which club?"

"It's a secret." Not really, but I enjoy teasing her too much to stop. "Just trust me."

Maria's brows pinch together. She glances at my pocket, the one holding my phone, and bites her lower lip. I've been waiting for her to ask, delaying the inevitable.

She's not going to like what I have to say. However, Maria doesn't ask about her friend's rescue. Instead, her gaze pops back to my eyes where she treats me to one of her amazing smiles.

I swear I could spend all day staring into those sapphire depths. Being on the receiving end of that smile is Nirvana manifested.

My hand squeezes hers, a soft reminder we're in this together. I love her humor. Talking to her is easy. Opening up about myself comes naturally. She's fun to be around. Not sure why that comes as a surprise to me, but it does.

I gaze down at her heart-shaped face and upturned nose. Her lips glisten and I'm hungry for another kiss.

Soon.

"New Orleans at night is a magical place." She squeezes my upper arm. "Although, I'm usually not out this late."

"Because of the creepers?"

"No, silly. Sybil and I like to party, but the realities of the job make that an infrequent thing. It's no longer possible to stay out all night like we did at Cornell. I can't run a company after a night with no sleep."

I guide her to our next destination, keeping her tight on my six while I scan the crowd for *unsavories* intent on ruining our good time.

"Hey, check these guys out." I pull Maria to a group of street performers. We've been slowly making our way from the restaurant to the first of several clubs of the evening, stopping along the way to watch the amazing talent of New Orleans street performers.

"Wow!" Maria gasps as one of the acrobats flies through the air. Launching over a dozen or so tourists who lie on the ground, he flips and spins, sailing an impossible distance before landing with plenty of room to spare as the awestruck crowd gasps and claps.

"Nicely done." I admire the skill that requires and reach into my pocket for a ten-dollar bill.

Making a living on the street is difficult. I should know, which is why I try to do what I can. Successful street performers can pull in substantial cash, but not all have such luck.

This crew is damn good, but it's nearly two in the morning. All the real money is already locked up tight in the hotel rooms of the tourists who know to stay off the streets of New Orleans after the bewitching hour. Predators are on the loose: lowlifes looking to take advantage of the innocent and defenseless.

One such predator prowls around the periphery of this crowd. I sense him first, then locate and track his movements a half a second later.

Leader of a crew of three, he checks out the various groups, looks for weakness and a big payoff.

Well, this ought to prove interesting, and I'm not against a small diversion from our evening's itinerary.

I keep my eye on the thief as I raise my hands over my head and clap. All eyes turn toward me, which is exactly what I need if I'm going to figure out who else is working with our potential mugger.

"Awesome job! Amazing!" I hold a ten-dollar bill over my head, flashing it to the crowd. "Best I've seen all night."

Striding toward the acrobats, I put the bill in a black hat that holds only coins. I've yet to figure out who the mugger and his crew are targeting, but I watch the crowd.

"Who wants more?" I need a better look at those gathered around, specifically who might be worth targeting.

At first, there are a few awkward chuckles, but I make a sweeping bow toward the hat, encouraging them to contribute. That's all it takes. One person drops a dollar bill. Another drops his loose change. Others come forward, filling the hat with coin and cash.

While the crowd donates, the street performers give me a nod of thanks. Stepping back, I move close to Maria. There's no way the muggers will come after me, but leave Maria on her own, and she'll be easy prey.

"We've got a situation." I lean down, keeping my voice pitched for Maria's ears alone. "How good are your skills?"

"My skills?"

"Your Krav Maga? Were you shitting me, or are you legit trained?"

"I'm trained. Or do you forget what happened in the van?" She grips my bicep. "Why? What's wrong?"

"Got a team checking out the audience."

Taking down criminals isn't normal date night material, but

tonight isn't technically a date. If I was with Lily or Jinx, I wouldn't think twice about engaging the thieves, but I'm with Maria. I have no idea what her capabilities are or what her liabilities might be. I'm also not willing to let an innocent person get mugged if I can prevent it.

"Where?" Maria scans the crowd, but it's clear she doesn't know how to pick out the thieves.

"Check out the guy in the black hoodie kicking up his heel next to that building. He's the lookout for those who will commit the crime. Over there, the one in the black pants with the long chain looping down to his knees?"

"I see him."

To Maria's credit, she doesn't make it obvious. She scans the crowd, like anyone would, not letting her gaze linger where it would draw attention.

"There's one more."

"Where?"

"He's in the crowd. Moving through." Headed toward an inebriated couple laughing and clapping with a little too much enthusiasm.

The man makes the mistake of pulling out his money clip and pulling off a bill rather than being discrete about it. From the wad of cash he carries and the Rolex on his wrist, he's prime for picking.

"What are we going to do?" Her fingers dig into my arm.

"That depends on you."

"What do you mean?"

"We can leave now, leave them to fate, or ..."

"We stop it." Her voice is pitched low, and I like her attitude. My girl doesn't hesitate.

"Not if it puts you at risk."

"You asked if I was lying about my skills, but I assure you, I know how to take care of myself. Defensive mostly. What if they have weapons?"

"I carry."

"I can disarm a knife, not sure about a gun."

She can disarm a knife? That rolled smoothly off her tongue, enough for me to believe it's true.

"You see a weapon and you run."

"Wouldn't be much of a partner if I ran."

"I'm serious, Maria. My job is to keep you *out* of danger, not put you in the thick of it."

"But if we do nothing, someone here is going to get mugged. Who's to say they won't have a knife or gun pulled on them. We can't walk away. I feel like we should do something."

"Let's see how this plays out. They may move on." But it's getting late. The evening crowd is thinning, which means there are fewer victims to target.

"If they don't ... we're going to do something, right?"

I've lost my mind, but I nod. Leaving someone to a fate like that simply isn't in my makeup. I'm compelled to intervene.

25

LIAM

THE ACROBATS START UP AGAIN, FLIPPING AND FLYING, IMPRESSING US with their skill. The thieves stand off to the side, out of the loose circle the audience forms.

The man with the Rolex, and a few too many drinks, steps away from the protection of the crowd. His wife, girlfriend, or date, stumbles after him, laughing when she trips over her own feet. Diamonds glitter around her wrist, dangle from her ears, and circle her throat.

What the hell are they thinking?

The man reaches out a steadying hand—not a total douchebag—but is too unsteady on his own to offer much support to his date. The two of them head down the deserted street with the glow of the man's cellphone illuminating his face.

Hopefully, he's calling for a car to take them to the protection of their hotel. Unfortunately, there's a block of darkness between them and the street, with far too few streetlamps to light their way.

The thieves wait for the couple to get a bit down the street before disentangling themselves from the crowd surrounding the performers.

Maria's grip tightens when she catches the kid leaning against the building kick off and amble behind the two other youths.

Yeah, this isn't their first mugging. They've got their system down pat, practiced and perfected just like the Guardians practice and perfect our missions before going live.

"We can walk away?" I give Maria an out, concerned for her safety.

"What's our play? We follow them and then what?"

"How good are you at playing drunk?"

The muggers took one look at me during their scan of the crowd and moved right on past. They didn't spare a glance for Maria.

"I can wobble in these shoes, if that's what you're asking."

"That works. You're two sheets to the wind, drunk off your ass. I'm going to gently escort you home. We'll hang back. When they make their move, I'll intervene."

"What about me?"

"I can take on all three. You're simply backup in case I need an assist."

"Backup? I know how to take care of myself in a fight."

"I'm not questioning your ability. This isn't male bravado. I asked. You answered. I trust your answer. Still doesn't mean I want you in the middle of it. You assist only if needed."

"Okay." She tugs a loose strand of hair out of her eyes, then gathers her hair together at her nape and secures it with a twist and a flip and a hairband she produced out of nowhere.

"Pretty impressive." I pull back, intrigued by how she did that. "That's got to be some female superpower. Where'd you get the hairband?"

I've seen women wear one on their wrists so it's always with them, but I've kissed both of Maria's wrists and there was no hairband.

"I'm not giving away all my secrets." Her angelic smile carries a hint of an impish grin in it.

I let it go, for the moment, then turn down the street our couple wandered down. The three youths keep to the shadows, walking independently. One veers left. The other holds to the right. Their lookout hangs back, scanning the area ahead.

Where he doesn't look is behind him.

Amateur.

Their technique is sloppy as shit.

Totally zeroed in on their prey, they don't notice me closing in from behind.

Unlike the sloppy threesome, I keep my head on a swivel. We're completely alone. No one's coming up from behind. Maria's technically not at risk. But I'm not used to leaving things to chance.

One against three? There will be holes in my periphery.

But Maria said she could defend herself. I have to trust her word.

First things first, take out their lookout—quietly.

I move up behind him, not as stealthy as I'd like, but he's too damn focused on the couple to notice me.

An armbar to his throat takes him to the ground. Gasping, he sucks wind. He'll be out of it for a few minutes. I point at the watcher, snapping my fingers, and hope Maria gets the hint.

His compatriots are completely oblivious to their fallen friend. That's the problem when you get laser-focused on a task. The rest of the world disappears.

I perform another quick scan of my surroundings. Unlike them, I'm trained. My situational awareness is spot on.

The youth on the left steps up the pace, trotting toward our drunken couple. His friend does the same.

When the man notices the thieves, he gives a shout.

The two youths put on a burst of speed and overtake their prey.

The couple doesn't belong out here this time of night. Not when they're drunk. Not after flashing that wad of cash. And not without a bodyguard, or some form of personal security.

They stagger drunkenly, reflexes delayed, reactions slowed, and come to a wobbly halt. The woman clutches the man. He holds up a hand, as if that's going to stop the attack.

Idiot.

I groan inwardly when one of the youths brandishes a knife. He announces his ultimatum.

"Your money, or your life."

The woman screams. Mr. Rolex might have peed himself. Hard to tell in the dark.

The knife-wielding lunatic's buddy holds his arms out, looking menacing, but doesn't appear to carry a weapon. He could have a gun tucked into the back of his pants, but he doesn't grab for it.

Eight out of ten, I give the first guy props for the knife. It's a broad-bladed wicked-looking monstrosity, but his grip's all wrong. Easy to disarm, he gets one out of ten for that. As for the *Your money, or your life* comment, I give his originality a two out of ten.

The couple look to flee. Real fear fills their expressions. The surge of adrenaline kicking along in their veins counteracts a little of their alcohol infused thoughts, speeding them up.

As for our would-be muggers, they may be old hats at relieving poor tourists of their excess cash, but Knife Guy isn't comfortable with his weapon. For lack of a better name, his friend, Tweedle Dee, keeps the couple from running off. Tweedle Dum, the look-out, is out of action, knocked out and *asleep* on the ground behind me.

Maria stands over him, her stance completely changed from a moment ago. Her weight shifts to the balls of her feet, ready to launch into action. She might actually know a thing or two about fighting.

I put her out of my mind, trusting her to have my back and focus all my attention on the two men in front of me.

Finally, Tweedle Dum's predicament registers on Knife Guy's face. His eyes round in fear and his mouth gapes. He may have pissed himself a little bit too. Hard to say, with it being dark and all.

I know what I look like to other men. I'm a scary motherfucker. Knife Guy isn't the first man to rethink his life choices when I turn my attention on him.

The man and woman look over their shoulders and do the exact same thing. I get it. I'm big and scary. But don't they recognize I'm on their side?

Probably not.

It's the alcohol flowing in their veins that makes every move deliberate and slow.

"This is when the two of you walk away." I point at the man and woman, urging them to move off.

What do they do?

Fuckers stand exactly where they are.

Terrified. Immobile.

They're in my way.

Since I've got time, I roll up my sleeves.

"And who the fuck are you?" Knife Guy juts out his chin.

After the initial shock of his friend K.O.'d on the ground behind me, a rush of ill-fated masculine bravado seals his fate.

Fucker's going down.

"I'm the guy you don't want to fuck with."

"You and what army?" He lifts his chin toward Maria, which really pisses me off. "She gonna jump in?" He waves the knife at me. "I'll cut her pretty face to ribbons."

"Wrong fucking thing to say." A growl escapes me as I fist my hands and flex my muscles.

"Look, we don't want any trouble." The victim finally wises up. He grips his date and drags her off to the side.

I ignore them and turn my attention to the young male needing serious reeducation.

"This isn't your night." I turn to the couple and speak to the man. "Get your woman off the street."

He staggers back, equal parts fear and alcohol. With a wide-eyed stare, he removes himself and his woman from this confrontation.

Anticipating Knife Guy's attack, I shift my weight to the balls of my feet. This is going to be fun.

Knife Guy rushes me.

Total idiot move.

Knife out, he exposes his wrist. I grab it, putting pressure on a nerve in his wrist until the knife slips out of his grip and clatters to the ground.

A swift kick and the knife skitters out of the way. I wrap my arm around Knife Guy's neck and use his momentum to toss him on the ground.

He goes down hard. Wide eyes stare up at me as his sluggish mind tries to catch up with what happened. He tries to get up, but I place the heel of my boot over his throat. It's a dick move but does what I need it to do.

I have no intention of crushing his windpipe, but he doesn't know that.

"Liam!" Maria's shout isn't necessary.

Tweedle Dee barrels into me, but I anticipate his move. He wants to knock me off my feet. Ducking his head, he rams into my chest.

I tense. He's headed for a wall of muscle. A little shift of my center of mass and I wrap an arm around his neck. He goes down in a flurry of arms and legs.

Taking a step back, I look at the men, wondering what they'll do next. If they're smart, they'll run away. The drunk couple did that, didn't stop to thank me, but that's okay. I'm not here for the credit.

I'm here to teach a lesson.

Knife Guy rolls to his feet. He looks for his weapon, but the knife is out of reach. He comes at me, arms and fists flying as he contacts solid muscle.

I take the blows, but only because I'm an asshole. Once he's done, I reward his pathetic attack with a string of punches that steal his breath.

Tweedle Dee comes at me. I shove him back, then slam my fist into his gut. I spin to pay attention to Knife Guy, landing a sharp uppercut to his jaw.

They stumble as one, tripping over their own feet, and fall to the ground where they lie motionless except for the rasp of their breaths. I shake my fingers out and stretch my neck, then turn toward the sounds behind me.

Holy hellfire, Maria is fucking fantastic.

The lookout, managed to get off his feet and attack her.

She lands a series of brutal blows to her attacker. A silly grin fills my face as Maria trades kicks and punches, landing four blows to every one of her opponent's. The idiot staggers as she moves in a blur around him, keeping him busy.

I should go to her aid, but there's no need. She glances at me, grin plastered to her face. Those heels, that skirt, none of it gets in her way. She deflects a string of punches aimed for her face and maintains focus like a professional.

Her technique is flawless. Can't believe I teased her about getting the rainbow when she told me she took karate. The woman has elite skills.

She spins and kicks, connecting solidly with the man's solar plexus. It's the hit that takes him down. He grunts and teeters on his feet, but he's done.

For the second time, he eats pavement.

I stare at the two men at my feet, wheezing and gasping for air. I saunter over to where I kicked away the knife, pick it up, and examine its edge. Really quick, I clean it on my pants then head over to Maria.

"Damn nice work. You've got good moves."

"Why, thank you." Barely out of breath, she props her hands on her hips.

I turn to the thieves, deliver a message, then take Maria's hand in mine and stroll off like nothing happened.

26

MARIA

I FEEL ALL BADASS.

I've never been in a real fight before.

My sensei said the constant practice would develop reflexive muscle memory, that I would eventually reach a point in my training where my body would flow through the moves, instinctually reacting to an attack.

I never believed him.

Honestly, I would've given it all up years ago, except for two things. First of all, it's amazing exercise, cardio and weights rolled into one. Second, I do it for my father. It was important to him, and some small part of my mind kept it up in memory of my father.

Now that the veil's been lifted, and I know what kind of business my father was involved in—most likely involved in—his desire to have me learn self-defense takes on a different meaning. Was he worried I might one day be at risk? That I would need to defend myself against his enemies?

Against his brother?

Wow.

My mind spins out scenario after scenario, my question growing more convoluted by the second. Everything I knew about my life takes on a different meaning.

"You kicked ass back there, princess." Liam pulls me close.

He drapes his arm over my shoulder, then locks me in a sudden armbar. I grab at his forearm, trying to dislodge him. Then I stomp down on his toe. He expects that, laughing at my pathetic attempt to free myself.

But I'm not done. While he laughs, my heel connects with his shin.

"Ow!" Liam releases me and I spin away from him, laughing.

"You deserve that." I point at him hopping around, holding his shin. Yeah, that's gonna bruise.

"And you deserve this." Head down, Liam charges me.

With a squeak, I turn around and try to run. He snags me by the waist, pulling me off my feet as I laugh and pull at his fingers.

Liam nuzzles my neck, licking a wet path from the tip of my shoulder, up the sweep of my neck, ending just below my ear.

"Ew! That's so gross. You slobbered on me!"

He puts me down on the ground. When he releases me, I wipe at the wetness.

"Just trying to keep up with expectations." A huge grin fills his face.

I wipe again at my neck, noting how my skin tingles. I'm breathy and giddy, feeling light-headed.

"I suddenly remember ..." He takes a step toward me. For no reason, I take a step back.

Liam lunges forward. One hand goes around my waist, the other grabs my nape. He closes the distance between us, until our lips are one breath away.

"Remember what?" That giddy sensation triples until I feel unsteady on my feet.

"How amazing you taste." Liam closes the distance between us, capturing my mouth in his.

The heat of his mouth sends sparks of electricity shooting through me. My hands find his biceps and grip tight as a low, needy moan escapes me. He bends me back, fully in control, and shows me how a real man kisses a woman.

Swoon-worthy.

My hands move of their own volition. Releasing my grip on his arms, my fingers walk their way to his broad shoulders and meander over to the hollow of his throat. From there, they move around to his nape. I twine my fingers in his hair as he shifts me to the side.

Liam lowers me into a dip, his lips glide over my mouth as my heart kicks in and my bloods rushes hotter than hot. He controls my head as my arms wrap around his neck. It's a kiss worthy of the movie stage.

His hot mouth lays a line of kisses up the curve of my neck, sucking and biting, as uninhibited moans escape me. He nuzzles my neck and the heat of his breath sends tingling chills racing down my spine.

"You taste like sin. Watching you fight that looser made me hard and hungry to taste the rest of you." Liam sucks my earlobe into his mouth, flicking it with his tongue.

My body practically combusts beneath the stimulation overload. I, too, am eager for more.

Is that wrong?

My skin tightens with anticipation as my core throbs and aches. I'm horribly turned on.

By a kiss?

Holy hell. I've never experienced anything like this before. My body is ready for more. Is this what foreplay is supposed to be like? If so, I've been sorely cheated out of it in the past.

Liam gently pulls me upright and steadies me on my feet. He bends down, kissing me one more time. Unlike the prior kiss, this one is reverent and unhurried.

"Damn, but you feel it, don't you?"

"I feel everything."

Indeed, I do.

I feel the night air flowing around us. The sparse traffic rushing past rumbles. Down the street, applause for the street performers carries on the air. Somewhere behind and to the left, a neon light flickers and buzzes.

It's sultry, steamy, and perfect.

Liam releases me. Our fingers interlace, and I spin off in a twirl, stopping when he pulls me back to him. He holds me, facing away from him, strong arms bracketing mine, hands hugging my waist.

Slowly, he starts to sway.

I tip my head back, close my eyes, and wish I met Liam on a different night, in a different place: a place far away from the ugliness into which I was born.

"We need to get moving," he whispers in my ear.

"I wish we could stay like this forever."

There's a distinct chance I may be falling for Liam.

Falling hard and fast.

It's going to hurt when I crash into the harsh reality that is the disaster of my life.

"Let's kick back and enjoy ourselves." Liam kisses the tip of my shoulder. "For tonight only, we're going to forget about the Guardians, forget about your family, forget about—"

"Don't say Sybil. I'll never let myself forget her for a second."

"About your friend ..."

"What about her? Do you have news? Have they found her? Is she okay?" I spin around until I face him. "I need to see her."

"Slow down, princess, and take a breath. No, I don't have any news, but I have every assurance they will rescue her. Guardians don't fail. But we should talk about *seeing* her."

"What do you mean?"

"There's no easy way to say this, but when they rescue her, Sybil won't be able to return to her normal life until we deal with ..."

"My family." I sense his hesitation, a need to break this news to me with sensitivity.

"Correct."

"So, what does that mean?"

"She'll be put into Guardian's Personal Protection Program."

"I don't understand."

"Are you familiar with witness protection?"

"I am." Then I pause. "Wait a minute." I take in a deep breath. "You're telling me I won't get to see her?"

"Correct."

"Can I speak to her?"

"That won't be possible."

"Why not?"

"Those that took her will want her back." He pauses, waiting—I suppose—for me to catch up. "She won't be safe until we deal with that."

"And any contact with me puts her at risk."

"Not just her." He takes my hands in his. "If your family knows Sybil reached out, they'll assume she told you everything about her abduction. It puts you at risk."

"You think my uncle might do something?" A sharp pain stabs my heart.

I want to go back to yesterday when I was oblivious to all of this.

"We can't rule out the possibility."

"This just stinks."

It does way more than that. It totally sucks.

"Let's make a pact." Liam takes my hands and leads me down the street.

"A pact?"

"Yes. When I get confirmation about Sybil, I'll share, but after that, we don't speak about her. It's too dangerous if anyone accidentally overhears. We don't talk about what happened on the twenty-fifth floor. We go back to the basics."

"Which are?"

"You and I have been dating. We're out tonight to have fun and get engaged."

"Do we have to do the engaged thing?"

"From what you've said about your mother, it's best to put that roadblock in front of her. Mitzy has access to Belvedere security systems. That will lead her down many paths. In my experience, however, the stuff people want no one to see ..." He rubs the back of his neck. "They keep that at home, far away from work. We need access to your uncle's home."

"I hate going there."

"But you do go there?"

"Every Sunday for brunch. Attendance required."

"What about your boyfriend? Your newly engaged fiancé?"

"My mother will drop dead."

"Perfect."

27

MARIA

After our encounter with the would-be muggers, Liam takes me to a nightclub.

A techno beat pumps through the speakers. Black lights flicker and flash, turning the inside of the club into an eclectic mix of color and sound. All around us, bodies bump and grind on the dance floor.

Liam takes me right to the center, where everyone can see his filthy moves.

The man's body is built for sin. If he can move like that on a dance floor, what can he do in the bedroom?

Not that I need to know.

Not that I should be thinking about that at all.

Not that it's exactly what I want to experience first-hand.

As far as clubbing goes, I'm not dressed for a night on the town.

Liam is.

He ditched the bulletproof gear but kept the black suit. I'm in a modest skirt, my favorite silk blouse, and sensible heels. The only reason we get into the club is because of Liam's megawatt smile.

"I'm done." I lift up on my toes and try to shout over the music.

I head to the bar, hoping to find a seat, but Liam yanks me back to his side, spinning me around as if he planned the whole move. I'm beginning to hate that about him.

In addition to being drop-dead gorgeous, my Hollywood hunk is Fred Astaire on steroids. He tears up the dance floor with moves that shouldn't be legal. He's the kind of dancer capable of compensating for his partner's weakness.

I'm an exceptionally inept dance partner. It takes a man like Liam to make me look good.

"We dance until dawn." Liam pulls me to him, spinning me like a top. The entire time, his steely gaze scans the room. "I don't see your friends."

By *friends*, he means my security detail. If they're worth half of what my uncle pays them, they should've found me by now.

The way Liam whispers in my ear is beyond amazing. The heat of his breath skates down my skin, making my fingers curl.

"Come on, princess, let's grind. Time to dance dirty." He leans in, towering over me as those hips of his go to work. Arms hanging loose, he's a sinuous gyration of shoulders and hips. Every female in the club stares at us.

At him.

When they look at me, jealousy and animosity shoot from their eyes. They'd eagerly claw my eyes out if they could, and they would. Except Liam makes it clear to every man on the dance floor that I belong to him. By the way he holds me, he tells every woman he has eyes only for me. That makes them hate me even more.

He's possessive, protective, and selfishly keeps me for himself. Those few men brave enough to make an attempt to lure me away, meet Liam's fierce stare and sinister growl. To a man, they back down like baby cubs.

Liam pulls me close. He wraps an arm around my waist, placing his palm flat against my back. We traverse the dance floor again. His hands slide up suggestively from my waist to my shoulders and continue on to the back of my neck, where his fingers tangle in my hair.

Controlling me by my head, he takes me for a series of spins. His dominant and determined moves make me look halfway decent.

But my feet hurt.

And I'm tired.

There's no news of Sybil, at least not that I know about. Liam hasn't checked his cell phone since we got in the club.

"I'm done dancing." I try to stop for a break, but Liam isn't having it.

"We're making a scene."

"I know. That's why I want to stop."

"That's why we can't."

"You sure?"

"The entire purpose of tonight is to be seen. That's why I won't let any of these assholes dance with you. You're all mine."

"What about you? Are you mine as well?"

"Have you seen me look at another woman?"

Come to think of it, I haven't, but I don't want him to know I'm insecure.

His left hand slides down to my hips. His other hand twines in my hair.

"I'm tired." I want to know how things are going with Sybil. The Guardians must have some kind of status update.

"Not yet." Liam leans down, growling into my ear.

The possessiveness of that tone makes my spine tingle. He releases my hair, letting it fall down my back, but that's only so he can grab my hips again. This music calls for suggestive moves, and Liam knows how to grind.

We practically fuck with our clothes on.

"Do you have to be so suggestive?" I blow out a breath as he wraps his arms around me.

"You don't like my moves?" He leans down, nuzzling my neck, as his hips gyrate, grinding against mine. His heated breath sends another wave of shivers rushing down my spine.

I shudder with the sensation and do my best to ignore the intense heat that follows. There's an intensity to Liam I'm not prepared to handle.

He should've come with a warning label.

When Forest suggested we pretend to be dating, what I had in mind was nothing like this. I thought about holding hands, not getting busy on a dance floor with a man I barely know.

Maybe a chaste kiss on the lips?

That's it.

If I thought he was hot when I first saw him, that's nothing compared to Liam making a scene. The man is a natural performer, flirtatious without making promises, gathering both men and women around him to dance.

There will be plenty of eyewitnesses for my uncle to question about how serious this thing is between me and Liam.

As for Liam, in addition to his creative pelvic thrusting, he's got the line dancing thing down pat. We're on our fifth or seventh version of the night. I swear he makes it up on the go, and everyone is having a total blast: falling in line, learning the moves, and taking it over from there.

As for that kiss?

His mouth has been all over me. From the tip of my shoulder to my more than ample cleavage, he's had either his lips, or his nose, buried there. All along my neck, and behind my ear, he's pressed his warm lips to my skin.

He flutters butterfly kisses over my eyes, presses his lips to my forehead, and kisses the inside of my wrist and the backs of my hands as if intimately acquainted with my body.

Like a lover would be.

And damn if there aren't moments when I close my eyes and dream what if?

What if this wasn't pretend?

What if I allow things to go that far?

What if I fall for this man?

Without fail, each time those thoughts enter my head, Liam

tenses. That's the only way to describe it. One moment, his body flows through his dance moves. The next, he's on high alert.

"Did you make up the line dance from the flash mob at the Belvedere?"

"I did not." Liam's hands shift from my waist down to cup my ass. He brings me in tight, guiding my hips to follow the movement of his. While he does that, he nuzzles my neck and nibbles on my ear.

It's hot. We're talking five-alarm fire, smoking hot.

"Could've fooled me." My arms dangle by my sides, swaying to the music, but I'm not really engaged.

Too nervous to let go, my body jerks instead of flows. I'm not a great dancer. I get along just fine, except when I'm in Liam's arms.

He drags his finger down my arm, swirling it around and past my elbow, until he reaches my wrist. As he lifts my arm, he whispers in that husky voice of his.

"Pretend you're having a good time, princess. Put your hands on me." He places my hand on his shoulder, then does the same thing to my other hand. Only this time, he pauses to kiss the inside of my wrist. "We're being watched."

I step on his toe, shocked by what he says.

"Sorry."

"It's okay. I can handle a few crushed toes."

Right, but only because he wears steel-tipped boots.

"Who's watching us?" With great effort, I refrain from looking around. I don't want the watchers to know I'm on to them. Not that I am. I'm completely oblivious to everything around me.

"Not sure."

"Has my security team found us?"

"It's possible. Let's see what they do when I kiss you." He leans down to kiss me.

The moment our lips connect, a burst of heat expands outward, tingling as it goes. He places my hand on his chest and kisses his way to my ear. While nibbling on my earlobe, making my toes curl, he whispers in my ear. "Drag your hand across my chest, then down over my abs."

"Why?"

"Because you're hot and bothered and thrilled to be out with your man. This is your night to be with me before returning to your strait-laced-and-chaste-like-a-virgin life."

"I'm no virgin." My words cut through the air, propelled by more anger and irritation than I intend. "Sorry."

I jerk my hand away from his chest, but he grips my wrist, turns it over, and drags his lips across the tender flesh of my inner wrist.

"I know." With his eyes locked with mine, he shamelessly brushes his lips across my knuckles.

He closes the distance between us, not that there was much distance to begin with. Pulling me tight, he squishes my boobs against his chest—soft meeting hard. "Reach around and squeeze my ass."

"You're kidding, right?"

"Not in the slightest. Hand on my ass, princess. Let's show these bastards how insanely attracted we are to each other."

Well, that's not a problem. This *job* would be a whole lot easier if he wasn't so goddamn good-looking. When he flashes that megawatt smile and follows it with a wink, he's a total lady killer. The man knows exactly what he brings to the table.

"It's just that I'm not used to this much PDA." I loop my arms over his shoulders and turn my head to check out the crowd around us. Every female on the dance floor watches me with unrestrained envy. Several have tried to pull Liam away from me. They all failed.

I see none of the men on my security detail.

"If you don't put your hands on my ass, I'm going to get very handsy and maul you on the dance floor."

How much *more* handsy can he get? No sooner does that thought go through my head, than Liam sweeps his fingers over the soft swell of my breast. I unlock my hands from around his neck and quickly put them on his waist.

"That's better, but my ass is lower than that."

"Why am I doing this?"

"Because our visitors are streaming this live."

My steps falter, not that it matters. Liam covers up my misstep by picking me up and twirling me in the air. Back on my feet, he whispers in my ear.

"Hands. Ass."

Through all of this, a gaggle of eager bitches approach. They giggle as they surround us, dancing suggestively. I'm not sure what they thought will happen, but Liam isn't having any of it.

His dismissal is cordial, a quick bump and grind, then he's right back with me. His message is clear. He's out to have a good time, but I'm with him.

He's not looking for anyone else. Normally, that kind of possessiveness would be a turn-on. Who doesn't like a protective male? But that's not what Liam is to me.

He's a pretend boyfriend I've been hiding from my family. An affair that will come to light in the morning when Liam returns me to work looking like I rolled out of bed with him still in it.

There are perks to this job.

I wish.

With the gaggle gone, I turn my attention to the crowd, both on the dance floor and off. If the men assigned to keep tabs on me are here, I don't see them.

I don't question Liam's instincts. If anything, the one thing I've learned in the past twenty-four hours is that my awareness of what happens around me is wholly inadequate.

By now, news of my all-nighter with Liam will have reached my uncle's ears.

Hopefully, he'll see tonight as proof I'm oblivious about what happened to Sybil. He'll have no reason to think I know anything about the other women.

That's the primary objective of this crazy night, and I hope my inexperience and gullibility doesn't ruin that piece of it.

28

MARIA

LIAM HOLDS MY HAND WHILE WE CROSS THE STREET.

The sky brightens toward the east. With our epic night behind us, and hundreds of photos splashed across social media, it's time to rejoin the land of the living.

It's time to face my family.

Normally, I love this time of day. In the predawn twilight, the sun hasn't had a chance to heat the air.

The festive atmosphere of the evening is gone. The streets are quiet; all revelry dissipated. Tourists returned to their hotels hours ago. Bars closed up shop after last call; both patrons and employees have long since sought the comfort of their beds. The storekeepers have yet to arrive to begin the process of opening their shops for the day.

Very few cars are out.

It's as if the city rests, holding its breath, until a new day dawns.

"What now?" I turn toward my very unusual date.

The only people on the street are an occasional drunk sleeping off one too many drinks and the homeless who survived another day on the streets.

"What do you normally do after you and Sybil go out?" Liam frees his hand from mine, but that's only to sling his arm over my shoulder.

He tugs me tight as he ambles down the sidewalk. I reach up and lace my fingers with his as I lean in loving the way he feels pressed up against me.

Despite all the dancing, my feet hold up rather well. Not that I don't want to stop and give them a break, but I'm good.

A few more blocks until we arrive at the Belvedere.

Liam stops for a homeless woman huddled on the steps outside of a drug store. I would normally hurry past, not wanting to get too close, but Liam strides right up to the broken woman.

"Good morning; how are you doing?"

The wretched-looking woman slowly brings her gaze up to meet Liam's eyes. Confusion and fear swirl in her face as she huddles on a stoop leading to a five-and-dime pharmacy.

When she doesn't answer, Liam holds out his hand. "My name's Liam. What's yours?"

"Patty ..." She offers nothing else and clutches at the rags covering her body.

"It's nice to meet you, Patty." Reaching into his pocket, he pulls out a five-dollar bill. "There's a great breakfast place a block from here. Clean restrooms."

Her brows practically climb her forehead, surprised by his charity. It takes a moment, but she slowly extends her hand. "Thank you." A tear slips down her cheek.

"My pleasure, Patty." Liam beams one of his Hollywood perfect smiles at the homeless woman. "It's a new day and anything is possible. It was nice talking to you."

Again, confusion ripples across her face. Her bony fingers curl around the bill, but then she opens her palm, staring at the money with awe.

"Thank you, sir." She sits a little straighter and glances around at her meager possessions.

Liam guides me away, keeping me tucked tight to his side, sheltered and protected from any possible threat.

"Why did you do that?" I told myself I wasn't going to ask, but I'm too curious. This isn't the first homeless person he's stopped to talk to during the night.

"Do what?"

"Ask for their name? Give them money?"

"Because they're a fellow human being. Asking their name tells them I see them as a person with value. The cash is for food."

"How do you know they won't blow it on drugs?"

"I don't."

"You're an enigma."

"We should never discount a person's worth because they've fallen on hard times. You never know how five dollars can turn a life around."

"That sounds oddly specific." I pull to a stop and turn in toward him.

When I stand this close, I have to crane my neck to look at him. Despite that, this feels normal rather than awkward.

"Sorry." I place my palm over his chest and close my eyes to the steady beat of his heart against my palm.

"Don't be sorry."

"If there's a story there, I'd love to hear it."

My eyes open when he puts the tip of his finger under my chin. Tilting my face to him, Liam sweeps down to brush his lips against mine.

I melt into the kiss. Unlike earlier tonight, this kiss is gentle and unhurried. My hands wrap around his midsection as our lips glide across each other.

He releases me from the kiss and takes off down the street, but not before taking my hand in his.

"I grew up poor. Incredibly poor. When I was five, my mother lost her home and we lived on the street for a couple of weeks."

"I'm so sorry." There's not a moment in my life when I haven't been surrounded by wealth. My comments seem incredibly insensitive now. "I didn't mean ..."

"It's okay, but I remember the day everything changed."

"What happened?"

"A man in a suit walked by. My mom sat much as that lady did there, only with me in her lap. I was cold, hungry, and crying. The man stooped down, looked me in the eye, and asked me my name."

"Wow."

"My mother pulled me back, afraid of strange men for good reason. The man looked at her, asked her name, then gave her five dollars. He told her there was a diner around the corner. It was open, had a clean restroom, and affordable food."

"What happened?"

"He left, but that stranger changed our lives."

"How?"

"My mother hadn't eaten for days. Any change she could scrounge went toward feeding me. She took me to that diner. The only thing she could afford was a kid's meal for me. The waitress brought my mother water and watched me eat. I remember the look she gave my mother."

"What kind of look?"

"Disgust. Like my mother was trash. Nothing but garbage to be taken out. The waitress kept trying to kick us out, but I knew to take my time and eat real slow."

"When the woman got more forceful, loud and mouthy about beggars being nothing but trash, a man came out from the back. He took one look at me, the one plate in front of me, and stared at my mother for the longest time."

"And?" I know there's more. There has to be.

"He walked right up to the mouthy waitress, fired her on the spot. I remember it like it was yesterday. He held out his hand, ordering her to give him her name tag and apron. The lady stormed out of the restaurant in a huff."

I keep still, hoping the story continues. I want to know what happened to his mother and what happened to him.

"The man turned toward my mother and asked if she wanted a job. The pay was minimum wage and the hours long. He said we could sleep in the back until her first paycheck came in, and I could sit in the back booth if I was quiet." Liam smiles wistfully. "My mother sat there, mouth open, stunned speechless. She shook her head and told me to get out of the booth. I didn't want to do that. The table had a bottle of syrup, and I wanted a little more."

"You can't leave me hanging like this. What happened?"

"He convinced my mother to take the job. When she finally agreed, he told her to wait where she was. When he returned, he brought this huge plate of food. Told her to watch him while she ate and learn what to do."

"That's incredible." I reach up to swipe away an errant tear.

I can't imagine Liam ever being small, but I see a small child, cold and starving, and a mother who sacrificed her needs to feed her son.

It's more than touching. It's overwhelming.

Liam continues with his story, ignoring the stray tear.

"That job saved us. It wasn't easy. She worked long hours and we slept in the diner until her first check. The manager helped her find an apartment. Within six months, I was going to school. I wasn't hungry. I wasn't cold. I had my own bed to sleep in."

"You're breaking my heart."

"Don't be sad." He stops and spins me to him. "We never had much, but we had each other. Five dollars from a stranger changed my life. That woman back there may spend it on drugs. She may spend it on booze. But she might spend it on a meal. I'll never know, but in my mind, that's the five dollars it takes to turn her life around. It's my way of paying back the charity my mother received."

"Wow." I shake my head, feeling incredibly small. "You are an amazing man."

"I believe in kindness."

"Yet you work in a job where you see the worst humanity has to offer."

"Only because I've been gifted with the ability to make a difference."

"Each time I think I know you, you throw in a curve ball like that and leave me speechless."

He kisses the crown of my head. "I know other ways I'd like to leave you speechless."

"Goofball."

"Princess."

We volley nicknames back and forth. I haven't settled on mine. Between Goofball and Hollywood, I don't know which one is a better fit.

"We should figure out how we're going to play this with your family."

"How do you mean?"

"Forest suggested fiancé, but maybe boyfriend is better?"

"Either way, my mother is going to rake you over the coals. She's protective."

And if what Forest thinks is true, my mother will want nothing to do with a man like Liam. Especially if she's working on a suitable match to be my husband.

"I can handle that."

"You don't know my mother."

"What about your uncle? How will he react?"

"It depends on our plans."

"Such as?"

"He wants controlling interest in the Belvedere. I understand a little better now why that may be. If our plans are to stay, he'll find a way to get rid of you. My mother will help. If our plans include moving away, he won't be a problem. But we'll still have to deal with my mother. She won't want to let me go."

"After you and Sybil would go out, what happened afterward?"

"What do you mean?"

"Your security detail?"

"Well, I would usually call my mother and check in with her while Sybil and I grabbed beignets and coffee for breakfast."

"Did she get angry?"

"Not really. I think she sees it as me getting all that wildness out of my system."

"Makes sense."

"And my security team eventually caught up with me."

"At the Belvedere?" Liam draws his hand down his chin, scraping against a night of stubble.

"Sometimes I caught them watching from the street while Sybil and I finished our coffee." Hot and scratchy, my eyes burn from lack of sleep. I try to swallow a yawn but lose the battle.

"You're exhausted."

"I'm okay. Put some coffee in me and I'm good to go."

"You have to sleep sometime." His eyes twinkle. "Have you thought of how you want to introduce me to your mother?"

I rub my hands on my skirt, trying to get rid of the nervous perspiration that comes on the heels of what Liam says. My gut feels all kinds of wrong.

"What does Forest think this accomplishes?" I'm still not sold on how this pretense works.

"He wants to put a Guardian close to your family."

"If I understand what I heard last night, Mitzy's already hacked into the security systems at the Belvedere. Bringing you along doesn't add anything."

"On the surface perhaps, but remember what Forest said."

"Forest said a lot of things I still don't understand." The struggle is real. I'm still trying to wrap my head around most of what Forest mentioned last night.

"You're correct about the Belvedere. That access is secure. What about the family home? There's your uncle's house, but you also mentioned the Hamptons?" He rubs at the back of his neck. "It's a bit of a drive ..." Mirth swims in the delectable depths of his eyes. The Hamptons is more than a bit of a drive; it's several hours by plane, days by car.

"We still have the house but don't use it like we used to. When Sybil and I were at Cornell, we drove down as often as we could. Spent all our summers there."

"Why the Hamptons if the family business is down south? That doesn't make sense." Liam scans the area around us. I follow the direction of his gaze, finding nothing concerning, but he's trained to identify threats.

"I'm originally from New York and if you're a wealthy family in New York, having a house in the Hamptons is required if you want to be taken seriously. My father always had business dealings in New Orleans, part of his shipping empire, but we lived in New York." I press a hand over my belly. Now that I know what those dealings are, it's hard not to get sick.

"When did he move the family down to New Orleans?"

"He didn't. My uncle took care of things down here while my father ran things in New York."

"Your mother moved here after your father's death?"

"Only because she married my uncle." Every time I think about my mother and uncle's marriage, my skin crawls.

"That makes sense." He runs his hand over the stubble of his beard. "What about the house in the Hamptons? Does it belong to your uncle? Your mother?"

"It's mine. I've been considering selling it, but it's the last thing I have of my father. I grew up in that house."

"And you came down here after graduating Cornell to be close to your mother?"

"I came because my father wanted me to run the Belvedere. My uncle has tried to take it from me several times, but the way my father put together his trust, I hold the controlling shares. It doesn't feel right to give that up."

"Yes, that's right." Liam's pensive for a moment, pulling at his chin again. "You said your father set up the twenty-fifth floor for his business. Did he ever bring any of that back to the Hamptons?"

"He was always doing business. I don't think his office has been touched, come to think of it. Sybil and I spent what time we could at the house, but I don't think my mother's been back since my father died."

"Why not?"

"I have a feeling their marriage wasn't as picture-perfect as I thought. It was almost like she couldn't move out fast enough."

"Interesting."

"Is there any chance your father may have left records behind at the Hampton house?"

"Maybe?" I shrug. "I wouldn't know."

"But if we went there, we'd be alone to look?"

"Doubtful."

"Why?"

"My security team."

"We'll just have to find a way to ditch them." He pauses for a second. "I have an idea ..." He fishes into his pocket and pulls out a diamond ring. "Maria Rossi, will you fake marry me?"

"When did you get that?" I yank the ring out of his hand and lift it up to the light. "How many karats is this?"

Smaller than the grotesque ring my mother wears, it's still a rock, easily seven to ten karats.

"Mitzy Magic." Liam shoves his hands in his pockets and rocks back on his heels.

"Mitzy said she'd quit if Forest made her find a ring."

"That's not all she said." His lip tips up in a smirk.

"I'm ignoring the first part of what she said. Seriously, when, where, and how did you get this?"

"Mitzy delivered it while we were dancing. Not Mitzy herself, but one of her many magical helpers."

"This is insane."

"You gonna put it on?"

"I can't." I shove the ring back at him.

"I asked you to fake marry me. You're going to break my heart if you don't fake accept."

"Fake accept your fake marriage proposal? I thought we weren't doing the fake engaged thing."

"Mitzy was busy all night long building my fake life. Your mother is going to be pissed, but I come from a reputable New York family." His brow arches.

"I see where you're going with this."

"Do you?" He gives me a look. It's more of a challenge.

I take in a breath and take a stab at it.

"Marriage to a wealthy husband is exactly what my mother desires. Getting me out of New Orleans is exactly what my uncle wants."

"You're doing pretty well, but there's one other bit."

"What bit?"

"Your security detail."

"Yeah, I don't get that."

"The only reason to have them, we assume, is to keep you off the twenty-fifth floor. I'll have my own security team."

"How?"

"Wolfe and Brady."

"I'm not following you here."

"It's a pissing contest; me against your uncle. If you're mine, then you're mine to protect. Once I tell him I have a protective detail on you, he can't have his team follow you."

"Sure, he could." I shrug, not getting it.

"It's an Alpha meet Alpha scenario."

"Still not connecting the dots."

"Think of it this way, if I pee on you, that means you're mine. He has to cede possession."

"Pee on me?" I shake my head, hoping I heard that wrong. "That's gross."

"It's a metaphor."

"Still gross, but I get what you're saying. If he doesn't pull his team, it's a slap in the face. I basically become a turf war."

"Now you get it."

"Just no peeing on me, okay? I'm interested in a lot of things, but that goes on my hard limits list."

"You have a hard limit list? Color me intrigued. What's on your green list?"

"Okay, that was a major overshare. What are the chances you'll forget that?"

"Just want to know if you prefer fuzzy cuffs or leather cuffs?"

"Don't get ahead of yourself, Hollywood. We're a long way from those kinds of conversations."

"Maybe not as far as you think." He nudges me with his shoulder. "Are you going to put on the ring?"

"Is it a real diamond?"

"Would I give my fake fiancée a fake diamond? It's real as they come."

With my hands shaking, I slowly slide the diamond ring onto my ring finger. It fits perfectly, but I'm not going to ask how that can be.

"I guess this makes you my fake fiancé."

"It does. Now, we're going to head back to the Belvedere. We're going to take a nap, then shower and get dressed for dinner tonight, and you're going to get me invited to Sunday brunch with your mother and uncle."

"What are you going to wear?" I glance at his suit. It's a bit tired looking from our night out.

"I took the liberty of having a few things delivered to your suite."

"No doubt you did, and I assume it comes with a bit of Mitzy Magic?"

"You're starting to learn." I bop her lightly on the nose with my forefinger. "You ready to face your mother?"

"I'm never ready to face my mother, but with you by my side, I can do anything."

"That's my girl." He holds my left hand and examines the diamond. "It looks good on you."

A yawn slips out of me.

"We get fake-engaged and you give me a yawn? Princess, you know how to bruise a guy's ego."

"Sorry, but I'm really tired."

"Let's go." Arm across my shoulders, he points us in the direction of the Belvedere. "Into the jaws of the beast."

Into the jaws of the beast?

I couldn't have said it better.

29

LIAM

AFTER OUR NIGHT OUT, I FEEL BETTER ABOUT THE ASSIGNMENT. AT THE last club, Mitzy sent one of her team members to hand off things I need: a new cellphone packed with her special tech gear, a dossier on my new identity, the ring for Maria's finger, and other things.

Unlike our fake engagement, that ring is very real.

Like Maria, I too am tired, but there will be very little rest.

"Do you want to get a car, or are you good to walk the last few blocks?" I take her hand in mine and admire the brilliance of the seven-karat stone glittering on her finger.

I don't know how Mitzy does it, but she's fucking badass. Although, this may be Forest's handiwork, considering what Mitzy said to him. Either way, it doesn't matter.

"I'm good. It's not that far." She takes my hand, threading her fingers with mine, and rewards me with one of her genuine smiles.

Those are my favorite because they lift the veil of her stoic exterior, allowing me a glimpse of her inner beauty.

The last few blocks, we walk in relative silence, each consumed by our own thoughts. There's not much to do today, other than stay by Maria's side. I almost make the mistake of thinking the offices of the

Belvedere will be deserted but remind myself Maria's hotel runs a twenty-four-seven operation.

"Are you nervous?" I lift her hand to my mouth and brush my lips across her knuckles.

"Very."

"What can I do to help?"

"Just stay by my side."

"I have no plans of leaving you alone." Before we get too far, we duck into a coffee shop for a pick-me-up. "Come, let's caffeinate ourselves." I use the word as a verb because I need a shot of caffeine if I'm going to keep my eyes open.

"I don't need coffee." The moment the words fall out of her mouth, a massive yawn takes over. She glances up at me, sheepishly. "Okay, maybe a cup or two."

We wander into a small coffee shop. Immediately, the rich aroma of coffee floods my senses. I take in a deep inhale. *Damn, that never gets old.* Just the scent of coffee is like a shot of adrenaline in my veins. I'm invigorated and ready to face the day.

The shop's sparsely populated. It's too early in the morning for the tourists to be up and about. There are plenty of tables, but I angle Maria toward a table stuck in a small alcove. I can put my back to the wall and keep the entrance and exits in sight. I settle Maria at a small table and step up to the counter to order two cups of the steaming brew. That done, I return to the small table.

I love coffee shops, even if I don't enjoy coffee all that much. The tantalizing aroma of fresh coffee percolating in the air is a welcome blanket on the senses. I could spend my entire day inside a coffee shop doing nothing other than breathing in the savory aroma.

Maria's gaze darts around the small shop, looking for threats that aren't there. The closer we get to the Belvedere, the higher her alert level grows.

"I have something for you." I pull out a small velvet pouch from my pocket. "Here."

"What is it?" Maria takes the pouch with a bit of hesitation.

"Look inside, silly. That's the best way to know what's it is."

She gives me a look, opens the silk drawstring, then reaches in and pulls out a stunning diamond and sapphire tennis bracelet.

"Wow." She stares at the bracelet, mouth agape and eyes wide. "I feel like I should say *You shouldn't have*, but I have a feeling this came from the Guardians?"

"You got it. Give me your wrist and I'll help you put it on."

The bracelet is nothing short of spectacular. Sapphires and diamonds alternate with one another along the length of the tennis bracelet. Like her ring, the stones are generous in size, and they're a perfect match to Maria's incredible eyes.

"A ring and a bracelet?" Maria admires her new jewelry. "Should I expect a tiara next?"

"Ha-ha, very funny, princess."

"It's very pretty. Thank you."

"You're welcome, but that's more than a pretty, shiny thing."

"Huh?"

"That bracelet holds a tracking device. If anything were to happen to you ..." I hate saying it like that because it makes it sound ominous, but there's no way around it.

"I get it." Her brows tug together. "It's for my protection."

I arch a brow, waiting for her to say something more. When she doesn't, I continue. "It's intrusive. I know. You're trading one protective detail for another, but I hope—"

"It's okay. I understand."

Following Mitzy's rule of *one to find and one to hide*, the tennis bracelet is the obvious place for suspicious individuals to locate a tracking device. Once they find that, if they find it, there's another device embedded in Maria's ring.

Actually, it wouldn't be such a bad thing for Maria's uncle to discover that tracking device. I want him to know what kind of over-protective asshole I can be. It's the easiest way to get him to relinquish his hold on his niece.

The barista calls out my name. I leave Maria with her thoughts and get our drinks. When I return to the table, a wistful expression fills her face as she admires both the tennis bracelet around her wrist and the diamond adorning her left ring finger.

One to find and one to hide.

I pray we never get in such a situation, but being over-prepared is our motto at Guardian HRS.

"Here you go." I place her coffee in front of her.

She wraps her fingers around the cup and leans forward to inhale the aromatic beverage.

"Coffee was a good call, and my feet thank you for the break."

I knew it.

"When we get to your place, I'll treat you to a special foot rub."

"Now that sounds wonderful."

She opens up several packets of sugar and dumps them into her coffee. Enough creamer follows to turn the dark liquid a light tan. Her eyes close as she brings the cup to her mouth.

"Perfection in a cup. That's what coffee is." Maria opens her eyes and glances at my untouched drink. "Aren't you going to have some?"

"Coffee isn't my favorite. You're welcome to it, if you want a second cup."

"I might take you up on that, but the coffee might do you some good." She takes another sip. Her eyes close like she's found heaven, then open again when she sets her drink down. "We didn't exactly come here for coffee, did we?"

"No. I wanted to get our stories nailed down tight." I already mentioned some of it. Hopefully, she remembers what I said. I'm also waiting for backup. There's no way I'm taking Maria back inside the Belvedere alone.

Over the next twenty minutes, we sip coffee and build our back-story until I'm satisfied she's got it locked down.

"Your friends are here." I glance outside the bistro at two men who loiter outside. They don't enter the coffee shop. I assume that's because they don't want to bother Maria.

"My friends?" Her spine stiffens, and I watch the battle she wages with herself not to spin around and look. "How many?"

"Two."

"I'm surprised they didn't show up at the club."

"Someone was at the club." I never saw a face, but we were being watched.

"Maybe they're getting sloppy?"

"You mentioned they never interfered with you and Sybil when you ducked out before. Maybe that's all it is?"

"Maybe." Maria doesn't look convinced.

I'm not either. I take her hands in mine. "This is probably a good time for a little of that PDA you dislike."

"Holding hands is far different from grinding on the dance floor."

"You know, you said you're a horrible dancer, but you held up pretty well."

"Thanks to a fabulous partner. You've got some moves."

"If you liked those moves, I have others." I squeeze her hands. "I'm still intensely curious about what's on that list of yours."

Her cheeks turn the prettiest shade of pink.

"I bet you are."

She lifts out of her seat and leans across the table. Her blouse gapes, giving me an amazing view of her cleavage. I'm almost too distracted by her tits to realize she's leaning over the table to kiss me, but I get it together for the kiss she plants on my lips.

She tastes like sugar and coffee, a delectable treat. Maria's kisses are nothing like mine.

I go all in.

She hesitates.

But the girl knows how to get a rise out of me. Her tongue slips between my lips, tentative and unsure, but far bolder than when we started this night.

Her kiss is also much shorter than one of mine. Before I know it, the kiss is over. Maria releases my hands, but only to lift her hand to admire the diamond glittering on her finger.

"Are they watching?" She cups her coffee with both hands, enjoying the heat of her drink.

"Are you telling me that kiss was just for show?" I should be disappointed, but her boldness reassures me.

Maria is willing to play up the lie we weave, fawning over the ring. A quick glance toward the window confirms what she says.

"Watching and calling it in." The man by the window holds a cell phone to his ear. "We've delayed long enough. Are you ready to enter the lion's den?"

I don't see my team, but we're running out of time.

"I actually am." She twists the ring on her finger, admiring the craftsmanship, then looks up at me. "Thank you for last night."

"It was my pleasure."

"That's not what I mean. I was nervous when Forest told me what he planned and knew there was no way I could pull something like that off."

"And now?"

"Spending the night with you helped, and I know it wasn't fun for you, but it really helped me to relax."

"Not fun for me?" I shake my head. "I had a blast." It's the truth. "You're a lot of fun to be around, and you make things easy."

"I know, but it's your job, and I just wanted to say thanks while I could. You know ... before we *really* have to put on a show."

"What if it's not a show?" I can't help but add that in. The longer I'm in her presence, the more I don't want any of this to end.

Movement outside catches my eye. Help has arrived. Wolfe saunters in and all eyes turn to him. The man is something else, simmering lethality comes to mind. Decked out in a black suit with a navy-blue tie, the man screams professional bodyguard, stay away.

Close on his heels is Brady, who barely made it out of the Cancun fiasco Bravo team faced.

He prowls into the coffee shop and steals every eye that latched onto Wolfe. The man is a built like a tank, solid, like Forest, and is the one Guardian who can look Forest Summers in the eye. Like Wolfe, he wears all black, except for an identical navy tie cinched tight at his neck. Unlike Wolfe, the left side of Brady's face is covered in scars from nearly getting burned alive.

While Wolfe heads to the counter, Brady angles over to me.

Maria's reaction to my friends is fun to watch. There's a gasp, a hitching of her breath, and sustained visual contact. I'd say eye contact, but there's no one in the coffee shop, with the exception of me, with the grit to maintain eye contact with Wolfe and Brady.

I take Maria's hands in mine. "Buckle up, buttercup, things are about to get interesting."

"Who ..." Her head tilts back as her eyes climb the impossible distance up to Brady's face. Mouth gaping, words seem to fail her.

"Maria ..." I lower my voice for her ears alone and give her hands a hard squeeze to get her attention.

"What?" She shakes her head and focuses on me.

"We're officially in play."

It takes her a moment, but then her eyes widen. She gives a shaky nod as Brady approaches the table.

"Sir." Brady gives a nearly imperceptible nod. He stands at parade rest, hands clasped behind his back, legs shoulder-width apart.

"Maria, I'd like to introduce you to Brady. He, along with Wolfe, will be your personal protective detail."

"My what?" Her mouth gapes.

"Remember, princess? We talked about this." I rub my finger over the diamond. We literally just talked about this.

It takes a moment, but then her eyes brighten and her mouth closes. She takes a sip of coffee and peeks up at Brady. Taking a moment to swallow, she smiles at him.

"It's nice to meet you, Brady."

"The pleasure is all mine, Miss Rossi."

"Please, call me Maria."

"Miss Rossi will do." Brady gives a sharp shake of his head.

Behind Brady, Wolfe arrives with two small black coffees in hand. He gives one of them to Brady, then holds his cup in front of him while I make introductions.

"It's nice to meet you, Miss Rossi."

This isn't the first time Maria's met Wolfe, but it may be the first time his name's been mentioned. I wait to see if Maria breaks character, but to my delight, she pretends this is the first time she's seen him.

"Likewise." Maria peeks around the massive form of Brady and her lips twist. "Looks like you have competition."

"How's that?" Wolfe shifts to a position where he can surveil the entire room.

Brady does the same.

The moment the two of them approach us, Maria's security team moves in. Hands tucked inside their suit jackets, they're not happy seeing Maria surrounded by Wolfe, Brady, and myself.

"Miss Rossi," the lead man says, "we're here to escort you home."

"Hey, Gerald." She gives a little flick of her fingers. "How are you?"

Gerald grits his teeth as he takes in Wolfe and Brady. They shift to protective positions, flanking Maria the moment Gerald and Stefan head our way.

"Are these men bothering you?" Gerald puffs out his chest. He's a large man, as men go, but nothing when compared to three Guardians.

His partner shifts on his feet, readying for a fight, but uncertain of the outcome. If he's smart, he weighs the odds and knows he's not only out-numbered, but out-manned as well.

As Guardians, we can't help a certain degree of bridled ferocity. It's in our blood, in the very makeup of who we are.

"Maria is under my protection. Who are you? And why are you here?" I glance up at Gerald, demanding an answer.

"We're her protective detail." Gerald swallows thickly.

"Protective detail?" I release Maria's hand and rise to my full height. My chair scrapes across the floor as I kick it out of the way. "Not such a protective detail when you lose your charge like you did last night. Fortunately, Maria was with me, but anything could've happened. You can tell whoever you work for that your services are no longer required."

Gerald does that thing again where he tries to swallow his Adam's apple and fails. He glances at Maria, trying to dismiss me, but I'm a hard man to ignore.

"Miss Rossi," the man does his best to ignore me, "your mother and your uncle were very worried last night when you disappeared."

"Why would that be?" Maria glances up at Gerald, completely nonplussed. A soft smile fills her face as she plays innocent. "I've been in very capable hands." She places her hands one on top of the other, showcasing the rock on her ring finger. It draws Gerald's eye.

"We thought you were abducted." He glances at me, uncertainty rampaging across his face.

"You thought I was kidnapped?"

"Yes, Miss Rossi." Gerald coughs into his fist. "We saw this gentleman yank you into a van and drive off."

"Oh, that." Her lashes flutter as she rolls her eyes. "It was nothing. We were just going out." She leans back, crossing her arms over her chest. "Gerald, it wouldn't be the first time I've ditched you and your men. Sometimes, a girl just wants to have fun."

"Miss Rossi, your mother is beside herself with worry."

"And, here I am, all safe and sound." Maria gives a flick of her fingers. "You can run along now. Tell her I'm perfectly fine."

"We've been instructed to ensure you make it home." Gerald isn't giving up.

She turns her attention to me. "See, I told you." Maria lobs the ball into my court.

To my surprise, she holds up incredibly well, falling right in line. I told her it was best to stick as close to the truth as possible. No lie ever withstands the test of time, or a true interrogation. The truth, embellished, is our friend.

"We're on our way back to the Belvedere as it is, so no reason for you to hang around. You should run along. I wouldn't want Maria's mother to worry unnecessarily, especially with our news. You can safely report that Maria is in good hands."

"And whose hands would those be?" Like a dog with a bone, Gerald is not letting this go, nor is he getting the hint.

"Liam." I shove my hand out. "Liam Cartwright. Now, if you don't mind, we'd like to finish our morning coffee unmolested."

"Miss Rossi." Gerald turns toward Maria, completely ignoring my extended hand. "You need to come with us."

30

MARIA

LIAM STANDS WITH HIS HAND OUTSTRETCHED, LETTING THE OFFENSE OF not having his handshake returned lengthen.

I've seen things like this before, intended snubs that leave a man, literally, hanging. Almost every time, the arm falls and a shift in the power balance goes toward the one who snubbed the first.

My uncle does that all the time. It's uncomfortable. Not just for whoever he's taking down a notch, but for those of us who witness the snub.

Liam doesn't let his hand drop. He keeps it outstretched, steady as a rock. Masquerading as a venture capitalist, everything about him screams power, wealth, pretense, and social standing.

"I'm going to say this as politely as I can." Liam takes a step toward Gerald, getting in his personal space. His hand remains up, but instead of a shake, Liam forcibly grasps Gerald's shoulder. "You have five seconds to leave me and my fiancée alone. Run back to your mistress like a good little dog. Inform her I will bring Maria back when I'm damn well ready and not a moment sooner."

Wolfe and Brady shift, closing in on Gerald and Stefan. It's a formidable thing to witness. I swear they barely move, but the tension in the room escalates a thousand-fold, brimming with lethality and male bravado.

I'm really glad there's practically no one in the coffee shop. The one couple who was sitting at the window grabbed their coffees and rushed outside the moment Gerald and Stefan entered. The baristas cower behind the counter, saying nothing, as the standoff escalates.

"Do we understand one another?" Liam's grip on Gerald's shoulder tightens.

Behind him, Wolfe unbuttons his jacket, revealing a shoulder holster and the weapon nestled inside. Brady does the same. Gerald holds up his hands, palms out. Stefan does the same.

"It would really be a shame for things to get out of hand here, don't you agree?" Liam releases his grip and pats Gerald's shoulder.

"We're not looking for any trouble. We just want to ensure Miss Rossi is safe."

"Miss Rossi is very safe ... with me." Liam's tone turns darkly possessive. "Unlike your shoddy protection, I would never lose her. You can also explain to Mrs. Rossi that Maria's with me now."

Stefan says nothing during the entire exchange. His face grows paler and paler by the second. Brady covers Stefan, while Liam and Wolfe focus their attention on Gerald.

"Miss Rossi ..." Gerald takes a step back, conceding ground. "You really should come with us."

"Please tell my mother that while I appreciate her concern, I'm a grown woman capable of making my own choices. Liam and I are enjoying spending time together. Lord knows we don't get nearly enough of it." I rise gracefully from my chair and move to stand beside Liam.

Surrounded by five overly large, overly muscular, overly alpha men, I feel about two-feet tall, but I've learned to fake confidence.

I gently grasp Liam's wrist and lift his arm up and over my shoulder. Leaning against him, I place my palm over his chest. Turning back toward Gerald, I have a little fun.

"In fact, why don't you tell mother I'll be busy the rest of the day? I'll see her at brunch tomorrow, and I'll be bringing a guest." I lift on tiptoe to kiss Liam's cheek while Gerald sputters. "It's definitely time to meet my mother."

"I'm looking forward to it." Liam returns the warmth of my smile, magnifying it a thousand-fold with his megawatt smile.

If I don't watch myself, I could fall for this man.

As for Gerald, he already knows he's lost, but he doesn't know how to back down gracefully. He sputters and coughs at my words. I add to them, sending a direct message to my mother. Even though it flows through Gerald, there's no doubt my mother will extract every word verbatim from his mouth.

"It's been a really long night, sweetie. I don't know about you, but I'm ready for bed." I leave my words flagrantly suggestive, realizing only after they leave my mouth how much I would enjoy such a thing.

If Liam doesn't shy away from showing his interest. Why should I?

Because, you're just a job to him, that's why.

Yeah, right.

It's easy to forget we're not actually out on a date. This sucks. I need to get out of here, away from my uncle's men, and find someplace quiet where I can think through everything that's happening.

With my active imagination, I plan out a really epic departure, but the execution of that plan turns comical in real life.

I imagine dragging Liam behind me as I squeeze past Gerald and head to the door, head high, shoulders back, completely in control. Liam and I would then head toward the Belvedere, unmolested and alone, where I would march him up to my apartment, close the door, take a much-needed nap, and maybe explore a few things on my adventurous list with Liam in bed.

That's not what happens.

I grip Liam's wrist. I try to lift his arm off my shoulder, but he tucks me in, closer to his side, and kisses the top of my head. He releases his grip on Gerald's shoulder. There's a moment where they stare at each other. I swear they growl at each other, but that might be my imagination at play.

After a tense moment, Gerald takes a step back, pivoting out of the way. Stefan does the same, only he takes two steps back. Liam pulls me into the breech as Wolfe and Brady fall in lockstep behind us.

I think we're headed to the Belvedere, but Liam angles me toward a black stretch SUV waiting by the curb. He holds the door for me as I climb in. Sitting inside the SUV is none other than Forest Summers, looking paler than I remember, and Mitzy, with her psychedelic hair.

"Hey, Maria. How're you holding up?" Mitzy's bubbly presence not only brings a smile to my face but drains all my tension.

"It's been a night." I slide across the leather seat to let Liam and the others inside. "You won't believe what we did."

"You taught a bunch of muggers a lesson. Tore up the dance floor. And faced down your uncle's men." She beams at me, looking pleased.

"How did you ...?" I look to Liam.

"Mitzy Magic." Liam kisses my cheek as he settles in. The car rocks as Wolfe gets in the driver's side and Brady settles himself in the passenger seat.

"Did you tell her?" I look at Liam, knowing he must have reported in along the way. When he did that, I don't know, but he must have.

"No silly." Mitzy grins. "I've got eyes everywhere."

"Okay." I don't believe her, but I'm willing to suspend disbelief, if only because I'm too tired to ferret out how she really knows.

"Everyone settled?" Wolfe looks through the rearview mirror, reminding me to strap in. It takes a moment, but I get the buckle fastened. Wolfe puts the car in gear and slowly turns out onto the nearly deserted street.

Outside, Stefan stares at us while Gerald lifts his phone to his ear. I do not want to be on the receiving end of whatever hellfire my mother rains down on those poor men. I kind of feel guilty, but they're the ones who signed up to work for Marco Rossi. If they have issues with the terms of their employment, they can bring it up with him.

In the meantime, I'm way off script. Instead of waltzing into the

Belvedere, ignoring my mother, and heading upstairs to crash, I find myself going for a ride in the back of a stretch SUV.

Like a limo on steroids, the back of the stretch SUV holds two bench seats facing each other. The bold and rich scent of leather floods my senses and screams far too much wealth.

"Is something wrong?" I hold Liam's hand and look to Forest.

His astute gaze cuts to me and slides down to my hand holding Liam's.

"Looks like it was a successful evening." His deep rumbly voice fills the back of the SUV. "The ring looks good on you, Maria."

I hold up my hand and spin the ring around my finger. "It's a bit much, don't you think?"

I don't say *Thank you for the ring*, because it's a loaner, and I don't ask the most pressing question on my mind. It feels as if I'm in a need-to-know situation, and I may not need to know about Sybil. Nevertheless, I rub my palm on my skirt and hold my question.

Forest leans forward, placing his elbows on his knees. "We rescued your friend. Sybil is unharmed."

"She is?" My heart goes off like a jackhammer.

All night, I've tried not to think about Sybil, what she endured, or the horrible fate she would meet if the Guardians failed.

Liam told me the Guardians never fail, but I don't believe the way he does.

"Liam said I can't talk to her ..." I'm hoping Forest's presence, and the fact he made a personal trip to give me the good news, means I can call my bestie.

"Unfortunately, that's correct. Her rescue makes your position more tenuous than before."

"How?"

Forest glances at Liam, a question implied in his expression. Liam looks at me, then returns a sharp nod.

If I knew what the question was, I might be able to interpret that exchange.

"Maria can handle it." Liam squeezes my hand, reassuring me.

Only I don't know why I need reassurance. My place in all of this is rather straightforward. I'm the Guardian's access to my uncle.

"Mitz ... the floor is yours."

31

MARIA

"Gotcha, boss." Mitzy flicks on the tablet she holds in her lap. "While the two of you were out having fun, I've been hard at work."

Mitzy doesn't look like a computer geek. Her bubbly personality doesn't make me think *smart*. I would've dismissed her abilities if I met her under any other circumstance. What she's capable of remains a mystery to me, for the most part, but I've glimpsed enough to know I've barely scratched the surface.

"First off, I want to reiterate what Forest said. Sybil was rescued, she's not injured—except for some bruising—but she's far from safe. We have her under a protective detail until we finish this."

"And by this?" I look to Forest.

"By this, we intend to break apart the Rossi empire."

"Why don't you grab my uncle and be done with it?" I squirm in my seat. Look at me telling the Guardians what to do. "I mean, I assume you're not against some vigorous questioning."

"Vigorous questioning?" Wolfe laughs under his breath. "Your woman is funny, Liam. Vigorous questioning indeed."

Beside me, Liam rolls his eyes.

"I didn't want to assume you'd resort to torture." I shrug. "I left it open ended."

"We question those who need it, but taking your uncle in for *vigorous questioning* will not accomplish our goals."

"It would end the trafficking of women and children. Get rid of him and—"

"Someone else will simply fill the void." Forest's low growl gets my attention. "We will deal with your uncle in time. Our goal is more than simply dismantling his operation. We need to know where his clients come from. How his services are advertised, and much more. Take him and we lose all the rest of it."

"What else is there?"

"We want to rescue those who've been taken." Liam grips my hand, giving it a squeeze.

His words make me feel like an ass. It never occurred to me to think about past victims. The Guardian vision is impressive.

"Correct." Mitzy jumps in. "We need access to client files, anything and everything associated with that part of his business."

"I take it you confirmed my uncle is, in fact, running this operation?" I remember what Forest said last night about jumping to conclusions and to assume nothing.

It seems like that conversation occurred months ago, but I sat in that library listening to Forest's story just last night.

"We confirmed that much." Forest's low voice rumbles inside the vehicle. "What we don't have are the buyers, and we're interested in one buyer in particular."

I remember him mentioning that. Something about what he said last night tickles a memory.

"What was the name of the girl? The one you rescued from the snuff film?"

"Zoe Lancaster." Liam answers instead of Forest. "Why do you ask?"

"I'm not sure, to be honest, but that name sounds familiar to me. Not Zoe, but her last name."

"Interesting." Forest leans back, looking as tired as I feel. He and Liam have another one of those nonverbal exchanges. "Looks like the two of you figured things out."

My brows pinch together, confused by what Forest says. I nearly ask him what we were supposed to figure out. Since I already feel overwhelmed by the combined brain power between Forest and Mitzy, I lean back and smile like I know exactly what's going on.

I don't.

Forest, Mitzy, and Liam carry on a rapid-fire conversation about tech and gear I have no context with to follow. After a few minutes, I give up trying to keep up with them and sit back and enjoy the ride. As far as comfort goes, I've definitely seen worse. While Mitzy explains the functions of yet another technical gadget, I let my mind wander.

I'm happy Sybil is safe, but I'd feel better if we could talk. I want to know what happened to her and how I can help her work through whatever it is she needs to work through.

The thing about Sybil is she's tough as nails. I have no doubt she'll find her path, but it feels as if I should be with her. From the age of twelve, I can count on one hand the number of times we were apart for longer than a few weeks.

After we met in Hawaii, her father arranged for Sybil to attend Prescott Academy, the college preparatory boarding school we attended. We went from that summer in Hawaii to surviving seventh grade together.

It physically hurts to be separated from Sybil for this long.

"And how are you going to get by his surveillance cameras?"

"I built this for you." Mitzy holds out her hand, which draws my attention back to the interior of the car.

Perched on her hand is a tiny drone. Made of something reflective —or see through?—its features are difficult to make out. My eyes *slip* over its shape. That's the only word I have to describe it.

"What is that?" I lean forward, pinching my eyes to make sense of what I'm seeing.

"It's a new drone prototype." Mitzy holds the tiny thing in the palm of her hand.

"Makes my eyes cross." I blink, thinking that will clear up what

I'm seeing. It doesn't. If anything, I'm more confused. It's there and yet *not* there.

"I'm trying out a new photo-optic material."

"Photo-what?"

"Visual camouflage. The skin has light-bending properties. I reached out to some of my Canadian friends who are working on an invisibility shield."

"You're kidding, right?" No way did Mitzy tell me she's cloaking a drone, making it invisible, but my eyes don't lie.

"Well, it's not enough to fool the human eye. You can kind of see it, but it's hard to make out what it is. For video surveillance systems, however, it's nearly invisible." Mitzy lets me hold the drone.

With my hands to help me see, I trace out the contours of a tiny drone.

"What is it for?"

"While you're at brunch tomorrow with your mother, hopefully, the drone will make a circuit of your uncle's house."

"Wow. I assume while it does that it will tap into whatever security they have?" I really don't see how a drone can tap into a security system, but I'm a Hotelly, not an engineer.

"Not necessarily their security systems. I'm looking for servers."

"Servers?"

"Computer servers." Mitzy sits back while I transfer the tiny drone to Liam.

Like me, he lifts it up, trying to get a better look at it.

"Maria, if you don't mind, I have a few questions for you."

"For me?" I point to my chest.

"Yes." Mitzy glances at Forest, who inclines his head, giving her the go-ahead. "What do you know about your father's death?"

That is not the question I expect. My fingers curl around Liam's hand.

"It's been years, what do you want to know."

"I've been looking into it and there's not much."

"I'm not surprised. As I understand it, he had a heart attack." My comment draws Forest back to the conversation.

He leans forward, intent gaze pinning me in place. "Why do you say it like that?"

"Like what?"

"Instead of stating that he had a heart attack, you said *As I understand it.*" He takes in a breath and blows it out nice and slow. "I'm curious as to your choice of words."

"I didn't mean anything cryptic. I wasn't there. Sybil and I were at Cornell when it happened. My mother called and gave me the news." I pause, letting Forest and Mitzy's words sink in. In the brief time I've known them, the one thing I've learned is no question is simple. They're looking for something.

Not wanting to make them dig, I give them everything I know.

"At the time, my father had several offices. He was a workaholic. Mother told him he needed to slow down, that he worked too hard." As the words come, my memory opens up like a book, and I see things from a different perspective.

"He had offices in New York, where most of his business was conducted, and of course, he had the Belvedere down here. He spent most of his time in New York, but I think that was so that he could stay close to me. Whenever we had time, most weekends in fact, he flew Sybil and me down to the Hamptons. Didn't matter if it was summer or the middle of the winter."

"Why do you think that was?"

"At the time, I thought it was me, and that's probably the truth of it. My parents weren't exactly getting along. They rarely fought, at least where I could hear, but they didn't spend much time together either. In the winter, my mother never joined us at the Hamptons."

"Did she stay in New York?"

"She did not." A funny feeling comes over me. "As a matter of fact, she came down here. That was one of the few times my mother and father were both in New Orleans. He was down here for about a week, then flew back to the Hamptons. For whatever reason, my mother returned with him."

"Was that unusual?"

"For them it was. Like I said, their relationship was ... strained.

Anyhow, they went to the Hamptons together. It was a day or two later that my father suffered a massive heart attack."

"And your mother didn't call you?"

"We were in the middle of prelims." At the confused look on Liam's face, I explain. "That's what we call mid-semester exams at Cornell. I guess she didn't want his death to affect my grades. She called me the next day. Sybil and I flew out that night."

"It was a quick funeral." Mitzy rubs the side of her nose. "A cremation?"

"Yes. My mother is a monster planner, and with it being so close to her infamous holiday parties, she wanted it done and over."

"I wondered about the cremation considering his religious views."

"I don't know what to say about that. I figured he and Mother discussed it."

"There was never an autopsy." Mitzy glances at Forest.

"Is that abnormal?"

"Typically, deaths at home are an automatic coroner's case. The cause of death needs to be established. I found it unusual that didn't happen in this case." Mitzy's voice holds a lot of unasked questions.

"Like I said, it never seemed strange to me. We went to the Hamptons and had a small funeral."

"And a year later your mother and uncle get married." Forest drums his fingers on his knee.

"Like I said, my uncle swore if anything happened to my father that he would take care of both my mother and me."

"Were you aware they were high school sweethearts?" Mitzy lobs that into the middle of the conversation, throwing me for a loop.

"Excuse me?" My brows pinch with confusion. "My mother and father dated in high school. He was a year older and had to wait a year before they could get married."

"Not your mother and father. I'm talking about your uncle and your mother." Mitzy keeps staring at me, like she's testing me.

"What about them?" If this is a test, I'm failing at it.

"They dated during high school." Mitzy's words make no sense.

"No. My mother married my father right out of high school. It was within a month of her graduation, as a matter of fact. My father dated her his senior year. My uncle was never in the picture like that."

"That's not true." Mitzy sits back and crosses her arms.

"How do you know?"

"I dig, but honestly, this was a simple thing to discover. I'm surprised you didn't know."

"Evidently, there are a lot of things I don't know. How did you find that out?"

"I talked to a couple of teachers from that school." Mitzy's flippant answer astounds me.

"Wow. That's thorough."

"I'm always thorough. Evidently, your mother and Marco Rossi dated until your mother's junior year. Everyone thought they'd get married, but all that changed your father's senior year."

"I've never heard of any of this."

"By the time your father graduated, he and your mother were engaged. A year later, they married."

"I knew that part. It always sounded romantic to me. High school sweethearts getting married."

"After you mentioned something being off between your father and uncle, I did some digging. Discovered that and more." Mitzy looks at her laptop.

"More? Such as?"

"What you mentioned about the Belvedere and the twenty-fifth floor. Your grandfather set aside that space, not your father. As you mentioned, your uncle ran things down here, under your father's supervision, while he managed his offices in New York. I don't think it's too much of a stretch to connect the dots from there."

"Do you think that's why my father insisted I run the Belvedere?"

"I don't like making assumptions, but I'll go out on a limb and say that sounds like the most plausible answer."

"And you think my mother and my uncle were carrying on an affair the whole time?"

"There's no proof, but it does tie everything together."

"And the questions about my mother and uncle ... are you insinuating foul play? You don't think they ...?" I struggle to swallow past the thick lump closing off my throat. "You don't think they had anything to do with it? Is that what you're trying to say?"

"I dislike assumptions or jumping to conclusions with insufficient data. I'm merely postulating ... or rather thinking out loud that there may be another reason behind your father's death."

"Is there any chance my father wasn't involved in human trafficking?"

"I wish I could say he wasn't, and while we have no direct evidence, I highly doubt he wasn't. I don't see how he couldn't have known."

"But if ..." I squeeze my eyes shut as I grasp for straws. I refuse to believe my father, the man I loved and admired growing up, would willingly kidnap young women and children and ... I can't even finish that thought.

Mitzy and Forest might suspect my father, but I hold on to hope and my belief that my father was a good man.

Lancaster.

The name rushes at me from somewhere in the depths of my mind. I know that name.

There it goes. The last vestige of hope I had left about my father's role in this snaps and floats away.

32

LIAM

Wolfe drives us in circles while Mitzy briefs me on the new tech and how best to use it. By the third circuit, I can no longer hold in my curiosity.

"Are they following us?" I resist the urge to twist around to look behind us.

Mitzy, who faces toward the back, glances over my shoulder, peering at the traffic behind us. She shrugs, oblivious to the tail I feel in my gut.

No way in hell did Gerald and Stefan leave us to our own devices. The moment Gerald called in to his boss, they were given instructions they dared not fail. All eyes are focused on the new man hanging around their precious princess.

I'm looking forward to meeting Marco Rossi and rub my hands in anticipation.

Forest keeps his council, remaining quiet for the duration of the ride. The formidable warrior seems somehow less than before.

Tired.

As if the weight of his burden to rid this world of those who seek to destroy innocent lives is slowly wearing him down.

I hate to see that in such a stoic man. He's our rock. The anchor which holds us steady on our path. We are the Guardians: his army of the righteous men and women who strive to rid the world of the evil which infests it. To see him shouldering the strain of that impossible task is a sucker punch to the gut. It's a reminder our heroes are human, after all.

Into that epic silence, Maria and I hold hands.

She grounds me.

She gives me strength.

She infuses me with the power to protect and defend as no one else can.

It's my solemn duty to fulfill that role and an oath I reaffirm right then and there. Whatever it takes, I will protect Maria.

She's quiet, immersed in her thoughts. No doubt she battles a vicious and bloody conflict warring within her. Turning against her family can't be easy. I wish there was something I could do to ease her pain. While she stares out the window, I sit beside her, lending what strength my presence might give.

I wish I could wrap her in my arms and take away her pain, but that is a path she needs to walk alone.

Her silence crashes all around me. Like thunder, it surrounds and drowns me. Instead of pulling her into my arms, I settle for threading our fingers together. My thumb rubs over the back of her hand. The heat of my body bleeds into hers. I'd give her more, if I could.

"Like merry little lambs." Wolfe looks at me through the rearview mirror. "I have a feeling their fear for Marco Rossi is greater than their fear of you."

"They'll learn." I drum my fingers on my knee, getting antsy to get going.

While not a fan of undercover ops, I have a unique flair for those particular jobs. It goes back to my high school days when I was a triple threat. I excelled in sports, academics, and dating all the hot chicks, but it was in drama and theater where I ruled the school.

Of course, I had a bit of a leg up considering my mother's atmospheric rise as an actress granted me the opportunity to explore years of child acting gigs. In the end, however, it wasn't for me.

I aspired to greater things, like walking in the footsteps of a man I never knew. When it became clear to my mother I didn't want to be an actor, she put aside her Hollywood dreams for her son and allowed me to pursue mine.

My father may have died in service to his country months before I was born, but it didn't matter to me. I wanted to travel his path, even if it meant sacrificing my life in service to my country like he ultimately sacrificed his.

I always get a kick over the L.A. stereotype that every waiter and waitress are either aspiring actors or out of work actresses. As often as it's true, the reverse happened for my mother.

She never aspired to anything more than taking care of her son and being the best mother possible. In those two things, she succeeded where many struggle or fail.

I have the best mother in the world.

She was a waitress, one of the few in L.A. not interested in acting, but for her the stars aligned. A late night of pouring coffee for a beleaguered director turned into the opportunity of a lifetime when he asked her to take a leap of faith. He saw something within her, a hunger to do more with her life, that piqued his interest. My mother took that leap. She turned in her apron and made history.

My mother went from living on the street and starving herself to feed her five-year-old son to million-dollar contracts and a mansion in L.A. She proudly displays her first tip from that tiny diner.

Framed in a dime-store picture frame, it sits alongside her Oscar on the mantle, and every Christmas the owner of that diner who took her off the street, and the director who allowed her to reach the stars, sit down for dinner at our table.

The tip was a measly fifty-three cents. Not a real tip. It was someone's discarded change, but it meant the world to her, and it changed our lives.

A year can mean a lot to people like us.

All that's to say, I know how to put on an epic performance and how to stay in character. Method acting always was my preferred style. I'm not worried about meeting Marco Rossi or standing toe to toe with him. It's all in the delivery, and I've got that down pat.

"Should we mess with them?" I can't help wanting to make Gerald and Stefan's life more difficult than it already is.

Obviously, Gerald called in our little conversation. Despite explaining how Maria is now under my protection, they remain dutiful dogs following their master's commands.

The only question I have is who gives them their marching orders?

Is it Marco Rossi or Maria's mother?

"Who's following us?" Maria twists in her seat.

"Your buddies." I never expected them to leave us alone, but the performance was required.

"Gerald and Stefan?"

"Yup." I pop the 'p' at the end, having fun. "Wolfe's been leading them in circles."

"And here I was wondering why I was getting car sick." Mitzy shakes her head and jabs Forest in the ribs. "You're looking kind of sick yourself."

"Just tired." Forest runs his hands through the thick mop of his ice-white hair. He gives me a grin, sitting straighter in his seat, but his shoulders slump a few seconds later.

As for Gerald and Stefan, I need to send a message to Marco Rossi there is a new alpha in town. As far as Maria's mother goes, if she doesn't know already, she'll know soon enough that there's a man out there ready and able to thwart the plans she has for her daughter.

I'm really looking forward to meeting Maria's mother as well.

It's going to be epic.

As for the mother-uncle union, the information Mitzy dug up on them is nothing short of shocking. Their marriage makes more sense with that bit of information.

Knowing human behavior as I do, both studying to be an actor, then later as part of my hostage interrogation training in the Navy, my mind is quick to form connections.

Mitzy abhors assumptions, but her life begins and ends with the technical world of zeros and ones. I'm a people person. My intuition never fails, and it's saying a shit-ton about Marco and Maria's mother.

I don't know whether to cheer what Milo did to his brother or condemn him. He did the unthinkable when he stole his younger brother's girlfriend. That takes balls, and as if that display of dominance wasn't enough, the bastard married Marco's girl.

Talk about putting your brother in his place. Milo did that and more. He moved his brother down to New Orleans, physically separating his wife and brother. No need for jumping to conclusions there; a thing like that never goes over well.

Did Milo do that to teach his brother a lesson?

Probably.

It sounds like a dick thing to do.

Was it a power move?

No doubt about that.

Maria mentioned things felt off between her father and uncle. We now know why that was, and why Marco is uncharacteristically cold toward his niece. The daughter of the woman he loves and the brother he hates, Maria is the living embodiment of Marco's impotence.

That kind of hatred grows roots that dive deep.

If Marco had the balls to kidnap Maria's best friend, there's little keeping him from taking the next, obvious step. Jealousy and animosity aside, Maria is no longer safe within the walls of the Belvedere. Yet that's exactly where we're headed.

33

LIAM

TAKING MARIA BACK TO THE BELVEDERE SCREAMS ALL KINDS OF WRONG. What we should be doing is keeping her far away from those who wish her harm. There's no doubt in my mind there will be a power move. What form that will take is anyone's guess.

At least, I won't be going in alone. I'm more than happy to have backup on this mission. I need another pair of eyes.

Two pair.

Brady is definitely a bonus on this mission. The guy is solid.

Maria shifts in her seat. Her brow furrows. Her deep sighs have me squeezing her hand, lending whatever support I can. She's not taking the news about her mother and uncle well. I have to think somewhere, buried deep in her subconsciousness, there have always been questions—a sense of wrongness. Or if not that, some idea there was more beneath the surface when it came to her father, uncle, and mother.

Now, she's inundated with answers that only complicate things further. Everything she knows about her life lays in ruin at her feet.

That kind of despair can be crippling.

"How are you doing?" I softly nudge her and squeeze her hand.

"I'm good. Tired? Overwhelmed? Processing?"

"I'm here, princess. I've got you." I cover her hand with mine and lean in close, lowering my voice, and whisper for her ears only.

Her fingers twitch. It's something. Not much, but some reaction is better than none. We can't afford for her to be shell-shocked when we engage with her family. All the work I did last night, getting her to feel comfortable around me, will be shot to shit if she can't snap out of the depressive fog Mitzy's words created.

I don't think Maria can take another shock to her system without shutting down completely.

"Thank you." She turns toward me, lying her head on my shoulder. One deep breath in and she relaxes. "Thanks for just being here."

I feel Maria's pain. She wants to believe in the good of her father, but we know the Rossi's are involved in criminal activities; human trafficking is merely the worst of them.

Honest men don't engage in questionable activities. Milo Rossi may have loved his only child, a daughter instead of a son, but he was as dirty as they come.

And it looks like his younger brother may have had the last laugh.

I bet millions Marco arranged for his older brother to meet an untimely end. The question in the back of my mind is how involved was the mother?

In many crime families, women and children are sheltered from the family's activities, leading lives oblivious to what contributes to their wealth.

Maria is a victim of that.

It shows in her face as each new blow lands.

In the space of twenty-four hours, everything she thought she knew about her family is gone.

Corrupted forever.

Mitzy adds more fuel to the destructive blaze sweeping through Maria's life when she suggests the death of Maria's father, more likely than not, was not the result of natural causes. I would have preferred to shelter Maria from that, but Mitzy doesn't hold back.

I pray her mother wasn't involved. I don't think Maria will come back from something like that.

Maria needs a win, even if it's a cold-hearted mother just as oblivious as Maria was.

"I was wondering why we were driving in circles. I thought it was just so Mitzy could brief you. Gerald and Stefan are going to be pissed." She snuggles against my side and draws my arm over her shoulder. "You smell nice."

"Good to know." After an evening of clubbing, I'm several seasons past fresh, but if Maria likes it, I don't mind one bit.

Wolfe has more fun with Gerald and Stefan, driving in circles and figure eights. By now, Gerald and Stefan, if they're any good, know we're fucking with them.

Up ahead, a line of horses and carriages wait for tourists eager for the experience of riding through the French Quarter in a horse-drawn carriage. We've driven past no less than three times, but an idea pops in my head.

"Hey, Wolfe ..."

"What?"

"Next pass around, stop at the carriages." I give Maria's hand a squeeze.

As a New Orleans resident, the chances she's indulged in the classic tourist activity is slim to none. What better activity for the newly engaged couple to enjoy?

Wolfe looks at me through the rearview mirror, one scruffy brow raised in question. I know what he's thinking. It's corny as shit and complicates his role as *bodyguard,* but I'm looking to kill time.

Originally, I planned on returning Maria to her apartment in the Belvedere, letting her get in a few hours of sleep before we engaged with her mother. After the confrontation in the coffee shop with her security team, I put myself in the position of making a power move when I told Gerald and Stefan I would do as I pleased, returning Maria when I was damn well ready.

Now, I have time to kill. I hope it's not too draining on Maria.

It may be time for more coffee.

Wolfe makes another circuit around the French Quarter, dragging

Gerald and Stefan behind us. As we return to the carriages, he pulls off to the side.

"You want us following on foot or stay in the car?" Dark hair, dark eyes, and scruff covering his jaw, I don't doubt Wolfe is also shy a night's worth of sleep.

"Would you kill me if I had you follow in a carriage?" It would be epic if I could force Wolfe and Brady to take a romantic carriage ride around the French Quarter together.

"Fat chance, asshole." Wolfe turns to Brady. "You up for a stroll watching the lovebirds?" He pulls up to the curb. He and Brady exit the vehicle, searching for threats like good little bodyguards, before signaling the okay for me to exit. Brady opens my door. After I climb out, I offer Maria my hand, then check in with Mitzy and Forest.

"You all set?" Inside the SUV, Mitzy crawls into the driver's seat.

"As much as possible." Tucked into a shielded pocket of my jacket, her tiny dragonfly drone waits for action. I have several other new gadgets I'm anxious to try. Wolfe and Brady carry the same stealth tech hidden on their person.

"You know the drill." Mitzy peers out of the SUV. "Check in as you're able."

"Not my first rodeo, sunshine."

"It's your first rodeo with me, dickhead. Don't fuck it up." Mitzy's quick to remind me this is my first solo operation with the Guardians.

Like I've said a million times, I prefer operating as a team. Not that I'm left with my ass hanging in the wind anymore. I've got Wolfe and Brady to watch my six. Ignoring Mitzy, I turn toward the carriages.

"Have you ever ridden in one of these?" I march to the head of the line, arm wrapped protectively around Maria's shoulders.

"Never. I've always wanted to, but there's never been time." Despite her fatigue, eagerness shines in her eyes.

"Well, we've got time to kill, and it's kind of romantic."

"It's romantic up until the moment the guy points out that it's romantic." She gives a playful jab to my ribs. "Looking to get lucky, lover boy?"

"What did I say about that name?" I spin her, facing her toward me, and playfully rub my knuckles on the top of her head. She giggles and dances out of my embrace. Rubbing her arms, she peeks up at me, fluttering those impossibly long, black lashes.

"Fine. Hollywood it is."

"I want a different nickname."

"Sorry."

"What do you mean, sorry?"

"You don't get to pick your nickname. You get what you get. What's it going to be? Lover boy or Hollywood?"

"How about I kiss you until you give in?" That first kiss I gave her flashes through my mind. I want more of that.

"You can kiss me all day, but I'm not giving ground on your nickname. Besides, you call me princess, and I distinctly remember asking for something else. All's fair in love and war."

"So it is."

Maria stops suddenly and surprises me. She places her hands on my shoulders and lifts on tiptoe to brush her lips over mine. It's almost a kiss—agonizingly *almost* a kiss. Then she whispers in my ear and throws me for a loop.

"If you behave, there's more where that came from." Then she ruins it as a yawn escapes her mouth. "Sorry." Maria covers her mouth and blinks sleepily. "That didn't exactly pan out the way I meant. It was a lot sexier in my head."

As much as a buzzkill as that yawn is, I can't help but laugh. Nor can I help but test the waters.

"I hope to explore more of *that*, but first, we have a show to put on for Gerald and Stefan."

"That we do." She grabs at my hand, much more comfortable touching me than when we began. Maria doesn't give a firm yes to the idea of taking this crazy, insane attraction we share for each other to the next level, but she's interested.

Another yawn escapes her.

"As for *that* ..." She covers her mouth. "You've got to be as tired as me. We've both been up for over twenty-four hours. I'm like a zombie, practically asleep on my feet. I think we need a nap before any of *that*. Do you think we can manage to share a bed and actually sleep?"

"Hardly." I pull up short and take both her hands in mine. "I'll crash on the couch. I don't think it's possible for me to share a bed with you without taking full advantage of it. If sleep is what you need, then I need to sleep on the couch."

"There will be time for more, Hollywood." She pats my chest and laughs. "Give it some time."

The sound of her lilting laughter is nothing short of spectacular. I could listen to that all day. Unfortunately, she's right. We're both running on empty. After we're rested, I'll see what she thinks about taking whatever this is between us to the next level.

I approach the lead carriage. The driver is decked out in all his finery, wearing a bright purple suit with a ruffled collar. His boots are black and worn, but his horse looks healthy and eager to spend a day outside. I feel a little sorry for the horses. What kind of life is it drawing a carriage down a street filled with noisy traffic and inconsiderate tourists? He tips his fanciful top hat, then removes it in a flourish.

"Beautiful day for a beautiful couple."

"It is at that." I take a moment to admire the horses and his carriage. "How much?"

I don't bother haggling with the guy. He mentions his price, and I pay double. After a few words in his ear, Maria climbs into the carriage with me right behind. Whatever she says leaves a smile on the man's face.

Wolfe and Brady give me a look. Wolfe rolls his eyes. Brady returns a cheeky grin.

I'm going to catch shit for being overly romantic with the guys, but I don't hardly give a damn.

Maria's worth it.

As for Wolfe, he's not happy being made to walk behind the carriage, but Wolfe knows the drill. It's all about making the right impression.

"Here, lean against me and close your eyes." I settle in the padded seat and pull Maria close. "You can catnap if you want."

"I might, but to be honest, I've always wanted to ride in one of these. Sybil said it was silly and for tourists only. I'd absolutely hate it if I missed out because I couldn't keep my eyes open. If I fall asleep, pinch me, okay?"

"Pinch? Is that on your green list?" I waggle my eyes suggestively. One day, I'll get her to tell me what's on that list and the others.

"I'm not telling you what's on my list."

"Never say never, princess. I can't wait to get into that dirty mind of yours."

"Not today." She grins, pleased with herself.

"But today is a special day. I'd say getting engaged allows us to break a few rules."

"I'm not telling you what's on my list."

"I can be quite persuasive." I lean back and take in the sights.

New Orleans is a pretty city, mixing old and new seamlessly. The steady *clop, clop, clop* of the horse's hooves is a gentle rhythm that will put me to sleep if I'm not careful. I blink against my fatigue and focus on the mission.

"Have you heard from Sybil?"

Maria stiffens beside me, surprised by my question.

"I hope she's okay." I continue, hoping Maria gets the hint. "Do you think something happened with her father? Is that why she didn't make the auction last night?"

Sybil's disappearance needs to be addressed. After Maria told me Sybil's father was sick, receiving treatment for leukemia, I figure that's good enough to use as an excuse. As for this conversation, it isn't for us.

It's for our carriage driver.

"I suppose." Maria sits straighter, letting me know she remembers our conversation about her friend.

"Are you going to call her?"

"I don't want to bother her. If she flew home, she'll call when she knows more."

"Right. In the meantime, it is a gorgeous day, and I plan on monopolizing all your time."

There's no lie about that. Bright, blue skies welcome the beginning of a new day. With sparse clouds covering the sky, it's going to be a scorcher, but I plan to have Maria indoors before the heat gets to be too much.

We talk about our engagement and plans for the future. Not because we have plans, but for the benefit of our carriage driver.

No doubt Rossi minions will descend on the poor guy demanding to know everything we talked about. I give him more than enough content to make it easy on him.

The steady *clop, clop, clop* of the horse's hooves makes me yawn. My eyes droop, making me forcibly blink against my fatigue. We both need more caffeine. What better way to grab some than a stop for beignets and more coffee at a New Orleans landmark?

34

LIAM

Wolfe and Brady keep up with the sedate pace of the carriage without difficulty. We pull up at the rear of the line of carriages and dismount. Eager tourists are out, queuing up for a morning carriage ride. I tug Maria to my side again. I can't get enough of holding her close.

"You hungry?" I kiss the crown of her head and angle toward beignets and coffee.

"A bit. I need more coffee if we're going to stay out much longer."

"How do beignets and coffee sound?"

"That sounds amazing."

Maria is blessed with the most beautiful smile in the world. Her sapphire eyes make her beauty all the more intense. Add to that her raven hair with its cascading waves and the girl is a knockout.

She brushes a wayward strand of hair out of her eyes, completely oblivious to the stares of others, and glances back at Wolfe and Brady, who trail behind us as the dutiful bodyguards they are.

"I feel bad for your friends."

"Why?"

"Having to follow us."

"That's what bodyguards do, love. They follow." I gently remind her Wolfe and Brady are not Liam Cartwright's friends but his employees.

"Sorry." She peeks up at me, then lowers her voice. "I'm not that good at this."

"You'll get better."

The beignet shop comes into view. Already, a long line extends outside.

"Whoa! That's a beast. Is there somewhere else you'd like to go?"

"Oh, that's not bad at all." She tugs me toward the end of the line.

"But the line snakes down the street."

"Yeah, but it moves really fast." She picks up her pace, suddenly invigorated.

"I was hoping to sit down and get you off your feet."

"Most of those people are picking up to go. I've never had problems getting a seat." She twists around. "What about them?"

"They're working." I lift her hand and kiss her knuckles.

"Sorry ..."

"It's okay. I love that you care. I take it having men protect you that you respect is much different from having them forced on you."

"Yes, much different."

We get in line, and to my amazement, the queue moves quickly. In less than a few minutes, we order and find a cozy table looking out on the street. Wolfe and Brady treat themselves to coffee but forego the beignets. They stand protectively outside, each with a different view of the street.

As for Gerald and Stefan, I don't see them. Either they gave up or are far better at hiding than I give them credit for.

"How long were you thinking we stay out?" Maria takes a bite out of a beignet. The powdered sugar coats her lips and she gets a bit of it on the tip of her nose.

"Enough to make my point." I lean across the table and swipe the powdered sugar off her nose. "Are you enjoying yourself?"

She plows away at the beignets. I didn't notice at first, probably because I'm only now relaxing around her, but she's not like other women I've dated.

Dated?

More like engaged in mutually pleasurable activities. That's a nice way to say I've only ever had fuck buddies: women for whom my interest extended only to the bedroom and never beyond. At the prerequisite wine-and-dine portion of the evening, those women picked at their food like tiny, little birds, as if what they ate, and how much they ate, made one bit of a difference to me.

Maria doesn't care what I think and dives in with gusto, enjoying the experience as much as the food. There's no apology. No mention of counting calories, carbs, or any of that silly stuff. There is, however, one big problem for me, and it's growing by the second.

For the nth time, Maria closes her eyes. She moans as she takes a bite of the confected pastry. My gaze fixates on her pert little mouth as my imagination takes me on a deliciously dirty path.

"You need to stop that." My words rumble in the air; a low, warning growl that makes the table of grandmothers sitting beside us jump.

"Stop, what?" Maria looks up at me, all doe-eyed innocence, but that's merely an act.

She's been pushing my buttons all morning long. If she's not careful, my iron-willed control will slip. I'm trying to be a professional here, whereas she's doing everything in her power to make me lose control.

"Making those noises." I cross my arms, serious about what I say.

"What noises?" Maria closes her eyes, takes a bite of beignet, and licks the powdered sugar off her lip with a succulent tease of her tongue.

I pick up a beignet. Like her, I close my eyes. Like her, I moan. Like her, I put my tongue to good use. I lick the powdered sugar the way I want to ravish her pussy.

Maria's lids pull back. Her pupils dilate, turning her sapphire eyes black with lust. She places a hand in her lap and squirms.

"Stop that."

"Stop, what?" I take another lick, flicking my tongue the way I'll tease her clit when the time comes.

"Liam!" She whisper-shouts and glances around the nearby tables.

We're starting to draw attention.

She may not be into public displays of affection, but I love them. Most of my exhibitionist days are behind me, but I'll resurrect that side of myself if it means getting a rise out of my girl.

A pink flush rises from her chest, travels up her neck, and settles in her cheeks. Her cheeks deepen from pink to the prettiest rosy red.

"What?" I turn the confectioned pastry around and lick at a fresh section of powdered sugar.

"You're making a scene." She grabs at my wrist, trying to pull the pastry from my mouth, but I'm far stronger, and win that exchange. I lick the beignet like a devil intent on despoiling his prize.

In that little tug-o-war, I win.

Perhaps this is the best time to show her what that will mean when we're alone?

I really should control myself. Put those urges on the back burner. But why?

I'm too far gone, with too much pent-up sexual frustration boiling within me. No way am I going to behave. Not when she entices and delights, fanning the flames of my desire.

When I force her to tell me the top ten things on her list, it's going to be the best moment of my life. I'm just waiting for the green light.

Christ, sweet innocent Maria Rossi made a list and titled it *Green*. That means there's a yellow and a red list. Fifty shades of what-ifs spread between us.

"Fair is fair." The thought of making her squirm, while I hold her down and turn those delicious moans into screams, fires up my pulse and sends licks of heat racing through my body.

Yeah, I'm a bit riled up.

We've been dancing around sex all night: first with that kiss at Rose Manor, then later on the dance floor where I taught her the joys of a bit of bump and grind. To my delight, she's interested, and I can't wait to explore our mutual attraction. I'll leave nothing on her body unexplored. Between my fingers, my mouth, and my dick, I plan on staking my claim.

Maria Rossi is mine. That's the beginning and the end of it, and if she doesn't watch out, I'll begin her demise right here and now.

A man can only take so much.

"What do you mean by *fair is fair?*"

"The way you're eating that beignet is positively sinful."

"I'm not ..." Her cheeks turn a deeper shade of red.

"You, my sweet princess, are a horrible liar."

"Am not."

"Luv, it's deliciously sinful watching you eat, but if you keep it up, I won't be responsible for what comes next."

"What comes next?" She flutters her lashes seductively.

"Other things." I shift in my seat and make a quick adjustment of my pants.

"Other things?" The pink tip of her tongue flicks her pastry as she maintains eye contact with me. Yeah, she knows exactly what she's doing.

"Yes. You're pushing me." I lift a brow suggestively, knowing she'll back down.

Maria is interested, but she's not bold enough to press.

"Really?"

Maria looks at the powdered sugar coating her index finger and sucks it into her mouth. Again, she maintains eye contact. It's cute watching her step outside her comfort zone, and I think nothing of it until she pulls her finger out of her mouth.

She deliberately dips it in the pile of powdered sugar on the plate and lazily swirls her finger in the white powder until the first and second joints of her finger are coated in white. Maria lifts her finger to her mouth. With her seductive gaze locked on my eyes, she pushes out the pink tip of her tongue while I swallow a groan and shift in my seat.

"It's not nice to tease. I'm warning you."

"I'm not teasing." Her tongue darts out, barely flicking the tip of her finger.

"I'm warning you." My pants grow tighter by the second as my dick takes notice. Fucker is eager, and hungry.

"Warning me about what?" Those magnetic eyes will be my undoing. With her lashes fluttering suggestively, she draws the tip of her finger into her mouth. Her cheeks suck in as she takes her finger deeper into her mouth. "It's a shame."

"What's a shame?"

"You mentioned needing a nap earlier." She lets out a dramatic sigh. "Imagine what we could do if you were well-rested? I could show you the first item on my list."

"You and that list of yours are going to be my undoing. As much as I'd love to see how far you're willing to take this little game, we are on the clock."

Maria grabs another beignet. "Look, if you want to take a nap, we take a nap. I get that you need sleep, but I'm ..."

Holy fuck.

Grabbing Maria's wrist, I haul her out of her chair.

"What—" Her luscious mouth parts, and I take advantage of the opportunity.

My lips crash down over hers, tasting the sweetness of her mouth as every nerve in my body vibrates with pent-up need. Maria grips my shirt and meets the ferocity of my kiss with her hot body and expert tongue. Gone are her tentative explorations from earlier.

I meet her heat, dealing relentless strokes as I claim her mouth. Her fingers reach up, curling in my hair—twisting, tugging, pulling. Christ, when did she start trembling?

I don't fucking care. Not with the delicious moans spilling out of her mouth that scream all kinds of *Yes!* and *Now!*

Aware we're in a very public place, I grab her hand and drag her away from the table.

My entire body aches to lick, to suck, and to take, leaving no part of her hot body unclaimed by my hungry mouth.

We make it as far as the street before I spin her around and back her up against a wall. Eager, needy, and hungry, I lean against her and cup her face. A groan vibrates deep in the back of my throat with the desire raging inside of me.

"If you don't want this to go where we're obviously headed, now is the time to say no." I give her an out.

"Will you just kiss me already." Maria lifts on tiptoe and meets every kiss, every lick, and every nip of my teeth with answering heat. Her fingers dig into my back, clawing my shirt, as I give her a glimpse of what's to come.

Her eagerness spurs me on as I kiss her lips, nip at her ear, and trail a line of heat down the gentle arch of her neck. I'm a slave to my lust, hanging on by a thread, as my adoration for her grows and my need becomes unbearable.

Maria's hands climb up my back until her fingers claw at my scalp, twisting in my hair and tugging on the roots. She follows me, keeping pace with my rising need until a low cough sounds behind me.

"Sir ..." Wolfe's interruption is a buzzkill. "This may not be the right place for that."

I look up, noticing how Wolfe and Brady shield us from the crowd. When he gives me a look, I return his stare completely unapologetic.

"Come, princess, it's time to take you home." I guide Maria down the sidewalk while Brady's muffled laughter turns into a snort and a wheeze.

The closer we get to the Belvedere, my senses heighten and adrenaline pulses into my bloodstream. I've felt like this before, moments before heading into battle and engaging with the enemy.

35

MARIA

As far as kissing goes, Liam does that very well. There's a rawness to his kissing, an unbridled passion that sweeps me off my feet. I've never experienced anything like it.

He can place his lips on the tip of my bare shoulder and my entire body quivers. When he touches my neck, sweeping his fingers up and into my hair, my breaths turn ragged, uncontrolled. My toes curl with anticipation when he grabs my waist to pull me close. My senses riot with an overload of sensation when we hover a kiss away.

Liam makes my body burn.

It's intense.

I'm not the only one affected. Virile power rages within him, a raw sensuality he barely contains. When he does unleash it, it explodes with the power to destroy everything I thought I knew about sex and turns it on its head.

Breathing in his dark, woodsy, decidedly masculine scent scrambles my brain. He makes me want more, and I know where I want this to go.

Last night, I pointed a gun at him, demanding he tell me what he'd done with Sybil. Now, there's a ring on that hand. We need to pump the breaks and slow things down, but considering I carry a ring on my finger, slow doesn't make much sense anymore.

Not that the ring is real. Not that there's anything but intense physical attraction drawing us together.

Every touch, every kiss, is a barrage of sensation raging like a firestorm within me. I'm both powerless to stop the devastation and eager to feel the burn.

Wolfe and Brady follow a few steps behind us. There's no sign of Gerald or Stefan. Either they're getting better at not being seen or Liam scared them into hiding.

We hold hands.

Actually, Liam holds my hand and I grip his arm, leaning into him as we weave through the tourists on our way to the Belvedere.

"That was pretty epic by the way."

"What was?" Liam glances down, brows tugged together.

"The way you dressed Gerald and Stefan down. I wanted to give you a fist bump. I've never had anyone stand up for me like that before. It was perfectly epic."

"Thanks. That was my intention all along."

"To be epic?"

"No, silly. To impress my girl."

My soft smile brings an answering grin to his face.

"Are you ready?" Liam reaches down, taking my hand in his. The reaffirming squeeze he loves to give is everything to me. In that touch, he lends me strength and tells me he's there if I need to lean on him.

My insides churn—not with the light, unsettled, and anxious feeling of butterflies in flight—but rather with a sickening, seething, swirling sensation of worms chewing on death and decay. Bile rises in the back of my throat, and I have to press my fingers to the hollow of my neck to make the sickening sensation go away.

"Maria?" Liam gives my hand another squeeze. "Are you okay?" He pulls me to a stop half a block away from the Belvedere. "We can turn around. You don't have to do this."

I want to turn around. I want to run screaming from this place. It's infested with evil where horrible things are done to innocent women ...

As a matter of course.

As a business enterprise.

As a routine daily event.

All of it occurring under my nose.

They took Sybil.

They kidnapped five others.

How many came before them?

Dozens? Hundreds? More?

The urge to empty the contents of my stomach nearly overwhelms me.

My uncle's been running this corruption from within the Belvedere for decades. How many lives has he ruined? How many people has he killed?

"I have to do this." I draw in a breath, tugging the humid air of the Mississippi Delta deep into my lungs. I may have grown up in New York, but New Orleans is my home.

And the Belvedere is *mine*.

Anger wells up from within me, seething with disgust and revulsion over what my uncle has done. I will avenge Sybil. I'll bring justice to the countless victims whose lives my uncle destroyed.

"We can find another way." Liam gives me an out, but I'm the key.

It all comes down to this.

Every step Guardian HRS has taken to end this operation led them to me.

To the Belvedere.

From the kidnapping of Zoe Lancaster to Sybil's abduction, it all ends with me.

Lancaster?

The name rings with familiarity, but I can't put my finger on why her name echoes in my head. Was she a fellow student at Prescott Academy? Sybil and I spent seventh through twelfth grade in the prestigious college preparatory academy.

Maybe?

Frustration grows within me because something important is trying to crawl out of my subconscious. A link? A connection? Some thread that makes sense?

"If I'm the only thing standing between my uncle and the Guardian's ability to take him down, I'll do my part." I inject strength into my voice, but I don't feel it.

Fear and weakness pull at me, growing stronger and more vocal as we draw near the hotel. It wouldn't take much to turn around and run.

But my father didn't raise a coward.

He trained me from a young age to become a leader and to fight for what was right. He groomed me to take over the Belvedere.

"The Guardians appreciate what you're doing, but if you have any doubts, now is the time to turn around. I support whatever you decide."

The sad thing about what Liam says is that it's true. Even me stepping aside cripples their ability to complete their mission, Liam will support my decision.

"I'm not turning back. I want to do this." I grip his arm. Steel beneath skin. He is my rock. "I *need* to do this."

Returning to the Belvedere brings all kinds of emotions boiling to the surface. Yesterday, this was my home. It was safe and my legacy; a place where I intended to make my mark on the world.

It's my father's gift to me, and I refuse to let that memory be soiled.

My love for my father runs deep—despite what the Guardians say about whether he may, or may not, have been a criminal—and I want to make him proud. Even if he's no longer with me.

Will I ever recover from the damage that's been done?

We round the corner, walking side by side, our stride in lockstep with each other. Behind us, Wolfe and Brady guard their wealthy client, Liam Cartwright, a venture capitalist with a portfolio in the billions.

My hotel is a gorgeous blend of iconic architecture unique to New

Orleans blended with a visionary eye to the future. My father built that with intent to give it to his daughter, when I was ready.

But I was barely a toddler when the Belvedere's doors opened to the public. My father entrusted the operation of the Belvedere to my uncle. Marco was to hold it in trust until I grew out of childhood and came into my birthright.

Somewhere along the way, holding the Belvedere in trust for his niece mutated into corruption and filth as my uncle used the Belvedere as a front to run the most vile industry on the planet.

I can't believe my father knew.

There's no way he could know and not have shut the whole despicable thing down.

The Guardians say otherwise, but I'm not ready to accept their version of reality.

After the events of the past twenty-four hours, I expect my uncle to meet me in person and greet my return with suspicion and distrust.

By now, my uncle will have received a thorough brief on the man standing by my side. I go over the details in my head, cementing the truths and lies Mitzy spun together to create Liam's backstory.

Despite my growing apprehension, there is no welcoming party. I glimpse Gerald and Stefan off to the side in the lobby, but they make no move to interfere as Liam and I head for the elevator.

"Do you want to go to my office?" A certified workaholic, it's not unusual for me to spend the day behind my desk. If not there, I can usually be found shadowing any of the hundreds of employees as I learn the ins and outs of their jobs.

"I was thinking we head to your place." Liam wraps his arm around me, tugging me close. The way his voice rumbles, wrapped in sin and masculinity, makes his desire abundantly clear to anyone who might be watching.

And there are many eyes on us.

In the lobby alone, over a hundred cameras imbedded in the walls and ceiling record everything that goes on. Our conversation is recorded along with all the rest.

I swallow against the lump in my throat as that stark reminder slams home. The security suite which monitors our guests against cheating at the tables is now zeroed in on every move I make.

It's too easy to forget.

"Sir, I would suggest obtaining your own room." Wolfe covers his mouth, hiding it from the cameras. He pitches his voice low.

"Maria's suite will be sufficient." Liam guides me the rest of the way to the elevator.

Still no welcoming party.

I can't imagine Marco isn't anxiously awaiting my return. He'll want to see how I deal with the disappearance of Sybil. Suspicious by nature, he's a smart man. He'll also want to know what Liam means to me and how that changes the power dynamic between me and him.

My job is easy.

Love-struck, all I have to do is swoon over the Hollywood heart-throb beside me. I think I can do that; no acting involved. I've already fallen head over heels for Liam. I told myself not to. I told myself to focus on reality instead of the fairytale. I told myself it was all pretend.

And I didn't listen to any of my own advice.

Like I said, the swooning part is a done deal.

The elevator doors open and Liam ushers me inside. Wolfe and Brady follow. Their fierce stares keep any guests from sharing our ride. When Marco doesn't accost me downstairs, I assume he's waiting to do so in a less public space.

It's another reason I opt for my office. It's a safer space than my private suite. Also, once in my office, we can take the private flight of stairs up to my rooms. Marco's never stepped foot in my private space before, and I intend to keep it that way.

My outer office stands empty, as it should for a Saturday.

I let my staff go on the weekends. Just because I'm a workaholic doesn't mean I force them to endure the long hours I put in. I also live and work at the hotel.

In many ways, I'm always at work. Mother thinks it's a show of weakness, not forcing my employees to work the weekend.

It's one of a million things on which we disagree.

With a breath of relief, I pass by my receptionist's desk and place my hand on the doorknob. When did I start trembling? I'm not ready to face my uncle or my mother.

I never will be.

What I really need is a shower, some rest, and a bit of action between the sheets.

Thinking about sex with Liam brings a smile to my face. It's one of those massive smiles that lights up a room. I feel invincible, like I can conquer the world. My steps quicken and my heart races with all the deliciously naughty thoughts swirling in my head.

With thoughts of sex on my brain, it takes a moment before I realize we're not alone.

I slam to a halt as my mother's imperious gaze sweeps over and through me. Disapproval and disappointment vibrate in the air between us.

Perched on the edge of my desk, Mother sits like a regal queen holding court from her throne. Back ramrod straight, her shoulders push back as her overly critical chin lifts, passing judgment on her imperfect spawn. Her imperious gaze rakes over me, scalding and burning, condemning my existence.

"Maria, where have you been?" Her voice is tight, as if scolding a recalcitrant child.

Her overly critical disapproval brings my shoulders to my ears as I seek to make myself as small as possible. Embarrassment heats my cheeks.

Why does she always have to do this kind of shit around other people?

I know the answer to that.

She wants to make me feel small, and damn if it doesn't work.

36

LIAM

MARIA'S MOTHER IS ONE IMPERIOUS BITCH. I SHOULD MIND WHAT I SAY, especially since I'm meeting my future mother-in-law, but *holy shit*. She blinks, ever so slowly, with gut-wrenching animosity seething in the background.

No one speaks to Maria like that.

No one.

I don't care if the vicious shrew in front of me is Maria's mother, there's no way anyone will speak to Maria like that when I'm around. My intent was to sweep Maria's mother off her feet the same way I do most women—with flattery and my irresistible charm—but that's not how this will go.

I'll deal with the fallout later.

If I can teach Muriel Rossi a lesson while I'm at it, then all the better for Maria. I get a strong feeling Maria's been a victim of that woman's wicked tongue since the day she was born.

How a mother can hold so much bitterness for her daughter is beyond me. My mother went days without food, feeding me whatever scraps she could scrounge. She used her body to shelter me when we lived on the street. She worked her body to the bone trying to turn our lives around.

My mother did everything possible to surround me with love. It was the one thing I never lacked and could count on when we had nothing.

Maria grew up with everything except her mother's love. I believe people put too much weight on material things. I have the benefit of knowing what it means to be dirt poor and comfortably rich.

The things I had, and those I didn't, meant little to me because I always had what was important.

My mother's love.

As for Maria, she mentioned tension between herself and her mother, but this exchange is arctic cold. Frigid comes to mind. My heart breaks for Maria as the room bristles with tension. Her cheeks flush with embarrassment, and she ducks her head, trying to make herself disappear.

There's no love, no compassion, nothing which speaks to a maternal bond. What compels a mother to speak to her daughter like that?

And with strangers in the room?

Complete lack of respect.

Wolfe and Brady shift behind me. They feel the glacial temperature plunging the room into icy stillness. They're probably wondering how I'm going to react.

I turn toward Maria and brush the back of my fingers against her wrist. She turns her hand around, desperately seeking my touch, needing reassurance. Or maybe, she tenders an apology for her mother's chilly reception. Maria hunches her shoulders and tucks in her chin.

Maria refuses to look me in the eye. Yeah, her mother's icy reception cut deep.

Our fingers twine together, joining as one.

"You must be Muriel Rossi." I flash my megawatt smile at the arctic bitch. "Maria goes on and on about her beautiful mother."

That, at least, is a truth I can speak without stretching things too far. Muriel Rossi is a beauty for the ages: a stunning amalgamation of great genes with a team of personal trainers, dietitians, and plastic surgeons to keep everything tight and tucked.

She gave the blessing of those genes to her daughter, where they magnified a thousand-fold.

Muriel Rossi's facial features, however, twist like a shrew—a pretty shrew, but a disgusting rodent nonetheless.

"Young man, I don't know who you are, nor do I care. I will speak to my daughter alone." She flicks her fingers, dismissing me as if I'll run away with my tail tucked between my legs. "Run along." Another flick of her fingers punctuates her words.

Her harsh gaze takes in the imposing presence of Wolfe and Brady, who stand two paces behind me. Her lids draw back, ever so slightly, not intimidated by my bodyguards but irritated by their presence.

That gives me pause. This woman lets very little get under her skin.

Wolfe, dark hair, dark eyes, monstrous in size, intimidates by breathing. We all do. Brady has that same vibe, but it isn't in your face like Wolfe.

Wolfe looks like the boy from the wrong side of the tracks who grew into the dangerous criminal everyone fears. What they don't know is his devotion for defending those weaker than himself. He's a righteous force for good in this world.

Brady is different.

He's the boy next door: a man with a smile you can't help but trust —and shouldn't. From his sandy-brown hair to the freckles dusting his cheeks, he's the all-American hero everyone loves...with scars.

It's a double-edged sword with him. If a person's not careful, they'll assume he's one of the good ones.

Which, in Brady's defense, he is.

Eagle Scout, All-Star Quarterback, and Homecoming King, he's the boy all the mothers and fathers trusted to keep their daughters safe. He's also the boy who deflowered those dainty little virgins while laughing his ass off when he delivered them safe and sound, minus their virginity and much more experienced in the ways of men, back to those same trusting parents. The man destroys his enemies without batting an eye, precisely because they trust him.

Muriel Rossi isn't affected by either of them.

She's not affected by me.

Damn, she's stone cold and unfeeling.

"I'd like to say I'm happy to finally meet the mother of the woman I love, but last I looked, I'm not a dog for you to order around, and your daughter deserves a far better greeting than that arctic frost."

Her cold eyes bristle. I expect shock, not this spine-chilling challenge. Cold is too warm of a word for this woman. She's dispassionate, dismissive, dangerous, and cold enough to freeze hell.

Mitzy's words return to me.

This woman married her boyfriend's brother.

Why?

What was the draw?

Did Milo Rossi offer her more power and prestige than his younger brother?

Not just a cold-hearted bitch then, but a power-hungry one as well?

That could explain the subsequent marriage to Marco Rossi after her husband's death. Used to the power of the Rossi name, maybe she did what she could to maintain her position as matriarch of the Rossi empire?

It's possible, and if that's possible, is it likely Muriel Rossi is involved in the true business dealings of the Rossi family? The woman is definitely used to people kowtowing to her demands.

She's really not going to like me.

"Young man, if you know what's best for you ..." Her frigid gaze turns to me, "you'll leave me and my daughter alone."

"I've been told I rarely know what's best for me, and I'm inclined to raise your *Young man* and fire back with *Old crone*, but I'm a gentleman and it doesn't feel right getting into a pissing contest with a woman I've just met. I'll keep my opinions to myself, but ..." No way is this woman scoring one point in our little exchange. "As for leaving Maria alone with you, that's not happening. We've had a long night.

Despite the excitement and the news we can't wait to share with you, Maria's practically asleep on her feet. I'm not going anywhere except to take her to bed."

Yeah, I slipped that one in. All Maria and I have done is hold hands and kiss a bit, but I'm definitely interested in more. That comment was more for Maria than her mother.

Maria's mother's lids draw back. I don't give her a chance to respond and roll right past whatever she was going to say. Her mouth shuts as her fury builds.

"You're in the way of me achieving that goal. I'm all for extending respect, but I won't tolerate anyone speaking to the woman I love the way you spoke to her just now." I hold out my hand and give a little flick of my fingers, gesturing toward the door. "Now, run along. You're not wanted, nor needed."

Muriel Rossi's face flushes with indignation. She opens her mouth to respond, but I don't give her a chance to utter a single word.

"You *do not* want to test me." I tug Maria to my side and hold her mother's fierce gaze.

It takes mere seconds for Muriel to crack. Although, it's more of a strategic retreat. She's outnumbered and knows it.

What Muriel needs are reinforcements. Leaving is the only way for that to happen, which means she must cede this first victory to me.

"You have no idea whom you're speaking to, *young man*. Your lack of respect for your betters will come back to bite you."

"A mother who tears into her daughter in front of strangers doesn't deserve my respect. The next time we see each other, perhaps our exchange will be more civil? Until then ..."

Wolfe and Brady take two steps back.

With a dramatic sweep of my arm, I gesture toward the door. Muriel slides off her perch, face screwed up like the shrew she is, but the woman is not defeated.

"This is not the end of our conversation, Mr. ...?" Her left brow arches in question.

Muriel Rossi knows exactly who I am. The moment Gerald and

Stefan left that coffee shop, news of my arrival shot straight up to
Marco and his wife, but Muriel will never admit to the deep dive they
took into my background.

"Liam Cartwright." Instead of proffering my hand, I lift Maria's
hand to my lips, specifically her left hand. The one with my ring on
her ring finger.

The diamond glitters beneath the decorative halogen lights overhead. Muriel catches the flash of light with a tight press of her lips.
She says nothing as her shoulders snap back and the muscles of her
jaw bunch.

"Perhaps when we meet for brunch tomorrow, we can begin on a
different, more congenial, note. I apologize for my brusqueness. Your
daughter means the world to me, and I may be a tad over-protective
when those around her treat her poorly. Add to that a lack of sleep,
and this may not be the best first impression. I assure you, however,
that after a bit of rest and self-reflection, things will not be so strained
in the morning. I'm looking forward to getting to know Maria's family
better. We have much to discuss."

"Discuss? Oh, no doubt we do. Since Maria's mentioned brunch,
the invitation is for two. Your goons are not welcomed and can stay
behind."

"I go nowhere without my bodyguards."

"You won't need them, and before tomorrow comes around, I
suggest you reflect on how it's best to address the mother of your
fiancée, or you will lose her."

"I doubt that very much but understood about brunch. Until
then." Maria mentioned a back staircase that leads up to her apartment, but for the life of me, I can't locate it. "Love, do you mind? I'm
ready to crash." Once again, I lift Maria's hand to my mouth.

Muriel's glacial gaze zooms in on the diamond adorning her
daughter's fingers. This is when a normal mother would react to such
a thing, but Muriel pushes her shoulders back, lifts her chin, and
glides out of the room as if it's her choice to do so.

Maria says absolutely nothing during the entire exchange, but
her mouth gapes as she watches her mother storm out. Once the door

to Maria's office shuts, Maria lets out a rush of breath and punches me in the arm.

"Holy cow. What the hell just happened?" She looks from me to the door and back again. "I've never seen anyone do that before. Not even my father. The very few times the two of them argued, he never managed to leave her speechless the way you just did." She spins around and places a hand on my chest. "You were *amazing*. I wanted to cheer when you told her not to speak to me that way. No one's ever stood up for me like that."

The sad thing is that's probably the truth.

"No one should ever speak to another human the way your mother spoke to you."

"Well ..." Maria lifts on tiptoe and kisses my cheek. "You're officially my hero."

Before she pulls away, I whisper in her ear. "Are there recording devices in here? Cameras? Microphones?"

"In my office?" Maria lowers herself down. Her gaze sweeps her office. "There shouldn't be."

"Wolfe, make a sweep." I bark an order to Wolfe, addressing him as I would someone who works for the bold and brash venture capitalist, Liam Cartwright.

Wolfe hides a snicker as he pulls out a device from the inside of his jacket. Brady does the same. They work in silence while I look at Maria and try to decide how much support she needs or wants from me.

"I hope I didn't overstep."

"Don't apologize to me. That dominant vibe is only one of the many things I love about you." Maria cups the side of my face. "I wish I was strong enough to speak to my mother the way you stood up for me."

"I said too much." If there are devices listening in, this is an exchange they would expect. It also serves to remind Maria we have a cover to maintain. "Your mother must hate me."

"You definitely made one hell of a first impression."

Brady signals he found a device.

"Just the one?" I glance between him and Wolfe.

"One what?" Maria flutters her lashes, pretending not to understand.

"It looks like someone has been listening in on you." I release Maria and close the distance with Brady.

He pulls a picture off the wall, flips it over, and exposes a bug. I pinch the small device and hold it up to my eye.

"Luv, were you aware of this?" I twist back to Brady. "Is this the only one?"

Wolfe completes his sweep for bugs on the other half of the room. He signals there are, in fact, three more hidden devices.

"No sir, I found another." Wolfe moves to a lamp beside the sofa. Like Brady, he removes that bug. Wolfe brings the device over to me, where the three of us examine the listening devices.

"What's that?" Maria grips my arm. "A bug?"

"Looks like." I make a show of examining the device.

There's no doubt in my mind every move we make is being recorded and transmitted in real-time to someone assigned to watch over us.

Hell, it may be Marco sitting on the other end of this feed.

After the interaction between me and his wife, Marco would be wise to watch me. He won't be happy with another alpha male sniffing around his territory. No doubt, he's got his security team performing a deeper dive into my background.

Mitzy left a few gems for him to find: things like a string of girl-friends for hire during my younger, more wild days.

I didn't like that bit of backstory inserted into my fake life, but I respect its purpose. Marco needs dirt to hold over my head. Hell, maybe he'll offer me an opportunity to bid at one of his auctions.

Those auctions used to be exclusive, invite-only events held in the private compound of Benefield, deep in the interior of Colombia. After Guardian HRS closed down that horrific operation, how did Marco Rossi pivot?

Is it all online? That exposes significant risk. Or did they open up a new location? These are only some of the questions Mitzy hopes to find answers to, and she needs us to gather that information.

"No cameras?" I hand the bug back to Brady, who crushes the device beneath the heel of his shoe. Wolfe follows suit with the device he found.

"Not that we found." Brady signals the remaining devices are both video and voice recorders.

Fucking hell.

No stretch of the imagination as to why the devices are here. Marco would want to keep an eye on his niece and ensure she doesn't make any move he doesn't know about. I respect his paranoia. It's something I would do if I were in a similar situation.

We could clear all four bugs.

I want Marco Rossi to know I care about my conversations being bugged, but he needs to know I'm fallible. He needs to sniff weakness.

That's what will make him underestimate me.

"Thank you." I pivot to face Maria. "Luv, how about we hit the sack? I don't know about you, but I'm exhausted."

"Sounds perfect." Maria's lack of reaction makes me wonder if she knew about the bugs in her office.

Once we're in a place where I can speak freely, I'll let her know about the remaining two bugs. She can decide what she wants to do about those later.

Maria heads over to a bookcase and presses on a hidden lever. That portion of the wall pushes out and slides to the side, revealing a set of stairs leading upward.

"After you, my love."

I enjoy calling Maria *princess*. Initially, it annoyed her, and I used it to get a rise out of her, but then it kind of grew on me.

It's our thing now, one of those things unique to a couple. Giving it up for *my love* doesn't sit well with me.

I'm not eager to surrender *princess,* but it feels as if Liam Cartwright would dote on his bride-to-be. For now, *my love* it is.

Some of what I said to Maria's mother is a whole lot truer than I'd like to think. In the short time Maria and I have spent together, she's doing far more than growing on me. I may, in fact, be falling in love with my princess.

If I was in love with her, however, I wouldn't be following her up a flight of stairs to her private quarters. I'd yank her out of the Belvedere so fast she wouldn't know what was happening, and then I'd tell Forest, Sam, CJ, and Mitzy to shove their plan up their respective asses. Because I'd never put Maria in danger if I truly *loved* her.

Instead, I admire her sexy legs as she climbs a few steps in front of me and commit myself to completing this mission.

"I'm looking forward to a bit of shut eye." I rub at the back of my neck.

"Are you?" Maria twists to look at me over her shoulder. "And here I was looking forward to a shower."

"I'm up for a shower."

"Are you?" The direction of her gaze shifts to my crotch. Her tone goes from teasing to downright seductive. "Who said you were invited to share my shower?"

With that, she gives a little wiggle of her ass while I eagerly close the distance between us.

Behind me, Wolfe and Brady groan.

37

MARIA

Giddy and walking on cloud nine, I can't believe what happened back there. The way Liam dressed my mother down does all kinds of things to my insides.

First, there was the mortification jelling my blood. Mother is her cruelest at the most inopportune times. It's almost as if she saves up for the moments where her words will cut the deepest.

Her weaponized words do that and more. Ripping and shredding from the inside out as she cuts me down and treats me as a recalcitrant child. I wanted to curl into a ball and hide under a rock.

I'm not sure what I expected Liam to do, but standing up for me was the last thing on my mind. Holy hell, he didn't hold his punches. I've never seen anyone dress MD down the way he systematically took the wind out of her sails. She tried putting him in his place, using a derogative name, and he didn't hesitate striking back.

The best part was watching my mother retreat.

She'll get reinforcements. There's no doubt she's doing that right now, but he shook her. Liam struck at her foundations and my mother felt the shifting in power.

As for what comes next, I'm not entirely sure what we're supposed to do for the rest of the day. I'm even more confused about brunch tomorrow. I *think* she said we could come, minus Wolfe and Brady, but I'm not sure.

Our entire mission depends on getting access to my uncle's house. Mitzy's certain the information the Guardians need to shut down his human-trafficking operation won't be found within the walls of the Belvedere. She wants records of all the women who've been sold.

After that interaction between Liam and my mother, that standing invitation should've been revoked, but there will be a face-to-face with my mother tomorrow.

She saw the ring.

A yawn slips out as I reach the top of the stairs.

"You doing okay?" Liam bends forward to place a kiss on my shoulder.

"Tired? Overwhelmed?" My body is beyond exhausted. I press my palm to the bio-lock on the door leading into my private rooms.

Liam enters after me, but Wolfe and Brady stay behind.

"What are they doing?" My brows tug together.

"Sweeping for more bugs."

"There won't be any in the stairwell."

"Were there supposed to be any in your office?"

"No." I nibble on my lower lip, thinking about it. "Maybe?"

Liam pulls me to him. His arms wrap around me, and his fingers interlock at the small of my back.

"Stop doing that." His voice rumbles with something needy and primal.

"Stop what?"

"Nibbling on your lip. Makes me want to kiss you."

"And that's a bad thing?"

I have an idea about what I want to happen next. It may even be enough to fill up the rest of the day.

I stop nibbling on my lower lip, but that's only to sweep my tongue out to moisten my lips.

"Woman, you will be the death of me." He rocks his groin against me, letting me know he's turned on.

"All clear." Brady exits the stairwell.

"Did you find any?" Liam's attention shifts to the dark opening.

"Nothing in the stairwell." Wolfe enters next. Both men immediately scan the room.

"Good." Liam jerks his head to the left, toward the bedroom. "Begin your next sweep in the bed and bath."

"On it, boss." Brady heads into my bedroom. I left in a hurry last night and hope I didn't leave too much of a mess behind.

Wolfe closes the door to the stairwell. "Does this thing have a lock, or can anyone with the right biometrics enter?"

"I'm not sure."

"Who else might have access to it?" Wolfe definitely doesn't shy away from grilling me.

"Me, and the security team, obviously."

"What about your uncle? Or mother?"

"I switched everything out when I moved in. They shouldn't."

"Shouldn't?" Liam releases me and wanders around my living room.

"My uncle is more than capable of obtaining a key to any part of the Belvedere. My mother wouldn't. She'd tell my uncle."

"This is a nice place." Liam spins around.

I'm a minimalist at heart and that reflects in my decor. Clean, straight lines define the place. There are few decorations: an art piece on the table, a painting on the wall, and virtually no personal touches. My view is stunning, looking out on New Orleans. I try to see my apartment through Liam's eyes. It's stark, empty, and barely lived in, but I like it. I abhor clutter.

"Thank you."

My apartment makes up a good chunk of the floor it's on. The only other thing on this level is the security suite.

"Wondering how to place my men." Liam turns to Wolfe. "Brady's sweeping the bedroom and bath for bugs. You should start in here. Once done, Maria and I will be retiring to the bedroom for the rest of the day."

Rest of the day? It's hours before noon. I almost ask what he means when it hits me. Those butterflies in my belly wake up and flutter their wings.

"Then I should go and double-check Brady's work. Wouldn't want someone seeing, or hearing, something they shouldn't. I see the two entrances. Are there any more?" Wolfe's attention cuts to me. There's a twinkle in his eye. The guy misses nothing.

"Just the two." My cheeks heat, and it takes everything within me not to cover them with my hands.

I'm embarrassed Wolfe and Brady know exactly what Liam and I will be doing in the shower, on the bed, and wherever else while they're one room away.

If that happens.

"Sir, if you would ..." Wolfe glances at the front door of my apartment.

"Sure." Liam spins around and marches over to the front door.

"What are you doing?" I trail behind Liam, confused.

Wolfe disappears, joining Brady in my bedroom to check for bugs.

"Standing guard." Liam shrugs.

"Is that something you do a lot?" I remind myself to stay in character. "Why have the bodyguards then?"

"Because sometimes, I need them to be doing something else. I'm not exactly a small guy and can take care of myself."

"You're definitely not small." My gaze cuts to the prominent bulge in his pants.

"Come here." Liam holds out his arms. I take no time in rushing to him. His strong arms fold around me. "Your mother is a piece of work."

"She's something, all right."

"Does she always speak to you like that?"

"Sometimes, it's worse." I tuck my head beneath his chin. Dang, but he smells amazing. His heart thumps solidly beneath my ear.

"I didn't mean to start off on the wrong foot, but I couldn't stand her treating you like that." He kisses the crown of my head.

"We may be uninvited for brunch tomorrow."

"I'm not worried about that."

"Why not?"

"This rock on your finger changes everything. Or didn't you hear what she said?"

"I'm not sure I'm following."

"She said my bodyguards weren't welcome tomorrow. You and I are most definitely expected." Liam reaches for my left hand. He lifts the diamond between us.

"I'll call her later and confirm."

"Sir, the bedroom and bath are finished. We'll begin our sweep in here." Brady returns from my room, palm up; three devices

Anger churns in my belly. I get why there might be recording devices in my office. Marco would want to know what was happening there. Or maybe, the devices were installed by my father to spy on his brother. Either way, those devices are highly offensive.

My bedroom? Where I undress? Who's been watching me?

Wolfe exits my bedroom palm open, adding two devices, which sit in his outstretched hand. One of them is a camera.

Liam and the others destroy the bugs. They left a few in my office, which makes sense in a weird way. Liam sends Wolfe and Brady to make a second sweep of my room.

Another yawn escapes me. It's one of those whole-body things that make me want to curl into a tight little ball and sleep for ages.

"Time to get you in bed." Instead of sultry, dark, and devastating, Liam's words are down to earth and practical. There's no mischief flashing in his eyes.

No eagerness.

There's nothing suggestive, almost as if he wants to go to bed.

"Shower first, then bed." It's been a long night. I drag my eyes away from Liam, disappointed, and pause as Wolfe and Brady search my living room.

Cameras and listening devices in my bedroom? I can excuse them in my office, thinking Marco has some kind of right to know what goes on there, but my personal quarters?

Paranoid much?

Perverted perhaps?

Whatever it is, it's gross. I need the shower to scour that filth off my body.

"How are you holding up?" Liam closes the door behind me.

I feel the muscular build of his body behind me and suck in a ragged breath. It's the first time we've really been alone. Head bowed, I close my eyes and try to take another breath.

"Maria?" Liam closes the distance. Standing behind me, he places a hand on my shoulder. It's a soft touch, concerned, and calming.

"Sorry." I spin around and wrap my arms around his waist. Leaning into him, my cheek rests against his chest. The beating of his heart comforts me. "Bugs in my bedroom?" I lean back to look him in the eye. "Why?"

Liam glances down at me with those gorgeous eyes. He sweeps the hair away from my eyes and bends down to place a tender kiss to my forehead.

"Who's to know the what and why behind it, except it's clear you are more of a threat to your uncle than we thought."

"But why?" I bring my hands around and place them against Liam's chest. "I'm a threat to no one."

"Your uncle doesn't believe that."

"What do I do with that?"

"We remove you as a threat, doing exactly what we're doing now."

"And what is that?"

"Convincing those who watch you that we're serious about each other."

"I don't get how that helps."

"Right now, your uncle is watching all his bugs getting systematically destroyed."

"Sorry, either I'm more exhausted than I feel or not connecting the dots. How does that help?"

"Your mother, more than likely, is telling your uncle what happened in your office. She's relaying to him how I stepped up to protect you, how I *hovered* protectively over you, but most importantly, how I dressed her down and took control of the situation. That will give your uncle pause."

"Okay?" I'm not convinced.

"He also received your security detail's report about my body-guards. Right now, he's realizing not only how thorough I am, but how capable my security is."

"How does he know that?"

"The sweep they're making for bugs."

"But you left bugs in my office ..."

"I did. I wanted him to know a few things."

"What things?"

"That not only do I suspect he bugs you, but that I won't tolerate it."

"I don't get it."

"Initially, I left a couple bugs in your office because I wanted him to know I thought of such things, but my ability to detect and remove them wasn't perfect. After that conversation with your mother, and after finding more bugs in your bedroom, I want him to know exactly how *competent* my men are. After Wolfe and Brady remove the bugs in your apartment, they'll head downstairs and remove the remaining bugs in your office."

"Wow." I can't help but shake my head at the amount of thought Liam, and the rest of his team, put into pretty much everything.

"Tomorrow, we'll work on the next step."

"And what's that?"

"We'll arrive for brunch, whether disinvited or not, and announce our engagement. I'm interested in his reaction."

"How so?"

"He knows Liam Cartwright's business is in New York."

"And?"

"The next question is what will you do after we're married? Will you stay here, continuing to run operations at the Belvedere? Or will you return to New York to live with me?"

"Ah, I get it. It takes the pressure off Marco. Or rather me."

"Exactly. We remove you from the picture and see what Marco

does. Before the day is done, Mitzy will be fully integrated with everything that happens in the Belvedere, including the twenty-fifth floor."

"How? I don't understand all the tech behind it, but I'm pretty sure whatever systems he has in place on the twenty-fifth floor are completely separate from the rest of the Belvedere."

"And you're most likely correct." Liam pulls out the little drone Mitzy gave him. "Remember these?"

"Yes?"

Liam glances at the ceiling and heads to an overhead vent. He pulls off the grate and does something to the drone, turning it on.

Whisper quiet, the tiny rotors barely make a sound as the thing lifts off his hand to hover in the air. The optical skin covering the miniature drone does that thing to my eyes, making them slip over the drone. If I didn't watch it lift from Liam's palm, it would be completely invisible.

"You're putting it in the vent?"

"Best way to gain access to pretty much everywhere. People watch rooms, but no one thinks about what's behind the walls." His attention shifts to the drone. "Ready?"

The tiny drone lifts and lowers its front section, as if answering Liam.

"Is someone flying that thing?" For some reason, I thought it was autonomous.

"Knowing Mitzy, she's probably the one at the controls, but it can honestly be anyone."

"Gotcha."

I try to follow the drone as it flies up and into the vent. Liam's right about the Belvedere's security systems. We watch the rooms, the halls, the elevators, and all the common areas, including the employee-only areas. To my knowledge, there's nothing monitoring the ventilation shafts.

"How long will it take?"

"For what?" Liam replaces the cover to the vent after the tiny drone flies in.

"To do whatever it's supposed to do?"

He shrugs. "Honestly, I don't know."

"Now I know why you call it Mitzy Magic." Another yawn slips out of my mouth. I cover it with my hand, but Liam misses nothing.

His attention shifts to the door leading to the bathroom. "How about we get you in that shower and to bed?" There's a twinkle in his eye.

It's completely devastating.

And for whatever weird reason, I'm suddenly incredibly self-conscious. I'm not sure what to do, what to say, or what to do next.

"Princess ..." Liam sweeps out his arm. "It can be just a shower. I'm not pushing for it to be anything more."

"You're not?" My brows pinch together, a bit surprised by the comment.

"I'm not." His voice turns husky, a low throaty sound that turns my insides to jelly.

"You don't want to ..." I let my voice trail off.

"Oh, I want ..." He closes the distance between us and takes my hands in his. "I very much want, but like I said, we're putting on a show for others. In public, we touch, we kiss, we invade each other's space. We're a couple in every way. That doesn't extend to what we do in private."

"It doesn't?" I'm really confused.

"What happens between us when we're alone is separate from what happens in front of others. I don't want you to feel like you have to do anything you don't want to do. We did just meet. I would never assume ..." The husky timbre of his voice grows deeper, sexier.

"Oh ..." Then I get it. He's trying to be a gentleman. If he only knew I was the queen of casual sex, he wouldn't try so hard to resist. Casual hookups are my thing. It's the relationship thing where I fail.

"Consider this the green light." I reach up and begin unbuttoning his shirt.

The moment my fingers brush across the heat of his skin, Liam's body tenses. He places his hand over mine.

"About your green light ... what's on that list of yours?"

"What list?" I bat his hand away and continue unbuttoning his shirt. A strangled moan escapes him.

"You will be the death of me."

He doesn't move as I untuck his shirt and continue with the buttons. After I'm done with the last one, I push his shirt to the side and run my hands up the hardened ridges of his muscular physique.

I take my time. Letting my fingers feather along the defined ridges and valleys of masculine perfection, I can't help but lean in and take a long, slow inhale of his potent essence: wonderfully dark and virile.

My toes curl.

I lean in and press my lips against his chest. It's a light, reverent kiss and lasts but a second. I push back and stare into the dark depths of his eyes where his arousal shimmers and swirls.

Liam makes no move, giving me the time I need to admire his chiseled perfection. Beneath my hands, however, his entire body vibrates with suppressed need.

My hands skate down his washboard abs and land on his belt buckle.

"Love where you're going, princess, but this is a one-way road from here on out. If this is what you want, you need to know one thing about me."

"What's that?"

"I'm not a follower. I don't do gentle and sweet. You've got your list, so you know what it means when I say I'm dominant in bed. If any of that scares you, or is on your other list, we stop here."

"I don't want to stop." I pull the end of his belt through the buckle and let my actions speak for themselves.

He's aroused and hard. With my hands where they are, and my attention fixed on his belt, there's no denying his eagerness.

Or my willingness.

Heat curls in my belly. Anticipation rises within me.

I'm not into all things associated with green, yellow, and red. I'm too independent to slip into the submissive mindset, but I'm perfectly fine with letting a man lead.

With his belt loosened, I flick open the button of his pants and grab the pull tab of the zipper. Before I can lower it, his hand slams down, covering mine as a low growl escapes him.

I tear my gaze from what waits for me behind that zipper. All evening, I've fantasied about this moment; when I finally get to see what he's been teasing me with all night.

Liam curls his fingers in my hair and leans in real close.

"First rule ..."

My breath hitches as the deep, rumbly sound from his throat hijacks my senses. A whole-body quiver begins at the top of my head and rolls through me all the way to my toes.

Liam leans down, the heat of his breath washes over my neck as he places his lips on the curve of my ear.

"Ladies always come first."

With that, Liam sweeps me off my feet and carries me to bed.

38

LIAM

From the moment Maria pointed her gun at me, I've thought about this moment.

There's something about a strong woman that gets under my skin. I love the power and confidence melded with feminine sensitivity and gentleness. It's a goddamn aphrodisiac.

Now, I'm a man on a mission, and I didn't lie. While I fuck like I fight; full of fire, passion, and determined to achieve results, the woman always comes first. If she's not happy, I'm not happy.

When I enter a woman, I engage my entire body, dedicating everything—not to fighting—but to dispensing pleasure.

But I don't fuck gently.

I didn't lie to Maria about that.

I'm as aggressive in the field as I am in bed; an assertive and unstoppable force, driven to achieve one objective—pleasure.

And I take what I need, whatever that may be in the moment.

Most moments, it's nothing more than satisfying a physical urge, first for my partner and then for me.

This isn't that.

Not by a long shot.

My entire being engages, driving not for a satisfying fuck with a woman who's name I won't remember in the morning.

Hell no.

That's not what this is about.

I'm going for complete domination, a joining of souls. I aim to sear my essence into every piece of Maria's mind, body, and soul. She'll never want another man after me.

That's my goal, and she's already done that to me.

I'm irrevocably tied to her. Now, it's my turn to show her why she belongs to me.

My days of playing the field and sowing my oats stopped the moment I tumbled into the sapphire depths of her turbulent gaze. My protective instincts flared, roaring to life in an explosion of possession and need I was helpless to evade.

"What about a shower?" Maria clings to me as I march toward her bed.

"Oh, you'll need a shower after I'm done with you."

I settle Maria on her feet at the foot of the bed.

"Why am I suddenly terrified?" Maria's cheeks are two shades past the pretty pink of her usual blushes.

"Because I'm about to erase the memories of all the men who came before me and ruin you for any man but me from here on out." I point to her pretty blouse, the one I've wanted to remove all night. "Take off your blouse."

She nibbles her lower lip, hesitating. It's cute seeing her turn from the sultry vixen, tearing off my shirt, to this shy creature standing in front of me.

I shake my head and deepen my voice to a rumbling growl. "Don't test me, princess. Second rule ..."

Her eyes widen and her pupils dilate. Those rosebud lips of hers part as she gets ready to say something. I place my finger over her lips and give another shake of my head.

"All I want you to do is feel. No words. Understood?"

It's a bold move, one that will wildly succeed or fail horribly. Despite her mention of having a list, I don't get the vibe she's really into the whole dominant/submissive game, but I'm willing to test her limits.

Maria slowly nods. Her lips press together, showing me she's at least willing to explore some limits.

"Now, as for that second rule. No hesitation."

"No hesitation?" Her left brow quirks up. "What does that mean?"

"You do as I say without hesitation."

Her chin trembles and her shoulders roll back in defiance, but she doesn't challenge me.

"If you're not up for it, you don't hesitate to tell me no. I'll readjust with no judgment. I'll never be upset with the truth, and you can't disappoint me. It's perfectly okay to say no. Is that understood?"

Her eyes shimmer. Women are emotional creatures I don't fully understand, and her tears slam into me like a physical force. A sucker punch to the gut, I stagger with her vulnerability and what we're about to do.

It's not about sex.

This is an emotional moment for us both. Yes, we're going to fuck —several times if I have my way—but this isn't about physical release and bodily pleasure.

This is about us becoming one.

I fold Maria into my embrace and marvel at my body's response. My dick is hard, harder than it's ever been. My heart races, excited for what comes next. My blood surges through my body, setting up every nerve for action.

I feel Maria deep within me, becoming a part of me. All her emotions swirl and tangle with mine, joining together where they dance and twirl and weave into something too complex for words.

"Maria," I lean back, "is that understood?" I can't move forward if she doesn't answer.

"Understood." Her lower lip quivers. Nearly imperceptible, it's there, nonetheless.

"Good." I release her and take two steps back. "Now, about that blouse." I deepen my voice, using vocal registers below a growl. "Take it off."

I could take it off myself. I considered it, but I want Maria to reveal herself to me. It would be too easy for me to lose control, and I'm barely holding on as it is. Every primal instinct inside me tells me to grab, rut, and claim.

I'll do that ... eventually.

But I'm not rushing our first time.

Maria glances down at her blouse, then peeks up at me, fluttering those phenomenal lashes of hers. The ring on her finger glitters in the light and I hate it.

I hate the pretense behind it—the lie it stands for. I hate that something fake glitters on her finger where there should be something of mine in its place.

And that's when I realize how far I've fallen. I stagger back as Maria releases the first of far too many buttons.

She looks up at me and our gazes crash together, tumbling about as our breaths deepen and our mutual arousal floods the space between us.

"All of them ..." Another low growl rumbles outward from my chest. I want to push further. A natural dominant, I'm used to controlling every facet of sex with a woman.

But I take my cues from Maria.

What I find is I'm slowly losing the battle to stay in control. All I want is to lunge forward, rip the offending fabric from her body, and enter her in one ravaging thrust. My mind swirls as my thoughts become muddy and my instincts struggle against my restraint.

To rut. To fuck. To claim. To take.

"Faster." My word comes out forcibly, an order she jumps to obey.

Her fingers flutter as the last of the buttons let go. Her chest heaves, deep breaths lift and lower the creamy swell of her breasts which makes it hard to swallow against the sudden lump in my throat.

"The bra." My fingers curl into fists as I struggle to contain myself.

Maria obeys immediately. She reaches behind her, doing what I should do, and the clasp of her bra releases. Holding her arms over her chest, the satin and lace of her bra stays in place, infuriating me.

"Drop it." I take half a step toward her, fingers tightening into fists as my need becomes intolerable.

The left shoulder strap of her bra slips off her shoulder. I ache to close the distance between us to kiss her creamy skin, but I resist. I know what I want, and patience is required.

I glare when she hesitates and growl low in the back of my throat. Then I rip off my shirt and toss it to the ground, demanding she bare herself to me as I bare my body to her.

"All of it." Another throaty growl escapes me. My cock throbs painfully as more blood races to fill it. "Unless you want me to tear it to shreds ..." I let my words trail off, letting her fill in what might happen next.

It's no secret. I'll lunge forward, obliterating the space between us, then I'll rip and shred her clothing until she's naked and mine.

Maria jumps, startled by my words, but she hastily complies. The bra flutters to the floor as she stands with her arms crossed in front of her.

I won't have that.

"Hands by your side, princess. Push those perky tits out where I can see them."

A moment passes while she wars with her inner demons. She's a proud and fiercely independent woman. While not against surrendering control during sex, it's not something that comes naturally. I love that I get to witness her inner struggle and the result that follows.

Maria sucks in a breath. Her arms move in short, jerky fits until they hang by her sides. Her rosebud nipples draw up into tight little buds, and the expanse of her chest, her neck, and her beautiful face flush the most perfect shade of pink.

I'm not against rewarding her. My fingers grasp the pull on my zipper. With her eyes widening as I make my intentions clear, I slowly ease down the zipper. Once down, I hook my fingers over the waistband of my pants, then look down at my shoes.

With a grin, I peek up at her, and can't help but laugh.

"Forgot the shoes."

Maria giggles as I hurriedly kick off my shoes, then stand as if that didn't happen. She mirrors my movement and toes off her heels. Her toes wriggle and dig into the carpet as she nibbles on her lower lip and waits for me.

Getting control of myself, my super sexy striptease ruined by that, I pretend it never happened and move right back into my dominant headspace. When I remove my pants, there's no way to hide my arousal.

My dick bobs eagerly behind the cotton of my boxer briefs. It aches for Maria. I can't help my rabid need to hurry this along and fist the shaft, squeezing hard to remind my dick which one of us is in control.

That gets Maria's attention.

Her eyes round as I fist my dick, and the tip of her tongue peeks out from between her luscious lips. Man, I can't wait to feel her mouth on me, but that comes later.

I wasn't kidding when I said ladies come first.

"The skirt." My skin tightens as she slowly lowers her skirt. Her pink, satin panties match the silk and lace of her bra. I should've had her lower the skirt before her bra. Now, I have to imagine what she'd look like in her panties and bra.

I'll save that for later. As she kicks away her skirt, Maria stands before me, nearly nude.

"Lie down." I point to the bed, then repeat myself when she doesn't immediately comply. "Lie down, princess. I'm not accustomed to repeating myself."

Eyes wide, mouth parted, Maria sits on the foot of the bed, then slowly inches her way back. She doesn't technically lie down, but I'll give her a pass for that. Before she scoots too far back, I hold up my hand.

"Far enough." I move to the foot of the bed, stopping when the mattress touches my legs. Here is where I pause, debating my next move.

My body is too keyed up. The slightest touch will set me off, and I intend to enjoy myself for the rest of the day, with no plans to leave this room.

"Do you want to see me?" I tighten my grip on my cock as it jerks, sending tiny electrical shocks to the base of my spine. It won't take much for me to come.

"Yes." Her breathy reply is like crack to my dick. It jerks again, sending more sensation to spark and sizzle at the base of my spine.

"Do you want to feel me?"

"Yes." Her lower lip curls inward and those sapphire eyes of hers are so blown out with lust that they're nearly black. "I want it all."

"Tell me what you want."

I could dive right in, rip those panties from her body and plunge right in, but I'm a fan of foreplay. I'm a fan of the mental games that come from hitching things up a notch and exploring mutual fantasies.

"I want to see it."

"It?" I can't help but laugh. "Do you mean my cock?"

"Yes, Liam. I want to see your cock. You've been teasing me with it all night long."

"I wouldn't say all night."

"Um, the dance floor?"

"What about the dance floor?" My grip tightens on my cock as it bucks and jerks, eager to dive into her mouth or slam into her pussy.

"Seriously?"

"Yes, seriously."

"Okay, I've fantasized about your cock all night long."

"What kind of fantasies?" I can't help but tease.

"Do you really expect me to answer that?" She can't keep her gaze off my cock.

"If I make it a command, will you answer?" I test her limits, curious how far I can push things.

Her lower lip curls inward again and her body shudders. There are certain things Maria likes and I love this process of discovery. She may be more submissive in bed than I initially realized.

This could be a lot of fun.

"It's no secret what I want." Her breathy answer makes me lean forward to make sure I heard right.

"Then tell me."

"I want you to fuck me. Hard and fast would be perfect. You're killing me right now, slowing this down."

"Is that all?"

"No, that's not all." She crosses her arms, covering her breasts. Then her head dips. Her lashes flutter.

"Tell me."

"I want my hands on you."

"Oh, I like that. Is that all?"

"No."

"What else?"

Maria drops her arms and shifts on the bed. Coming to her knees, she crawls to me.

Holy-ever-loving-fuck-me, but that's fucking hot.

"Maria ..." My tone is low, warning, and strained to the breaking point. She suddenly turns the tables on me, and I'm not ready for that.

Maria on her hands and knees is the most incredible thing I've ever witnessed. She reaches the edge of the bed and looks up at me. With a flick of her lashes, she seals my fate.

"Let me show you what I want." Maria practically glides down to the floor. There's no other way to describe it. I may be functioning on two working brain cells, but I swear she floats to the floor. All the blood in my body rushes to my cock, as she kneels before me.

She reaches for the waistband of my briefs and pulls them down. I still grip my cock, too afraid to let go. I'll embarrass myself if she touches me. Gritting my teeth, I do everything in my power to hold back my impending release.

And she still hasn't touched me.

Maria pauses when I don't release my grip. Her lashes flutter as she looks up at me. I about jump out of my skin when her hand grazes my cock. She releases my grip, finger by finger, as I huff against the need rising within me.

This is not how I wanted tonight to go. I wanted to bury my face between her creamy legs, taste her sweet essence, and listen to her scream my name as I made her come on my tongue, my mouth, my face, and eventually my cock.

With my grip released, Maria slowly removes my briefs, helping me step out of them as my cock bobs between us, eager and weeping for stimulation of any kind.

I try to rally my command of this situation but jerk violently as she presses her lips to the crown. I stagger back, then look down as her head bobs forward. She grabs me at the base of my cock, and her sinfully hot mouth slowly encases me as my toes curl and my fingers grasp at her hair.

The familiar feel of a condom makes me groan.

Holy fucking shit, she puts it on with her mouth. When did ...?

My eyes roll into the back of my head as she takes me fully into her mouth. Her fingers finish the job of sheathing me as her mouth draws back, making my entire body shake.

Shit, I'm going to fall on my ass if she continues.

Maria kneels before me, hand on my cock, eyes dancing with amusement.

"Bet you didn't expect that?" Oh yeah, she's fucking pleased with herself.

I give her props for knocking me off my game. This may not go the way I planned, but it's still moving full steam ahead.

"For the record, my answer is yes," she says.

For the life of me, I can't remember what question she's answering. My fingers curl in her hair as she leans forward and takes me fully into her mouth.

The heat of her mouth wraps around me and surrounds me as she swallows me whole. Fuck, but the woman has a talented mouth, and what she does with her tongue? That swirling, flicking thing? She sends me up and up and up. I rock up on my toes as she sucks my cock. My thighs tremble as her tongue flicks all the best spots. When her hand wraps around the base of my cock, I practically levitate off the floor.

I don't embarrass myself, but only just. Within minutes, my entire body shakes as my release plows through the last vestiges of my restraint. But then Maria takes things one step further as she presses down hard just behind my balls.

Holy fucking intense.

It doesn't stop. On and on, pleasure sweeps through me.

"Holy fuuuuck!" I call out as my hips buck and jerk.

My fingers dig into her hair, tugging and pulling as the world spins and rushes toward me. With one last spasmodic jerk, my release is spent. Out of breath, and on wobbly legs, I barely control my body as I hook my hands under her arms. I lift her up and toss her onto the bed.

I'm a man on a mission and she is mine.

Before she can even bounce, I'm on her. My fingers claw at her panties. The fabric rips as I tug it down and around her hips. Her heady essence floods my nostrils as I slide the fabric down her legs.

With my hands beneath her knees, I fall to mine, hitting the floor with a thud. I tug her ass to the edge of the bed, hook her knees over my shoulders, and spread her creamy thighs. Her glistening pussy calls to me, and I dive right in.

With a lick of her slit, her hips buck. With my mouth on her clit, the first of her cries fills the room. My tongue lashes mercilessly, driving her higher and higher. I bring my fingers into play, thrusting them deep into her pussy. Thrusting in and out, I curl my fingers until I hit *that* spot.

Her back arches. Her tits push up. I give one last lick of her slit.

It's time to end this maddening dance. A man can only stand so much. The need to be inside of her is all-consuming.

I place a tender kiss to her inner thigh. It will be the last tender thing I do, then crawl up the expanse of her luscious body.

Making a detour at her tits, I can't help but nuzzle and lick.

"You're fucking amazing, princess."

"You're not so bad yourself." Her fingers twirl in my hair, twisting lazily as I fully acquaint myself with her breasts.

"Don't judge yet."

"I wasn't ... I just meant ..."

"Luv, we're just getting started." I wedge myself between her legs, letting the broad flare of my cock bounce at her entrance.

Her eyes round as I make my intent clear. Yeah, we're done with the slow and gentle thing. Now that she took the edge off my insatiable need, I can take things slow.

But slow doesn't mean gentle, not when it comes to me and sex.

39

MARIA

Phenomenal doesn't begin to describe Liam's brand of lovemaking. I thought long and hard about how our first time would go. Each potential scenario is one I tossed out, looking for something that would be memorable.

It's rare that I go down on a man before we've had sex, but I wanted to do that for Liam. Somehow, I knew he was the kind of lover who put his partner's needs above his own. I wanted to tip that on its head and surprise him.

I'm pretty pleased with how well the blowjob went. It surprised Liam. Score one for me. I thought it would give me a sense of control. In many ways, he scares me. I figured if I could just control that one thing, then I wouldn't be scared to surrender the rest of me afterward.

I don't know what I was thinking. Liam wrung out one of the most explosive orgasms I've ever experienced with nothing but his mouth and that wicked tongue of his.

He takes his time getting to know my body. My nerves fire off constantly, little zings of electricity that coil in my belly and build from there. I sense him everywhere. The heat of his body sinks into mine. His heady scent, something dark and masculine, floods my senses until I breathe him in and out. His breath flutters across my chest, drawing my nipples into tight little buds. Heat from his mouth makes me arch into him. Then a cold chill makes me shiver when he withdraws.

Fucker is having fun with me.

His nose brushes against my ear, and his husky whisper makes me squirm.

"You are incredible, princess. Fucking amazing."

"You're not so bad yourself."

"Luv, I've barely begun ..." And with that, Liam shifts his weight.

The broad head of his cock presses against my slit and I can't help the shameless whimper escaping my lips. I'm both excited and terrified of what comes next. He's on the larger side of things when it comes to cocks; definitely the biggest I've experienced.

Liam holds himself over me. His heavy body barely touching mine. Skin to skin, I feel him everywhere. My eyes close. I nibble on my lower lip ... waiting for what comes next.

"Maria ..."

"Yes?"

"Last chance to put a stop to this. Fair warning, once I'm inside of you, you're going to come like you've never come before. Pleasure, like you've never known, will rush through you. I aim to ruin you for all other men. My cock will be the only one that matters from here on out."

The possessiveness of his tone brings goosebumps to my skin, making me shiver with the weight of what he means. I press my lips together and do my best to think. Which is impossible when all I feel is Liam surrounding me and drowning me in pleasure unlike anything I've known before.

"There's one other thing you need to know." He shifts slightly, adjusting his weight. The plump head of his cock bounces against my folds. I want to move my hips, change the angle, and impale myself on his cock.

But Liam holds me down.

"What?" My thoughts move slowly in my lust fogged state.

"You're mine. Now and forever, you're mine." With those words, his hips thrust forward.

His cock breaches my walls and slams all the way home. His half-hooded eyes close completely as he buries himself to the hilt. Chest to chest, he keeps most of his weight off of me. His powerful arms bracket me. Tight and toned forearms press against my head. He stares down at me, mouth a whisper away as he seats himself as deeply as he can.

"Do you feel me, princess?" He changes the angle and slides in deeper. "That's me making you mine." That mouth of his brings a smile to my face. Those full, pillowed lips, along with that wicked tongue of his, pull screams of pleasure from my throat.

But that's nothing compared to the heat coiling in my gut. Liam settles over me, staring down at me as my entire body quivers. Suddenly, he stops.

"What's wrong?"

"Nothing's wrong." His eyes twinkle as he stares down at me. "I'm simply enjoying how you feel wrapped around me. I'm savoring the moment."

"Don't savor it for too long. I need you to move."

"You do?"

"Yes." I'm breathless for no reason, but it's a struggle to string more than a few words together.

He wiggles his hips. The motion sends tingles of pleasure shooting through me. It's not enough. Not enough by a long shot. I grab his ass and pull him to me while I strain to rise up to meet him. If he's not going to fuck me, I'll do what I can.

I need more friction. More movement. I need to feel him lose control.

His low, throaty chuckle leads to me punching at his chest.

"It's not funny."

"Luv, there's no way in hell I'm letting you set the pace. Your only job is to feel. Nothing else matters."

"Then move already." I'm not against begging. "I need you to fuck me."

"I'm literally buried balls deep right now. I'd say this counts as fucking."

"You know what I mean." I punch him softly on his arm. "You're killing me."

He shifts to the side, freeing one hand. Cupping my face, his thumb circles over the skin of my cheek. His touch ignites a riot of sensation, pure unadulterated pleasure surges within me. Tiny tremors make my body shake as the slow, sensual slide of his fingers against my skin makes me close my eyes and float in a sea of pure bliss. He teaches my body how to crave him, and I know he's right about ruining me for any other man.

Liam lifts his head. Our eyes lock for a second before he lowers his mouth to my breast. The heat of his mouth brings a moan to mine. Then a screech as his teeth clamp down on my nipple. Before I process that pain, he shifts to the other breast, kissing and suckling, until my entire body shakes.

His hot mouth and talented tongue bring a rush of heat to my skin. From my breasts to my neck, he lays a devastating path behind him. My fingers dig into his scalp, pulling and tugging at his hair as I try to swallow the moans escaping my mouth.

Holy hell, another release coils in my belly. My skin draws tight as my entire body trembles. A light sheen of sweat covers our bodies, unusual because we aren't exactly exerting ourselves.

At least, I'm not.

I lie beneath him, captured and contained, while he licks and sucks, leaving no part of my body unexplored. Pleasure curls within me, coiling into a tight spiral, that when it releases, will leave me forever changed.

"Liam ..." Breathless, I pant with the need for more.

"Yes, princess?"

"Please."

"Please, what?"

"Please fuck me."

"That is my intent."

"No, I mean now. Put me out of my misery and *fuck me.*"

"Misery?" He huffs a low laugh. "But I'm not done staking my claim." He licks up the side of my neck and nibbles on my earlobe. A low, keening wail escapes me, equal parts frustration and need. "You are incredible. Sinful. Addictive. I'll never get enough of this."

The heat of his breath whispers across my skin. My nostrils flare with the heady scent of him. I miss the moment everything changes, but his cock drags against the walls of my pussy and then stabs forward in one powerful thrust. Gasping with sensation, he sheaths himself to the base of his cock. Liam doesn't stop there. He rocks in and out, picking up speed. His breaths turn to low, determined grunts as he goes deep, fucking me.

My hands move of their own accord. They're everywhere, grappling to hold on while his body ruts and fucks. I spread my legs as wide as I can, encouraging him to go as deep as he wants.

His thrusts turn savage, animalistic, primal ... as he slams in and pulls out. He builds up a rhythm that makes my body writhe beneath him. There's pleasure. There's pain. There's the strangest amalgamation of the two. He hits my g-spot with lethal precision, obsessive in his goal to drive me wild.

I've had sex before. I've been fucked rough before. But I've never been possessed in the way Liam takes control. He fucks with a beautiful and unapologetic brutality, forcing me to feel every inch of him as his essence floods my body and claims every cell within me.

He kisses while he fucks, tongue tasting, teeth nipping, mouth sucking with fevered intensity. My senses can't keep up with what he delivers. My breathing turns ragged and uneven, and just when I don't think he can go any deeper, he proves me wrong.

Stretching me with those powerful thrusts, he pins me to the bed, making it impossible for me to move.

"Fuck, but you feel like heaven." His hips buck, surging harder, faster. He pulls back, only to ram his steely cock deeper and deeper.

His hand reaches up, gathering my hair in his fist. Controlling my head, he claims my mouth as he takes and takes. He's merciless in his plunder. Ravenous with his need. And he claims with heat and virility, a dominant male who gives as good as he takes.

And just like that, he destroys everything I've known about sex. I've never felt anything like this before. In surrender, I find strength. Everywhere he touches me turns into a blaze of heat surging through me. A firestorm of need and want heats my blood as my insides twist and tighten. My nerves are overwrought, sizzling as pleasure courses through them to settle in a fiery blaze deep within me.

Liam's demanding rhythm falters above me. I gasp into the gap and dig my nails into the skin of his shoulders.

"Yes. More. Please. Don't. Stop." I've been reduced to uttering single words.

Liam regains his rhythm, controls it, and slows it down. My hands stay on his shoulders, holding on. Pleasure sparks within me, then rushes out all at once, obliterating me as it burns through me. My grip tightens as I curl around him, then I let go, my back arching as wave after wave of pleasure sweeps through me.

Over top of me, Liam's legs tremble as he chases his release. With a shout, his body bucks as he chases his release and joins me on the other side of Heaven.

My mouth is dry. My lips cracked from breathing through my mouth. But there's a smile on my face. I press a hand over my heart, feeling the glowing presence Liam left behind. He inscribed himself on my heart, forever joined together no matter what comes next.

We lie in a twisted pile of limbs, talking about nothing and everything. He holds my hand, tracing out the lines on my palm. We make love again, softer this time, less frantic and rushed, almost as if we have all the time in the world.

Eventually, there's no escaping the fatigue chasing us. My lids bounce and beside me Liam's breath turns even as sleep overtakes him. I lie beside him for some time, admiring the man beside me and laughing at the way our lives intersected.

Soon, my breathing slows, and I lose the battle to keep my eyes open. I curl around Liam's powerful frame, my back pressed against his front. He shifts in his sleep and wraps his arm around my waist. Tugging me tight against him, I feel delicate and fragile, sublimely feminine. What I don't feel is weak or needy.

Breathing in his unique scent, I silence the chaos in my head and the fear in my heart. Slowly, fatigue draws me under, and I fall asleep in Liam's embrace.

Evil may walk the world, but in this moment, in Liam's arms, everything is absolutely perfect.

40

LIAM

KNOWING WOLFE AND BRADY GUARD OUR PRIVACY, I LINGER IN THE beauty that is Maria Rossi. For the past hour, I've watched her sleep, unwilling to wake her before she's ready. She looks so fragile and delicate, yet I've seen the woman fight. I've seen her stand up for her friend even while the rest of her world crumbled around her. I wish I could protect her from her family, but I sense she needs to fight that battle alone.

It's hard for me to step aside. I'm a Guardian. Dedicated to saving those in need. If I can't fight her battles for her, I will stand by her side, lending what support I can.

Feeling better after a brief nap, restless energy surges within me. I need to get up and check in with my teammates, but I'm loathe to slip out of bed. I don't want to leave her, even for a second.

Miss Maria Rossi, my princess, somehow you worked yourself into my heart.

I don't regret taking a break from the mission. We both needed sleep, but it's getting late. Later than I'd like, but probably best for our little act. Marco Rossi is watching every move we make, trying to assess what kind of threat I pose and how much Maria knows about the kidnapping of her friend.

They're going to see nothing but the truth. We're two lovebirds spending the day in bed. Funny how our fake engagement doesn't feel that fake anymore.

I never understood why my teammates fell for their women. It always felt rushed, like they dove headfirst into the abyss, mindless of the jagged rocks waiting below—oblivious, or uncaring, of the danger they faced.

There's a reason I don't do relationships ... or didn't. Maria got to me. She tunneled right into my heart, where she filled in all the empty bits inside. She's a part of me now.

I understand why Axel fell for his girl. He and Zoe share a history. Not a good one. Axel was a royal asshole to Zoe growing up. He thought her infatuation nothing but an annoyance, never realizing his true feelings.

Her abduction released whatever needed to be knocked loose in Axel's head. The man was driven to rescue his childhood friend, then realized Zoe stole his heart somewhere along the way.

The same can be said for Griff. Moira is a fighter, a survivor. She knows how to take care of herself. He was with us when we rescued Moira in the Philippines, then trained her at The Facility in the art of self-defense. She had no idea who her Guardian trainer was, but Griff always made sure he was paired with her. I think he's been soft for her since her first rescue. It hurts to think that Moira suffered so much for so long. She still fights those demons. But Griff's love is exactly what she needs to heal.

When Max found Eve, he thought she was the enemy. She was taken by Benefield, held hostage for months, and did what she needed to survive. During her captivity, she never gave up hope of rescue. And not just for herself.

It's due to Eve's foresight that the Guardians are as close as we are now to bringing down the Rossi's human-trafficking operation. She found the ledgers with the lists of client names and the women who were purchased. That list ultimately led us to the Belvedere and the Rossi's.

Knox and Lily started off as adversaries. She thought he worked for criminals bringing drugs into the USA. When she learned the truth, the two of them became partners, then lovers.

Wolfe and Jinx decoded the ledgers Eve discovered, working brilliantly together once they stopped fighting their attraction for each other. They uncovered the names of six girls who were slated to be taken and sold.

Sybil's name was on that list.

The Guardians came to that information late, and we nearly lost those women. Alpha team, augmented by two of our new Protectors, rescued Sybil and the other two women, while Wolfe and I, along with Jinx and Lily, rescued the remaining three. That brought me face to face with Maria and the barrel of her gun pointed at my chest.

Looking down at Maria, I want endless moments like this. I can't help myself from kissing her shoulder, a light touch, which doesn't wake her. She looks so fragile and innocent. I wish I could hold her in my arms forever, but I can't. There's work to do.

I slip out of bed, without disturbing her, and take a quick shower. Rather than put on the clothes I wore last night, I head out into the living room with a towel wrapped around my waist.

Wolfe looks up at me from a recliner but says nothing. Brady stretches out on the couch. Thick blankets cover his face. I get it. They split the shifts. Brady's on the night shift.

My buddy points to the dining room. I stroll over, happy to see clothing was provided while I slept. With my back to Wolfe, I drop the towel and slowly get dressed. He says nothing, although I expect some kind of dig from him. Maria and I weren't exactly quiet earlier, but if he says anything to disrespect Maria, I will take him out.

"What's the status on Mitzy's drones?" I zip my pants and move to the buttons of my shirt. With Brady sleeping in the other room, I keep my voice low. The drones we launched into the air ducts have had a couple of hours to do their thing.

"Nothing to report." Wolfe places his hands behind his back and widens his stance. "No servers for her to scour. No hidden rooms with other victims."

"Seems too clean."

"I agree."

"He can't hide from Mitzy."

"I'd say your gut is true as far as Marco Rossi goes, but whatever dirt he's hiding, it's not at the Belvedere."

"Anything I need to know?"

"Mitzy's recalling the drones come morning. She wants as much time as possible in case there's something she missed. Is brunch still on for tomorrow? Or did you get yourself disinvited the way you dressed down her mother?"

"I'm not sure, but I doubt it. Her mother's scrambling, trying to find out everything she can about Liam Cartwright." I fasten the cuffs on my sleeves and tuck in my shirt. "Maria's still sleeping. We'll have to wait and see when she wakes up."

"What are your plans for tonight?" Wolfe arches a brow.

A quick glance at my watch reveals we have an evening to kill.

"What do you think? Safer to stay here and eat in? Should we dine in one of the hotel restaurants? Or should we go out?"

"Mitzy has an idea about that."

"She does?"

"She wants you to play at the tables."

"I'm not much of a gambler."

"No, but you've got the best eyes to help you out."

"Too risky. I don't want to get caught cheating. That's a sure-fire way to cut this operation off at the knees."

"Then play to lose. Winning or losing isn't really the point."

"Then what is?"

"That you are too fucking rich to care if you drop a hundred grand at the tables."

"Hate to lose that much cash."

"You might win." Wolfe doesn't give a damn one way or the other. Easy for him to blow through Guardian cash. He won't be the one everyone's laughing at. "What are you best at? Poker? Blackjack?"

Poker is more Max's thing. He fooled all of us, making us think he had a gambling addiction. The truth is far different and sobering.

Me?

Not so much.

"How about craps or roulette?" Wolfe doesn't let up.

"Suck and suck some more. Why not go out?"

I was thinking of doing something extravagant.

"Mitzy suggested we stay in the hotel, limit our excursions outside where we have less coverage. If you want to play craps or spin the wheel, it's up to you. Shit, you can feed quarters into a slot machine for all I care."

"Slots aren't a Liam Cartwright worthy endeavor." I roll my shoulders back and sniff with indignation. It's time to get serious and fully embrace the persona Mitzy built for Liam Cartwright.

"Your pick. Meanwhile ..." Wolfe joins me in the dining room. "Mitzy sent info on Marco's home. It's ..." His voice trails off.

"It's what?"

"Impressive." Wolfe gives a slow shake of his head.

"How so?"

"It's a fucking fortress." Wolfe pulls up a set of schematics on his computer. "Unique architecture."

"That does sound interesting." I peer at the drawings, not impressed at first ... but then I see the understructure.

Not a basement. Nothing so simple. The complex structure laid out before me is nothing short of jaw-dropping.

"What the fuck is that?" I point to an underground tunnel and drag my finger to the edge of the screen.

"What the fuck indeed?" Wolfe clasps my shoulder. "It has to be him. I mean, we know it's him." He rubs at the back of his neck. "Right?"

"It's him." I feel it in my gut. We're on the right path.

Take Marco Rossi down, undermine his *distribution* network, and the world is a little better off. That's what drives us. It gets us out of bed each and every day.

We're the Guardians. Men who will do whatever it takes to rescue those who've been taken. The hope for a better tomorrow is what drives all of us.

My brows scrunch together, not liking the questions swirling in

Wolfe's head. His uncertainty isn't something I ignore. The man has killer instincts.

We're missing something, but for the life of me, I can't figure it out.

Wolfe's a smart guy. He worked in Navy Intelligence before becoming a SEAL. Whipcord smart, he sees through a different lens than the rest of us.

"The money runs through the Belvedere." He pulls up a map of the twenty-fifth floor. "Mitzy confirmed it, but the twenty-fifth floor is exactly what it appears to be."

"You're kidding."

"I wish I were. Mitzy's drone made several passes while you were ... otherwise occupied." He covers his mouth, coughing, but the twinkle in his eyes says what's on his mind.

"You better think real careful about what comes out of your mouth next."

I'm not playing. Wolfe's my teammate. He's my friend. I trust him with my life, but I'll kill him if he disrespects my woman.

"Take it down a notch, lover boy." Wolfe slugs me in the arm. "It's about time the love bug took a bite out of you."

Not sure how to respond to what he says, so I don't. Instead, I focus on the screen.

"So, the room the women were held in is what then?"

"An opportunistic office that was repurposed." Wolfe rocks back on his feet.

We interrupted their normal operations when we took out Benefield's operation in Columbia. That left them scrambling to fulfill the last set of orders he arranged but failed to deliver on: specifically, six women.

"They took a major risk bringing the women here."

"No shit." Wolfe stares at the computer screen. "But that whole floor is nothing but offices. Not that Mitzy isn't digging for dirt. If she finds something, she'll turn things over to the FBI."

Our assumption is Marco Rossi operated the illegal side of his many business ventures out of the twenty-fifth floor. Wolfe and I rescued three women from there. The other three were shipped out on *Caviar Dreams*.

We assumed that was the base of his operations.

"We have to get into Marco's home ..." I tap the top of the table.

"Yeah, time to lay on some of that Hollywood charm of yours. I hope to hell you haven't fucked up your brunch invitation. You didn't hold your punches when speaking to her mother."

No, I did not. I grasp the back of my neck and squeeze my tense muscles.

I was never technically invited to brunch with Maria's family, but that's beside the point. I flick back to the blueprints of Marco's home and subterranean fortress.

"I'll fix the invite."

"You better. We need to know whatever the fuck that is ..." Wolfe drags his finger along the screen, tracing out the tunnel leading to a secondary structure buried underground.

I don't disagree, but I'm more concerned about the reception I'll receive by Maria's mother and uncle.

"You do realize you're walking into a trap." Wolfe's deep voice rumbles, vibrating the air and sending chills racing down my back.

"Yeah, let's talk about that."

41

MARIA

I WAKE TO AN EMPTY BED, FEELING REFRESHED AND GLORIOUSLY FUCKED. The sheets beside me are cold, with no evidence of Liam's lingering body heat. I give a little sigh, wondering if I should be disappointed he didn't wake me.

A little bit of wake-up sex would've been nice, but I understand there's more going on than ensuring my sexual needs are met.

The low rumbling of men's voices filters through the closed door of my bedroom. Indistinct, but unmistakable, Liam's out there talking to his teammates.

I wrap myself in a robe and pad over to the door. Opening it a crack, Wolfe and Liam stand by my dining table, looking at a computer screen. Brady's asleep on my couch. At least, I assume that's him beneath the lump of blankets.

Not wanting to head out there looking freshly fucked, I go to my bathroom where I see Liam took a shower. Following suit, I crank on the hot water and lather up with soap. Is it weird that I don't want to wash away his scent?

Probably.

In general, I take quick showers. This is no exception. A glance at my watch reveals we slept the afternoon away. It's early evening and my stomach grumbles, reminding me we skipped lunch in favor of *other* things.

Not knowing what Liam plans for the evening, I put on a basic red dress that I can dress up, or down, in seconds. Picking something in the middle of the road, I grab a colorful scarf and tie it around my waist. It brings my look up a notch.

With a quick twist and flip, my hair is tucked up and out of the way in a classy French twist. I take a moment to put on barebones makeup that I can touch up as needed. But that's it. I'm eager to see Liam and curious as to what our next step might be.

With a final look in the mirror, I'm pleased with my results. I look classically understated and elegant; ready for anything from an afternoon stroll around the French Quarter to an upscale dining experience.

My phone rings in the other room. The dour tone tells me it's Mother. I debate letting her call go to voicemail, but that will only irritate her more. With a deep breath, I pad into my bedroom and accept the call.

"Mother." I don't say hello. There are no pleasantries. I brace for a verbal tongue lashing and questions about Liam.

"Good evening." My mother's response is short and clipped.

When I don't say anything, she blows out a breath in irritation.

What does she expect me to say?

"We need to talk about what happened earlier." Her caustic tone sends shivers down my spine.

I'm not afraid to fire that shot right back at her. From her imperious tone, she's ready to dress me down and verbally whip me into submission. But I'm tired of that, and I don't deserve having anyone talk to me like that.

Even if it's my mother.

"Are you referring to the way you humiliated me in front of Liam? Because I agree, we need to talk about that."

"I didn't ..."

"Mother, you dressed me down in front of the man I intend to marry. That's the news Liam wants to share with you. Instead, you ruined it."

"I ruined nothing. You went out again and ditched your security. I was worried about you. It's not my fault if he took exception to that."

"You've never once been worried about me." Anger churns in my gut and it's a struggle to keep it contained. Spouting off at my mother does nothing other than prove I'm incapable of containing my emotions.

"You're being overly dramatic."

"I'm frustrated." I take in a deep breath and try to force my body to stop shaking. "I wanted to share our news and you made that impossible." I wait, but she doesn't say anything about the engagement ring. "Aren't you going to congratulate me?"

"You're not marrying that man." Her comment is dismissive and final.

"I am marrying that man." My breath hitches because those words ring with truth. I might not marry Liam now, but there's a future between us. "You can either accept it, or not."

"This isn't something we should discuss over the phone."

"Would it kill you to be happy for me? I love Liam and we're going to get married."

"How well do you know this person?" Her challenge is undeniable, but expected. The way she says 'person' dehumanizes Liam.

Thankful for the backstory Mitzy created, and the little bit of practice Liam and I did, I'm confident in the lie I tell my mother.

"We've been dating for months. I know him well."

We've known each other for less than twenty-four hours and it's insane to consider a future with Liam.

Yet, I am.

"He doesn't even live here." Her dismissive tone continues. Her choice of words tells me she's looked into Liam's past. Fingers crossed Mitzy's backstory holds up.

"He lives in New York."

"And what are you going to do when you marry? What about the Belvedere?"

Ah, here it is. The hook that will smooth everything.

"That's one of the things we want to discuss. I realize things didn't go well between you and Liam this morning, but he's a good man. Good for me. He wants to sit down with you and Uncle Marco to announce our engagement and what it means for us."

"Us?"

"Yes."

"How does it affect us? Other than the obvious?"

"What does that mean?"

"I've gone to great lengths to secure an appropriate match, something that increases Rossi—"

"I don't care what you secured for me, who he might be. I'm not marrying a man I don't know. The days of arranged marriages are long gone. If you're looking for a merger, you can do that without me. In fact, you don't need me at all."

"Be careful how you speak to me."

"Why? You've never been kind to me."

"A parent's role isn't to be kind to their children."

"You're right. It's to shower them in so much love they feel they can do anything, but you never did that for me." My fingers practically cramp from how tight I hold the phone. This conversation is veering off track and I need to pull it back around. "Look, I don't want to argue with you. Liam and I are getting married, with or without your blessing. That's going to change things around here. We want to discuss what those changes might be with you and Uncle Marco, tomorrow at brunch. If we're still invited."

"You want to bring that man into my home? After the way he spoke to me?"

"You mean the man who stood up for me? I'd like to think that's the kind of man you'd want your daughter to marry."

"I'm surprised you'd let anyone speak to your mother the way he spoke to me."

"Honestly, Liam wasn't wrong, and he'd say the same thing about the way you treated me and the way you spoke to me." I run a finger through my hair. "Look, he's not happy with how things went, but we're getting married. He wants to sit down with you and Uncle Marco and talk about options for buying me out."

"Buy you out?" My mother fails to contain her surprise. Her tone turns from dismissive to gleeful.

"It doesn't make sense for me to stay on as the CEO if I'm moving back to New York. But this is a conversation best done face to face. Unless you say otherwise, Liam and I will be at Sunday brunch noon tomorrow. We'll discuss what all of this means and what timeframes we're looking at. Until then, you can brief Marco."

"This is what you want? To leave New Orleans? You've been adamant about staying."

"It's what I want."

"When?"

"As soon as possible."

I may be spinning out a lie, but it feels like the truth. There's no way I'm staying in New Orleans after everything I've learned. As to what I'll do once this is all over and done with, I don't have a clue, but I'll figure something out. I cross my fingers and pray we didn't ruin our chance of getting Mitzy's tech into my uncle's home.

"Then, we'll see you at brunch?"

"Brunch is served promptly at noon." Her concession comes grudgingly, but it does come.

Success!

"Your uncle has some business in the morning. I'll be with him." Her tone is terse, but I can't help but smile.

"What happened to no business on Sundays?"

That's always been a rule; no business on the Lord's day.

"Don't use that flippant tone with me. Your uncle is dealing with a crisis."

I can guess at what crisis that might be. The Guardians rescued all six of the women my uncle intended to sell.

"I'm sorry. I didn't mean to be disrespectful." It's time to return to my role of dutiful child.

"Are you really willing to give up the Belvedere for this man?"

"It doesn't make sense when I'm not going to be living here.

Besides, Uncle Marco has wanted to take over my shares since the beginning. The only reason I didn't was because the Belvedere is the only thing I had from Father. I've since come to realize I was holding onto it for the wrong reasons."

"Your uncle will be pleased you finally realized the Belvedere was too much for you."

"I'm sure he will."

Too much for me? She didn't hear a word I said.

"I look forward to seeing you tomorrow. Liam really is an amazing man."

"If you say so." It's the closest my mother will get to agreeing with me. "Like I said, your uncle has business in the morning. I'll be with him. If we're not home, you have the codes to let yourself in. But just you and him. There's no need for his men."

"Thank y—" Before I can finish, she ends the connection.

I take another look in the mirror before heading out to see what Liam is up to. Satisfied with how I look, I take in a deep breath.

My hand shakes as I grip the doorknob and the faintest flush makes my cheeks heat.

There's no way to hide or deny what Liam and I did, so I brace myself for whatever rude comments may come my way and open the door.

During my shower, Brady got up from the couch. The blanket is neatly folded and drapes over the back of the couch. My entrance doesn't go unnoticed. All three men turn as one to stare as I step into the room.

"Hi." I give a little half-wave and bite down on my lower lip.

Liam's mouth gapes and his eyes round as he takes me in from head to toe. He hesitates for a moment, then rushes toward me. He wraps me in a hug and lifts me off my feet.

"You look fucking amazing." Lowering his voice, he whispers in my ear. "I want to rip off that dress and spend the rest of the day in bed."

I can't help but giggle as he nuzzles my neck. It's a ticklish spot for me, one he's becoming well acquainted with.

"It's almost five. I'd say we've lost the day." I cup his cheek and stare adoringly into his eyes. "Do we have work to do?" Although, whatever that work might be is lost on me.

"Some. Mitzy wants us to stay in tonight. No more making a splash on the town. She suggested we have dinner here and spend time at the tables."

"I can't gamble."

"I'm not much of a gambler myself, but it's all for show."

"You don't understand."

"Understand what?" Liam gives me a look.

"I'm actually really good at poker and blackjack, but since I work here, I'm not allowed to gamble here. It's a rule that pertains to all our employees."

"Hmm." Liam scratches his head. "Does that mean you can't be with me if I gamble?"

"I can be eye candy on your arm—"

"Eye candy?" Wolfe snorts.

Liam gives him the eye.

"Hey! She said it, so it's cool. Don't bust my balls over something your woman said." Wolfe points at me.

"Anyway ..." My attention shifts between Liam and Wolfe. There's more subtext there than I'm aware of. Nevertheless, I continue. "It doesn't look good to my employees. If you win, they'll think ..."

"Don't worry about him winning." Brady huffs a laugh and joins Wolfe at the table.

"Huh?" I don't understand that comment.

"Don't mind them." Liam tugs me to his side. "They're being a couple of assholes."

"Were you going to lose on purpose?" Wolfe snickers and Brady tries to cover his laughter with a cough. "Okay, what's up with them?" I hook a thumb toward Liam's teammates.

"Like I said ... they're assholes." Liam pulls me close, eyeing my dress. His expression heats. "If gambling is out ... I can think of another way to spend the night."

"Before we get ahead of ourselves, I have news." I glance down at the computer screen. "What's that?"

"That is your uncle's house." Liam points to the screen.

"Um, that's not his house." I've spent far too many Sunday brunches at that house and know it intimately.

"That's the structure underground?"

"Underground? Like a basement?" I've never been in the basement of my uncle's house before. There was never a need.

"Not the basement, princess. That's a stronghold."

"Really? How did you ..." My voice trails off and I hold up a hand. "Don't tell me ... that's a bit of Mitzy Magic?"

"Gotcha there. Mitzy got a hold of the architectural plans for the house and this little gem showed up."

"Wow. That's impressive." I lean forward, trying to make sense of the underground structure. "At least I have good news."

"You do?"

"Despite how it went between the two of you, brunch is still on. I told Mother about our engagement and that we wanted to talk to my uncle about giving up my interest in the Belvedere."

"I bet that got her interest."

"You should've heard the way her voice cracked. But there's a catch."

"What's that?"

"Wolfe and Brady are not welcome. Mother made that very clear."

"Well, we can adjust." Wolfe taps his chin. "How about we stay in, order room service, and figure out how we're going to tackle tomorrow morning?"

"Sounds good to me." I pipe up, agreeing easily. I'm up for hiding out until the last minute. "Everyone up for room service?"

"Dining in sounds just fine." Liam's voice heats and there's no mistaking the subtext in his tone.

Wolfe and Brady pretend they don't hear Liam, but they do. I'm beginning to really adore Liam's friends. These tough guys are soft where it counts.

"One other thing ..." I tug on my hair, twirling a strand around my finger.

"What's that?"

"Mother said Marco was dealing with a crisis and he has business in the morning. Brunch is always at noon, but she said we could let ourselves in."

"What does that mean?"

"Well, I assume the *crisis* Marco faces is six missing women. For whatever reason, Mother will be with him for whatever *business* he needs to take care of."

"So, you're telling us you have the access codes to Marco Rossi's house?" Wolfe runs his fingers through his thick mop of hair.

"I do."

"Well, shit. Why didn't you say so sooner?" Wolfe gives me a look. "We need to get those codes to Mitzy and CJ."

"Why?"

"We can do a little recon tonight." Wolfe taps the table.

"That's not a good idea. If Marco's dealing with a *crisis*, he'll have locked down security. Not that I'm telling you how to run a mission, but that could turn into a shitstorm pretty damn quick."

"I have to agree with Maria." Liam backs me up. "But we can show up early?"

"Seems like what we need are eyes on the house." Brady joins in. "Once Marco and your mother are out of the house, you and Liam can go in."

"That'll work." Wolfe pulls on his chin. "Let's rope in Sam and CJ, see what they think, and see if Mitzy has anything to add."

"Meanwhile, I'll order dinner." I take a look at each of the men. "Any special requests?"

"Strawberries and whipped cream." Liam responds lightning quick while Wolfe and Brady laugh.

"Not subtle, dude. Not subtle at all." Wolfe smacks Liam in the arm. "How about I handle dinner while the three of you call Overwatch?"

We split up the tasks. I show Wolfe my stack of takeout menus as well as the menus of all five of the restaurants in the Belvedere. Wolfe and I wind up ordering a five-star meal from our showcase restaurants, while Liam and Brady call back to base.

Most of the rest of the night is dedicated to planning our course of action in the morning. The plan is relatively simple. Liam and I will arrive an hour early, release Mitzy's drones, and poke around the house; specifically, Marco's study.

Once our food arrives, the four of us sit down in front of the television, where we argue over what to watch. We settle on some shoot 'em up, smash 'em up movie. I last through the first half, then find myself yawning.

Shortly after that, Liam carries me to my room, where he shows me how inventive he can be. I reward his efforts with the first item on my list and spend the rest of the night tied up and subject to his mercy.

42

MARIA

I STAND ON THE THRESHOLD OF MY UNCLE'S STUDY, SHIVERING AS THE icy-cold, recycled air gives me goosebumps and lifts the fine hair on my arms.

The study looks like it should be warm and inviting. Massive leather couches fill the room. They accent the heavy mahogany furniture and bookshelves that fill the walls. The heady aroma of cedar, leather, and old books mingles with the faintest scent of roses.

Pretty blooms fill the vases to overflowing. Plucked from the expansive estate gardens, those are my mother's signature touch. Maybe it's my mother's touch that turns warm and cozy into cold and frigid?

"Nervous?" Liam presses his hand to the small of my back. It's meant to be reassuring, but it feels like he's shoving me into the room.

I naturally push back. I have reservations about this room. As for the shivering, I'd like to think the chills racing up and down my back are from the cool air, but there's more to it than that.

"It's an interesting room." Liam stands slightly behind me as we stand at the threshold. "It looks warm on the surface, but it definitely doesn't welcome visitors."

"You're right about that." I try to see the study through Liam's eyes, as someone who never visited here as a child—someone not traumatized as a child. "I've always been afraid of this place."

"Why's that?" He steps around me, seemingly oblivious to my hesitation, and scans the rows of books lining the shelves. His fingers trail over the polished wood. Every now and then, he grabs a book by the spine, tilts it out to scan the title, then eases it back in place.

He's searching for something. That much is clear, but for the life of me, I don't know what it could be.

"I don't know. It was just forbidden."

"Really?"

The thick carpet beneath my feet swallows all sound, hiding my transgression as I step fully into the room. This is the one place that always filled me with dread when I was a child, and an ominous foreboding hovers over me now. I instinctually hunch my shoulders, wary and more than a little frightened.

"Yeah, and forbidden made me curious. That didn't end well."

"So, you peeked?" His tone is light, teasing, but the expression on my face pulls him up short. "What happened?"

Tiffany lamps illuminate the dark space, casting puddles of soft light, which makes the furniture glow. Normally, such an esthetic should make the study welcoming, but it only makes me want to curl into myself even more. I make a quick circuit of the room, knowing my mother and uncle will be here soon.

I'm nervous. Beyond nervous.

"I think we should leave." I glance toward the hallway outside. I feel jumpy. It's evident in the lightness of my steps, my stooped posture, and in the way I keep looking toward the hall. I want to be out there.

"The few times we traveled to New Orleans, my father would take me aside before visiting here."

"Why?"

"He told me I needed to be on my best behavior and follow all the rules. That it would be really bad if I broke any of them. The way he said it scared me."

"What was he worried about?" Liam doesn't understand the dynamics of my family.

"Like I said, his relationship with Marco was never quite right. All I knew was I needed to be on my best behavior and follow all the rules. Mother demanded it, of course, and I rarely disobeyed her, but my father desperately wanted me to be perfectly behaved. Looking back, it's like he had something to prove to Marco. Regardless, since that's what my father wanted, I wanted it too."

"And you never broke the rules?"

"The one, and only, time I disobeyed was the last time I stepped foot in this house as a child. I mean, I've been back. Obviously ..." I gesture vaguely toward the hall. "But that was only after my father died and after I moved to New Orleans for good. Since then, it's been Sunday brunch at noon like clockwork."

"What happened when you were a kid?" His expression darkens, revealing his protective side.

"My mother dragged me outside, screaming about disrespecting her privacy."

"Her privacy? I thought this was Marco's house?"

"It never made sense to me."

"Are you sure that's what she said?"

"I was seven, so my memory might not be perfect." I shrug, although I'm certain about what she said.

"Or maybe, your memory is spot on. What did she do?"

"She grabbed a switch from one of the rose bushes and whipped me with it. The thorns cut and left gouges in my skin. I still remember the little trails of blood dripping down my legs."

"That's horrible. Your mother abused you. I have to say it, I hate your mother."

"I don't hate her, but there's definitely little to love. And it's not like it happened again."

"How so?"

"My father heard my screams. He ran out, stopped my mother, and rushed me to the emergency room. It was the last time I ever came here as a kid."

"I'm sorry. I didn't know." He continues with the books, tilting them out one by one.

"My father took me back to the Hampton house. Left my mother here. They didn't speak for weeks, and she didn't return home until after school started in the fall."

"She stayed with Marco?"

"Yes." I glance around the room, looking for something, anything that feels out of place. "I don't know when they started their affair, but things are different now when I look back."

"I bet."

"Sorry, my life's a bit of a mess."

"With all that history, why do you come here for brunch every Sunday?"

"Because Mother demands it, and it makes sense."

"In what twisted universe does it make sense?" Liam's fingers curl and his muscles bunch. With no one to direct his anger at, some of it slips toward me.

I respond defensively as tension builds.

"Because I *have* to work with my uncle. The Belvedere is mine, but the family business ..." My voice trails off as I listen to the words coming out of my mouth. How easy it is to fall back on old habits, believing Rossi family holdings are nothing more than a series of jointly held companies? "Well, it used to make sense." I spin in a slow circle, taking in the dark study. "Nothing makes sense now, and I don't know what we're doing here. I will say this ..."

"What's that?"

"I feel like a little kid snooping where I don't belong, and I'm terrified of getting caught."

Liam moves to the next set of bookcases, where he taps at the molding.

"What are you doing?" His odd inspection of the bookcases can no longer be ignored.

"Looking for hidden things."

"What makes you think there are any hidden compartments?"

He spins his finger in the air, gesturing at nothing in particular.

Somewhere within the house, Mitzy's little dragonfly drones evade the security systems with their light-bending camouflage. I hope she finds what she needs and that we can leave this wretched place.

"Right." I feel foolish forgetting about the drones.

While he checks out the bookcases, I sit down behind my uncle's desk and shamelessly check out the way Liam's ass fills out his trousers. I want more of that. Screw sneaking around in my uncle's house. I'd rather be in bed, exploring more of what Liam has to offer.

I lean way back to prop my feet on Marco's desk. The chair wobbles beneath me and kicks out, dropping me unceremoniously to the floor. Liam comes running.

"Are you okay?"

I hold my hand to my temple where one of the casters, or maybe it was the arm of the chair, whacked me. The spot is tender to the touch, but there's no blood.

"That's going to leave a mark." Already, I feel the skin swelling. "How am I going to explain this to my mother?"

"Screw your mother." Liam squats down and places his hand on my arm. "Here, let me help you out."

A sprawl is not my best look. I wave Liam off and spin around until I'm on all fours. I get ready to push myself off the floor when an odd compartment under the desk catches my eye.

"Liam?"

"Yeah?"

"What's that?"

My uncle's desk is a massive piece of carved mahogany. Inlaid wood covers the top of the desk, and delicate carvings decorate the four corners. Every surface is polished to a high shine, including the wood underneath the desk.

Just to my right, tucked under the desk, is a door with a brass lock securing it in place.

43

LIAM

I GET ON ALL FOURS AND SHOVE MY HEAD UNDER THE DESK, TRYING TO see what Maria found.

"Here." I hand her my cellphone. "Give me some light."

While she turns on the light of my phone, I pull out my multi-tool. It's basically a Swiss Army knife on steroids, loaded with all kinds of extras, courtesy of Mitzy. Lock pick in hand, I get to work on the lock.

It doesn't take long before that satisfying *snick* unlocks the hidden compartment.

The building schematics indicate a secret tunnel exiting this room. It leads to the underground bunker we saw on the files Mitzy sent earlier. I was looking for a lever, or release, when Maria took her spill.

"What's inside?" Maria lowers her voice to a whisper, although there's no need.

Thanks to our Guardian team, Marco and Muriel Rossi are conveniently stuck in traffic. Which gives us time to do a little recon before they arrive to the party. I estimate we've got an hour before they work their way free of that mess.

I open the door and pull out a painted wooden box. It looks to be decades old. Deep grooves mar the black and silver metallic finish. There's a lock on the box; the brass finish worn smooth over the years. I hand it back to Maria.

"It's locked." Maria turns the box in her hands. About a foot in every dimension, it's a bit too large for her to handle. She drops the box on the floor and something rattles inside, several somethings.

"Let's open it." I crawl out from under the desk and spin around to place my back against the heavy wood. Maria hands me the box and I make quick work of the lock. Once the lock is opened, I hand the box back to her, knowing she needs to be the one to open it.

"It's like finding hidden treasure." She places her hand over the lid. "What do you think we'll find? Cash? Jewels?" She's making this more of an adventure than it needs to be. "Deeds to stolen land? Barron bonds? Are those even a thing?"

I love the way her eyes light up when she's excited. I give her a little nudge, wishing I was close enough to give her a kiss. It feels like it's been weeks, rather than hours, since I held her in my arms.

"Open it and let's find out."

She lifts the lid, and her brows draw together.

"What the hell?"

Maria pulls out an old video recorder, a relic from an earlier time when VCRs were all the rage. DVDs took over soon after that. Floppy discs ushered in the computer age, and even floppies were pushed to the side as thumb drives took over. Now, even those are mostly obsolete. With everything stored in the cloud, there's no need to keep storage of any kind.

She pushes the red power button and to our surprise, the thing turns on.

"Whoa, that's weird." She holds it away from her, as if it's a poisonous snake that will bite her. "It's fully charged." Turning it around, she peers at the archaic display. "How can it be fully charged?" She digs inside the box. "There's no charging cord."

The skin on the back of my neck itches. It's a warning I've come to respect. I glance around, looking for a charging station that would help make this odd find make sense.

I take the box from Maria while she examines the controls.

"There are several videotapes." Each one is painstakingly labeled, along with a collection of thumb drives. I scoop the thumb drives into my hand and hold my hand palm up.

"What are you doing?"

A soft, nearly imperceptible whirring sound disturbs the air. I locate the tiny drone by ear and by a rippling disturbance in the air. Invisibility cloaks no longer belong in the realm of movies such as Harry Potter. The tech is out there, and it's no surprise Mitzy leads the forefront of deploying that tech into the field.

The drone lowers, hovering over my palm by less than a foot. A gentle downward breeze is the only sign it's there, at least until a miniature grappling device lowers down from its belly.

"What the hell?" Maria jumps when a fine cable, not much larger than a strand of spider's silk, spools out of the drone. Her eyes blink several times as she searches for the nearly invisible drone. It's not an easy feat.

The grapple makes contact with my palm. I do nothing but hold still while the drone slowly loads the small collection of thumb drives into a tiny bay hidden inside itself.

"What's it doing?" Maria locates the drone by following the cable up.

"Taking these out for analysis."

"We don't even know what's on them. Shouldn't we put them back where we found them?"

"And miss finding something important?" I point to the video recorder. "Let's play a couple of those tapes. I'm curious what your uncle would hide under his desk."

"Can't the drones carry these out?"

"No. They're too big to fit inside the drone."

The drone finishes loading the last of the thumb drives. The grappling hook reels back up into the drone, and I lower my hand to the floor. I don't hear it leave, but I know it's on its way out of the house with its precious cargo.

Taking the box from Maria, I reach inside and pull out several of the tapes. One name, in particular, catches my eye. I hand it over to Maria, then second guess the wisdom of that choice. Too late, she inserts the tape into the old video recorder and presses play.

With the tiny flip screen, I scoot around until I sit behind Maria. Cradling her in my arms, I provide something for her to lean against. An image fills the screen of a younger version of the woman I love lounging poolside at an impressive estate.

"That's me." She peers at the screen.

"Do you recognize where that is?" An impossibly lavish pool fills the background.

"Yes. That's my home in the Hamptons."

"When was this taken?" An unsettled feeling stirs in my gut.

"Oh, I don't know ... Oh wait." She adjusts her position, leaning against my shoulder. "There's Sybil."

Indeed, a young version of her friend fills the screen. The two of them are poolside, wearing tiny bikinis. They laugh and wave to whoever is recording the video.

Maria watches the recording, and a smile fills her face. "Lord, we were so young. I can't believe my mother let me out of the house in that. Although, technically, we were still on the grounds."

"Maria?" I try to get her to focus. Assumptions are a bitch, but I've already formed mine. "When was this taken?"

Maria thinks this is nothing but an innocent summer video, but there's no reason Marco would hide something innocent in a locked compartment under his desk. I brace for the moment the video reveals its true purpose.

I know men like Marco, and I know what they like. Nubile young girls tend to be at the top of their list.

"Oh, it had to be the summer of our sweet sixteen."

Her smile is brighter as Sybil moves to the edge of the pool. Pulling at her bikini bottom, Sybil glances coyly at the camera. Eyes fluttering, she places her hands over her head and gracefully dives into the pool.

The camera cuts from the edge of the pool to follow Sybil's

graceful form underwater. She swims to the other side of the pool where the photographer records everything.

Popping up out of the water, she blinks as water sluices down her face, then props her arms on the side of the pool, lifting her body enough out of the water to reveal rather impressive cleavage. As expected, the cameraman's view goes right to Sybil's tits.

Maria has yet to react. I don't think it hits her, but I remember every word of what she told me about the summer of her sweet sixteen.

The video cuts out, then picks up a few seconds later. It's night-time. The grounds are lit up in bright lights, ostentatious floral arrangements are everywhere. Light and airy fabric flutters in the breeze as what looks to be the party of the season seems to be in full swing. Despite the summer heat, the men wear dark suits, and the women compete to wear the skimpiest and most revealing dresses.

After panning through the crowd, the camera zooms in on the dance floor where Maria and Sybil dance together. They laugh and shout. They drink far too much champagne. Maria checks out one of the busboys while Sybil turns to the camera and gives a little wave of her fingers where Maria can't see.

The feed cuts out again. It's replaced a moment later with a view of carpet as the camera swings. A suit jacket falls to the floor. It lands in a clump of fabric. Then Sybil's skimpy dress joins it.

"Maria ..." I place my hand on her arm, only now noticing how her reminiscent smiles have turned into shock and horror.

"Is that ..." She blinks, as if that can erase what she's seen.

The camera falls to the floor where it's covered with an errantly placed sock. The screen goes dark for a moment, but then the camera is on the move. The view jostles about as the cameraman places it on the dresser. All we see is a hairy chest, but then Marco takes a step back and checks his shot.

Sprawled on the bed, Sybil waits for her first lover.

Maria shuts off the video camera and covers her mouth.

"Sybil's first was Marco?"

I want to hold Maria, provide some sort of comfort. I remembered

Maria's recounting of the pact she and Sybil made to lose their virginity when they were both sixteen.

Maria picked a busboy.

Sybil chose an older man.

"How could she?"

"Did she know who he was?"

"I don't know." Maria shrugs. "Maybe?" Her brows knit together, and she chews on her fingernail. The fake engagement ring glitters on her finger with an all too real treasure of a diamond. "Come to think of it, Sybil did seem a bit surprised at breakfast. I can't believe she never told me."

"Maybe she was embarrassed?" There are hundreds of reasons why Sybil never told her best friend the identity of the man who took her virginity.

That's not my concern.

My concern is Marco willingly seduced a sixteen-year-old virgin. He was easily twice her age, and there's no state where that kind of shit is legal. If Marco had a taste for young girls, then, how have his tastes matured over the ensuing years?

He's involved in human trafficking and fulfilled the last set of orders Benefield took in before the Guardians stormed the facility in Colombia. Benefield lost his life in that raid, and the Guardians obtained a set of ledgers detailing every transaction. Six names were at the end of that list. Six orders for sex slaves that had yet been fulfilled.

Those clients paid outrageous sums to Benefield and expected delivery. Marco had no choice but to fulfill the orders, but what else did he fulfill?

We still don't know who ordered the deaths of six innocent women, young things taken off the streets of Cancun and brutally murdered while a client watched the whole thing. We saved only one during that mission. Zoe Lancaster was tortured and on the brink of death by the time we stormed that compound.

I want the person who ordered the deaths of those girls for their perverted pleasure. I want to watch them suffer the way those girls suffered.

Maria presses the play button.

"You sure you want to watch that?"

"I'm going to fast forward. There might be something important on the rest of the tape."

It's a bad idea, but I keep my thoughts to myself as I continue to watch from over Maria's shoulder. The tape shows Sybil and Marco in bed together having sex. Maria fast forwards the explicit scene until static fills the screen.

Taking in a deep breath, she lowers the camera to her lap. Right as she does, another video begins to play.

"Lord, there's more?" Maria huffs out a breath. "I can't watch any more of that." She lifts the camera up, giving it to me.

"Um, Maria?"

"What?" She lifts the camera again. "You can take it."

"Maria ..." I wrap an arm around her waist. This isn't good. "That's not Sybil.

The couple on screen are not Sybil and Marco, but rather a younger version of Maria's mother having sex with her uncle. Her mother gyrates over Marco, riding him. Her face contorts with pleasure as she lifts up and slams down. Muriel Rossi looks up into the camera and smiles. It's not a smile filled with joy; nothing as innocent as that. It's a smile of sublime satisfaction.

Maria's silent, processing what she sees. I take the opportunity to look through the other tapes as her mother's head bends back as she moans through an orgasm.

"How long was she cheating on my father?" Maria leans against my chest. "Is there anything about my life that isn't a total fucking disaster?"

Another name catches my eye. I pull out a tape labeled *Z. Lancaster.*

Holy fucking shit. This needs to be called in. I know only one Zoe Lancaster, and Axel needs to know what we've found.

44

LIAM

"What's that?" Maria looks at the tape in my hand. I let her take it from me. "Z. Lancaster? I swear there's something familiar about that name." Brows pinched, and a little nibble of her lower lip, the woman is something else.

My thoughts turn back to yesterday when I kept her in bed the entire afternoon. I wish we were there now, instead of this wretched place.

Maria inserts the tape and presses play.

She amazes me. There's no other way to describe how completely enthralled I've become by all things Maria. The way she deals with this discovery not only impresses me, but it shows the depth of her character.

Maria is strong inside and out.

The video plays out. Zoe wanders through a rose garden, stopping every now and then to smell the beautiful blooms.

We don't have sound. For some reason, that's not working, but Zoe picks one of the roses and turns toward the camera. As she approaches, the video zooms in on her cleavage.

Whoever filmed these videos is a tits man.

The view shifts and an older man comes into view. I've seen him before.

"That's Zoe's father."

"Her father?"

"Yes. Do you know where this video was taken?"

"It was taken here." She points to the screen. "Those are the rose gardens out back." Maria twists around. "What does her father do?"

"He's a lawyer. He hired the Guardians to rescue his daughter, but they live in California, not here. What would he be doing out here? And why would he bring his daughter? That doesn't make sense."

"This video is a few years old." Maria leans in to peer at the screen. "Maybe he was doing something for my uncle? Or my father?"

"Your father?"

"Yes. My father was still alive when this was taken." She points to the lower left of the screen, where there are numbers too tiny for me to see.

"Well, Zoe's finishing up college now. If your father was alive when this was taken, she had to have been in high school." I shrug.

I don't date college co-eds precisely because high school girls know how to dress up and look years older than they are. Unlike Marco, jailbait holds no interest for me.

"Well, from this, I'd say about sixteen in this video."

A chill runs down my spine. Zoe would've been the same age as Sybil was in that previous video, but Zoe wouldn't go after Marco like Sybil did.

According to everything Axel says, Zoe crushed on him since she was the age of five. I don't see her suddenly jumping into bed with an older man. Although, Axel wouldn't have been around when Zoe was sixteen. He's several years older than her and had enlisted in the Navy by then.

It's a weird connection and I don't like weird connections. There's always a thread; something that pulls it all together. I add it to the list of things I want Mitzy to take a look into.

Despite my concerns, there's nothing revealing on the tape with

Zoe. It looks like whoever filmed this was just having fun videotaping a pretty girl.

The film cuts out and static fills the screen.

"I'm sure these things have sound." Maria examines the video camera.

"Considering what we've seen, do you really want to listen in on any of it?"

"Not the sex parts. But if this Zoe is somehow connected to my family, don't you want to hear what they're talking about?" Maria twists the video camera around, checking out all the buttons. "There's got to be a button somewhere ..." Her voice trails off as she turns the clunky video camera upside down and every which way. "Ah, here it is." She flicks a tiny switch and garbled static fills the room.

New footage plays.

Maria gasps.

It's another sex tape.

Muriel and Marco make a second appearance. This time Marco goes down on Muriel.

Maria doesn't turn away. Her brows pinch as I try to imagine how something like this must feel. Her mother's adultery has to hurt.

When the whole disgusting thing is over, Muriel gets off the bed and pulls on her robe. With the sound finally turned on, we hear every disgusting word that comes out of her mouth.

* * *

"*THAT WAS FUN.*" SHE FACES THE CAMERA AND GRINS IN A CRUEL RICTUS of victory. Muriel crosses the distance, closing in on the camera, as her cold eyes flick to the side. "*What about you, honey? Did you enjoy watching your brother fuck me? Did you hear the way he makes me scream? The way he ate me out was divine. Don't you think?*" The camera shakes as she spins it around.

Tied up on a chair, gag in place, Milo Rossi stares at her with rabid hatred. His muffled shouts are unintelligible, but fury fills his features.

"*Do you know what the perfect heart attack drug is?*" She runs the back of her bony fingers along Milo's cheek. Muriel leans down to kiss him, then turns her face to the camera. "*Cocaine.*"

He struggles wildly in the chair.

"*And did you know it can be especially dangerous for men who are predisposed to heart attacks? Isn't that what your doctor said? You're at risk? Need to slow down? Make some lifestyle changes? Well, I want to help you make a permanent lifestyle change.*" She tosses her head back and cackles.

Kneeling down, she messes with something outside of the camera angle. When she stands, she holds a box of plastic wrap. She opens the box and pulls on the plastic film. While Milo Rossi bucks in his seat, becoming more frantic, she calmly wraps the film over his mouth and around his head, leaving his eyes and nose exposed.

"*Let me educate you on the dangers of cocaine. Your heart will beat faster. The drug will constrict your blood vessels, making it harder for your heart to pump. That strains your heart as it's forced to work harder to move blood through your body. Cocaine also spikes your blood pressure. You might stroke out before you die.*"

She finishes wrapping his head and steps back to admire her handiwork. In the background, Marco swings his legs around to sit on the edge of the bed. His hand goes to his groin where he slowly strokes his cock.

"*I've been reading up since you went to the doctor. Did you know that over a quarter of the people who die suddenly after using cocaine have atherosclerosis? Isn't that what the doctor said? You have atherosclerotic coronary artery disease?*" She leans in close, whispering in his ear. "*Cocaine can be deadly for someone like you.*"

She holds up a small tray with a mound of white powder on it.

Milo's eyes widen.

"Don't worry, love. All you have to do is breathe."

Milo bucks, thrashing his head back and forth.

Marco slips off the bed, fully nude and fully aroused. His cock bobs between his legs as he moves around to the back of the chair. He grabs Milo's head, immobilizing him, as Muriel places the cocaine under Milo's nose. He snorts, blowing a cloud of fine white dust into the air. Muriel jumps back and laughs.

"You fool. That's nothing to me."

Before Milo can take a breath, she slams the coke up against his nostrils. Milo has no choice but to inhale the drug, snorting it into his nasal passages as he takes a breath.

"You thought you could steal her from me, brother. Force me to step aside?" Milo's grip tightens as he leans down and speaks into Milo's ear. *"But now you know. She's always been mine. Each time you slipped your dick inside my girl, she thought of me. You raped her and forced her to bear your despicable kid. Now, you'll pay, and you'll go to Hell knowing I took everything from you."*

Muriel forces Milo to breathe in more of the cocaine. If he doesn't have a heart attack, the overdose will kill him.

Beside me, Maria watches in horror as her father's pupils constrict.

"Oh love, we're not so cruel." Muriel lowers the empty tray and removes her robe. *"Your ride to Hell will be rapturous."*

Milo sags in the seat, huffing and sweating profusely as the drug kicks in. His brother steps around to the front of the chair, in perfect view of the camera.

"I want you to watch your wife, brother." Marco snaps his fingers and points to the ground. His attention shifts to Maria's mother. *"On your knees, love."*

Muriel doesn't hesitate. As she lowers down to her knees, she looks at Milo in disgust. *"Watch how I obey him, my wretched husband. Watch how I willingly service a better man than you."* She kneels before Marco, a look of abject adoration on her face as she opens her mouth.

* * *

THAT'S ENOUGH. I DON'T WANT MARIA SUBJECTED TO ANOTHER SECOND of this filth.

"Maria ..." I place my hand on her arm. "Stop the tape."

But Maria doesn't stop the playback. Tears stream down her face while the tape plays on.

"I'm so sorry. I'm so sorry." Maria rocks back and forth, saying it over and over again as she watches her father's face turn blue and his body go limp. "I'm so sorry." Tears run down her face, and I fear they'll continue to fall until she has no tears left.

45

MARIA

I watch every frame of the tape, forcing myself to listen to every spiteful word my mother says. I know she can be cruel, but this is beyond brutal. Every nuance in my mother's voice strikes like a physical blow.

My mother poisoned my father. She killed him.

She overdosed him on cocaine until his heart gave out. While he dies from a heart attack, she gives my uncle a fucking blowjob?

A blowjob?

She's psychotic. A sociopath. She terrifies me.

I don't know the woman on the screen. That's not the mother I know. I can't imagine the depravity of such an act.

My uncle's release comes while my father watches. Sweat beads on his brow and pain creases his forehead.

Watching my mother murder my father isn't as big of a shock as I feel like it should be. Their relationship was always distant. My father doted on me, while my mother barely tolerated my presence.

I finally understand where her hatred stems from, and in some strange twist of fate, I find peace in that knowledge.

It isn't me.

It was never me.

She hated me for something I couldn't control. All my hopes for some small scrap of maternal love were in vain. Like any child, I wanted my mother's love. Never having it made me feel defective.

But I'm not.

I'm not defective.

I never was.

"Give it back." I reach for the video camera, but Liam pulls it away.

"Don't."

"Give it back." My tone turns serious.

"You don't need to torture yourself." He grips the video camera. "Don't you see what this means?"

"My mother is a monster? My uncle is too?"

The thing is, I already know this. I think I always have known it on some small level.

"It means we can put them away for murder. They documented their crime. We can put them away forever."

"Give me the camera." I flick my fingers, demanding.

He's right and he's only trying to protect me, but I need to watch it one more time. I feel like I need to witness my father's last moments.

"I really don't think—"

"I don't care what you think." I place my hand on his arm. "You're amazing—beyond amazing—and I love that you want to protect me. I love everything about you, but I need to watch to the end."

I need to see my father die and bear witness to this act.

"Ah, princess." Liam cups my face and stares into my eyes. "You're stronger than you know." He hands me back the video camera.

I rewind the tape and watch the whole wretched scene again, listening to every nuance of my mother's voice. She enjoyed it. She set the whole thing up. A lot of planning went into my father's final moments.

Finally, I turn off the camera and eject the tape. Cradling it in my hands, I stare at it for what seems forever.

"What do we do now?" I turn the tape over and run my finger over the label on the front. "Do we turn it over to the police? Or will they just bury it, bought by my uncle to ensure things like this disappear?"

Liam takes the tape and tucks it into his inner coat pocket.

"We do what we must."

An overhead drone catches my attention, but only because there's a fluttering and a pneumatic whisper of a sound. One of those grappling hooks descends out of thin air, suspended by a fiber no larger than a strand of spider's silk.

"I have a feeling a recording of that tape is already on its way to the right people." Liam sees the drone and glances around the room.

They're near invisible. We could be surrounded by the things and not know it.

"The cops?" I nibble on my lower lip. The Belvedere is a frequent off-duty hangout for the cops. I always thought that was cool, but I have a feeling there was far more to it than I knew. No doubt, Marco pads the pockets at all levels within the police department.

"More likely the FBI." Liam fishes the cassette out of his jacket and places it on his palm. Like before, the tiny grappling hook grabs hold. Only this time, it doesn't retract all the way. The tape is too large for the drone to carry in its tiny compartment. Instead, it flies back to the ventilation duct and disappears inside.

I breathe a little easier knowing that tape is on its way.

My mother is a murderer.

It's going to take a minute to process.

I uncross my legs, and when I do, my foot kicks the box. One last tape falls out.

"What do you think is on this one?" My hand shakes as I insert the tape. I try to still my breathing, but it's hard. I'm too keyed up to pretend whatever's on that tape won't come as a complete shock.

Liam rolls his wrist and his entire body goes on high alert. "We need to get going."

"Wait, I want to see this." I press the play button.

"They bypassed our team." Liam jumps to his feet and bends down to help me. As he does, the first frame begins.

"What the ever-loving fuck?" I stare at an impossible image. My heart pounds as I cover my mouth.

"What?"

There are no words for what I see. Instead, I hold the video camera up to Liam. "Holy shit." He staggers back and puts his fist to his mouth. I swear, Liam almost hurls. I get it.

I totally get it.

My stomach churns with what's on that tape.

I'll never be the same again.

A noise in the hallway gets my attention. Liam reaches for his gun as I spring to my feet.

"I wouldn't do that if I were you." My uncle cocks his weapon and points the muzzle of his gun at me.

Liam holds his hands up and out.

My mother and uncle stand in the threshold, but all I can see is a killer and a psychopath.

"What are you doing in here?" That imperious voice is one I know well.

My mother steps into the room. Her long, slender fingers curl like talons; a bird of prey swooping in for the kill, and her brittle voice makes my blood run cold. Her gaze cuts to the video camera.

"Where did you get that?" She spits the words at me with poisonous intent.

"Does it matter?" All I can see is the young woman on the tape being stabbed to death while my mother and uncle have sex.

My mother knows exactly where we found it.

"I know what you did." I shift my attention back and forth between them, not sure which one of them I despise the most.

"You shouldn't have snooped." My mother takes a step.

Liam shifts toward me. Hands still in the air, he moves to place me behind him. The man is a Guardian, a sworn protector, and in this moment, I know he'll willingly give his life to save mine.

But I can't let that happen.

I'm having some difficulty breathing. Blood roars past my ears as I gasp for air and try to make myself breathe through a panic attack. My heart pounds in my chest as I fail to calm myself.

"Ah, Maria ..." My uncle steps into the study. "You should never have seen those." Middle-aged, my uncle is a classically handsome man with thick, wavy hair constantly threatening to cover his dark and intense eyes.

"You killed my father. You killed that woman."

"Technically, your mother killed that pathetic waste of flesh."

"And the woman?" I eject the tape and hold it up. "The two of you ..." I can't make the words come. "While she ..."

They fucked while someone killed her. That goes beyond psychopathic to insanity.

"You're not getting away with this." My voice sounds bolder than I feel.

"This is unfortunate." My uncle clucks his tongue and glances at my mother. "Darling Muriel, you know what needs to happen."

"Marco ..." My mother clasps her hands in front of her. "We can't. She's my daughter."

"She's my brother's spawn. Or did you forget how many times he raped you? Day after day? Month after month? And year after year? Forcing you to raise his child?"

"But ..." My mother's voice vibrates with an emotion I've never heard before. She's genuinely scared.

"You are going to do exactly what I say, or the brat dies." Marco waves his gun at me, but his words are for Liam. "Reach in real slow and place your weapon on the desk."

"And if I do?" Hands up, Liam shifts again, closing the distance between us.

"This isn't an *If I do* kind of scenario, but let me spell it out for you. You do it, and she lives. You don't do it, and she dies. The choice is yours." My uncle's hard gaze doesn't waiver. His finger moves from the trigger guard to the trigger itself.

Liam takes half a step forward, getting closer to me. I'm not sure what he's planning. He could easily take my uncle out. I've no doubt his aim is impeccable, but can he pull his weapon from his shoulder holster before my uncle puts a bullet between my eyes?

I don't think so.

Is disarming himself any better?

We'll be defenseless.

"Don't make me repeat myself." Marco gives a little shake of his weapon.

"It's going to be okay." Liam looks at me, his expression stern and focused.

I wish I believed him.

"What are you going to do to us?" I wring my hands, desperate for some way out of this madness.

Marco reaches into his back pocket and pulls out another gun. He hands it to my mother, then looks at me.

"Maria, pretty Maria ... I don't want you distracting your fiancé. Step away and take a seat on the couch."

"Do as he says, Maria." To my horror, my mother lifts the gun and points it at me.

"Liam?" My voice cracks, but I don't move. I can't. My feet are rooted in place.

"It's okay." His voice is low, steady as a rock. There's not an ounce of fear in his expression or in the way he holds his body. He lowers his voice. "We're not alone."

Not alone?

It sure as shit looks like we're alone. Wolfe and Brady are somewhere outside, doing a piss-poor job as lookouts. Why didn't they warn us my uncle and mother bypassed the traffic stop?

Where are the elite Guardians now? How did they fail so epically?

I don't hear any of Mitzy's drones, and I don't see any of the visual distortions wrinkling the air. Not that a tiny drone does us any good.

We're very much alone.

"Mother ..." I try to plead to whatever scrap of maternal instinct that may still exist within the woman standing in front of me. "This isn't you. You're better than this."

Better?

Better than having sex while a young woman is brutally slaughtered in front of her? I don't know who the woman standing before me is, but she can't be my mother.

"You have no idea who I am or what I endured at your father's hands." Her voice hardens and her grip on the pistol tightens. "Sit down."

"And what are you going to do? Are you going to kill me like you killed my father? Is that what you're going to do?"

Mother glances at my uncle. "Marco, there has to be another way."

"My darling, you know ..."

"We take them to the basement. We'll figure something out. She's a Rossi. She's our legacy." Her voice changes timbre, hardening and growing cold. "As for him ... we don't need a witness."

A cold sweat breaks out on my forehead. I try to even out my breathing, but that proves impossible. I stand before a sociopath and a psychopath. There's no reasoning with that kind of madness.

Then I see something that steals my breath. My uncle stares at me completely devoid of emotion. He's a cold, calculating machine who knows nothing about caring for another human being, but in my mother's eyes, I see fear for the very first time. I see the tiniest glimmer of love for a daughter she hates.

"You do anything to Liam and I don't care what you have to say. You'll have to kill me too."

"Marco ..." My mother turns to my uncle while my stomach churns.

I shouldn't let them know how much Liam means to me. It gives them too much power.

"We take care of this ourselves." Marco takes a step forward, gun leveled at Liam. "We'll get rid of them the same way we got rid of my brother."

All the blood in my face drains away, leaving me lightheaded and wavering on my feet. This can't be happening. I'm going to wake up any minute and realize this is all one horrible dream.

My mother's fingers clench the gun. Her trigger finger sits far too close to the trigger for my liking. It won't take much for the gun to go off.

"Maria, for once in your life, do as you're told." My mother bites off each word, her voice growing stronger, more controlled. "Sit on the goddam couch."

I glance at Liam, knowing that's the last thing I should do. We can't let them separate us. To my surprise, he gives a gentle nod. Fear flows in my veins. It bangs away inside my heart. But there's no fear in Liam's expression. He's steady as a rock.

Hands up, he reaches inside his suit. He grabs his weapon and slowly draws it out. With my mouth gaping and eyes practically bugging out of my head, I can't believe he's disarming himself.

He places the weapon on the edge of the desk.

"Push it toward me." Marco's compassionless voice sends chills racing down my spine.

I've yet to move. Somehow, if I let them separate us, it'll be the end of us.

Liam pushes his pistol, sliding it across the desk.

"Now, wasn't that easy?" Marco sneers at Liam. He reaches into his back pocket and pulls out a heavy set of zip ties. Tossing them onto the desk, his lips stretch into a grin. "Hands behind your back. Put those on. And Maria, since you can't seem to follow directions, you get to tighten them."

Liam bends forward and grabs the set of zip ties. He fastens one into a loop, then threads the end of the second one through it, forming two loose loops. He places one hand through one of the loops, then tightens down the tie. The *zip*, as it ratchets in place, makes me jump.

Every movement Liam makes is deliberate and slow. He once again holds his hands up, palms out. The zip tie dangles on his left hand. Moving methodically, he places his hands behind his back.

He shifts slightly as he pulls up on the back of his pants, then feeds his free hand through the remaining loop.

"It's okay ..." The confidence in his voice, while reassuring, doesn't make sense to me.

There's nothing okay with what's happening now.

"Maria!" My mother snaps at me. "Fasten his hands behind his back."

My hands shake as I move to obey. If Liam has some plan hashed out in his head, he doesn't share it with me. I zip the ties tight around his wrists. Not too tight, but tight enough to pass inspection.

I step back, hands up like Liam earlier, and turn to face my mother.

"What now?"

46

LIAM

Maria's fear is palpable. It rolls over and through me. I don't know how to tell her not to worry, that the Guardians are on top of this, so I don't. Which makes me feel like a royal jerk.

Due to the nature of our work, Maria's not privy to the conversations between me and the rest of the team. Mitzy's drones made a complete circuit of Marco's house, hacking into his systems while Maria and I explored the library.

Mitzy tried sending her drones into the vast bunker beneath the house, but couldn't get them in, due to mesh covering the air intakes. Which means, I need to get down there; me and the three drones attached to my person.

Two sit on my shoulders; one on each side. A third hangs between my shoulder blades. The idea is to walk them into the bunker complex, but the only way to do that is to get caught.

I wish I could explain all of this to Maria, but her fear needs to be real. Her reactions need to be spot on.

And I hate Mitzy and Forest for putting me in the position where I have to lie to Maria. Not that I've said anything untrue, but a lie of omission is a lie, nonetheless.

"Muriel," Marco gestures to his wife. "Tie her hands." He steps away, backing up toward the entrance. Keeping the gun trained on me, he reaches into his suit pocket and retrieves his cellphone. "We're coming down ..." His voice trails off, presumably listening to whoever is on the other end of that call.

This is a moment of truth. I'm trussed up, hands behind my back, which limits my movements, but I'm a considerable threat. Maria is not—or at least that's the assumption I hope Marco makes.

To my relief, Muriel secures Maria's hands in front of her rather than behind her back. That's a stroke of luck, which will serve us well later on—I hope.

I take a lot on faith, but it's not a random gamble. Reading people is one of my special skills, and I'm nearly a hundred percent certain Marco thinks very little of Maria and what she can do. That arrogance will be his biggest mistake.

"You can't kill him." Maria cries out and tries to reason with her mother. "I love him. Don't you see how wrong this is?"

Those three little words nearly bring me to my knees. They resonate with something deep within me, something I've barely acknowledged due to the fear it'll interfere with my focus.

She loves me. Shit. I think I love her too.

Muriel takes a step back to admire her handiwork. Bitch tightened the zip ties enough to cut off the circulation to my hands. Already, my fingers tingle.

Marco continues his phone conversation, telling whoever it is to expect us momentarily.

"Was there ever a time when you loved me?" Tears brim in Maria's eyes. "How can you hate me? I'm your daughter."

"You don't understand." Muriel slowly turns to face her daughter.

"Then explain it to me." Maria continues with the waterworks.

What confuses me the most is not knowing how much of what Maria says and does is real versus pretend?

"You live in a different world than I did. You've been pampered and protected your whole life." Muriel's tone actually softens. It sounds wistful, almost regretful, and it humanizes her. "You've had a better life than me, but now it's time to step up do your part, like I did."

"I don't understand?"

"No doubt you don't." Muriel's face twists into a rictus of disgust.

"Mother, you're not making sense. Why?"

"Why, what?"

"Why marry father if you didn't love him? Why didn't you marry Marco?"

"Milo wanted me and since he was the elder brother that was the beginning and end of it. What I wanted had nothing to do with it."

"That makes no sense."

Unfortunately, to me, it makes perfect sense. Evidently, Milo sheltered his daughter from the realities of mob life. Muriel doesn't seem to have had that kind of protection when she was younger.

We're missing a crucial bit of information. What did a marriage to Muriel do to strengthen the Rossi crime empire? There has to be something. The wedding between Milo and Muriel had to have been sanctioned by their parents. What did Muriel's family bring to the table?

I wish Mitzy was here to find those answers.

"Milo was not the kind and gentle man he led you to believe. You were his daughter and he doted on you. To me, he was cold and hard, brutal and uncaring. He deserved what he got."

"Murder?"

"He hurt me. Raped me. Forced me to witness ..." Muriel's eyes narrow. Her words cut deep. She doesn't complete her sentence but rages on. Her fists curl and her eyes rage with a deep-seated hatred, which persists to this day. "He kept me from the love of my life and flaunted it every day. Your father was a monster. His death was too kind, and he deserved far worse. You have no idea what he was capable of, the things he did, or how many lives he ruined. I did the world a favor the day he died."

"That's not true."

"You doubt me?" Muriel's words turn caustic. "You led a sheltered and protected life, given everything and anything you desired by that horrible man."

"But this?" Maria gestures to the video camera.

Maria's innocence hurts. I've experienced the depravity of the world firsthand. It no longer surprises me what one person can do to another. The same cannot be said for Maria.

She's still processing what she saw on those tapes. I see the way her mind struggles to wrap itself around the crimes her mother committed and wish I could make it all go away.

Maria is a kind and gentle person who sees goodness and light in those around her. It goes against her nature to accept darkness. I have a horrible suspicion about who ordered the murders of all those young women, but I'll hold my judgment until presented with irrefutable proof.

"Please, Maria, no more questions." Her mother's voice is brusque and dismissive, but there's something else there as well.

A trace of humanity? Is it possible Maria uncovered the light within her mother?

"Why?" Maria sobs with her question. Tears run freely down her cheeks, but her mother doesn't care.

"Because you're useful."

"I don't understand what that means."

"It means that if you shut up and stop acting like a spoiled brat, you may live to see another day."

"You're going to kill me no matter what. What does it matter if I ask questions?"

"Because, despite any of this, you're still a Rossi." Muriel places the tip of her finger under Maria's chin and forces Maria to look at her. "You have value."

"Value? How?"

"The same way I had value once I turned eighteen."

"That doesn't make sense."

"Pathetic thing? Can't you guess?"

Maria shakes her head.

"It's what's between your legs that has value. We sell that to the highest bidder, and we not only secure Rossi holdings but also expand operations. It's what was done to me and how you'll serve your family the way I served mine. My poor, sweet, innocent spawn, your father did you a disservice when he led you to believe your life was your own. We're not going to kill you." She tosses her head back and cackles. "We're going to use you."

"No. That's a lie. And you're crazy." Maria shouts at her mother and stands, only to be shoved back on the couch by her mother.

"Silence! For once in your life, shut up and listen. You're going to be the perfect Rossi princess."

"I'd rather die."

"I don't think so, but he might." Muriel spins and glares at me. A sinister smile spreads across her face. "Behave, and do as you're told, and we'll make his death short and sweet, nearly painless."

"No."

"Be a disobedient brat and Marco will ensure he suffers. Do you know how long we can keep a man alive? Your fiancé will suffer horribly if you don't play your part."

"You're both monsters. I'll never do what you say. There's absolutely nothing you can do to make me do what you want."

"And here, I thought you loved him?" Muriel cocks her head, thinking. Then that serpentine smile is back. "Evidently not, but I do know one person who you'll do anything to keep safe."

"I will never do what you say. You'll have to kill me because the moment I get free, I will run to the cops and tell them everything I know."

"Oh, my foolish girl. What do you think Sybil will think about that?"

"Don't bring her into this." Maria snaps at her mother.

"Darling, Sybil is already involved. Why do you think she never showed up at the benefit?"

I cringe and wait for Maria's reaction. If she plays this wrong, we're all dead.

"She didn't show up because her father finished chemo. She wanted to be there for him."

"Yeah, about that ..." Muriel looks over her shoulder, eyes spinning with mania. "Marco, be a dear and tell her where Sybil is?"

"About now, up on an auction block for real." His cold, dispassionate words are delivered with zero emotion.

"No." Maria's eyes round in fear. "That's not true. She's in Hawaii. She got the call right before she left to get ready. She's in Hawaii." Maria surprises me with her acting, hitting it spot on.

Even I believe Sybil received a call from her parents and is safe in Hawaii. I'm curious how Marco will react.

Will he buy the lie? Or does he suspect Maria knows the truth?

"Her fate is in your hands, daughter." Muriel grins in victory. "You will do as I did ... exactly as you're told."

"You get ahead of yourself, my dear." Marco rejoins us.

With me trussed up and Maria subdued, Marco closes the distance. He feels safe. It's a mistake he'll come to regret. "Your fiancé knows things. Things I need to know." I get the worst feeling in the pit of my stomach. We've misjudged Marco Rossi.

"What are you talking about? He knows nothing." Maria's shock is real, if a little over the top. It's enough to increase her uncle's suspicions rather than ease them.

"Oh, he knows a great deal. Don't you, Alpha-six?"

My entire body stiffens at his use of my designation. Marco Rossi knows far too much, and now he wants to pull that information out of me.

Things just got interesting, but not in a good way.

Marco knows who I am, or at least who I work for. He'll keep me alive until he extracts what he needs to know.

No problem.

My job is to endure and survive.

Marco presses a switch underneath the edge of the desk. An entire wall of bookcases slides to the side. Beyond, a concrete ramp angles down into darkness.

"After you." Marco waves his gun, gesturing for me to head down to the basement.

I brace against the slight breeze coming up from below. It carries the musty scent of earth and reeks of putrid decay.

Having been a party to all manner of interrogations over the years, this will be my first time on the wrong end of one.

Interrogating a prisoner requires a certain amount of finesse. My question is how much practice has Marco had?

All Guardians are recruited after serving in the military. Most of us are team guys. SEALs predominate in the Guardian community, but we have all comers. Green Berets, Air Force Special Ops, Delta guys, name the specialty, there's one who became a Guardian.

What this means is we're all well versed in enhanced interrogation techniques. That's the politically correct term for torture. Griff likes to call it *how-to-fuck-with-people-so-they-tell-you-shit,* and the man is a master in the art of torture. He's a big, fucking guy. Intimidating and scary as shit.

Marco is not physically intimidating, but he still worries me. Unlike Griff, there's very little humanity in the flat stare he gives me as he forces me at gunpoint down into the extensive bunker complex beneath his home.

As part of my training as a SEAL, I attended—and survived—SERE. It's the quintessential survival training program that is so comprehensive that it's universally adopted by the CIA, the military, and military defense contractors. Proving challenging training in evading capture, surviving inhospitable environments, and escaping captivity, the simulated torture during the captivity portion is considered by most to be the most challenging; physically and mentally.

Torture comes with one, and only one, objective. Strip a man, or woman, down to their breaking point until they spill their secrets. SERE simulates torture, but it's not real. We all know it will end.

Nothing simulates real fear.

As strong as I am, my imagination runs wild, conjuring all manner of things meant to cripple, maim, and kill, but that's not what I fear. I don't care what they do to me.

It's a body. It'll heal. Or, I'll be dead.

I fear what they'll do to Maria. She has none of my extensive training and none of the mental tricks I've learned to survive torture.

"Keep moving." Marco jabs the muzzle of the gun between my shoulder blades, motivating me to put another foot forward.

And another.

Maria's softer footsteps sound behind me. I want to comfort her. At a minimum, I want to prepare her for what's to come. It's going to suck major monkey balls. Fuck the monkeys. We're talking elephant balls for this one. Already, I put the shields in place I'm going to need.

As we descend, the dampness increases, and offensive aromas clot the air. The metallic tang of copper is the most noxious.

Copper means blood.

We come to the end of the tunnel. Thus far, Mitzy's drones have been silent, riding on my shoulders while I carry them down. In the dim light, their unusual optical camouflage makes them nearly invisible. They provide some reassurance. On the other side of those drones, my team waits.

They're planning and they'll be here soon.

All I have to do is buy my team the time they need to rescue us.

The tunnel evens out and ends at a massive bank vault door blocking our way.

"Open it." Marco barks an order at Muriel, and she jumps to obey. One of the tiny drones lifts off my shoulder. No need to crack open the vault when Mitzy can watch Muriel spin the dial and get the combination.

I don't have a good feeling about Muriel and Marco. Madness swims between them, feeding on each other. It's an ugly, nasty beast snarling with ravenous hunger for me.

Dangerous as shit.

Marco appears to be in charge, but I have a feeling Muriel is the true threat. She hides behind her femininity. The woman craves power, but she's mentally unstable—a sociopath, or psychopath. Not that it matters. That woman is off in the head.

At least we know why she forsake Marco in favor of his older brother. The woman is whipcord smart and a force not to be dismissed, but even she bends to the will of her family.

She's also quite facile at opening the vault door.

This isn't her first time down here.

47

MARIA

MY MOTHER'S SIGNATURE SCENT, ROSES AND LAVENDER, SOMETHING I always associated with home, is now a rank and odiferous assault on my senses. Add to that the dank mustiness of wherever we are, and my nose is ready to give up.

Speaking of ... what the hell is this place? A hidden fortress beneath my uncle's home? Has it always been here?

Liam walks beside me, a bastion of strength, while I struggle to breathe and not lose my ever-loving mind. Panic swims in my blood and surges in every breath.

They know he's a Guardian.

How do they know?

More importantly, what are they going to do to him?

My imagination conjures brutal scenes of torture and death. My instincts tell me to make a break for it, but my rational brain says that's the surest path to death.

Besides? Where am I going to run? And there's no way in hell I'll leave Liam behind.

I can't help but hope there's some way out of this.

For both of us.

Several times, Marco says Liam won't be making it out alive. My mother says the same. The woman walking beside me terrifies me. My mother's always been cold and distant, but this?

It's madness. The kind of mental instability that goes beyond reason. I want to plead and beg her to reconsider, but the woman walking beside me is not the woman I thought I knew.

She's a monster.

How can Liam walk like he doesn't have a care in the world? I'm dying over here, jumping at every sound, startling at every stray breeze. He looks like he's on a Sunday stroll while I have ants in my pants.

My mother opens the massive bank vault door and we're ushered through at gunpoint. The moment we're inside, a whirring disturbs the air beside my ear and the slightest breeze lifts my hair.

Is that ...? But it can't be?

I want to cheer and shout.

If the drones are here, we're not alone.

Hope surges within me. Rescue will come, but will it be in time?

Marco waves his gun, forcing us deeper underground. I consider pleading for Liam's life, but decide silence is my best weapon right now.

Two men join us on the other side of the door. I thought we were headed to a basement, but we've entered a massive underground structure.

The poured concrete walls leach the heat out of my body. I shiver uncontrollably, but the chill in the air doesn't seem to affect my mother. She's a cold-blooded creature, comfortable in sleeveless gowns and cocktail dresses, when I'm grabbing for a wrap.

Marco forces Liam forward. The two brutes bracket him in from either side. My mother walks beside me, mouth pinched and regal shoulders proudly rolled back. She looks like a queen entering her kingdom.

But that can't be right.

Marco's the one in charge.

We enter a room meant for one purpose: torture.

I flinch at an assault of noxious stimuli. The concrete walls have chunks taken out of them. Either something was ripped out of the walls, or slammed into them, shattering them. Blood, and other bodily fluids stain the walls, the ceiling, and spread across the floors.

In front of me, the concrete floor angles down to a dirty drain. Several dark stains flow toward it; blood from previous victims. A single, crudely made chair sits in the center of the room, away from the drain. I assume that's so the hapless victim can watch their blood as it disappears down the drain.

"Sit." Marco orders Liam to sit on the single chair filling the room. When he doesn't move, the men to either side of him grab his arms and drag him forward. They spin him around and force him onto the chair with a sucker punch to the gut that doubles him over.

Liam's face twists with the pain as he falls back and lands with a hard thud on the chair. It wobbles beneath him, far too rickety to hold his weight.

But it does. It holds up just fine.

Liam adjusts himself and glares at Marco. He scoots forward, perching on the edge, unable to sit back due to his hands tied behind his back.

I want to comfort him, but I'm afraid to say anything. Our gazes connect across the distance. He doesn't blink. His expression is completely flat and lifeless, but our connection spans the space between us.

In that look, he somehow tells me everything will be okay. Or maybe, that's what I want to believe, too terrified that I desperately cling to false hope.

The door behind me slams shut and locks. The vibration sends a shiver down my spine. The thick, malodorous smell in this room is rich in layers of fear-stench, unwashed bodies, piss, vomit, and blood. It's overwhelming and makes me sway while trying not to hurl. The noxious stimuli is a physical assault and layered upon that is something worse.

The acrid coppery tang of blood is so fresh, I taste it in the back of my throat. I gag and nearly spew the contents of my stomach all across the floor.

The two goons take up position beside Liam while Marco spins toward me. His face twists and I draw back, horrified by the visage of a man I thought I knew.

"You have nothing to fear from me." Marco strolls across the room until he stands toe to toe with me. "Your mother wants you alive, and that's the way you'll stay. Behave and Sybil will stay that way too." His attention shifts to my mother, who makes a choking sound at that last comment.

"That's not what we agreed." My mother's eyes practically pop out of her face. Her beautiful face twists, but Marco silences her with a single upraised finger.

"Her life for her friend's." A stare-off commences between the two of them. He tilts his head sideways as a grin spreads across his face. "That's my price, but we can renegotiate terms."

"That won't be necessary." My mother snaps back at him, eyes storming with fury and hatred.

What the hell?

I try to piece together what that means, but Marco's despicable mouth keeps flapping, spilling venom into the air.

"As for your *fiancé* ..." His lip lifts into a sneer. "His fate depends on the answers he gives. I'll grant him an easy death, or something much more satisfying."

"Kill him and you get nothing from me." My fists curl, tightening until my fingernails cut into my skin.

"You have nothing I need." He clucks at me; *tut-tut-tut*. "Milo really did you a disservice letting you believe your life was yours to decide. Sybil lives by my pleasure. She suffers by my pleasure. Now you do as well." Once again, his gaze cuts to my mother.

I'm too slow to see the expression she returns, if any, but I sense Sybil is a sore spot between them.

"We had a deal ..." My mother grinds out the words.

"And I've had a change of heart." He points toward me. "Your daughter is too high-strung. This is how we control her."

"You could keep the man alive ... Kill Sybil as we agreed." My mother fires back. "If she loves him ..."

Kill Sybil? My mother wants Sybil dead? Why?

Then it hits.

My mother's jealous.

Jealous of Sybil.

Because he took her virginity? That was years ago. Unless ...

"Silence!" Marco's shout reverberates painfully in my ears as it bounces off the walls and amplifies.

I wince while my mother grinds her teeth, clearly upset by Marco's command. She spins around and marches to the far wall. Arms folded, she leans against one of the few unstained spots of concrete and glares at Marco.

"She's right." I'm not afraid to go up against Marco. "If you kill him, you'll get nothing from me, and you want something from me." I snarl at Marco, furious and determined to make him pay for his part in murdering my father. He wants the Belvedere back. He wants that and so much more.

"I'm offering you a gift." He runs his fingers through wavy, black hair, combing them into some semblance of control.

"Gift? In what twisted world is Liam's death a gift?"

My attention cuts back to Liam. He gives me nothing. There's no encouragement. There's no warning. There's nothing. It's as if he's trying to disappear.

Then I get it. He's buying time by not drawing attention to himself. In letting my uncle engage with me, he drags out the seconds, piling them up behind us.

Time is what we need; time for the Guardians to launch a full-scale assault.

"Because, my sweet, darling niece ... you get to decide *how* he dies. Are we going to do this slow? Or ..."

"Maria ..." Liam's softly spoken word draws my gaze. "Don't listen to a word he says. Have faith."

"Faith?" Marco tosses his head back and belts out a cackling laugh. "You're going to need a lot more than belief in the supernatural to get you out of this." His deep, throaty growl raises the hairs at the back of my neck.

"You're nothing but a piece of shit I'm going to permanently remove from this world." Liam spits on the ground, emphasizing his point.

The urge to do the same and spit in Marco's eye overwhelms me, but I resist the temptation. There's no need to make Marco any angrier than he is, but there is a desperate need to stall.

"Tie him down." Marco redirects his gun, aiming for Liam's chest.

All I need to do is get free of the zip ties and gain control of one of the guns. I didn't lie. My father enrolled me in every self-defense course possible, and after his death, I continued to learn. Getting out of zip ties is child's play.

As for my defensive training, I've never gone up against four people before. If the men holding Liam down get their hands on me, I'm done. I can probably take Marco out, but not with those two in the room.

The whirring in my ear is back.

The Guardians are on their way.

48

LIAM

WHILE LISTENING TO MARCO'S CONVERSATION WITH MARIA, IT'S CLEAR Sybil means something to him. An argument, or arrangement, occurred between him and Maria's mother about Sybil's fate, and he just reversed it.

It's a betrayal that cuts deep ... if I'm reading the expression on Muriel's face right. And I'm pretty damn certain if looks could kill, Marco would be a dead man right about now.

Unfortunately, that concludes their conversation, which means it's time for Marco to turn his attention to me. I have no idea how long it'll take Mitzy and the rest of my team to come up with an action plan, but it's not going to be easy, or quick.

Which means, my life's about to really suck.

Grin and bear the suckage!

It's a phrase we used often during BUDS.

As for my current state, let the torture begin. I'd rather get started than sit around waiting for it.

"You're going to tell me about your employers. What they know? What they're doing sniffing around me? And what their next move will be. Most importantly, I'm going to send one hell of a message." He stops in front of me, expression fierce, eyes as crazy as the lunatic he is, and smacks his fist into his opposite palm. It's a power move meant to intimidate and instill fear.

I'd laugh, but I'm not a total idiot. There's no reason to poke the bear. I resort to flowery language.

"Fuck off." I have a role to perform, and I'm going to give this asshole one hell of a performance.

Marco may not know about stress positions.

Griff loves those.

Putting people in uncomfortable positions places strain on their bodies. Griff's favorite is a hogtie. He used that on the men in Cancun when we were looking for Zoe, tying arms and legs behind their backs. About an hour of that makes shoulders, knees, thighs, and hips burn. I feel some of that in my shoulders right now, and I only have my hands tied behind my back.

"You ready to start?" Marco's grin is a gruesome thing contorting what would otherwise be a handsome face.

"Fuck off." I decide to limit my answers and like how that sounds.

Marco looks to his men. They grab my legs and secure my ankles to the chair legs. Because they're pricks, they slam me against the back of the chair, but I expect the dick move and brace.

That brings a grin to my face, and I flash that smugness right back at Marco.

Poor choice.

Marco leaps into action, surprising me with a roundhouse kick. He plants his foot firmly against my chest with enough force to send the chair skittering along the concrete floor. I fly back and suck wind. The bastard knocks the breath out of me.

The chair wobbles, then cants back. Knowing what's coming, I tuck my chin to my chest as the chair crashes backward. Staring up at the stains in the ceiling, I'm not happy.

Where is my team?

How much of this shit do I have to endure?

Marco crosses the distance. The heels of his shoes sound loudly in the bare room, echoing in my ear. He stands over me, lips twisted into a rictus of revulsion.

That's okay, buddy. I hate you too.

My position sucks. I'm too vulnerable. I stare up into the visage of a monster and return his angry scowl. More interested in my pain than any information he might extract, he's determined to make me suffer. I'll use that to my advantage.

Walking around the chair, his next move lacks creativity. He kicks me in the ribs, making me huff against the pain. Five seems to be the magic number because he waves his men over to set the chair back on its legs after kicking me five times.

The moment I'm upright, one of them punches me in the gut. It hurts, but I tense. Not happy about my midsection being as exposed as it is, there's nothing to do about it. At least, Marco decides to leave his kicking for my chest and ribs instead of my head.

Marco expects me to lash out. He's a cocky fucker, leaning in close. My body's not tied to the chair. Only my feet. I could lunge forward and cause serious damage.

I think that's what he wants.

I've discovered over the years, little is accidental when it comes to torture.

My breath returns after the sucker punch. Marco is good, but he's got nothing on Griff. That man is brutally beautiful when it comes to getting his victims to sing. All Marco accomplishes is making me mad.

My anger makes me clam up. Not that I'll ever break. Not for a man like Marco. When it comes to a battle of wills, I've got him beat, hands down.

I lean on my SERE training, resisting interrogation.

My training was ... thorough.

What Marco does is child's play compared with what I endured during SERE. While nothing can really prepare a person for the real thing, I'm confident in what I can endure and know my strengths.

I also know where the chinks in my armor make me vulnerable. Marco is yet to discover my weakness.

When he does, I'm toast.

Which is why I make zero eye contact with Maria.

She stands alone and forgotten, huddled against the far wall. Her mother stormed off to the other side of the room, angry eyes shooting daggers at Marco.

She's really pissed about Sybil. It's as if Marco stole her favorite toy. There's definitely more to that story, but first ...

Marco slams his fist into my jaw, jerking my head to the side. He plows into my midsection with well-timed punches that leave me sweating and huffing for breath.

I'm okay with getting the shit kicked out of me. Marco lets his fists fly, tenderizing my face with brutal punches that make my head spin and have my eyes seeing stars. The acrid tang of blood fills my mouth after a particularly well-placed punch that cuts the inside of my cheek.

I spit out clots of blood and glare defiantly at Marco. He continues with the punches, asking a question, punching me, asking again. We go 'round and 'round like this for what seems like forever but can only be a few minutes.

That's the thing with torture.

It *feels* like forever.

"I assume Liam Cartwright is not your real name?" Marco cracks his knuckles.

"Don't you know better than to assume? It makes an ass out of you and me."

"You think you're smart?" Marco kicks my shins like a grade school bully in the schoolyard.

I shrug. It's the only answer he'll get from me.

"I assume you're not a venture capitalist either?"

Instead of a shrug, I reward him with a glare.

He's not a stupid man. Mitzy built an awesome cover, but it's not perfect.

It was never meant to be perfect.

"Which means those bodyguards you left behind are not bodyguards. They're on your team."

I go back to the shrug.

Interrogation is an art form. There are several distinct phases, each one directed at wearing down the victim. Each successive phase builds on that momentum until victims are suggestive, malleable, and loquacious.

Loquacious.

That's a big word for saying they overshare.

Fortunately for me, I know how this is going to go down. Not that Marco read the playbook on interrogation techniques, but people tend to develop their own unique style, building upon what worked for them in the past.

Right now, we're in the *getting to know you stage*. Meaning, he's not asking anything he doesn't already know. This is merely his way of establishing that he is, indeed, the questioner, and I'm his prisoner.

It's a bit overkill, if you ask me. We sorted that shit out when he marched me down here at gunpoint, but it's part of the game. Things are going to get bad before they get worse.

Judging by the bloodstains on the ceiling, walls, and floor, this isn't Marco's first rodeo, but he's not a pro.

He's not a perfectionist like Griff.

Things may look bad for me right now, but I have a leg up. I've read this playbook hundreds of times, and I've watched Griff. He's Alpha team's go-to torture guy, uniquely suited to getting people to tell him shit they don't want him to know.

All I have to do is hang on, and while I'm getting the shit kicked out of me, I have a few questions of my own.

"Do you enjoy ruining lives? Selling women to the highest bidder? Is that what gets you hard?" My questions are answered by a flurry of his fists. Blackness crowds my vision after a particularly nasty uppercut to my jaw. My ears ring as I try to shake it off.

"It makes me rich." Marco preens, overly pleased with himself. "Low overhead. High return on investment."

"Is that for the ones you pluck off the streets in Cancun? The special orders? Or the snuff you sell to the highest bidder?"

Marco's eyes flicker. He covers up the tell, but not before I see it.

It's the confirmation we need. There's more we need to know;

things I won't get out of him, but I'm confident this whole situation will turn itself around soon enough.

"You got greedy, and that greed made you sloppy." I can't help but egg him on. The more I can stoke his anger, the more likely he'll slip up and tell me something important.

"And your stupidity made you sloppy." Marco shows me exactly how sloppy with a barrage of fists to my face and a series of kicks to my midsection. "Or are you confused as to why you're down here?"

"I thought I was down here because you needed a punching bag." My flippant reply makes his anger flare. I have a sense very few people talk back to him and live to tell about it.

It's just a body.

I hope one of Mitzy's three drones stayed in here. We couldn't get more of a confession than that.

It's been a long, hard road getting to this point.

Alpha team has definitely worked our asses off to *snuff* out this particular organization, and I don't use that word lightly.

Human trafficking is the least of Marco's crimes.

He's the leader of the operation responsible for not only the kidnapping of innocent women, but orchestrating disgusting snuff films, which took far too many lives.

"Who do you work for?" Marco clocks me in the jaw, snapping my head violently to the left.

My teeth chomp down, taking another chunk out of my inner cheek. Spit and blood spray in an arc upward.

I'm beginning to see how those stains got on the ceiling.

My answer is a sloppy grin.

"What do you know about my organization?" He shakes out his fists. Marco's sweating with his exertion. That says a lot. I have a feeling Marco isn't generally this one-on-one when it comes to torture.

Reverting to the shrug, it's almost time to expand my repertoire of responses.

I'd wipe the blood from my chin, but my hands remain tight behind my back. My shoulders ache—ah, the joys of a stress position

—and I roll my ankles, making sure to circulate blood to my feet. Eventually, they'll go numb, which will make it difficult to stand.

"Marco, please ..." Maria pleads from the far side of the room. "Stop."

My gaze cuts to Maria, begging her to remain silent. She was doing so well, practically ignored in the corner. She'll only make things worse if she draws attention to herself.

I won't let that happen.

Marco spins, delivering another devastating roundhouse kick that sends me and the chair careening back to the floor. I land hard on my shoulder and barely keep my head from smacking the concrete floor. Marco's goons lift me back into position.

"Who are you working with?" Marco does a bit more tenderizing with his fists.

I brace for each blow, but he's a strong man, packed solid with muscle. His blows sting.

My lip swells, split from the heavy ring on his finger. The inside of my cheeks bleed from multiple cuts. My left eye waters, forcing me to blink to clear my vision. That ring on Marco's finger cuts my forehead, sending blood streaming down my temple.

I hack and spit and blink, then hack and spit some more. Meanwhile, Marco fires off question after question. His frustration rises with my stoic silence.

"Are you with the men who rescued Sybil?" Whatever he's going to say is cut off when his attention suddenly shifts to Maria's mother.

"The men who what?" Muriel screeches at Marco.

Did Marco forget to tell Muriel about Sybil?

This just got interesting.

"She was to be mine." Muriel's eyes burn as a murderous rage overcomes her. "You promised. Now, she's gone." She launches at Marco.

Muriel is a mess of arms and legs as she throws herself at him, clinging to his body. Interestingly, the two goons beside me make no move to intervene.

Fingers scratch at his face and pull at his hair. Dark clumps fall to the floor. Damn, the woman is bat-shit crazy. Marco barely reacts. He holds his arms out to the side as she clings to him. Then with a breath in, and a breath out, he calmly lifts her off his chest and slams her down on the floor.

Muriel jumps to her feet and seethes as Marco holds out his hand.

"Don't push me. I'm not in the mood."

Using my reprieve from Marco's fists, I process what I see. None of it makes sense.

Marco dusts off his shirt and spins toward me.

"Enough with this. You start talking or ..." Marco walks in a slow circle around me, then draws a wicked blade.

I spit out another wad of blood and give him the *Or what* look. To my horror, Marco turns toward Maria.

Fuck.

49

MARIA

My uncle beats the hell out of Liam.

Liam's face is a mess of bruises. A cut to his temple bleeds freely. His left eye swells along with a cut over the curve of his cheekbone. His mouth is full of blood. Every time he opens it to say something, he has to spit on the floor first.

There's a lot of blood on that floor.

I stand against the far wall, as far from the door, and escape, as possible.

Not my choice.

It's where I was put and where I stay. I hug the wall and cringe while Marco lands blow after blow.

Marco's men watch Liam, holding him down when necessary, but they keep their eyes on me.

Liam and Marco go another round. Liam says something. Suddenly, Marco turns toward me, dark eyes swirling with hatred.

It's terrifying.

But that's not what makes me suck in a breath.

The curved blade in his hand makes my entire body quiver with fear, even more so when he takes a step toward me.

Well, shit.

Liam goes crazy, bucking in the chair, thrashing as he tries to free himself. The two men beside him hold him down.

"The girl knows nothing." Liam spits blood. "She's nothing more than my ticket in."

"You sure about that?" Marco spins back around. "Looks like she's a bit more than that."

"She led me straight to you." Liam spits again. "Gullible little girl. Easy to fool. Easy to fuck. Bad in bed."

The words hurt.

Although, I understand what Liam's doing.

Unfortunately, it doesn't stop Marco.

"You've been nothing but an annoyance since the day you drew your first breath." He closes the distance while I prepare to fight for my life.

What can I do?

How can I help Liam?

I take a step away from the wall and focus on what my self-defense instructor taught me. I've got seconds before Marco closes the distance. I don't like that knife.

During practice, we duct-taped my wrists to protect my skin. What I'm about to do can cut deep, but I'd rather slice my wrists than face Marco and that knife with my hands tied together.

The first thing is counterintuitive.

I bring my wrists up to my mouth. Keeping the locking bar in the middle of my wrists, I bite down on the free end of the zip tie and tighten it down until it's tight enough to cut off the circulation to my hands.

Next, I reach overhead. Finally, I chop down violently toward my waist, imagining my shoulder blades touching as the zip tie snaps under the sudden stress.

My fingers curl as I remember another lesson my instructors taught. Like I told Liam, I'm proficient in self-defense.

Marco should know this, but he's cocky. He's enraged. All he sees is a woman much smaller than him.

With nowhere to go, I take another step away from the wall and move toward him.

His face twists into a grimace as hatred thunders through his body. Madness swims in his eyes; a terrifying darkness I face all on my own.

From the far side of the room, my mother shrieks as Marco charges toward me. I've got two choices.

I can use the side of my hand to chop down on the side of his neck where the tendons with their vulnerable nerves underneath sit. That move will drop anyone. All I have to do is follow through.

But I'm short. Marco is much taller than me, which makes that logistically impracticable. I go for an alternate technique, but one I have far less experience with.

Knife raised, he comes at me. My left arm sweeps out, pushing the knife out to the side. I put everything I have into driving the heel of my hand under his chin.

His teeth smack together with a loud *crack*.

His head snaps back.

The shockwave to his brain knocks him back, making him stagger. As he falls, however, unimaginable pain rips through my midsection.

I follow my uncle to the floor, crying out in agony.

Liam is somehow up. He wings his arms high up on his back and violently slams his wrists against his bowed back. The zip tie rips, and Liam's hands are free. The two men grab Liam, placing their hands on his arms.

My fall seems to go on forever as everything around me slows down. Blackness crowds inward, stealing my sight. Liam battles the guards as I crumple on the sticky wet floor.

Sticky?

Wet?

A slow blink brings the unforgiving concrete into focus. That's a lot of blood.

My blood.

A screech sounds over me. My mother races to my side. She grabs my shoulders, turning the pain in my side to white-hot agony. She lifts me into her arms, cradling me against her chest.

My arms flop as she holds me, crying into my ear.

The lights overhead flicker, and a loud cracking of wood pulls my sluggish gaze to where Liam battles for his life. Somehow, he split that rickety chair in two. With his ankles still attached to the front legs, the wood flies through the air as he lands one roundhouse kick after the next.

The men who fight him move in slow motion compared to the deadly blur that is Liam. Their reflexes come a second too late as he spins and kicks. His powerful fists smack into solid muscle, unstoppable and lethal.

He spares a look for me and pays for it with a hit to his jaw. All I see are the whites of his eyes and ... fear?

Movement at the door draws my eye.

Something flies into the room.

A tiny canister.

It lands with a *plink,* then a *pop.* A *hiss* follows.

Two more canisters follow.

Plink. Pop. Hiss.

Plink. Pop. Hiss.

Thick smoke billows out of the first canister, followed by more from the other two. The smoke rushes inward, a roiling wave of smoke fills the room.

I blink, not believing my eyes. Six shadows materialize out of the smoke. From head to toe, they're lethal wraiths cloaked in black. Guns raised, they spread out.

In the center of the room, Liam grabs one of his assailants by the ears, bends him forward, and jabs his knee into the guy's gut. The man goes down in a jangle of limbs.

Liam turns to the last man standing.

That man looks at the shadow shapes and takes a step back. His hands go up in surrender, but Liam lays the man out cold with a kick to the head.

I blink, my thoughts sluggish.

Smoke obscures everything.

My mother's tears splash on my cheek. Each time she rocks back, the pain in my abdomen makes me nearly blackout. The lancing agony, however, makes unconsciousness impossible.

A heaviness fills my arms. My thoughts turn sluggish as warmth spreads across my midsection. I know what's happening.

I'm bleeding out.

So tired.

My lids bounce, staying closed longer while I seem to float.

An ear-piercing shriek brings me back.

My mother's lifted up and away.

I slide toward the floor, only to be caught by strong arms and the comforting scent of the man I love. Liam lowers me down, laying me out on the floor.

He reeks of blood and sweat, but damn if it doesn't smell like coming home. I drift in and out of consciousness, crying out when something hard presses down on my midsection.

"Medic!" Liam cries out. "Axel, get your ass over here."

Closing my eyes, I can no longer fight the bone-deep fatigue pulling at me.

Darkness envelops me as I let go.

50

LIAM

THE MOMENT MARCO PULLS THE KNIFE, MY GUT CLENCHES, AND MY heart leaps. When he turns toward Maria, I lose my shit.

Marco closes the distance between him and my woman while my stomach churns and the bottom of my world drops out beneath me. Bile rises in the back of my throat, and blood roars past my ears. I spit out more blood and see nothing but red as Marco closes in on Maria.

There's no way I can reach her in time.

But my princess is a warrior.

She steps away from the wall. Like me, her hands are tied together with zip ties. Unlike me, her hands are bound in front of her body. She raises her hands above her head, then cuts down sharply, chopping like an axe.

Holy hell. I know that move. I teach that move to our rescues at The Facility.

The zip tie snaps, and her hands are free.

But, it's too late.

Marco is too close.

He raises that wicked knife.

Maria, however, shows no fear. She leans forward, placing her weight on the balls of her feet, then brings her hand up across her midline. Sweeping out, she blocks his knife arm, but Marco isn't done. He sweeps the knife out in an arc, then back toward Maria.

Her body stiffens as the knife slices into her, but my girl isn't done. She rams the base of her palm up, against his chin, snapping his head sharply back. A shockwave ripples through Marco's body. His hand shakes and his fingers loosen their grip on the knife. He staggers back half a step, then drops like a load of bricks.

Maria grabs her waist and cries out as she falls.

The whole thing happens in slow motion as Maria slowly crumbles to the floor. A powerful rage erupts deep within me and draws forth my most primitive, animalistic self.

Kill him.

Protect her.

Any thoughts of self-preservation fly right out the goddamn window.

With my woman in danger, I ride a powerful wave of adrenaline surging through my veins.

Strength amplifies.

Senses enhance.

Rage comes front and center.

I rise out of the chair like a man bent on murder.

Using a similar technique to the one Maria employed, I lift my bound hands as far up my back as possible. Bending forward, I turn my hands into a wedge by pressing my palms together and curling my fingers; this strains the zip tie.

Next step ... a sharp, downward jerk cuts the skin of my wrists but also snaps the zip tie.

My hands are free.

As for the chair, it shatters beneath me. I kick away chunks of wood except for the two front legs, which remain attached to my ankles.

Delaying for my team to get here no longer matters.

Save Maria.

Now.

There's no thought behind my actions. I simply react and let muscle memory take over.

I take out the man to my left with a brutal sequence of kicks and punches, then turn to the other man, ready to kill if that's what it takes.

Muriel Rossi, however, shrieks like a banshee and runs to her daughter. It distracts me, something I pay for with a fist to my gut. I trade blow for blow with my assailant, but the broken chair hampers my movements.

The lights overhead flicker in a pattern I know well. It's code. A series of short blips and longer flashes, similar to an S.O.S., it tells me my teammates are on their way.

I fight my assailants. Dull and slow, they can't keep up as I spin and kick, landing powerful strikes of fist, foot, and knee into vulnerable places.

I spare a look for Maria and pay for it with an uppercut to my jaw. Maria's mother cradles Maria in her arms as blood ... far too much blood ... pools on the floor beneath her.

A smoke canister flies into the room. It lands with a *plink,* then a *pop* and a *hiss* as it releases the contents inside. Thick smoke billows into the room.

I blink against the noxious cloud and turn my attention to the men in front of me. I grab one of them by the ears, knee the guy and take him out. Then I turn to the last man standing.

He looks over my shoulder, and there's no need to spin around to know what he sees. He sees the men of Alpha team and just about shits his pants. Hands up, he breaks away from our fight, surrendering like a coward.

The thick smoke fills the room, making it impossible to see, but I don't need my eyes to know where Maria lies. I race over and pause only long enough to bodily yank her mother out of the way and deposit her unceremoniously on the floor a foot away.

I catch Maria and lower her softly down to the ground. She's injured and I need help.

"Medic!" I call out, falling back on my team days. "Axel, get your ass over here." I shift to the side where far too much blood seeps out of a deep gash across her midsection. I apply pressure to the wound and wait for my teammate.

Axel is there within two breaths. He wastes none of those breaths on words. Pulling his medical pack out, he unzips the bag and rolls out his gear.

"Report." He moves quickly but is methodical and well-trained.

"Knife to her midsection. Shit-ton of blood." I keep my hands on Maria's wound, holding pressure, until Axel tells me otherwise.

Behind me, my team secures the room. The men I fought are bound, arm—*and legs*—behind their backs.

Max and Knox take hold of Muriel and pull her away kicking and screaming. Wolfe and Griff take care of Marco Rossi. They drag him away, giving Axel room to work.

"Is she ..." I don't want to finish that thought.

"She'll make it." Axel grabs my wrists and forces me to let go.

When I do, blood rises to the surface, and I lunge forward to stem the bleeding, but Axel pushes me away.

"I've got this." He cuts away Maria's shirt then wraps a bulky bandage around her midsection.

I brush the hair from Maria's face and place my lips against the curve of her ear.

"I'm here. You've got this." I reach for her hand and curse. "Axel, her hand is cold."

"She's in shock." He ties off the pressure bandage, then calls in to Command. "Overwatch. Need medical."

"Copy that." CJ's voice crackles through the radio.

A slight pause follows then Skye Summers comes on the line. "What do you have?"

I lose track of their exchange, but Axel reports what he found, and they talk through what to do next. I don't like the way Axel grits his teeth.

Behind me, my team does what they do best.

My body buzzes, amped up on adrenaline. The need to do something rages within me. Axel's busy with Doc Summers, taking care of my girl. There's nothing more I can do for Maria ...

Except be with her.

Hold her hand.

Tell her you love her.

But there is one thing I need to do first.

"I'm going to check in with Max." I tap Axel on the shoulder and push off the ground. Then I locate the knife.

Axel clasps my arm. "She's good."

My faith in my teammate is unshakable. Those two words mean the world to me. Maria won't be alone. If she's with Axel, then she's with a part of me.

I take a step and realize the chair legs are still tied to my ankles. I use the knife to cut the zip ties and march over to the rest of my team.

They congregate around four people: three men and one crazy lady.

"My daughter. Maria ..." Muriel looks up at me, eyes watering, nose running. "Is she ..." Her voice trails off, unable to form the question.

I want to tell Muriel Rossi to fuck off, but my mother's gentle face flashes before me. I'm one of the lucky ones. My mother is an amazing woman. Her unwavering love and affection carried me through the worst of times.

Maybe her presence now is to remind me to be compassionate and kind?

I sway on my feet, knowing I'm hallucinating.

All that excess adrenaline has yet to burn itself out. That energy needs an outlet, and I know exactly where to direct it.

But first, I show an ounce of compassion.

"Maria will live." I hope that's not a lie.

Muriel Rossi breaks down in soul-rending sobs. She's nothing like the cold-hearted bitch I met yesterday. If she loves her daughter enough to cry over Maria's injuries, why didn't she show Maria some of that love before?

I turn to Marco Rossi. Griff and Wolfe stand over him, weapons trained on a monster, a murderer, and a pathetic excuse of a human being.

I close the distance.

Rage burns in my veins and bunches in my muscles. Griff and Wolfe step aside as I rear back and kick him in the head.

The bastard goes down.

"Tenderizing him for me, I see." Griff huffs out a laugh. "Thanks."

"That bastard doesn't deserve to draw breath."

"Well, let's leave him breathing for a bit longer." Wolfe taps me on the back. "Forest has some questions for the man."

No doubt.

"You look like shit." Wolfe arches a brow. "What happened to your face?"

"I was getting the shit kicked out of me. What the fuck took you guys so long?" I spit out a clot of blood and fold my arms across my chest.

"Oh, you know ..." Wolfe gives me one of his wolfish grins. "Just dillydallying. Taking our time. Puttering around. Hemming and hawing. Figured you had it covered."

"Does this look like I had it covered?" I point to my face.

Now that I'm not worried about life and death things, I pack that animalistic side of me back where it belongs. The pain of my beating starts to rear its ugly head.

My temple throbs. My eye is tender to touch. Tight, and swollen to goose egg proportions, I wince as I gingerly feel the damage. My lip is split, thickening as it swells. My ribs feel like they got the shit kicked out of them, which they did, and my abs feel even worse.

"What Wolfe is trying to say," Griff joins in, "is we met a bit of resistance on the way here."

"You mean the vault?"

"Huh?"

"Didn't you see the fucking door?" I look between them. "How many people do you know with a bank vault under their fucking house?"

"We didn't see a door." Wolfe looks at me, confused.

"The one that belongs in a bank?" I look between them. "The one with the combination?" No recognition on either of their faces. "Mitzy's drone watched Muriel open it? You had the combination?"

"Oh, that?" Griff waves dismissively. "We didn't enter from the house."

"Then how?"

"Air shafts." Wolfe snickers. "It was the only place not under active surveillance. We slipped down the air ducts and found some interesting things. Didn't want them to know we were here."

"What kind of interesting things?" My eyes keep bouncing between the two of them.

"All kinds of things that Mitzy's crew are going to have a fucking field day with." Griff places his hand on my shoulder. "We hit pay dirt. Thus, the dillydallying. Met some resistance. Took care of shit. Locked other shit down."

"You didn't do that yourselves." No way would they leave something like that unsecured.

"Bravo team stepped up. Max and Brady figured since most of Bravo team was already on-site, why not stand the team back up. They're securing the building. Forest has others securing the house."

Max wanders over. "Got a minute?" He squeezes the back of my neck and looks me in the eye.

"Uh, yeah?" I glance around. There's nothing left for me to do, other than see how Maria is doing. There's something in Max's tone, however, that puts me on alert. "What's up?"

"Just need a moment." He looks at Wolfe and Griff. They take two steps back, letting Max and me pass. Max leads me to the other side of the room. He stops and releases me.

"What the fuck?" The air handlers make quick work of the smoke from the canister, but it still reeks down here. Or, maybe it's me that stinks to high heaven. "What's wrong?"

"I just wanted to talk."

"About?"

He glances at our prisoners and presses his lips together.

"About what?" I press him to get on with it.

"There's really no way to say it." Max takes in a deep breath.

"Then spit it out." I shrug. "What's up?"

"It's about the snuff." The way he looks at me makes me pause.

"What about it? From the videos of Sybil and Zoe, Marco's our guy." Yes, Muriel was there, but Marco is the real monster.

I've been thinking about it ever since Maria and I discovered the videos. Both Sybil and Zoe were placed with the young women who were to be killed. We barely saved Zoe, and because of what Eve's father, Carson Deverough, spilled, we knew Sybil was to be killed as well.

Marco videotaped both Zoe and Sybil when they were young. He slept with Sybil. I don't know if he slept with Zoe, but I feel like that probably didn't happen. But Marco was obsessed with both girls. I assume that obsession turned into something darker.

Max takes a breath which hitches on its way in. He ducks his head and finds something overly interesting about the bloodstains on the floor. I tap him on the shoulder. He looks up and rubs at his jaw.

"Marco didn't commission the snuff films."

"Then we sic Griff on him and force him to tell us who did."

"We don't need Griff for that."

"Why?" I scratch my head. "What aren't you telling me?"

"They were ... executions."

"Not snuff?" I take a step back. "What did any of those girls do to get themselves executed?"

We've all seen the tapes of what was done to the women in Colombia when we rescued Zoe. Using the strict definition of the word, *snuff* is a pornographic movie of an actual murder. I suppose it wasn't snuff.

Just torture and death.

"It's snuff, just not in the way you'd think." Max glances over at Maria. "Mitzy told me not to say anything, but I couldn't not tell you."

"Mitzy? What does she have to do with this?"

"She said you'd lose your shit. Promise me you've got a handle on your emotions."

"My emotions?" I scrunch my brows. "We having a *Kumbaya*

moment here? My emotions are locked down tight, like they always are."

"We'll see about that." Max's scowl darkens. "We reviewed the videotapes you watched in the library with Maria, but it's what's on the thumb drives that makes this some fucked up shit."

"What's on the thumb drives?"

"Files of the six girls killed when we saved Zoe and other ... things." Max's hesitation sends chills down my spine

"What other things?"

"Video of who paid for them."

"Video of what? Of them watching?"

"Yes." Max gives me a look.

"It was Marco. No secret there. Maria and I watched one of the tapes."

Max glances back at Marco, Muriel, and the goons. It takes me a few times to realize who he's looking at, and it isn't Marco.

"Holy fucking hell." I run my fingers through my hair, embarrassed that they shake. "Muriel is the client?"

I blame it on the excess adrenaline still circulating in my blood rather than the monster sitting in plain sight.

51

MARIA

I'm not sure how I got out of Marco's weird subterranean bunker or how long I was passed out.

I wake in a plane.

Not an ordinary plane. It's a massive jumbo jet kitted out with plush, leather seats, computer screens attached to the bulkheads, and what appears to be a mini-medical suite.

"Where am I?" I try to sit, but a hand to my shoulder holds me down.

"Stay put, princess." Liam leans over me, filling my vision with his perfect face swollen and cut up in several places.

"What happened to you?" I reach up, then realize plastic tubing hangs from my arm. "What happened to me?"

And what's that low droning sensation I feel more than hear?

I'm in a bed with a crisp white sheet pulled over me. IV tubing snakes from my arm and attaches to half-empty bags hanging from an IV pole.

"You're in one of Guardian HRS's jets. We're flying you back to headquarters."

"Headquarters? Where's that?"

I'm in a jet, so I'm guessing New Orleans *is not* the correct answer.

"California."

Liam takes my hand in his and cups it between his massive hands. He lifts my hand to kiss the back and rewards me with a twinkle in one eye. His other eye is swollen shut.

"You look like crap. Are you sure you're okay?" I reach for his face, but he's too far away. "Shouldn't you be in bed instead of me?"

"As much as I'd like to crawl into that incredibly small bed, that's going to have to wait."

"I didn't mean *with* me." Then it all comes rushing back. Marco wailing on Liam, then lifting the knife to ... "What happened to me?"

"First off, you're safe. Secondly, you're going to be okay."

"Firstly, tell me what the hell happened. I *hate* being treated like I can't handle whatever it is I need to handle." The thing is, I feel pretty good. Too good come to think of it. "Am I on drugs?"

"Only the best painkillers on the planet." Again, his one blue eye twinkles.

"I guess that's why I don't feel any pain." I curl my fingers around his hand. "Liam, what happened? And don't sugarcoat it for me. I can take it."

"Your uncle cut you. You lost a lot of blood. Axel stabilized you, and Doc Summers patched you up. You're on painkillers and a shit ton of medicines I can't pronounce to help against infection."

"Hi, Maria." Skye Summers approaches from the foot of my bed. "How's my patient doing?" She squeezes my toes and I pull back.

"Hey, that hurts."

"Good." Skye writes something down on a tablet. "Capillary refill brisk. Your perfusion is improved. Now, if I can get your Guardian to step aside, I can see how you're really doing."

"I don't remember what happened."

"Liam, if you don't mind?" Skye turns toward Liam. "There are a few doctor-patient things we need to do."

"I'm not leaving her side." Liam nearly growls at the doctor.

"Not asking you to leave, but how about we shift positions? Let me at the head of the bed and you take the foot?" Her soft voice isn't one to dismiss. The woman speaks with quiet confidence she'll be obeyed.

"Fine." Liam bends down to kiss my forehead. Then he moves around to whisper in my ear. "I hope you're ready because I'm never letting you go."

Skye pretends not to hear and goes about performing a thorough examination. "You were cut with a knife over the left side of your body. Unfortunately, it cut deep and nicked your bowel. I had to go in and fix that and stop some internal bleeding. You lost a lot of blood, and we're replacing that with saline. I don't think you'll need a transfusion, but we'll figure that out once we land." Skye goes on to tell me everything she did while I try to absorb what she says.

I drift off and wake up sometime later. Instead of Liam standing over me, there's someone else.

"Hi." Wolfe smiles down at me. "Looks like you're going to pull through."

"Thanks to you."

He holds my hand and gives a little squeeze of my fingers. "Don't tell Liam I told you this, but he was a total basket case while Doc Summers stitched you up. We practically had to put him in a straitjacket to get him to stay out of the sterile field."

"It feels like you're speaking English, but I don't understand one word in ten." Indeed, my thoughts are muddied, swimming with the painkillers Skye pumps into my veins. "Thanks for rescuing us."

"Hey, it's what we do." Wolfe cocks his head to the side.

I slip in and out of consciousness during the rest of the flight and for a good part of the next few days. My body takes its sweet time to heal, and I battle a nasty infection from the knife wound that keeps me holed up in the hospital longer than I'd like.

Finally, I get the all-clear and I'm free to leave.

But I have nowhere to go. My home is in New Orleans.

"Hey, princess." Liam knocks on the door. "Hear you're getting the old heave ho' from the doc."

"Looks like." I sit up in bed, feeling strong enough to do so on my own. I still get dizzy when I stand, but the feeling passes soon enough.

"I brought gifts." He winks and flashes that devastatingly handsome smile. Most of the swelling on his face is gone. The bruising is still there, making him look like he got his ass handed to him, but it only makes him look even more handsome than before.

"What kind of gifts?"

"Nothing special. Mostly clothes because Doc Summers said I had to, but I brought you this." He pulls out a small flowering cactus from behind his back.

"You brought me a plant?"

"Well, I know chicks dig flowers and shit like that, but after a few days they wither and die. Feels kind of weird giving a girl a gift that's supposed to symbolize your love only to have it die. I figured a cactus was better."

"Better?" His words make my stomach flutter. He definitely used the L-word.

"Yeah. First off, it's practically impossible to kill. Secondly, it has a beautiful flower that lasts for a month. Or, at least, that's what the lady said at the garden shop."

"It looks beautiful." I hold out my hands. "Let me see."

Liam crosses the distance from the door to my hospital bed and sits down beside me. He hands me the fist-sized cactus and squirms like he's nervous.

I'm missing something.

I turn the cactus this way and that and catch the back of my hand. Something's missing on my finger. I don't know when I lost the ring, or when the Guardians reclaimed it, but it makes me sigh.

Liam and I have known each other less than a week, but it feels like forever. And while whirlwind romances rarely last, for the briefest moment, I dared to let myself dream of a future with Liam by my side.

"Do you like it?" Liam leans forward as I spin the cactus in my hand.

"I do." I'm not sure if I'm a fan of cacti—their spikes don't really scream love—but I agree with him about the flowers.

"And ..." He leans forward ... expectantly.

"And ... what?" I look at him, knowing I'm clearly missing something.

"Look closer." He pushes the small cactus closer.

It's the size of a small spud with long thorns radiating outward from every tiny inch of the spiky plant.

"What am I looking for?"

"Seriously?" He takes the cactus from me, looks at it closely, then spins it around and hands it back. "Don't tell me you don't see it. If you do, I'll have to tell Doc Summers there's something wrong with your vision."

"Don't do that." I wasn't really that impressed with the cactus and may not have really looked at it. To humor Liam, I do that now.

Something shiny catches my eye.

"What is that?" My breath catches.

"Pick it up and see."

"Oh no. No way am I putting my fingers in there." I shove the cactus back at him while trying to regain a little composure.

"You don't have to ..." He looks at the cactus. "Well shit, that wasn't supposed to happen." He tries to pull out the ring but only succeeds in getting impaled by the cactus. "Damn, that fucking hurts."

"Is that supposed to be ..." I can barely finish my sentence.

"Consider it a promise ring for my princess."

"A promise ring? Since when is a solitaire princess cut diamond called a promise ring?"

"I didn't want to scare you off with a full proposal and shit. I didn't want to assume. I mean, I want to be with you, but if you need time ... it's nothing more than a promise. Or more. It can be more if that's what you want."

"You're hopeless." I can't keep the tears from my eyes.

"So, what do you say?" The hopeful expression on his face doesn't match his Guardian physique.

"To what? Are you proposing or promising?"

"I guess that depends on you."

"Me?"

"Which one are you willing to say yes to?"

"Liam, you're a total goofball, and I love everything about you."

"And I love everything about you too. So ..." His brows scrunch together. "Is that a yes?"

"Most definitely."

"To which one?" His smile falters.

"I guess that's something you need to figure out. Now, as far as this hospital bed goes, I'm eager to get out of here, take a real shower, and do absolutely nothing for a couple of days."

I don't ask where I'll be staying. I assume it's with him, and I assume we'll be doing a whole lot of getting reacquainted in his bed.

I change into real clothes and sign the discharge paperwork. Liam gets my prescriptions filled. I worry about the medical bill. Only there is no bill. The hospital belongs to the Guardians.

My thoughts turn to Sybil. It's been nearly a week since we last spoke. So much has happened. I need to tell her about Liam and how I fell in love with the man I held up at gunpoint demanding he take me to her.

I really hope Sybil's okay. She's the sister I never had. We share everything, and I feel disconnected. So much has happened.

As I think about her, my phone rings.

I glance around, not sure where it is, and not really sure who would be calling me. If it's work, I need to answer.

"Do you see my phone?" I pat the covers, getting frantic as it rings and rings. On the sixth ring, it'll go to voice mail.

Liam helps me search. I'm still stiff and sore from my surgery and recovering from sepsis. "Here it is." He finds it on the hospital tray table shoved in the corner.

"Answer it." Something stirs in my gut, a sense that I need to answer that call.

Liam accepts the call then hands me the phone.

"Hello?"

"Maria!"

"Sybil? Oh my God! I was just thinking about you." My hand shakes, nervous for how she's doing. "Where are you? Are you okay?"

"I only have a minute."

"Are you hurt? Are you safe?"

Liam told me Sybil was rescued, but that's it. I have no details. I *need* details. I rattle off a dozen questions, barely pausing to let Sybil answer. Her soft laughter is the light of my life through the phone. My friend is okay.

"I'm good. I'm safe. You wouldn't believe what I've been through."

"Tell me everything. Are you really safe?" My voice cracks and catches on itself as emotion overwhelms me.

"I am. I was rescued, and I've been with a protector for the past week. It's been crazy. Insane actually. It's a conversation that needs several bottles of wine." Sybil pauses. "Look, I've got less than thirty seconds. I just needed to hear your voice, but I'm good. How are you?"

"Girl, you will not believe what's happening here. When you went missing, I had a coronary. I barged into security. Had them track you down. Watched you at the elevator, then nothing. You disappeared. They scrubbed the feeds—fuckers—but I knew you were headed to the garage. They didn't scrub those feeds. When you never made it to the garage ... Well, let's just say I'm so sorry. I didn't know." I pause to take a breath.

"Hey, it's okay."

"No. It's not. I need to tell you something about my family." A lump forms in the back of my throat. All the horrible things that happened to Sybil are because of my family. "Everything people said about my family is true. They're thieves and criminals."

"What people, Maria? Who are you with?"

"They call themselves Guardians. They're like freedom fighters."

"Oh, the Guardians. Brett is one of them. He's my Protector. He rescued me, and then we were on the run. There was an alley and a tunnel with rats. We hid out in the desert of all places. There was even a robotic dog. Oh, I have so much to tell you, but I gotta go." Sybil breathes a sigh of relief on the other end of the phone.

"Where are you?"

"Pennsylvania of all places. Listen, I have to go."

"But I haven't told you about Liam." Liam arches a brow when he hears his name. I can't help the goofy smile filling my face.

"Liam?"

"He's a Guardian, and since you have your very own Protector, you know exactly what that means." My voice turns breathy.

Swoony.

"Maria ..." Sybil's tone turns protective. "What are you doing?"

"Nothing." I sound all kinds of guilty. When I glance at the poor cactus with the princess cut diamond in the thorns, I can't help but smile. There's a whole lot more than nothing happening between me and Liam.

"I know exactly what that means." This time, her voice turns breathy too.

"We need to trade stories."

"We will, just as soon as Brett and the Guardians say I can leave protective custody."

With my uncle under questioning by the Guardians, I have a feeling she won't need to hide out too much longer.

"I love you."

"Love you back."

"Bye! X-o-x-o." My flippant goodbye is absolutely perfect, totally us.

"Bye, luffs you." With that, Sybil cuts the connection.

My heart swells with the knowledge Sybil is not only safe, but it seems she found someone special.

For the first time in over a week, I feel like I can breathe again. As usual, we're totally in sync with each other. We're both up to no good, and I can't wait to hear all the gory details.

Until then, I look at the ring trapped inside the cactus. I give Liam a look.

"Now, how exactly are you going to get that out of there? And don't you dare tell me you're going to hurt that poor cactus."

"I thought you didn't like the cactus."

"Are you kidding!" I grab the poor plant out of his hands. "It's everything to me." And that's the truth.

Liam's proposal-that-isn't-a-proposal is perfectly imperfect, but it's perfect for us. I'll make him stew for a few days before giving him a proper answer.

As soon as he liberates that ring from the cactus, it'll be on my finger. Until then, I'll pinch myself several times a day. I can't believe this is my life.

52

MARIA

1 MONTH LATER

I can't believe it's been over a month since I held a gun on Liam. I'll never forget him yanking me into that van and turning the tables on me.

Who knew the sexy Hollywood heartthrob would become everything to me?

But that's where we are.

He's my heart, my love, my soulmate.

He's my other half, and in a few months, we'll be married in Hawaii. I wanted to get hitched in Vegas, but Sybil wants a dual wedding at her family's resort in Hawaii.

Although, it seems to be a Guardian tradition—and that of our hosts—to get married fast in places like Vegas or Niagara Falls. For some, they didn't even know they were getting married. I look at Skye and can't help but wonder how that happened.

As for me, I have a whole new family to replace the one I lost.

My sister from another mother, Sybil, sits beside me. We exchange a glance that says everything and nothing all at once. It's not possible to be this deliriously happy, but somehow, we found a way; Sybil with her Protector and me with my Guardian.

"Tell me again," Sybil shouts to be heard above the voices of so many people. She directs her attention to Forest as he tosses another log on the massive bonfire. "How did this all begin?"

"This?" Forest's pale gaze sweeps around our loose semicircle.

We gather around a bonfire on a rocky beach along one of the most rugged coastlines in California. The surf pounds against the rocks, and a steady breeze blows in off the ocean bringing a salty tang to the night air and feeding the fire. The sun is set and night rushes in.

The bonfire crackles and pops, throwing off tons of light and heat for those gathered. Behind me, a trolley car squeals on the tracks as it heads back up the steep cliff to bring down more visitors for the night.

Visitors?

Those visitors are the owners of *Insanity*. Specifically, the members of the mega rock band, Angel Fire. We're their guests on their secluded beach.

Evidently, Skye and Forest Summers live, work, and play with the mega rock band, Angel Fire. Forest happens to be their manager. I'm really curious about how that happened.

Somehow, the band created a group residence and all live together. To my surprise, not only is Skye married to their lead singer, but Mitzy's married to their keyboardist.

It's one massive, interconnected family.

I can't wait to learn their stories.

Forest is part of a throuple.

I never heard of a throuple until a few hours ago. He married his assistant, Sara, and is in some kind of lifestyle dynamic with a Dominant named Paul. I don't begin to understand that, but if it works for them, it works for me.

The band is late to the party because they're coming off a European tour and just landed.

As for the rest of us, all of Alpha team is in attendance. We're celebrating the arrests of my uncle and the woman I no longer call mother. A court date's been set and we're nearly certain of dual convictions with multiple life sentences with no chance for parole.

If I thought the dissolution of my family wasn't bad enough, it pales to what happened when my mother's role in the whole disgusting operation was revealed.

Worse than a kidnapper, rapist, or murderer, she bought young women only to watch them murdered for her pleasure; and that's the sickest part. We are talking *pleasure.*

She's a sociopath and psychopath. Now, she's locked up behind bars forever. I should feel some kind of loss over that, but once Sybil and I were reunited, and after her parents flew out to make sure we were both okay, I realized I already had the best parents in the world. Sybil's parents adopted me, and I adopted them.

Not to mention all the other members of my new, extended family.

"You pinching yourself again?" Sybil leans over and whispers in my ear.

"I'm deliriously happy."

And I am.

I glance around the fire and smile at all the new people in my life. People who will drop everything to save me, many who risked their lives so that I might be free.

There's Axel and Zoe, Griff and Moira, Max and Eve, Knox and Lily, Wolfe and Jinx, and finally my Liam and Sybil's Brett. We're joined by CJ and his wife, Melissa, then finally by Sam, who leads the Guardians.

Of course, there wouldn't be Guardians if not for Skye and her amazing brother, Forest Summers.

"I can't believe this is my life."

"Well, it is, and I want to hear the story." Sybil jumps to her feet. "Forest, you're not getting away without telling me what brought the Guardians to my sister's doorstep."

Tonight's a night of celebration, and I consider myself an exceptionally fortunate guest, but I'm a bit anxious about the retelling of that story. Considering my father, mother, and uncle's role in the whole thing, my shoulders lift to my ears.

In many ways, I'm an outsider. I may have been brought into the fold, but the sins of my family weigh heavily on my shoulders.

"Well, let's see." Forest's deep rumbly voice carries over the crackling of the fire, the pounding of the surf, and the boisterous conversation all around us. "Once upon a time, there was a girl who didn't believe nightmares were real. But the girl woke up, trapped in a nightmare."

"That girl was me." Axel's girl, Zoe, stands and presses her hands to her lower back. "Thirteen girls were kidnapped. Six lost their lives. Six went missing. The last girl was me. I nearly died that day, but the Guardians swooped in to save the day."

"And I got shot in the ass." Griff cups his mouth with his hands and calls out.

"It wasn't your ass." Moira stands and moves to Zoe. "He got shot in the leg."

"Doesn't matter. Skye wouldn't let me operate. Put me in *support*." Griff uses air quotes and turns to Skye, scowling. But it's all for show.

"Right, and somehow *support* meant you went in guns blazing to save your girl." Skye fires right back at him.

"Technically, I saved myself." Moira corrects Skye. "I just didn't know how I was going to get off that container ship. Fortunately, the Guardians came to the rescue ... again." She wraps an arm around Griff and lifts on tiptoe. "He swooped out of the night sky, scared me to death, then lifted me off that ship. My hero."

"Then what happened?" I'm with Sybil. I want to hear the story behind the Guardians showing up on my doorstep.

"Well, Eve was one of the missing girls." Max grabs Eve's hand. He turns it over and kisses the back of her hand. "Her douchebag father arranged to have his own daughter kidnapped as a way to launder money. The only problem was Benefield didn't want to give her back."

"How did you know about Benefield?" Many of these names are still new to me.

"Well, that required some detective work and a bit of questioning of Julian Townsend by Griff," Mitzy pipes up; her high-pitched voice carries easily on the night air. "And you know how Griff likes to *have chats* with our prisoners."

"Who's Townsend?" Now that's a name that is new to me.

"Townsend is the asshole who got me and Zoe kidnapped the second time." Moira rubs at her arms.

"Townsend is a rich, entitled prick who set his eyes on Moira years ago in the Philippines. We rescued Moira from that hell, and she was well on her way rebuilding her life, when that prick paid for the privilege to abduct her again." Griff tugs her to his side and wraps his arm over her shoulder. "After he lost her during that raid, he couldn't let her go. Soon as he could, he reached out to Benefield to kidnap her again. Fortunately, we caught him instead. It was a bit of a sting operation. Once I got him alone, he sang like a goddamn canary."

"That's Griff's way of saying he terrorized the poor fool." Moira punches Griff in the chest. "Townsend told the Guardians about Benefield, and a bit of Mitzy Magic led them right to Benefield's door."

"By them, Moira means me and Knox." Max and Knox exchange a look impossible to interpret. "I had to go undercover as a slave buyer. I *thought* I was going to buy Eve. Instead, I ran into her looking nothing like a woman being held against her will."

"That's because I was trying to survive. Hello." Eve shakes her head and looks at me. "Benefield had an active interest in keeping me alive. Every month, he sent proof-of-life photos to my dad. My dad paid the ransom, at least until it became clear Benefield wasn't going to release me. That's when he called the Guardians." Eve points at Mitzy. "Speaking of Mitzy Magic, Mitzy used those photos to find Benefield's compound in the middle of Colombia."

Mitzy returns a smug smile. "It's not magic, guys. It's called technology."

"Well, Eve's father didn't tell us the whole story," Lily chimes in, adding a new voice to the story. "Jinx and I used to work for the DEA, and we thought Knox was a drug runner. Turns out that wasn't true.

The container we thought we were busting wasn't filled with drugs. It was filled with girls."

"There was a bit of a turf war." CJ clears his throat. "Nothing Sam and I couldn't sort out. Once we got Lily working on our side, she managed to crack Deverough wide open."

"It wasn't me." Lily stands and collects empty containers and deposits them in the trash can. "Deverough cracked like I thought he would, and yeah, he moved the case forward, but it was really Eve who brought everything together. Without her foresight, we'd still be chasing our tail."

"I don't understand." I glance around the bonfire, confused.

The fire pops, sending sparks up into the night sky. They look like the fireflies of New Orleans. I press a hand to my chest, missing my home, but I like California.

I love the family that found me and welcomed me with open arms, despite what my family did to them.

"All I did was get the ledger." Eve dismisses Lily's comment. "It was Jinx really, and Wolfe, who figured out what was inside. Benefield kept a ledger of every transaction and every order that came in. That's what brought the Guardians to your doorstep."

"Wow." Sybil runs her hands down her arms. "That gives me chills. You're saying I was in that ledger?"

"Unfortunately." Jinx rocks back, hugging her knees. The fire lights up her face, a golden glow for a beautiful woman. "Sorry."

"It's not your fault." Sybil dismisses Jinx's comment.

Sybil's name on that list is a touchy, and awkward, subject. My mother put her name there, like she put the name of every girl Marco ever slept with. There was nothing random about the women who died. Each one was handpicked by my mother.

And that's not the worst part.

She forced Marco to have sex with her while she watched the murder of each girl. Marco's proclivity for young teens was not restricted to the sordid affair he and Sybil maintained.

That was something new I learned, but I don't fault Sybil. My uncle twisted her mind and played to her fantasies. They continued their affair up until the night of my mother's wedding to Marco.

I guess that was the last straw and what earned Sybil's name on that ledger. Somewhere in the twisted, psychotic mind of my mother, that was Marco's punishment.

As for Zoe, I've wracked my mind around that one. Zoe and Marco never had a sexual relationship, but he did obsess over Zoe when she was much younger.

That piece of the puzzle finally came to me in the middle of the night, waking me up from a dream.

Mitch Lancaster was my father's accountant. He was the man responsible for taking all the dirty money and funneling it into various legitimate business ventures, such as the Belvedere, until it came out the other side squeaky clean. Those business meetings brought Zoe and her father to my home in the Hamptons, and that's where Marco's obsession over Zoe began.

My mother thought he slept with Zoe, and why wouldn't she? Marco slept with a lot of sixteen-year-old girls.

I take in a deep breath and glance around the fire. These faces are new to me but more familiar as the days pass.

There's nothing I can do about my father, my mother, or my uncle. I'm not one of them, and I've made a decision.

I know what I want.

As they trade stories of each of the missions that led to them bringing down a massive human-trafficking organization, I find Forest. He stepped away from the fire and stares out toward the ocean.

"Forest?" I don't want to startle him.

The massive man spins around and smiles. "Are you settling in? Feeling like you need to get back to New Orleans?"

"Actually, that's what I want to talk to you about."

"How's that?"

"Liam asked me to visit The Facility."

"Ah, what do you think of the place?"

"It's phenomenal, but I think you're outgrowing the space."

"Yeah." Forest rubs the back of his neck. "We're looking at expanding."

"Well, if you decide to expand and need someone with experience running a hotel ..."

"The Facility isn't a hotel."

"I know it's not." I hold up my hand. "And I didn't mean to imply it was. It's just that I have some ideas about The Facility. I have a vision for making it more."

"More?"

"If I'm not overstepping?"

"You're not overstepping. I'm always open to new ideas. It's what moves us forward and brings us together. I take it this means I won't be losing a Guardian to New Orleans?"

There's been a lot of speculation about whether Liam will stay with the Guardians or join me back in New Orleans.

"For too long, I couldn't see giving up the Belvedere." Forest is easy to open up to. He's the big brother I never had. "But I can't stay there and run a business touched by the filth of my family."

"Your family's crimes are not yours."

"I know that up here." I point to my head. "But I'm still coming to terms with it in here." I point to my chest. "I'm not giving up the Belvedere. I'll keep it under the umbrella of my corporation, but I don't need to be the CEO. I have other plans. Other dreams. And those dreams are here, with Liam, and with the Guardians."

"I'm very happy to hear you say that, and you're welcome to stay. There's a place for you here. Set up a meeting with me and Skye, we'll talk it over. In the meantime, I think there's someone who wants to talk to you." Forest pivots and gestures behind us. Liam is light on his feet, always sneaking up on me. "Looks like another one bites the dust. You've got yourself a good one here, lover boy."

With those words, Forest leaves Liam and me alone. Liam holds out his hand and I take it. Our fingers intertwine just like our hearts wrap around the other.

"What were the two of you talking about?"

"I was asking for a job."

"A job? What about the Belvedere?"

"It's not home anymore." I snuggle into Liam's embrace. "You are."

Behind us, the Guardians and their women laugh into the night, trading insults, stories, and tall tales with love and faith in the bonds that tie them together. In front of us, the ocean extends toward the horizon and to a new life we'll forge together.

"I'm the luckiest man on earth." Liam tugs me close and kisses the crown of my head.

It's a simple gesture filled with more love than my heart can bear. But I will bear that burden. I'll bear it happily with the man I love.

"I'm the happiest woman on earth."

"Well, aren't we the sappiest couple ... on earth." Liam laughs at that. "Come, you ready for a treat?"

"Is it time for S'mores? I was promised S'mores."

"Later, but the band is here." Liam points to the top of the cliff where the gondola begins its slow descent. "Ever hung out at a bonfire on the beach with rock legends?"

"No." I spin around until I face him. Lifting up on tiptoe, I gently press my lips to his.

Liam's grip around my waist tightens and a low groan spills into the night. S'mores, bonfires, and rock legends are pretty damn impressive, but they pale in comparison to the man I love.

"Forever and always."

I lean against Liam, snuggling into the warmth of the man with whom I can't wait to share tomorrow and all the days that follow.

"Forever and always," Liam repeats our phrase, turning it into a promise.

It's a promise that leads to a beginning, and I can't wait to begin our new life ... together.

Forever and always.

53

BRADY

GUARDIAN HOSTAGE RESCUE SPECIALISTS: BRAVO ONE

One Year Ago

"Bravo One to Overlord. In position." The radio squawks in my ear.

I crouch behind thick vegetation on the outskirts of the bustling port in Cancun. Intel says one of the hundreds of shipping containers out there contains a dozen girls, young women, who are bound for Colombia and a fate worse than death.

Bravo Team's job is to locate that container and rescue those girls. We're in position and merely hold for Mitzy's technical team to locate the container holding the girls.

They'll do that using *Smaug*, a large drone loaded with specialized tech, like heat sensors. It makes another pass overhead, scanning for the girls.

"Copy that." CJ answers from Command and Control. *"Overwatch in position. Scanning."*

"Good copy." I glance back at my team.

Decked out in the best gear on the planet, we're a formidable force. Bravo Two, my best buddy, Booker, squats behind me, while Rafe and Hayes reference a schematic of the shipyard. Once we get confirmation of which cargo container holds the girls, they'll determine our path through the maze of containers. Alec and Zeb hold the rear.

"Overlord to Bravo One, target identified." CJ rattles off grid coordinates that Rafe and Hayes copy down.

"Good copy." I turn around. "Bravo Three, we set?"

"Affirmative." Rafe gives me a thumbs up.

"Status of patrols?" My comment is for Overlord.

Cancun's port is busy, but they shut down at night, unlike many other ports around the globe. In those places, massive flood lights push back the darkness, turning night into day. Here in Cancun, there are shadows upon shadows in the pervasive darkness.

Dressed in our black tactical gear and equipped with night-vision goggles, that darkness means nothing to us.

"None in your vicinity." CJ reports back what I already know, confirming our approach is clear.

During recon, we discovered security at the port is minimal. It's a joke, to be honest. They focus only on the entrances and exits. We arrived from the water, infiltrating the port after securing our black RIBs to pylons under the docks. We brought three six-man RIBs, splitting our team into pairs, as they will be our transport out.

"It's quiet." Booker taps me on the shoulder.

"You got a concern?" I rely on my team and always listen to what they have to say.

"Feels off, that's all."

"How?"

"Dunno. Like I said, it's quiet." Booker doesn't explain more than that.

I get his concern. The shipyard should buzz with activity. Tomorrow, they will load all these containers onto a ship and begin their journey to Colombia.

"I need more than that."

Scanning what I see of the shipyard, there are no guards milling about, no dockworkers making last-minute adjustments to the containers, and there's nothing but the wind blowing in my ear.

"That's all I got." Booker glances around.

"It's not enough to call the op."

If we call it, they will load those girls on the cargo container ship.

We have another window to attempt recovery, but sea operations are far more complex than dealing with this on the ground.

"*Status?*" CJ's voice crackles through the comms.

I glance at Rafe who gives me the thumbs up.

"We've got a route. Sending now." I report back, and as I do, Rafe uploads the path we'll take to the designated container.

"*Copy that.*" There's a slight pause, then the radio squawks again. "*Received.*"

"Bravo Two says it's too quiet. Any concerns on your end?" Even though Booker can't vocalize what he feels, I respect his instincts. Lord knows they've saved our asses before.

"*Not from our end.*" CJ replies. "*We'll do another sweep to be sure.*"

"Good copy." Hopefully, that will satisfy Booker.

We wait in silence while *Smaug* makes another sweep of the docks.

"*Bravo One, all's quiet on our end. Your call.*"

Booker shrugs.

"We're going in." I glance at Rafe. He gives me a thumbs up and packs up his gear.

I give the signal to move out.

Falling into line, we move as we train; silent and deadly.

All of us are former US Navy SEALs, recruited out of the military by the organization that is Guardian HRS. Besides being a SEAL, I operated as a Delta team operative. I did a lot of hostage rescue in Delta.

This feels like old times.

Rafe guides us through the maze. Lifting my fist in the air, I call a halt. The shipping container is right in front of us. We pause, taking in how it sits a little apart from the other containers.

All around us, containers stack three to five high, but not this one.

It's odd, but I can understand. Inside that container, precious cargo waits for delivery. The men in charge will do whatever they can to ensure those women reach their destination alive.

"Bravo One to Overlord, we're in position."

"Copy that." CJ doesn't waste breath on unnecessary chatter. *"Confirmed ten inside."*

"Ten?"

"Correct."

Two less than expected.

Behind me, Hayes pulls out his bolt cutters. Alec and Zeb climb the nearest container. They'll provide cover if things come down to that.

"The op is yours." CJ tells me all subsequent mission commands are mine to make. *Smaug* will support only.

With a signal to Booker, Rafe, and Hayes, I give the command to move out.

We move as one, four highly trained operatives used to working together. Once we reach the door of the container, Bravo Two and I turn toward defense. Meanwhile Bravo Three gets the bolt cutters ready,

I scan the area, see nothing, then turn to watch Rafe place the bolt cutters on the lock. That's when I see the wire.

"Freeze!" I shout, but it's too late.

Rafe cuts the lock.

I shoulder him out of the way and shove him behind me.

A bright, fiery flash sears my retinas. Flames engulf me. Intense heat burns through me as my entire world goes dark.

***

I HURT ALL OVER WITH NO FREAKIN' IDEA WHAT HAPPENED, OR WHERE the hell I am.

"He's conscious." A muffled voice speaks from what seems to be a great distance.

"Push more morphine."

My eyes are open, but I can't see a damn thing. When I try to speak, there's something in my throat, choking me.

My arms don't move. My legs don't either. Panic surges through me, then fades away as my body floats on a morphine high and consciousness fades away.

"Will he survive?"

"I don't know. The burns are extensive. They cover the entire left side of his body with second and third-degree burns. With luck... we'll see."

***

UNRELENTING PAIN CONSUMES ME, MORNING, NOON, AND NIGHT. IT'S the worst during the debriding sessions, when they scrape off dead tissue.

Hydrotherapy is a curse word in my world right about now. It's where they remove all the devitalized tissue. I've taught many of the newer nurses creative and colorful curse words.

Fucking worst pain of my life.

The days blend into one another, but I've got the best burn doctors working on me. At least that's what I remember in my brain fog and morphine fueled dreams. I float in a morphine fog most days, letting unconsciousness take me when things are their worst.

I've lost count of the number of surgeries. Evidently, early excision and grafting of burns is vital to recovery. I say, they've tortured me through a few too many of those.

"How are you doing today?" Margaret is my nurse, and I meet her cheery smile with a growl and a scowl.

"Fuck you."

"I see." She ignores my mood and goes about her fucking business like she's not about to torture me until I pass out. "Let's look at what we've got."

"How about we not?"

"A comedian today." Margaret begins the laborious process of unwrapping the bandages which cover the burns. "Looking good. No signs of infection."

"Yippie ki yay." I'm falling off the sharp cliff of my narcotic high. "How about some juice before my daily dose of torture?"

"I've already given you some."

"What?" I missed her injecting it into my medline. "Well, fuck me sideways and don't hold back. Can't we up the dose?" I'm becoming a freaking addict.

"Pain is good."

"Have you ever had your skin slough off?"

"No."

"Then don't fucking tell me pain is good." I close my eyes and go to my happy place as pain sinks into every fucking breath.

Debridement.

I hate it, but the docs say it's necessary.

Dermal preservation.

That's the goal. To achieve that goal, they remove the burned tissue layer by layer until reaching viable tissue. Early excision of my burns is supposed to decrease healing time, reduce my discomfort, and prevent infection. It's supposed to improve my overall outcome.

It fucking hurts like a living motherfucker on a skyway to Hell.

"How's he doing today?" The soft voice of Dr. Skye Summers interrupts my living hell.

"He's a ball of warm fuzziness today." Margaret continues her task.

"That bad?"

"Yes. Says the morphine isn't touching him."

"He's on a really high dose."

"Hey, I may be the patient, but I'm right fucking here. Don't talk over me."

"Sorry, Brady." Skye comes to stand closer to the side of my bed. "I spoke with your doctors."

"Thought you were my doc."

"I'm an emergency and trauma doc. I deal with burns on the front end, but this requires a level of expertise far outside my wheelhouse."

"Well, what do the fucking experts have to say?"

"That your vocabulary needs a major overhaul."

"I'm entitled to be grumpy."

"There's grumpy and then there's you."

"So?"

"I know this sucks, Brady. I really do, but you're doing incredibly well. So far, we've avoided infection setting in. The debriding is going well. The grafting looks good. All in all, you should recover near full mobility."

"You telling me I'm going to live?"

I remember a dream fog where there was some debate whether I'd survive.

"Don't lie to me, doc. When you say functional, what does that mean? Will I be an invalid?"

"Not an invalid. I know things look bad. This is the worst of what you're going to face."

"The worst of it was having that container blow up in my face." I remember nothing of the explosion. Well, not nothing. There was a flash, intense heat, then nothing. I blacked out.

"Touché." Skye covers the irritation in her voice poorly, but she takes my bad attitude in stride. "You will have scarring. There's no way around that, but things look good for rehabilitation."

"Rehabilitation? What kind of rehab are we talking?"

Will I be able to operate? If I can't be a Guardian, life's not worth living.

That is the only question that matters, but I'm not strong enough to ask it. I'm too afraid of the answer.

"Months at least."

"Months?"

"Maybe longer."

"Longer?" My heart can't take that. "So... you're basically telling me I'm screwed? I'm done."

"That's not what I'm saying at all. Look, the road to recovery is going to be long and hard. You're in for the hardest fight of your life. I sugarcoated nothing for you. You'll have scars, but with proper burn care, grafting, and fingers-crossed, no infections to complicate healing, you'll be out of here within a month."

"A month?"

"Two at most?"

"Two?"

"I'm sorry. It is what it is and I—"

"I know, you'll tell me the truth." I grimace as Margaret exposes my burned skin to the air. "You sure I can't have more morphine?"

"I'll up the dose a bit." She turns to Margaret and rattles off another dose of morphine. "You've got this Brady. You're one of the strongest men I know. Tenacious as shit and bull-headed in the extreme, but you've got this."

"But I'm out of the Guardians?" I mean to say it as a statement of fact. I'd rather hear the bad news coming out of my mouth than out of hers. If she says it, I'm done.

"Out of the Guardians? Why would you think that?"

"Why wouldn't I?"

"Because I'm going to do everything in my power to get you back as Bravo One."

A flood of adrenaline? Relief? I don't know what that floaty feeling is, but Doc Summers gives me hope. Or maybe I'm just riding another morphine high.

"You wouldn't shit me, would you?"

"No, Brady. I wouldn't lie about this."

Whatever else she says fades away. My lids grow heavy and all I want is to disappear.

* * *

ALPHA TEAM'S STORY IS DONE FOR NOW, BUT JOIN BRAVO TEAM AS THEY recover from their injuries and take on new missions, new adventures, and find their soulmates.

Read Brady's story, Rescuing Angie, and let the adventure continue.

ELLZ BELLZ

ELLIE'S FACEBOOK READER GROUP

If you are interested in joining the ELLZ BELLZ, Ellie's Facebook reader group, we'd love to have you.

Join Ellie's ELLZ BELLZ.
The ELLZ BELLZ Facebook Reader Group

Sign up for Ellie's Newsletter.
Elliemasters.com/newslettersignup

ALSO BY ELLIE MASTERS

The LIGHTER SIDE

Ellie Masters is the lighter side of the Jet & Ellie Masters writing duo! You will find Contemporary Romance, Military Romance, Romantic Suspense, Billionaire Romance, and Rock Star Romance in Ellie's Works.

YOU CAN FIND ELLIE'S BOOKS HERE:

ELLIEMASTERS.COM/BOOKS

Military Romance

Guardian Hostage Rescue Specialists

Rescuing Melissa

(Get a FREE copy of Rescuing Melissa

when you join Ellie's Newsletter)

Alpha Team

Rescuing Zoe

Rescuing Moira

Rescuing Eve

Rescuing Lily

Rescuing Jinx

Rescuing Maria

Bravo Team

Rescuing Angie

Rescuing Isabelle

Rescuing Carmen

Rescuing Rosalie

Military Romance

Guardian Personal Protection Specialists

Sybil's Protector

Lyra's Protector

The One I Want Series

(Small Town, Military Heroes)

By Jet & Ellie Masters

EACH BOOK IN THIS SERIES CAN BE READ AS A STANDALONE AND IS ABOUT A DIFFERENT COUPLE WITH AN HEA.

Saving Abby

Saving Ariel

Saving Brie

Saving Cate

Saving Dani

Saving Jen

Rockstar Romance

The Angel Fire Rock Romance Series

EACH BOOK IN THIS SERIES CAN BE READ AS A STANDALONE AND IS ABOUT A DIFFERENT COUPLE WITH AN HEA. IT IS RECOMMENDED THEY ARE READ IN ORDER.

Ashes to New (prequel)

Heart's Insanity (book 1)

Heart's Desire (book 2)

Heart's Collide (book 3)

Hearts Divided (book 4)

Hearts Entwined (book5)

Forest's FALL (book 6)

Hearts The Last Beat (book7)

Contemporary Romance

Firestorm

(KRISTY BROMBERG'S EVERYDAY HEROES WORLD)

Billionaire Romance

Billionaire Boys Club

Hawke

Richard

Brody

Contemporary Romance

Cocky Captain

(VI KEELAND & PENELOPE WARD'S COCKY HERO WORLD)

Romantic Suspense

EACH BOOK IS A STANDALONE NOVEL.

The Starling

~AND~

Science Fiction

Ellie Masters writing as L.A. Warren

Vendel Rising: a Science Fiction Serialized Novel

ABOUT THE AUTHOR

ELLIE MASTERS is a multi-genre and Amazon Top 100 best-selling author, writing the stories she loves to read. These are dark erotic tales. Or maybe, sweet contemporary stories. How about a romantic thriller to whet your appetite? Ellie writes it all. Want to read passionate poems and sensual secrets? She does that, too. Dip into the eclectic mind of Ellie Masters, spend time exploring the sensual realm where she breathes life into her characters and brings them from her mind to the page and into the heart of her readers every day.

Ellie Masters has been exploring the worlds of romance, dark erotica, science fiction, and fantasy by writing the stories she wants to read. When not writing, Ellie can be found outside, where her passion for all things outdoor reigns supreme: off-roading, riding ATVs, scuba diving, hiking, and breathing fresh air are top on her list.

She has lived all over the United States—east, west, north, south and central—but grew up under the Hawaiian sun. She's also been privileged to have lived overseas, experiencing other cultures and making lifelong friends. Now, Ellie is proud to call herself a Southern transplant, learning to say y'all and "bless her heart" with the best of them. She lives with her beloved husband, two children who refuse to flee the nest, and four fur-babies; three cats who rule the household, and a dog who wants nothing other than for the cats to be his best friends. The cats have a different opinion regarding this matter.

Ellie's favorite way to spend an evening is curled up on a couch, laptop in place, watching a fire, drinking a good wine, and bringing forth all the characters from her mind to the page and hopefully into the hearts of her readers.

FOR MORE INFORMATION
elliemasters.com

facebook.com/elliemastersromance

twitter.com/Ellie__Masters

instagram.com/ellie_masters

bookbub.com/authors/ellie-masters

goodreads.com/Ellie_Masters

CONNECT WITH ELLIE MASTERS

Website:
elliemasters.com
Amazon Author Page:
elliemasters.com/amazon
Facebook:
elliemasters.com/Facebook
Goodreads:
elliemasters.com/Goodreads
Instagram:
elliemasters.com/Instagram

FINAL THOUGHTS

I hope you enjoyed this book as much as I enjoyed writing it. If you enjoyed reading this story, please consider leaving a review on Amazon and Goodreads, and please let other people know. A sentence is all it takes. Friend recommendations are the strongest catalyst for readers' purchase decisions! And I'd love to be able to continue bringing the characters and stories from My-Mind-to-the-Page.

Second, call or e-mail a friend and tell them about this book. If you really want them to read it, gift it to them. If you prefer digital friends, please use the "Recommend" feature of Goodreads to spread the word.

Or visit my blog https://elliemasters.com, where you can find out more about my writing process and personal life.

Come visit The EDGE: Dark Discussions where we'll have a chance to talk about my works, their creation, and maybe what the future has in store for my writing.

Facebook Reader Group: Ellz Bellz

Thank you so much for your support!

Love,

Ellie

DEDICATION

This book is dedicated to you, my reader. Thank you for spending a few hours of your time with me. I wouldn't be able to write without you to cheer me on. Your wonderful words, your support, and your willingness to join me on this journey is a gift beyond measure.

Whether this is the first book of mine you've read, or if you've been with me since the very beginning, thank you for believing in me as I bring these characters 'from my mind to the page and into your hearts.'

Love,
Ellie

THE END

* * *

Printed in Great Britain
by Amazon

31750930R00247